Charles M. Sheldon

In His Steps

The Classic Bestseller and the Contemporary Retelling
Complete in One Volume

What Would Jesus Do?

Garrett W. Sheldon

Inspirational Press • New York

Previously published in two separate volumes:

IN HIS STEPS
Foreword copyright by Garrett W. Sheldon
Text design by Steven Boyd and copyrighted by B & H

WHAT WOULD JESUS DO?
Copyright © 1997 by Broadman & Holman Publishers

First Inspirational Press edition published in 1998.

Inspirational Press
A division of BBS Publishing Corporation
386 Park Avenue South
New York, NY 10016

Inspirational Press is a registered trademark of BBS Publishing Corporation.

Published by arrangement with Broadman & Holman Publishers.

Library of Congress Catalog Card Number: 98-72393

ISBN: 0-88486-219-4

Printed in the United States of America.

Contents

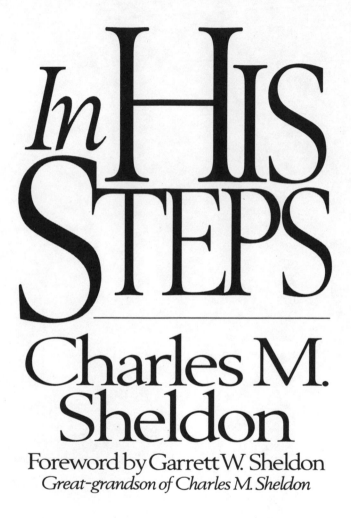

In HIS STEPS

Charles M. Sheldon

Foreword by Garrett W. Sheldon
Great-grandson of Charles M. Sheldon

Preface to the 1935 Edition

THE STORY "IN HIS STEPS" WAS WRITTEN IN 1896, AND it was read a chapter at a time to my young people, Sunday evenings in the Central Congregational Church, Topeka, Kansas. While it was being read it was being published in the *Chicago Advance,* a religious weekly, as a serial. The publisher did not know the conditions of the copyright law, and he filed only one copy of the *Advance* each week with the department, instead of two, which the law required. On that account the copyright was defective, and the story was thrown into the "public domain" when the Advance Company put it out in a ten cent paper edition. Owing to the fact that no one had any legal ownership in the book, sixteen different publishers in America and fifty in Europe and Australia put out the book in various editions from an English penny to eight shillings. Mr. Bowden, the London publisher, sold over 3,000,000 copies of the penny edition on the streets of London.

The book has been translated into twenty-one languages, including a Russian publication which has been banned by the Soviet. A

Turkish translation in Arabic is permitted circulation by the government and is being read all over Turkey.

The story has been made into the drama form and is being used by groups of young church people and by college students. And while conditions have changed in the years since the story was written, the principle of human conduct remains the same. I do not need to say that I am very thankful that owing to the defective copyright the book has had a larger reading on account of the great number of publishers. I find readers in every part of the world where I go. And I am informed by the *Publishers Weekly* that the book has had more circulation than any other book except the Bible. If that is true, no one is more grateful than I am, as it confirms the faith I have always held that no subject is more interesting and vital to the human race than religion.

May I be allowed to add a word of appreciation for the courtesy of the publishers of this gift edition who have through these years recognized the moral rights of the author and have kindly permitted him a share in the financial sales of the book. I hope for this edition a hearty and kindly welcome from the readers, old and young, who believe that in the end of human history Jesus will be the standard of human conduct for the entire human race.

Charles M. Sheldon
Topeka, Kansas, 1935

Foreword

In His Steps BY CHARLES M. SHELDON IS THE MOST widely-read Christian book, after the Bible. Since its publication in 1896, this little book, written by my great-grandfather, has sold an estimated thirty million copies and has been translated into fifteen languages, including Russian, Arabic, Chinese, Greek, Hindu, Japanese, and Turkish.

Because of its reputation as a book that people "passed around," *In His Steps* has been read by two or three times the thirty million copies sold.[1] Ironically, because of a faulty copyright, the Reverend Sheldon earned almost no royalties on this best-selling Christian novel, but he rejoiced that it was so popular and so effective in inspiring millions to a more personal, direct Christian discipleship and lifestyle.

The story in *In His Steps* is simple. A group of people in an ordinary church, led by their pastor, take a pledge to ask the question "What would Jesus do?" whenever each of them makes a decision. The effects of this personal, immediate, conscious following "in the steps" of Jesus are dramatic.

One of the characters in the story is Ed Norman, publisher of the city newspaper, and the effects of asking what Jesus would do in the media leads to drastic change in how he reports the news and finances his business. Another character, Rachel Winslow, is a beautiful young singer who struggles with career and marriage choices after asking what Jesus would have her do with her life. All of the people in this book find their way of viewing hundreds of daily situations radically changed by asking the simple question, "What would Jesus do in my place?"

The results will amaze you and convince you that such personal, immediate Christian living is not only possible; it is the key to growing in the faith and being used of God to the fullest. The challenges and unexpected blessings that confront these modern-day disciples of Christ will inspire you.

The minister of Central Congregational Church in Topeka, Kansas, Charles Sheldon wrote *In His Steps* as a "sermon story" that he delivered to the church youth during the Sunday evening services.[2] The Reverend Sheldon found that reading a dramatic story illustrating Christian principles in the everyday lives of ordinary people, like Jesus' parables, drew crowds of young people to the church on Sunday evenings. Each night he would leave off at an exciting point in the story, encouraging the audience to return the next Sunday to hear how it came out.

While Dr. Sheldon was reading chapters of *In His Steps* on Sunday evenings in the fall of 1896, it was being published serially in a small church magazine, *The Advance*. Soon the editor of this magazine was receiving hundreds of letters from all over the country praising the theme of *In His Steps* and urging that it be published as a book. The author went to Chicago and offered the manuscript of *In His Steps* to three large publishers, all of whom turned it down! Finally, *The Advance* magazine brought it out in book form, which quickly sold hundreds of thousands of copies.

About a year later, other publishers discovered that *In His Steps* was not copyrighted (as nothing in *The Advance* was), so they were free to publish and sell it without permission or paying the author any royalties. Soon, sixteen publishers in America were printing *In His Steps* and sales were in the millions. Foreign translations were being made and sold all over the world. In 1898, several editions were published in Britain and soon sold six million copies. Throughout the British Commonwealth, *In His Steps* spread like wildfire, igniting revivals in New Zealand and Wales. A printer in Kingsport, Tennessee, printed millions of copies to be sold in Woolworth's stores. An Arabic translation was read throughout the Moslem world. It was translated into Russian but banned by the Soviet government. A Hindu translation of *In His Steps* appeared in India. As Sheldon's biographer, Timothy Miller, wrote, this "simple but perceptive little novel . . . catapulted Sheldon . . . to world renown."[3]

Newspapers and magazines serialized *In His Steps*. This simple but inspired religious novel changed the world in the early twentieth century. Eric Goldman included it in the list of thirteen books that changed America, along with *The Federalist Papers* and *Uncle Tom's Cabin*.[4] In England, a town council voted to ask "What would Jesus do?" in political matters.

Sheldon's church and church groups around the world took the book's pledge to ask "What would Jesus do?" He received dozens of letters a day relating how that pledge had changed lives, restored families, strengthened relationships, cleaned up business practices and politics, and given peace and joy to countless believers. This success proved to Sheldon that "religion is the most interesting subject known to the human race" and "the standards of Jesus . . . are the greatest we can ever know."[5] As individual believers seek God's will in their lives and let the Spirit of Christ lead them in day-to-day decisions, "Jesus will conquer and draw all men up unto Himself."[6]

A dramatic version of *In His Steps* was written in 1910 and performed as a play all over the country. My great-grandfather always hoped a film version would be produced, as I have hoped a movie of my contemporary *What Would Jesus Do?* will be made.

In his autobiography, Charles Sheldon clearly states that he did not on his own dream up the captivating theme of *In His Steps,* but that it was given to him, inspired by God, and so all the glory should be given to Him. "But for all and any influence the book may have had," he wrote, "all the praise and wonder of it belongs to Him who alone among the sons of man is King of kings and Lord of lords."[7] The evidence of this divine quality of *In His Steps* was, for my great-grandfather, the "regeneration of thousands of lives" as they pledged to accept Jesus as their Lord and Savior and received the guidance of Christ's Word and Holy Spirit.[8]

The message of this novel is not original, but just a reforming of the traditional Christian message of seeking God's will for our lives, being obedient to His will through the power and love of His Spirit, and experiencing the joy and peace of Christ's salvation. "The question, 'What would Jesus do?' is not a new question; it is an old one. It has been asked repeatedly by some of the best Christian men and women in the world. The Bishop of Exeter, many years ago, wrote a hymn which was sung in England by his people, and the last line was 'What would Jesus do?'"[9]

And this, for the Christian, is the secret of happiness: "becoming Christlike, learning of his nature and character, loving God with all our mind and loving neighbors as ourselves."[10]

A life following in the steps of Jesus is the most exciting, satisfying life. With His faith and love, relying on the conviction, guidance, and comfort of His Holy Spirit, and seeking and finding all of God's blessing for you—who knows the true "desires of your heart" better than you do?

As I have spoken to churches of all denominations all over America, I have been surprised to find some of the most devout Christians afraid to take the pledge to ask "What would Jesus do in my place?" for fear of not being able to follow through on it. But that's the whole point! As we strive to be Christlike and realize our own inability of showing the fruits of His Spirit (love, patience, kindness, gentleness, etc.) we come to rely more and more on Him and allow the Holy Spirit to work His miracles through us! Those weaknesses and failures then serve the humbling effect of Paul's "thorn in the flesh," reminding us of our own inadequacies without Christ and building our gratitude for His forgiveness of our sins. As my great-grandfather put it:

> All over the world today can be found thousands of men and women who are dating a new life, new impulses, and new joys from the asking of the question, "What would Jesus do?" It has not proved to be a discouragement to them, . . . but it is overwhelmingly true that practically asking the question has been a source of daily encouragement. Those who have honestly asked it have not felt overawed by the divine superiority but rather helped by the human sympathy.[11]

As we rely on the Holy Spirit to convict us of our shortcomings, but also to provide the comfort and reassurance of Christ's love and forgiveness, living out the question, "What would Jesus do?," can strengthen and deepen our Christian walk every day. It did for thousands of brothers and sisters in Christ that wrote to my great-grandfather with personal stories of God's power and goodness as they obediently followed Jesus: restored relationships, bitterness cleansed away, being able to believe and love again.

Charles Sheldon's own life exemplified this personal, immediate discipleship, where our Christian faith is tested best by how we relate to those closest to us: in our families and with our friends, co-workers, acquaintances, and strangers we encounter. He wrote that social improvement is only possible as individual men and women become transformed into "new creatures" of Christ. "A new humanity is the only hope of a better world. And a new humanity cannot come to the world except it come through the Christ of God."[12]

I grew up hearing stories of my great-grandfather's character, his reverence for God, and the love and kindness he showed to friend and stranger alike. My favorite story about him was told me by my father, Charles M. Sheldon II. Whenever the Reverend Sheldon visited his grown son, M.W. Sheldon, a wealthy and prominent businessman, he would greet the family and then immediately go to the kitchen and visit with the cook and other servants.

He always showed Christ's love and respect for the humble and poor. Despite worldwide fame, he always retained God's view of the world's riches, vanity, and pomp—their dangerous and worthless quality when compared to fellowship with Jesus Christ. Growing up on a farm in North Dakota never left Charles Sheldon.

As I read and reread his books, articles, and letters, I'm also struck with the wonderful humor of this evangelist. He loved to laugh. He appreciated a good joke. He was a jovial companion, with the joy of the Holy Ghost. He saw the humorous side of this often sad world, the folly of human pride, and the gift that God gave us in a sense of humor. His one regret about the book *In His Steps* was that it didn't have more humor in it. I have tried to remedy that in my sequel, *What Would Jesus Do?*, believing, as he did, that Christ came to free us from sin and sorrow. "The joy of the Lord is our strength."

My hope and prayer for this centennial anniversary edition of *In His Steps,* along with my updated version of this classic, *What Would Jesus Do?*, is that they will both be used of God to once again inspire many to a closer, personal walk with our Lord and His ways of faith, love, peace, joy, forbearance, reproachment, and forgiveness. As they do, they will personally come to know what saints have known for almost two thousand years—God delights to lead them, cherish them, and protect and bless them. Although the world may despise and persecute Christ's children, Jesus triumphs over the world. My own experience of following "in His steps" has proven to me that it is the greatest source of what Peter called "that joy unspeakable and full of glory." I know it will be for you too.

Garrett W. Sheldon

Wise, Virginia

Notes

1. Timothy Miller, *Following in His Steps: A Biography of Charles M. Sheldon* (Knoxville: University of Tennessee Press, 1987), 86–87.

2. Charles M. Sheldon, *The History of "In His Steps"* (Topeka, Kan., 1938), 2–3.

---

3. Miller, *Following in His Steps,* 66.

4. Ibid., 94.

5. Sheldon, *The History of "In His Steps,"* 19.

6. Ibid., 22–23.

7. Charles M. Sheldon, *Charles M. Sheldon: His Life Story* (New York: George H. Doran Company, 1925), 107.

8. Charles D. Crane, ed., *A Charles M. Sheldon Yearbook* (Topeka, Kan.: Crane & Company, 1909), 9.

9. Ibid., 155.

10. Ibid., 230–31.

11. Ibid., 278.

12. Ibid., 323.

I

"For here unto were ye called; because Christ also suffered for you, leaving you an example, that ye should follow his steps."

———

IT WAS FRIDAY MORNING AND THE REV. HENRY MAXwell was trying to finish his Sunday morning sermon. He had been interrupted several times and was growing nervous as the morning wore away and the sermon grew very slowly toward a satisfactory finish.

"Mary," he called to his wife, as he went upstairs after the last interruption, "if any one comes after this, I wish you would say I am very busy and cannot come down unless it is something very important."

"Yes, Henry. But I am going over to visit the kindergarten and you will have the house all to yourself."

The minister went up into his study and shut the door. In a few minutes he heard his wife go out, and then everything was quiet. He settled himself at his desk with a sigh of relief and began to write. His text was from 1 Peter ii. 21: "For hereunto were ye called; because Christ also suffered for you, leaving you an example that ye should follow his steps."

He had emphasized in the first part of the sermon the Atonement as a personal sacrifice, calling attention to the fact of Jesus' suffering

———

in various ways, in His life as well as in His death. He had then gone on to emphasize the Atonement from the side of example, giving illustrations from the life and teachings of Jesus to show how faith in the Christ helped to save men because of the pattern or character He displayed for their imitation. He was now on the third and last point, the necessity of following Jesus in His sacrifice and example.

He had put down "Three Steps. What are they?" and was about to enumerate them in logical order when the bell rang sharply. It was one of those clock-work bells, and always went off as a clock might go if it tried to strike twelve all at once.

Henry Maxwell sat at his desk and frowned a little. He made no movement to answer the bell. Very soon it rang again; then he rose and walked over to one of his windows which commanded the view of the front door. A man was standing on the steps. He was a young man, very shabbily dressed.

"Looks like a tramp," said the minister. "I suppose I'll have to go down and—"

He did not finish his sentence but he went downstairs and opened the front door. There was a moment's pause as the two men stood facing each other, then the shabby looking young man said:

"I'm out of a job, sir, and thought maybe you might put me in the way of getting something."

"I don't know of anything. Jobs are scarce—" replied the minister, beginning to shut the door slowly.

"I didn't know but you might perhaps be able to give me a line to the city railway or the superintendent of the shops, or something," continued the young man, shifting his faded hat from one hand to the other nervously.

"It would be of no use. You will have to excuse me. I am very busy this morning. I hope you will find something. Sorry I can't give you something to do here. But I keep only a horse and a cow and do the work myself."

The Rev. Henry Maxwell closed the door and heard the man walk down the steps. As he went up into his study he saw from his hall window that the man was going slowly down the street, still holding his hat between his hands. There was something in the figure so dejected, homeless, and forsaken that the minister hesitated a moment as he stood looking at it. Then he turned to his desk and with a sigh began the writing where he had left off. He had no more interruptions, and when his wife came in two hours later the sermon was finished, the loose leaves gathered up and neatly tied together, and laid on his Bible all ready for the Sunday morning service.

"A queer thing happened at the kindergarten this morning, Henry," said his wife while they were eating dinner. "You know I went over with Mrs. Brown to visit the school, and just after the games, while the children were at the tables, the door opened and a young man came in holding a dirty hat in both hands. He sat down near the door and never said a word; only looked at the children. He was evidently a tramp, and Miss Wren and her assistant Miss Kyle were a little frightened at first, but he sat there very quietly and after a few minutes he went out."

"Perhaps he was tired and wanted to rest somewhere. The same man called here, I think. Did you say he looked like a tramp?"

"Yes, very dusty, shabby and generally tramp-like. Not more than thirty or thirty-three years old, I should say."

"The same man," said the Rev. Henry Maxwell thoughtfully.

"Did you finish your sermon, Henry?" his wife asked after a pause.

"Yes, all done. It has been a very busy week with me. The two sermons have cost me a good deal of labor."

"They will be appreciated by a large audience, Sunday, I hope," replied his wife smiling. "What are you going to preach about in the morning?"

"Following Christ. I take up the Atonement under the head of sacrifice and example, and then show the steps needed to follow His sacrifice and example."

"I am sure it is a good sermon. I hope it won't rain Sunday. We have had so many stormy Sundays lately."

"Yes, the audiences have been quite small for some time. People will not come out to church in a storm." The Rev. Henry Maxwell sighed as he said it. He was thinking of the careful, laborious effort he had made in preparing sermons for large audiences that failed to appear.

But Sunday morning dawned on the town of Raymond one of the perfect days that sometimes come after long periods of wind and mud and rain. The air was clear and bracing, the sky was free from all threatening signs, and every one in Mr. Maxwell's parish prepared to go to church. When the service opened at eleven o'clock the large building was filled with an audience of the best dressed, most comfortable looking people of Raymond.

The First Church of Raymond believed in having the best music that money could buy, and its quartet choir this morning was a source of great pleasure to the congregation. The anthem was inspiring. All the music was in keeping with the subject of the sermon. And the anthem was an elaborate adaptation to the most modern music of the hymn,

"Jesus, I my cross have taken,
All to leave and follow Thee."

Just before the sermon the soprano sang a solo, the well-known hymn,

"Where He leads me I will follow,
I'll go with Him, with Him,
all the way."

Rachel Winslow looked very beautiful that morning as she stood up behind the screen of carved oak which was significantly marked with the emblems of the cross and the crown. Her voice was even more beautiful than her face, and that meant a great deal. There was a general rustle of expectation over the audience as she rose. Mr. Maxwell settled himself contentedly behind the pulpit. Rachel Winslow's singing always helped him. He generally arranged for a song before the sermon. It made possible a certain inspiration of feeling that made his delivery more impressive.

People said to themselves they had never heard such singing even in the First Church. It is certain that if it had not been a church service, her solo would have been vigorously applauded. It even seemed to the minister when she sat down that something like an attempted clapping of hands or a striking of feet on the floor swept through the church. He was startled by it. As he rose, however, and laid his sermon on the Bible, he said to himself he had been deceived. Of course it could not occur. In a few moments he was absorbed in his sermon and everything else was forgotten in the pleasure of his delivery.

No one had ever accused Henry Maxwell of being a dull preacher. On the contrary, he had often been charged with being sensational; not in what he had said so much as in his way of saying it. But the First Church people liked that. It gave their preacher and their parish a pleasant distinction that was agreeable.

It was also true that the pastor of the First Church loved to preach. He seldom exchanged. He was eager to be in his own pulpit when Sunday came. There was an exhilarating half hour for him as he faced a church full of people and knew that he had a hearing. He was peculiarly sensitive to variations in the attendance. He never preached well before a small audience. The weather also affected him decidedly. He was at his best before just such an audience as faced him now, on just such a morning. He felt a glow of satisfaction as he went on. The church was the first in the city. It had the best choir.

It had a membership composed of the leading people, representatives of the wealth, society and intelligence of Raymond. He was going abroad on a three months vacation in the summer, and the circumstances of his pastorate, his influence and his position as pastor of the First Church of the city—

It is not certain that the Rev. Henry Maxwell knew just how he could carry on that thought in connection with his sermon, but as he drew near the end of it he knew that he had at some point in his delivery had all those feelings. They had entered into the very substance of his thought; it might have been all in a few seconds of time, but he had been conscious of defining his position and his emotions as well as if he had held a soliloquy, and his delivery partook of the thrill of deep personal satisfaction.

The sermon was interesting. It was full of striking sentences. They would have commanded attention printed. Spoken with the passion of a dramatic utterance that had the good taste never to offend with a suspicion of ranting or declamation, they were very effective. If the Rev. Henry Maxwell that morning felt satisfied with the conditions of his pastorate, the First Church also had a similar feeling as it congratulated itself on the presence in the pulpit of this scholarly, refined, somewhat striking face and figure, preaching with such animation and freedom from all vulgar, noisy or disagreeable mannerism.

Suddenly, into the midst of this perfect accord and concord between preacher and audience, there came a very remarkable interruption. It would be difficult to indicate the extent of the shock which this interruption measured. It was so unexpected, so entirely contrary to any thought of any person present that it offered no room for argument or, for the time being, of resistance.

The sermon had come to a close. Mr. Maxwell had just turned the half of the big Bible over upon his manuscript and was about to sit down as the quartet prepared to arise to sing the closing selection,

"All for Jesus, all for Jesus,
All my being's ransomed powers,"

when the entire congregation was startled by the sound of a man's voice. It came from the rear of the church, from one of the seats under the gallery. The next moment the figure of a man came out of the shadow there and walked down the middle aisle. Before the startled congregation fairly realized what was going on the man had reached the open space in front of the pulpit and had turned about facing the people.

"I've been wondering since I came in here"—they were the words he used under the gallery, and he repeated them—"if it would be just the thing to say a word at the close of the service. I'm not drunk and I'm not crazy, and I am perfectly harmless, but if I die, as there is every likelihood I shall in a few days, I want the satisfaction of thinking that I said my say in a place like this, and before this sort of a crowd."

Mr. Maxwell had not taken his seat, and he now remained standing, leaning on his pulpit, looking down at the stranger. It was the man who had come to his house the Friday before, the same dusty, worn, shabby-looking young man. He held his faded hat in his two hands. It seemed to be a favorite gesture. He had not been shaved and his hair was rough and tangled. It is doubtful if any one like this had ever confronted the First Church within the sanctuary. It was tolerably familiar with this sort of humanity out on the street, around the railroad shops, wandering up and down the avenue, but it had never dreamed of such an incident as this so near.

There was nothing offensive in the man's manner or tone. He was not excited and he spoke in a low but distinct voice. Mr. Maxwell was conscious, even as he stood there smitten into dumb astonishment at the event, that somehow the man's action reminded him of a person he had once seen walking and talking in his sleep.

No one in the house made any motion to stop the stranger or in any way interrupt him. Perhaps the first shock of his sudden appearance deepened into a genuine perplexity concerning what was best to do. However that may be, he went on as if he had no thought of interruption and no thought of the unusual element which he had introduced into the decorum of the First Church service. And all the while he was speaking, the minister leaned over the pulpit, his face growing more white and sad every moment. But he made no movement to stop him, and the people sat smitten into breathless silence. One other face, that of Rachel Winslow from the choir, stared white and intent down at the shabby figure with the faded hat. Her face was striking at any time. Under the pressure of the present unheard-of incident it was as personally distinct as if it had been framed in fire.

"I'm not an ordinary tramp, though I don't know of any teaching of Jesus that makes one kind of a tramp less worth saving than another. Do you?" He put the question as naturally as if the whole congregation had been a small Bible class. He paused just a moment and coughed painfully. Then he went on.

"I lost my job ten months ago. I am a printer by trade. The new linotype machines are beautiful specimens of invention, but I know six men who have killed themselves inside of the year just on account of those machines. Of course I don't blame the newspapers for getting the machines. Meanwhile, what can a man do? I know I never learned but the one trade, and that's all I can do. I've tramped all over the country trying to find something. There are a good many others like me. I'm not complaining, am I? Just stating facts. But I was wondering as I sat there under the gallery, if what you call following Jesus is the same thing as what He taught. What did He mean when He said: 'Follow me!' The minister said," here the man turned about and looked up at the pulpit, "that it is necessary for the disciple of Jesus to follow His steps, and he said the steps are 'obedience, faith, love, and imitation.' But I did not hear him tell you just what he meant that to mean, especially the last step. What do you Christians mean by following the steps of Jesus?

"I've tramped through this city for three days trying to find a job; and in all that time I've not had a word of sympathy or comfort except from your minister here, who said he was sorry for me and hoped I would find a job somewhere. I suppose it is because you get so imposed on by the professional tramp that you have lost your interest in any other sort. I'm not blaming anybody, am I? Just stating facts. Of course, I understand you can't all go out of your way to hunt up jobs for other people like me. I'm not asking you to; but what I feel puzzled about is, what is meant by following Jesus. What do you mean when you sing 'I'll go with Him, with Him, all the way?' Do you mean that you are suffering and denying yourselves and trying to save lost, suffering humanity just as I understand Jesus did? What do you mean by it?

"I see the ragged edge of things a good deal. I understand there are more than five hundred men in this city in my case. Most of them have families. My wife died four months ago. I'm glad she is out of trouble. My little girl is staying with a printer's family until I find a job. Somehow I get puzzled when I see so many Christians living in luxury and singing 'Jesus, I my cross have taken, all to leave and follow Thee,' and remember how my wife died in a tenement in New York City, gasping for air and asking God to take the little girl too. Of course I don't expect you people can prevent every one from dying of starvation, lack of proper nourishment and tenement air, but what does following Jesus mean? I understand that Christian people own a good many of the tenements. A member of a church was the owner of the one where my wife died, and I have wondered if following Jesus all the way was true in his case. I heard some people singing at a church prayer meeting the other night,

> 'All for Jesus, all for Jesus,
> All my being's ransomed powers,
> All my thoughts, and all my doings,
> All my days, and all my hours,'

and I kept wondering as I sat on the steps outside just what they meant by it. It seems to me there's an awful lot of trouble in the world that somehow wouldn't exist if all the people who sing such songs went and lived them out. I suppose I don't understand. But what would Jesus do? Is that what you mean by following His steps? It seems to me sometimes as if the people in the big churches had good clothes and nice houses to live in, and money to spend for luxuries, and could go away on summer vacations and all that, while the people outside the churches, thousands of them, I mean, die in tenements, and walk the streets for jobs, and never have a piano or a picture in the house, and grow up in misery and drunkenness and sin."

The man suddenly gave a queer lurch over in the direction of the communion table and laid one grimy hand on it. His hat fell upon the carpet at his feet. A stir went through the congregation. Dr. West half rose from his pew, but as yet the silence was unbroken by any voice or movement worth mentioning in the audience. The man passed his other hand across his eyes, and then, without any warning, fell heavily forward on his face, full length up the aisle. Henry Maxwell spoke:

"We will consider the service closed."

He was down the pulpit stairs and kneeling by the prostrate form before any one else. The audience instantly rose and the aisles were crowded. Dr. West pronounced the man alive. He had fainted away. "Some heart trouble," the doctor also muttered as he helped carry him out into the pastor's study.

2

HENRY MAXWELL AND A GROUP OF HIS CHURCH MEM-
bers remained some time in the study. The man lay on the couch
there and breathed heavily. When the question of what to do with
him came up, the minister insisted on taking the man to his own
house; he lived near by and had an extra room. Rachel Winslow said:

"Mother has no company at present. I am sure we would be glad
to give him a place with us."

She looked strongly agitated. No one noticed it particularly. They
were all excited over the strange event, the strangest that First Church
people could remember. But the minister insisted on taking charge of
the man, and when a carriage came the unconscious but living form
was carried to his house; and with the entrance of that humanity into
the minister's spare room a new chapter in Henry Maxwell's life began, and yet no one, himself least of all, dreamed of the remarkable
change it was destined to make in all his after definition of the Christian discipleship.

The event created a great sensation in the First Church parish.
People talked of nothing else for a week. It was the general impres-

sion that the man had wandered into the church in a condition of mental disturbance caused by his troubles, and that all the time he was talking he was in a strange delirium of fever and really ignorant of his surroundings. That was the most charitable construction to put upon his action. It was the general agreement also that there was a singular absence of anything bitter or complaining in what the man had said. He had, throughout, spoken in a mild, apologetic tone, almost as if he were one of the congregation seeking for light on a very difficult subject.

The third day after his removal to the minister's house there was a marked change in his condition. The doctor spoke of it but offered no hope. Saturday morning he still lingered, although he had rapidly failed as the week drew near its close. Sunday morning, just before the clock struck one he rallied and asked if his child had come. The minister had sent for her at once as soon as he had been able to secure her address from some letters found in the man's pocket. He had been conscious and able to talk coherently only a few moments since his attack.

"The child is coming. She will be here," Mr. Maxwell said as he sat there, his face showing marks of the strain of the week's vigil; for he had insisted on sitting up nearly every night.

"I shall never see her in this world," the man whispered. Then he uttered with great difficulty the words, "You have been good to me. Somehow I feel as if it was what Jesus would do."

After a few minutes he turned his head slightly, and before Mr. Maxwell could realize the fact, the doctor said quietly, "He is gone."

The Sunday morning that dawned on the city of Raymond was exactly like the Sunday of a week before. Mr. Maxwell entered his pulpit to face one of the largest congregations that had ever crowded the First Church. He was haggard and looked as if he had just risen from a long illness. His wife was at home with the little girl, who had come on the morning train an hour after her father had died. He lay in that spare room, his troubles over, and the minister could see the face as he opened the Bible and arranged his different notices on the side of the desk as he had been in the habit of doing for ten years.

The service that morning contained a new element. No one could remember when Henry Maxwell had preached in the morning without notes. As a matter of fact he had done so occasionally when he first entered the ministry, but for a long time he had carefully written every word of his morning sermon, and nearly always his evening discourses as well. It cannot be said that his sermon this morning was striking or impressive. He talked with considerable hesitation. It was evident that some great idea struggled in his thought for utterance, but it was not expressed in the theme he had chosen for his preaching. It was near the close of his sermon that he began to gather a certain strength that had been painfully lacking at the beginning.

He closed the Bible and stepping out at the side of the desk, faced his people and began to talk to them about the remarkable scene of the week before.

"Our brother," somehow the words sounded a little strange coming from his lips, "passed away this morning. I have not yet had time to learn all his history. He had one sister living in Chicago. I have written her and have not yet received an answer. His little girl is with us and will remain for the time."

He paused and looked over the house. He thought he had never seen so many earnest faces during his entire pastorate. He was not able yet to tell his people his experiences, the crisis through which he was even now moving. But something of his feeling passed from him to them, and it did not seem to him that he was acting under a careless impulse at all to go on and break to them this morning something of the message he bore in his heart.

So he went on:

"The appearance and words of this stranger in the church last Sunday made a very powerful impression on me. I am not able to conceal from you or myself the fact that what he said, followed as it has been by his death in my house, has compelled me to ask as I never asked before 'What does following Jesus mean?'

"I am not in a position yet to utter any condemnation of this people or, to a certain extent, of myself, either in our Christ-like relations to this man or the numbers that he represents in the world. But all that does not prevent me from feeling that much that the man said was so vitally true that we must face it in an attempt to answer it or else stand condemned as Christian disciples. A good deal that was said here last Sunday was in the nature of a challenge to Christianity as it is seen and felt in our churches. I have felt this with increasing emphasis every day since.

"And I do not know that any time is more appropriate than the present for me to propose a plan, or a purpose, which has been forming in my mind as a satisfactory reply to much that was said here last Sunday."

Again Henry Maxwell paused and looked into the faces of his people. There were some strong, earnest men and women in the First Church.

He could see Edward Norman, editor of the Raymond *Daily News*. He had been a member of the First Church for ten years.

No man was more honored in the community. There was Alexander Powers, superintendent of the great railroad shops in Raymond, a typical railroad man, one who had been born into the business. There sat Donald Marsh, president of Lincoln College, situated in the suburbs of Raymond. There was Milton Wright, one of the great merchants of Raymond, having in his employ at least one hundred men in various shops. There was Dr. West who, although still comparatively young, was quoted as authority in special surgical cases. There was young Jasper Chase the author, who had written one successful book and was said to be at work on a new novel. There was Miss Virginia Page the heiress, who through the recent death of her father had inherited a million at least, and was gifted with unusual attractions of person and intellect. And not least of all, Rachel Winslow, from her seat in the choir, glowed with her peculiar beauty of light this morning because she was so intensely interested in the whole scene.

There was some reason, perhaps, in view of such material in the First Church, for Henry Maxwell's feeling of satisfaction whenever he considered his parish as he had the previous Sunday. There was an unusually large number of strong, individual characters who claimed membership there. But as he noted their faces this morning he was simply wondering how many of them would respond to the strange proposition he was about to make. He continued slowly, taking time to choose his words carefully, and giving the people an impression they had never felt before, even when he was at his best with his most dramatic delivery.

"What I am going to propose now is something which ought not to appear unusual or at all impossible of execution. Yet I am aware that it will be so regarded by a large number, perhaps, of the members of this church. But in order that we may have a thorough understanding of what we are considering, I will put my proposition very plainly, perhaps bluntly. I want volunteers from the First Church who will pledge themselves, earnestly and honestly for an entire year, not to do anything without first asking the question, 'What would Jesus do?' And after asking that question, each one will follow Jesus as exactly as he knows how, no matter what the result may be.

"I will of course include myself in this company of volunteers, and shall take for granted that my church here will not be surprised at my future conduct, as based upon this standard of action, and will not oppose whatever is done if they think Christ would do it.

"Have I made my meaning clear? At the close of the service I want all those members who are willing to join such a company to remain and we will talk over the details of the plan. Our motto will be, 'What would Jesus do?' Our aim will be to act just as He would if He was in our places, regardless of immediate results. In other words, we propose to follow Jesus' steps as closely and as literally as we believe He taught His disciples to do. And those who volunteer to do this will pledge themselves for an entire year, beginning with to-day, so to act."

Henry Maxwell paused again and looked out over his people. It is not easy to describe the sensation that such a simple proposition apparently made. Men glanced at one another in astonishment. It was not like Henry Maxwell to define Christian discipleship in this way. There was evident confusion of thought over his proposition. It was understood well enough, but there was, apparently, a great difference of opinion as to the application of Jesus' teaching and example.

He calmly closed the service with a brief prayer. The organist began his postlude immediately after the benediction and the people began to go out. There was a great deal of conversation. Animated groups stood all over the church discussing the minister's proposition. It was evidently provoking great discussion.

After several minutes he asked all who expected to remain to pass into the lecture-room which joined the large room on the side. He was himself detained at the front of the church talking with several persons there, and when he finally turned around, the church was empty. He walked over to the lecture-room entrance and went in.

He was almost startled to see the people who were there. He had not made up his mind about any of his members, but he had hardly expected that so many were ready to enter into such a literal testing of their Christian discipleship as now awaited him. There were perhaps fifty present, among them Rachel Winslow and Virginia Page, Mr. Norman, President Marsh, Alexander Powers the railroad superintendent, Milton Wright, Dr. West and Jasper Chase.

He closed the door of the lecture-room and went and stood before the little group. His face was pale and his lips trembled with genuine emotion. It was to him a genuine crisis in his own life and that of his parish. No man can tell until he is moved by the Divine Spirit what he may do, or how he may change the current of a lifetime of fixed habits of thought and speech and action.

Henry Maxwell did not, as we have said, yet know himself all that he was passing through, but he was conscious of a great upheaval in his definition of Christian discipleship, and he was moved with a depth of feeling he could not measure as he looked into the faces of those men and women on this occasion.

It seemed to him that the most fitting word to be spoken first was that of prayer. He asked them all to pray with him. And almost with the first syllable he uttered there was a distinct presence of the Spirit felt by them all. As the prayer went on, this presence grew in power.

They all felt it. The room was filled with it as plainly as if it had been visible.

When the prayer closed there was a silence that lasted several moments. All the heads were bowed. Henry Maxwell's face was wet with tears. If an audible voice from heaven had sanctioned their pledge to follow the Master's steps, not one person present could have felt more certain of the divine blessing. And so the most serious movement ever started in the First Church of Raymond was begun.

"We all understand," said he, speaking very quietly, "what we have undertaken to do. We pledge ourselves to do everything in our daily lives after asking the question, 'What would Jesus do?' regardless of what may be the result to us. Some time I shall be able to tell you what a marvelous change has come over my life within a week's time. I cannot now. But the experience I have been through since last Sunday has left me so dissatisfied with my previous definition of Christian discipleship that I have been compelled to take this action. I did not dare begin it alone. I know that I am being led by the hand of divine love in all this. The same divine impulse must have led you also.

"Do we understand fully what we have undertaken?"

"I want to ask a question," said Rachel Winslow. Every one turned towards her. Her face glowed with a beauty that no physical loveliness could ever create.

"I am a little in doubt as to the source of our knowledge concerning what Jesus would do. Who is to decide for me just what He would do in my case? It is a different age. There are many perplexing questions in our civilization that are not mentioned in the teachings of Jesus. How am I going to tell what He would do?"

"There is no way that I know of," replied the pastor, "except as we study Jesus through the medium of the Holy Spirit. You remember what Christ said speaking to His disciples about the Holy Spirit: 'Howbeit when He the spirit of truth is come, He shall guide you into all the truth; for He shall not speak from Himself; but what things soever He shall hear, there shall He speak; and He shall declare unto you the things that are to come. He shall glorify me; for

He shall take of mine and declare it unto you. All things whatsoever the Father hath are mine; therefore said I, that he taketh of mine and shall declare it unto you.' There is no other test that I know of. We shall all have to decide what Jesus would do after going to that source of knowledge."

"What if others say of us, when we do certain things, that Jesus would not do so?" asked the superintendent of railroads.

"We cannot prevent that. But we must be absolutely honest with ourselves. The standard of Christian action cannot vary in most of our acts."

"And yet what one church member thinks Jesus would do, another refuses to accept as His probable course of action. What is to render our conduct uniformly Christ-like? Will it be possible to reach the same conclusions always in all cases?" asked President Marsh.

Mr. Maxwell was silent some time. Then he answered, "No; I don't know that we can expect that. But when it comes to a genuine, honest, enlightened following of Jesus' steps, I cannot believe there will be any confusion either in our own minds or in the judgment of others. We must be free from fanaticism on one hand and too much caution on the other. If Jesus' example is the example for the world to follow, it certainly must be feasible to follow it. But we need to remember this great fact. After we have asked the Spirit to tell us what Jesus would do and have received an answer to it, we are to act regardless of the results to ourselves. Is that understood?"

All the faces in the room were raised towards the minister in solemn assent. There was no misunderstanding that proposition. Henry Maxwell's face quivered again as he noted the president of the Endeavor Society with several members seated back of the older men and women.

They remained a little longer talking over details and asking questions, and agreed to report to one another every week at a regular meeting the result of their experiences in following Jesus this way. Henry Maxwell prayed again. And again as before the Spirit made Himself manifest. Every head remained bowed a long time. They went away finally in silence. There was a feeling that prevented speech. The pastor shook hands with them all as they went out. Then he went into his own study room back of the pulpit and kneeled. He remained there alone nearly half an hour. When he went home he went into the room where the dead body lay. As he looked at the face he cried in his heart again for strength and wisdom. But not even yet did he realize that a movement had begun which would lead to the most remarkable series of events that the city of Raymond had ever known.

3

"He that saith he abideth in Him ought himself also to walk even as He walked."

EDWARD NORMAN, EDITOR OF THE RAYMOND *Daily News,* sat in his office room Monday morning and faced a new world of action. He had made his pledge in good faith to do everything after asking "What would Jesus do?" and, as he supposed, with his eyes open to all the possible results. But as the regular life of the paper started on another week's rush and whirl of activity, he confronted it with a degree of hesitation and a feeling nearly akin to fear.

He had come down to the office very early, and for a few minutes was by himself. He sat at his desk in a growing thoughtfulness that finally became a desire which he knew was as great as it was unusual. He had yet to learn, with all the others in that little company pledged to do the Christlike thing, that the Spirit of Life was moving in power through his own life as never before. He rose and shut his door, and then did what he had not done for years. He knelt down by his desk and prayed for the Divine Presence and wisdom to direct him.

He rose with the day before him, and his promise distinct and clear in his mind. "Now for action," he seemed to say. But he would be led by events as fast as they came on.

He opened his door and began the routine of the office work. The managing editor had just come in and was at his desk in the adjoining room. One of the reporters there was pounding out something on a typewriter. Edward Norman began to write an editorial. The *Daily News* was an evening paper, and Norman usually completed his leading editorial before nine o'clock.

He had been writing for fifteen minutes when the managing editor called out:

"Here's this press report of yesterday's prize fight at the Resort. It will make up three columns and a half. I suppose it all goes in?"

Norman was one of those newspaper men who keep on every detail of the paper. The managing editor consulted his chief in matters of both small and large importance. Sometimes, as in this case, it was merely a nominal inquiry.

"Yes—No. Let me see it."

He took the type-written matter just as it came from the telegraph editor and ran over it carefully. Then he laid the sheets down on his desk and did some very hard thinking.

"We won't run this to-day," he said finally.

The managing editor was standing in the doorway between the two rooms. He was astounded at his chief's remark, and thought he had perhaps misunderstood him. "What did you say?"

"Leave it out. We won't use it."

"But—" The managing editor was simply dumfounded. He stared at Norman as if the man was out of his mind. "I don't think, Clark, that it ought to be printed, and that's the end of it," said Norman, looking up from his desk.

Clark seldom had any words with the chief. His word had always been the law in the office and he had seldom been known to change his mind. The circumstances now, however, seemed to be so extraordinary that Clark could not help expressing himself.

"Do you mean that the paper is to go to press without a word of the prize fight in it?"

"Yes. That's what I mean."

"But it's unheard of. All the other papers will print it. What will our subscribers say? Why, it is simply—" Clark paused, unable to find words to say what he thought.

Norman looked at Clark thoughtfully. The managing editor was a member of a church of a different denomination from that of Norman's. The two men had never talked together on religious matters although they had been associated on the paper for several years.

"Come in here a minute, Clark, and shut the door," said Norman.

Clark came in and the two men faced each other alone. Norman did not speak for a minute. Then he said abruptly, "Clark, if Christ was editor of a daily paper, do you honestly think He would print three columns and a half of prize fight in it?"

"No, I don't suppose He would."

"Well, that's my only reason for shutting this account out of the *News*. I have decided not to do a thing in connection with the paper for a whole year that I honestly believe Jesus would not do."

Clark could not have looked more amazed if the chief had suddenly gone crazy. In fact, he did think something was wrong, though Mr. Norman was one of the last men in the world, in his judgment, to lose his mind.

"What effect will that have on the paper?" he finally managed to ask in a faint voice.

"What do you think?" asked Norman with a keen glance.

"I think it will simply ruin the paper," replied Clark promptly. He was gathering up his bewildered senses, and began to remonstrate, "Why, it isn't feasible to run a paper nowadays on any such basis. It's too ideal. The world isn't ready for it. You can't make it pay. Just as sure as you live, if you shut out this prize fight report you will lose hundreds of subscribers. It doesn't take a prophet so see that. The very best people in town are eager to read it. They know it has taken place, and when they get the paper this evening they will expect a half page at least. Surely, you can't afford to disregard the wishes of the public to such an extent. It will be a great mistake if you do, in my opinion."

Norman sat silent a minute. Then he spoke gently but firmly.

"Clark, what in your honest opinion is the right standard for determining conduct? Is the only right standard for every one, the probable action of Jesus Christ? Would you say that the highest, best law for a man to live by was contained in asking the question, 'What would Jesus do?' And then doing it regardless of results? In other words, do you think men everywhere ought to follow Jesus' example as closely as they can in their daily lives?" Clark turned red, and moved uneasily in his chair before he answered the editor's question.

"Why—yes—I suppose if you put it on the ground of what men ought to do there is no other standard of conduct. But the question is, What is feasible? Is it possible to make it pay? To succeed in the newspaper business we have got to conform to custom and the recognized methods of society. We can't do as we would in an ideal world."

"Do you mean that we can't run the paper strictly on principles and make it succeed?"

"Yes, that's just what I mean. It can't be done. We'll go bankrupt in thirty days."

Norman did not reply at once. He was very thoughtful.

"We shall have occasion to talk this over again, Clark. Meanwhile I think we ought to understand each other frankly. I have pledged myself for a year to do everything connected with the paper after answering the question, 'What would Jesus do?' as honestly as possible. I shall continue to do this in the belief that not only can we succeed but that we can succeed better than we ever did."

Clark rose. "The report does not go in?"

"It does not. There is plenty of good material to take its place, and you know what it is."

Clark hesitated. "Are you going to say anything about the absence of the report?"

"No, let the paper go to press as if there had been no such thing as a prize fight yesterday."

Clark walked out of the room to his own desk feeling as if the bottom had dropped out of everything. He was astonished, bewildered, excited and considerably angered. His great respect for Norman checked his rising indignation and disgust, but with it all was a feeling of growing wonder at the sudden change of motive which had entered the office of the *Daily News* and threatened, as he firmly believed, to destroy it.

Before noon every reporter, pressman and employee on the *Daily News* was informed of the remarkable fact that the paper was going to press without a word in it about the famous prize fight of Sunday. The reporters were simply astonished beyond measure at the announcement of the fact. Every one in the stereotyping and composing rooms had something to say about the unheard of omission. Two or three times during the day when Mr. Norman had occasion to visit the composing rooms the men stopped their work or glanced around their cases looking at him curiously. He knew that he was being observed, but said nothing and did not appear to note it.

There had been several minor changes in the paper, suggested by the editor, but nothing marked. He was waiting and thinking deeply.

He felt as if he needed time and considerable opportunity for the exercise of his best judgment in several matters before he answered his ever present question in the right way. It was not because there were not a great many things in the life of the paper that were contrary to the spirit of Christ that he did not act at once, but because he was yet honestly in doubt concerning what action Jesus would take.

When the *Daily News* came out that evening it carried to its subscribers a distinct sensation.

The presence of the report of the prize fight could not have produced anything equal to the effect of its omission. Hundreds of men in the hotels and stores down town, as well as regular subscribers, eagerly opened the paper and searched it through for the account of the great fight; not finding it, they rushed to the news stands and bought other papers. Even the newsboys had not all understood the fact of omission. One of them was calling out "*Daily News!* Full 'count great prize fight 't Resort. News, sir?"

A man on the corner of the avenue close by the *News* office bought the paper, looked over its front page hurriedly and then angrily called the boy back.

"Here, boy! What's the matter with your paper? There's no prize fight here! What do you mean by selling old papers?"

"Old papers nuthin'!" replied the boy indignantly. "Dat's to-day's paper. What's de matter wid you?"

"But there is no account of the prize fight here! Look!"

The man handed back the paper and the boy glanced at it hurriedly. Then he whistled, while a bewildered look crept over his face. Seeing another boy running by with papers he called out "Say, Sam, le'me see your pile." A hasty examination revealed the remarkable fact that all the copies of the *News* were silent on the subject of the prize fight.

"Here, give me another paper!" shouted the customer; "one with the prize fight account."

He received it and walked off, while the two boys remained comparing notes and lost in wonder at the result. "Sump'n slipped a cog in the Newsy, sure," said the first boy. But he couldn't tell why, and ran over to the *News* office to find out.

There were several other boys at the delivery room and they were all excited and disgusted. The amount of slangy remonstrance hurled at the clerk back of the long counter would have driven any one else to despair.

He was used to more or less of it all the time, and consequently hardened to it. Mr. Norman was just coming downstairs on his way home, and he paused as he went by the door of the delivery room and looked in.

"What's the matter here, George?" he asked the clerk as he noted the unusual confusion.

"The boys say they can't sell any copies of the *News* to-night because the prize fight isn't in it," replied George, looking curiously at the editor as so many of the employees had done during the day. Mr. Norman hesitated a moment, then walked into the room and confronted the boys.

"How many papers are there here? Boys, count them out, and I'll buy them to-night."

There was a combined stare and a wild counting of papers on the part of the boys.

"Give them their money, George, and if any of the other boys come in with the same complaint buy their unsold copies. Is that fair?" he asked the boys who were smitten into unusual silence by the unheard of action on the part of the editor.

"Fair! Well, I should— But will you keep this up? Will dis be a continual performance for de benefit of de fraternity ?"

Mr. Norman smiled slightly but he did not think it was necessary to answer the question.

He walked out of the office and went home. On the way he could not avoid that constant query, "Would Jesus have done it?" It was not so much with reference to this last transaction as to the entire motive that had urged him on since he had made the promise.

The newsboys were necessarily sufferers through the action he had taken. Why should they lose money by it? They were not to blame. He was a rich man and could afford to put a little brightness into their lives if he chose to do it. He believed, as he went on his way home, that Jesus would have done either what he did or something similar in order to be free from any possible feeling of injustice.

He was not deciding these questions for any one else but for his own conduct. He was not in a position to dogmatize, and he felt that he could answer only with his own judgment and conscience as to his interpretation of his Master's probable action. The falling off in sales of the paper he had in a measure foreseen. But he was yet to realize the full extent of the loss to the paper, if such a policy should be continued.

4

DURING THE WEEK HE WAS IN RECEIPT OF NUMEROUS letters commenting on the absence from the *News* of the account of the prize fight. Two or three of these letters may be of interest.

Editor of the *News:*
Dear Sir—
I have been thinking for some time of changing my paper. I want a journal that is up to the times, progressive and enterprising, supplying the public demand at all points. The recent freak of your paper in refusing to print the account of the famous contest at the resort has decided me finally to change my paper. Please discontinue it.

Very truly yours,

——————.

Here followed the name of a business man who had been a subscriber for many years.

Edward Norman,
Editor of the Daily *News*, Raymond:
Dear Ed.—

What is this sensation you have given the people of your burg? What new policy have you taken up? Hope you don't intend to try the "reform business" through the avenue of the press. It's dangerous to experiment much along that line. Take my advice and stick to the enterprising modern methods you have made so successful for the *News*. The public wants prize fights and such. Give it what it wants, and let some one else do the Reforming business.

Yours,

——————.

Here followed the name of one of Norman's old friends, the editor of a daily in an adjoining town.

My Dear Mr. Norman:

I hasten to write you a note of appreciation for the evident carrying out of your promise. It is a splendid beginning and no one feels the value of it more than I do. I know something of what it will cost you, but not all. Your pastor,

Henry Maxwell.

One other letter which he opened immediately after reading this from Maxwell revealed to him something of the loss to his business that possibly awaited him.

Mr. Edward Norman,
Editor of the *Daily News:*
Dear Sir—

At the expiration of my advertising limit, you will do me the favor not to continue it as you have done heretofore. I enclose check for payment in full and shall consider my account with your paper closed after date.

Very truly yours,

——————.

Here followed the name of one of the largest dealers in tobacco in the city. He had been in the habit of inserting a column of conspicuous advertising and paying for it a very large price.

Norman laid this letter down thoughtfully, and then after a moment he took up a copy of his paper and looked through the advertising columns. There was no connection implied in the tobacco merchant's letter between the omission of the prize fight and the withdrawal of the advertisement, but he could not avoid putting the two together. In point of fact, he afterward learned that the tobacco dealer withdrew his advertisement because he had heard that the editor of the *News* was about to enter upon some queer reform policy that would be certain to reduce its subscription list.

But the letter directed Norman's attention to the advertising phase of his paper. He had not considered this before.

As he glanced over the columns he could not escape the conviction that his Master could not permit some of them in his paper.

What would He do with that other long advertisement of choice liquors and cigars? As a member of a church and a respected citizen, he had incurred no special censure because the saloon men advertised in his columns. No one thought anything about it. It was all legitimate business. Why not? Raymond enjoyed a system of high license, and the saloon and the billiard hall and the beer garden were a part of the city's Christian civilization. He was simply doing what every other business man in Raymond did. And it was one of the best paying sources of revenue.

What would the paper do if it cut these out? Could it live? That was the question. But—was that the question after all? "What would Jesus do?" That was the question he was answering, or trying to answer, this week. Would Jesus advertise whiskey and tobacco in his paper?

Edward Norman asked it honestly, and after a prayer for help and wisdom he asked Clark to come into the office.

Clark came in, feeling that the paper was at a crisis, and prepared for almost anything after his Monday morning experience. This was Thursday.

"Clark," said Norman, speaking slowly and carefully, "I have been looking at our advertising columns and have decided to dispense with some of the matter as soon as the contracts run out. I wish you would notify the advertising agent not to solicit or renew the ads that I have marked here."

He handed the paper with the marked places over to Clark, who took it and looked over the columns with a very serious air.

"This will mean a great loss to the *News*. How long do you think you can keep this sort of thing up?" Clark was astounded at the editor's action and could not understand it.

"Clark, do you think if Jesus was the editor and proprietor of a daily paper in Raymond He would permit advertisements of whiskey and tobacco in it?"

"Well—no—I don't suppose He would. But what has that to do with us? We can't do as He would. Newspapers can't be run on any such basis."

"Why not?" asked Norman quietly.

"Why not? Because they will lose more money than they make, that's all!" Clark spoke out with an irritation that he really felt. "We shall certainly bankrupt the paper with this sort of business policy."

"Do you think so?" Norman asked the question not as if he expected an answer, but simply as if he were talking with himself. After a pause he said:

"You may direct Mark to do as I have said. I believe it is what Christ would do, and as I told you, Clark, that is what I have promised to try to do for a year, regardless of what the results may be to me. I cannot believe that by any kind of reasoning we could reach a conclusion justifying our Lord in the advertisement, in this age, of whiskey and tobacco in a newspaper. There are some other advertisements of a doubtful character I shall study into. Meanwhile, I feel a conviction in regard to these that cannot be silenced."

Clark went back to his desk feeling as if he had been in the presence of a very peculiar person. He could not grasp the meaning of it all. He felt enraged and alarmed. He was sure any such policy would ruin the paper as soon as it became generally known that the editor was trying to do everything by such an absurd moral standard. What would become of business if this standard was adopted? It would upset every custom and introduce endless confusion. It was simply foolishness. It was downright idiocy. So Clark said to himself, and when Mark was informed of the action he seconded the managing editor with some very forcible ejaculations. What was the matter with the chief? Was he insane? Was he going to bankrupt the whole business?

But Edward Norman had not yet faced his most serious problem. When he came down to the office Friday morning he was confronted with the usual program for the Sunday morning edition. The *News* was one of the few evening papers in Raymond to issue a Sunday edition, and it had always been remarkably successful financially. There was an average of one page of literary and religious items to thirty or forty pages of sport, theatre, gossip, fashion, society and political material. This made a very interesting magazine of all sorts of reading matter, and had always been welcomed by all the subscribers, church members and all, as a Sunday morning necessity.

Edward Norman now faced this fact and put to himself the question: "What would Jesus do?" If He was editor of a paper, would He deliberately plan to put into the homes of all the church people and Christians of Raymond such a collection of reading matter on the one day in the week which ought to be given up to something better and holier? He was of course familiar with the regular arguments of the Sunday paper, that the public needed something of the sort; and the working man especially, who would not go to church any way, ought to have something entertaining and instructive on Sunday, his only day of rest. But suppose the Sunday morning paper did not pay? Suppose there was no money in it? How eager would the editor or publisher be then to supply this crying need of the poor workman? Edward Norman communed honestly with himself over the subject.

Taking everything into account, would Jesus probably edit a Sunday morning paper? No matter whether it paid. That was not the question. As a matter of fact, the Sunday *News* paid so well that it would be a direct loss of thousands of dollars to discontinue it. Besides, the regular subscribers had paid for a seven-day paper. Had he any right now to give them less than they supposed they had paid for?

He was honestly perplexed by the question. So much was involved in the discontinuance of the Sunday edition that for the first time he almost decided to refuse to be guided by the standard of Jesus' probable action. He was sole proprietor of the paper; it was his to shape as he chose. He had no board of directors to consult as to policy. But as he sat there surrounded by the usual quantity of material for the Sunday edition he reached some definite conclusions. And among them was a determination to call in the force of the paper and frankly state his motive and purpose. He sent word for Clark and the other men in the office, including the few reporters who were in the building and the foreman, with what men were in the composing room (it was early in the morning and they were not all in) to come into the mailing room. This was a large room, and the men came in curiously and perched around on the tables and counters. It was a very unusual proceeding, but they all agreed that the paper was being run on new principles anyhow, and they all watched Mr. Norman carefully as he spoke.

"I called you in here to let you know my further plans for the *News*. I propose certain changes which I believe are necessary. I understand very well that some things I have already done are regarded by the men as very strange. I wish to state my motive in doing what I have done."

Here he told the men what he had already told Clark, and they stared as Clark had done, and looked as painfully conscious.

"Now, in acting on this standard of conduct I have reached a conclusion which will, no doubt, cause some surprise.

"I have decided that the Sunday morning edition of the *News* shall be discontinued after next Sunday's issue. I shall state in that issue my reasons for discontinuing. In order to make up to the subscribers the amount of reading matter they may suppose themselves entitled to, we can issue a double number on Saturday, as is done by many evening papers that make no attempt at a Sunday edition. I am convinced that from a Christian point of view more harm than good has been done by our Sunday morning paper. I do not believe that Jesus would be responsible for it if He were in my place to-day.

It will occasion some trouble to arrange the details caused by this change with the advertisers and subscribers. That is for me to look after. The change itself is one that will take place. So far as I can see, the loss will fall on myself. Neither the reporters nor the pressmen need make any particular changes in their plans."

He looked around the room and no one spoke. He was struck for the first time in his life with the fact that in all the years of his newspaper life he had never had the force of the paper together in this way. Would Jesus do that? That is, would He probably run a newspaper on some loving family plan, where editors, reporters, pressmen and all meet to discuss and devise and plan for the making of a paper that should have in view—

He caught himself drawing almost away from the facts of typographical unions and office rules and reporters' enterprise and all the cold, businesslike methods that make a great daily successful. But still the vague picture that came up in the mailing room would not fade away when he had gone into his office and the men had gone back to their places with wonder in their looks and questions of all sorts on their tongues as they talked over the editor's remarkable actions.

Clark came in and had a long, serious talk with his chief. He was thoroughly roused, and his protest almost reached the point of resigning his place.

Norman guarded himself carefully. Every minute of the interview was painful to him, but he felt more than ever the necessity of doing the Christ-like thing. Clark was a very valuable man. It would be difficult to fill his place. But he was not able to give any reasons for continuing the Sunday paper that answered the question, "What would Jesus do?" by letting Jesus print that edition.

"It comes to this, then," said Clark frankly, "you will bankrupt the paper in thirty days. We might as well face that future fact."

"I don't think we shall. Will you stay by the *News* until it is bankrupt?" asked Norman with a strange smile.

"Mr. Norman, I don't understand you. You are not the same man this week that I always knew before."

"I don't know myself either, Clark. Something remarkable has caught me up and borne me on. But I was never more convinced of final success and power for the paper. You have not answered my question. Will you stay with me?"

Clark hesitated a moment and finally said yes. Norman shook hands with him and turned to his desk. Clark went back into his room, stirred by a number of conflicting emotions. He had never before known such an exciting and mentally disturbing week, and he felt now as if he was connected with an enterprise that might at any moment collapse and ruin him and all connected with it.

5

Sunday morning dawned again on Raymond, and Henry Maxwell's church was again crowded. Before the service began Edward Norman attracted great attention. He sat quietly in his usual place about three seats from the pulpit. The Sunday morning issue of the *News* containing the statement of its discontinuance had been expressed in such remarkable language that every reader was struck by it. No such series of distinct sensations had ever disturbed the usual business custom of Raymond.

The events connected with the *News* were not all. People were eagerly talking about strange things done during the week by Alexander Powers at the railroad shops, and Milton Wright in his stores on the avenue. The service progressed upon a distinct wave of excitement in the pews. Henry Maxwell faced it all with a calmness which indicated a strength and purpose more than usual. His prayers were very helpful. His sermon was not so easy to describe. How would a minister be apt to preach to his people if he came before them after an entire week of eager asking, "How would Jesus preach? What would He probably say?" It is very certain that he did not preach as

35

he had done two Sundays before. Tuesday of the past week he had stood by the grave of the dead stranger and said the words, "Earth to earth, ashes to ashes, dust to dust," and still he was moved by the spirit of a deeper impulse than he could measure as he thought of his people and yearned for the Christ message when he should be in his pulpit again.

Now that Sunday had come and the people were there to hear, what would the Master tell them? He agonized over his preparation for them, and yet he knew he had not been able to fit his message into his ideal of the Christ. Nevertheless no one in the First Church could remember ever hearing such a sermon before. There was in it rebuke for sin, especially hypocrisy, there was definite rebuke of the greed of wealth and the selfishness of fashion, two things that First Church never heard rebuked this way before, and there was a love of his people that gathered new force as the sermon went on. When it was finished there were those who were saying in their hearts, "The Spirit moved that sermon." And they were right.

Then Rachel Winslow rose to sing, this time after the sermon, by Mr. Maxwell's request. Rachel's singing did not provoke applause this time. What deeper feeling carried the people's hearts into a reverent silence and tenderness of thought? Rachel was beautiful. But her consciousness of her remarkable loveliness had always marred her singing with those who had the deepest spiritual feeling. It had also marred her rendering of certain kinds of music with herself. To-day this was all gone. There was no lack of power in her grand voice. But there was an actual added element of humility and purity which the audience distinctly felt and bowed to.

Before service closed Mr. Maxwell asked those who had remained the week before to stay again for a few moments of consultation, and any others who were willing to make the pledge taken at that time. When he was at liberty he went into the lecture-room. To his astonishment it was almost filled. This time a large proportion of young people had come, but among them were a few business men and officers of the church.

As before, he, Maxwell, asked them to pray with him. And, as before, a distinct answer came from the presence of the divine Spirit. There was no doubt in the minds of any present that what they purposed to do was so clearly in line with the divine will, that a blessing rested upon it in a very special manner.

They remained some time to ask questions and consult together. There was a feeling of fellowship such as they had never known in their church membership. Mr. Norman's action was well understood by them all, and he answered several questions.

"What will be the probable result of your discontinuance of the Sunday paper?" asked Alexander Powers, who sat next to him.

"I don't know yet. I presume it will result in the falling off of subscriptions and advertisements. I anticipate that."

"Do you have any doubts about our action? I mean, do you regret it, or fear it is not what Jesus would do?" asked Mr. Maxwell.

"Not in the least. But I would like to ask, for my own satisfaction, if any of you here think Jesus would issue a Sunday morning paper?"

No one spoke for a minute. Then Jasper Chase said, "We seem to think alike on that, but I have been puzzled several times during the week to know just what He would do. It is not always an easy question to answer."

"I find that trouble," said Virginia Page. She sat by Rachel Winslow. Every one who knew Virginia Page was wondering how she would succeed in keeping her promise. "I think perhaps I find it specially difficult to answer that question on account of my money. Our Lord never owned any property, and there is nothing in His example to guide me in the use of mine. I am studying and praying. I think I see clearly a part of what He would do, but not all. What would He do with a million dollars? is my question really. I confess I am not yet able to answer it to my satisfaction."

"I could tell you what you could do with a part of it," said Rachel, turning her face toward Virginia.

"That does not trouble me," replied Virginia with a slight smile. "What I am trying to discover is a principle that will enable me to come to the nearest possible to His action as it ought to influence the entire course of my life so far as my wealth and its use are concerned."

"That will take time," said the minister slowly. All the rest of the room were thinking hard of the same thing. Milton Wright told something of his experience. He was gradually working out a plan for his business relations with his employees, and it was opening up a new world to him and to them. A few of the young men told of special attempts to answer the question. There was almost general consent over the fact that the application of the Christ spirit and practice to the everyday life was the serious thing. It required a knowledge of Him and an insight into His motives that most of them did not yet possess.

When they finally adjourned after a silent prayer that marked with growing power the Divine Presence, they went away discussing earnestly their difficulties and seeking light from one another.

Rachel Winslow and Virginia Page went out together. Edward Norman and Milton Wright became so interested in their mutual conference that they walked on past Norman's house and came back together. Jasper Chase and the president of the Endeavor Society stood talking earnestly in one corner of the room. Alexander Powers and Henry Maxwell remained, even after the others had gone.

"I want you to come down to the shops tomorrow and see my plan and talk to the men. Somehow I feel as if you could get nearer to them than any one else just now."

"I don't know about that, but I will come," replied Mr. Maxwell a little sadly. How was he fitted to stand before two or three hundred working men and give them a message? Yet in the moment of his weakness, as he asked the question, he rebuked himself for it. What would Jesus do? That was an end to the discussion.

He went down the next day and found Mr. Powers in his office. It lacked a few minutes of twelve and the superintendent said, "Come upstairs, and I'll show you what I've been trying to do."

They went through the machine shop, climbed a long flight of stairs and entered a very large, empty room. It had once been used by the company for a store room.

"Since making that promise a week ago I have had a good many things to think of," said the superintendent, "and among them is this: The company gives me the use of this room, and I am going to fit it up with tables and a coffee plant in the corner there where those steam pipes are. My plan is to provide a good place where the men can come up and eat their noon lunch, and give them, two or three times a week, the privilege of a fifteen minutes' talk on some subject that will be a real help to them in their lives."

Maxwell looked surprised and asked if the men would come for any such purpose.

"Yes, they'll come. After all, I know the men pretty well. They are among the most intelligent working men in the country to-day. But they are, as a whole, entirely removed from church influence. I asked, 'What would Jesus do?' and among other things it seemed to me He would begin to act in some way to add to the lives of these men more physical and spiritual comfort. It is a very little thing, this room and what it represents, but I acted on the first impulse, to do the first thing that appealed to my good sense, and I want to work out this idea. I want you to speak to the men when they come up at noon. I have asked them to come up and see the place and I'll tell them something about it."

Maxwell was ashamed to say how uneasy he felt at being asked to speak a few words to a company of working men. How could he speak without notes, or to such a crowd? He was honestly in a condition of genuine fright over the prospect. He actually felt afraid of facing those men. He shrank from the ordeal of confronting such a crowd, so different from the Sunday audiences he was familiar with.

There were a dozen rude benches and tables in the room, and when the noon whistle sounded the men poured upstairs from the machine shops below and, seating themselves at the tables, began to eat their lunch. There were present about three hundred of them. They had read the superintendent's notice which he had posted up in various places, and came largely out of curiosity.

They were favorably impressed. The room was large and airy, free from smoke and dust, and well warmed from the steam pipes. At about twenty minutes to one Mr. Powers told the men what he had in mind. He spoke very simply, like one who understands thoroughly the character of his audience, and then introduced the Rev. Henry Maxwell of the First Church, his pastor, who had consented to speak a few minutes.

Maxwell will never forget the feeling with which for the first time he stood before the grimy-faced audience of working men. Like hundreds of other ministers, he had never spoken to any gatherings except those made up of people of his own class in the sense that they were familiar in their dress and education and habits. This was a new world to him, and nothing but his new rule of conduct could have made possible his message and its effect. He spoke on the subject of satisfaction with life; what caused it, what its real sources were. He had the great good sense on this his first appearance not to recognize the men as a class distinct from himself. He did not use the term working man, and did not say a word to suggest any difference between their lives and his own.

The men were pleased. A good many of them shook hands with him before going down to their work, and the minister telling it all to his wife when he reached home, said that never in all his life had he known the delight he then felt in having the handshake from a man of physical labor. The day marked an important one in his Christian experience, more important than he knew. It was the beginning of a fellowship between him and the working world. It was the first plank laid down to help bridge the chasm between the church and labor in Raymond.

Alexander Powers went back to his desk that afternoon much pleased with his plan and seeing much help in it for the men. He knew where he could get some good tables from an abandoned eating house at one of the stations down the road, and he saw how the coffee arrangement could be made a very attractive feature. The men had responded even better than he anticipated, and the whole thing could not help being a great benefit to them.

He took up the routine of his work with a glow of satisfaction. After all, he wanted to do as Jesus would, he said to himself.

It was nearly four o'clock when he opened one of the company's long envelopes which he supposed contained orders for the purchasing of stores. He ran over the first page of type-written matter in his usual quick, business-like manner, before he saw that what he was reading was not intended for his office but for the superintendent of the freight department.

He turned over a page mechanically, not meaning to read what was not addressed to him, but before he knew it, he was in possession of evidence which conclusively proved that the company was engaged in a systematic violation of the Interstate Commerce Laws of the United States. It was as distinct and unequivocal a breaking of law as if a private citizen should enter a house and rob the inmates. The discrimination shown in rebates was in total contempt of all the statutes. Under the laws of the state it was also a distinct violation of certain provisions recently passed by the legislature to prevent railroad trusts. There was no question that he had in his hands evidence sufficient to convict the company of willful, intelligent violation of the law of the commission and the law of the state also.

He dropped the papers on his desk as if they were poison, and instantly the question flashed across his mind, "What would Jesus do?" He tried to shut the question out. He tried to reason with himself by saying it was none of his business. He had known in a more or less definite way, as did nearly all the officers of the company, that this had been going on right along on nearly all the roads. He was not in a position, owing to his place in the shops, to prove anything direct, and he had regarded it as a matter which did not concern him at all. The papers now before him revealed the entire affair. They had through some carelessness been addressed to him. What business of his was it? If he saw a man entering his neighbor's house to steal, would it not be his duty to inform the officers of the law? Was a railroad company such a different thing? Was it under a different rule of conduct, so that it could rob the public and defy law and be undisturbed because it was such a great organization? What would Jesus do? Then there was his family. Of course, if he took any steps to inform the commission it would mean the loss of his position. His wife and daughter had always enjoyed luxury and a good place in society. If he came out against this lawlessness as a witness it would drag him into courts, his motives would be misunderstood, and the whole thing would end in his disgrace and the loss of his position. Surely it was none of his business. He could easily get the papers back to the freight department and no one be the wiser. Let the iniquity go on. Let the law be defied. What was it to him? He would work out his plans for bettering the condition just before him. What more could a man do in this railroad business when there was so much going on anyway that made it impossible to live by the Christian standard? But what would Jesus do if He knew the facts? That was the question that confronted Alexander Powers as the day wore into evening.

The lights in the office had been turned on. The whirr of the great engine and the clash of the planers in the big shop continued until six o'clock. Then the whistle blew, the engine slowed up, the men dropped their tools and ran for the block house.

Powers heard the familiar click, click, of the clocks as the men filed past the window of the block house just outside. He said to his clerks, "I'm not going just yet. I have something extra to-night." He waited until he heard the last man deposit his block. The men behind the block case went out. The engineer and his assistants had work for half an hour but they went out by another door.

At seven o'clock any one who had looked into the superintendent's office would have seen an unusual sight. He was kneeling, and his face was buried in his hands as he bowed his head upon the papers on his desk.

6

WHEN RACHEL WINSLOW AND VIRGINIA PAGE SEPA-
rated after the meeting at the First Church on Sunday they agreed to
continue their conversation the next day. Virginia asked Rachel to
come and lunch with her at noon, and Rachel accordingly rang the
bell at the Page mansion about half-past eleven. Virginia herself met
her and the two were soon talking earnestly.

"The fact is," Rachel was saying, after they had been talking a few
moments, "I cannot reconcile it with my judgment of what Christ
would do. I cannot tell another person what to do, but I feel that I
ought not to accept this offer."

"What will you do then?" asked Virginia with great interest.

"I don't know yet, but I have decided to refuse this offer."

Rachel picked up a letter that had been lying in her lap and ran
over its contents again. It was a letter from the manager of a comic
opera offering her a place with a large traveling company of the season. The salary was a very large figure, and the prospect held out by
the manager was flattering. He had heard Rachel sing that Sunday
morning when the stranger had interrupted the service. He had been

much impressed. There was money in that voice and it ought to be used in comic opera, so said the letter, and the manager wanted a reply as soon as possible.

"There's no great virtue in saying 'No' to this offer when I have the other one," Rachel went on thoughtfully. "That's harder to decide. But I've about made up my mind. To tell the truth, Virginia, I'm completely convinced in the first case that Jesus would never use any talent like a good voice just to make money. But now, take this concert offer. Here is a reputable company, to travel with an impersonator and a violinist and a male quartet, all people of good reputation. I'm asked to go as one of the company and sing leading soprano. The salary—I mentioned it, didn't I?—is guaranteed to be $200 a month for the season. But I don't feel satisfied that Jesus would go. What do you think?"

"You mustn't ask me to decide for you," replied Virginia with a sad smile. "I believe Mr. Maxwell was right when he said we must each one of us decide according to the judgment we feel for ourselves to be Christ-like. I am having a harder time than you are, dear, to decide what He would do."

"Are you?" Rachel asked. She rose and walked over to the window and looked out. Virginia came and stood by her. The street was crowded with life and the two young women looked at it silently for a moment. Suddenly Virginia broke out as Rachel had never heard her before:

"Rachel, what does all this contrast in conditions mean to you as you ask this question of what Jesus would do? It maddens me to think that the society in which I have been brought up, the same to which we are both said to belong, is satisfied year after year to go on dressing and eating and having a good time, giving and receiving entertainments, spending its money on houses and luxuries and, occasionally, to ease its conscience, donating, without any personal sacrifice, a little money to charity. I have been educated, as you have, in one of the most expensive schools in America; launched into society as an heiress; supposed to be in a very enviable position. I'm perfectly well; I can travel or stay at home. I can do as I please. I can gratify almost any want or desire; and yet when I honestly try to imagine Jesus living the life I have lived and am expected to live, and doing for the rest of my life what thousands of other rich people do, I am under condemnation for being one of the most wicked selfish, useless creatures in all the world. I have not looked out of this window for weeks without a feeling of horror toward myself as I see the humanity that passes by this house."

Virginia turned away and walked up and down the room. Rachel watched her and could not repress the rising tide of her own growing definition of discipleship.

Of what Christian use was her own talent of song? Was the best she could do to sell her talent for so much a month, go on a concert company's tour, dress beautifully, enjoy the excitement of public applause and gain a reputation as a great singer? Was that what Jesus would do?

She was not morbid. She was in sound health, was conscious of her great powers as a singer, and knew that if she went out into public life she could make a great deal of money and become well known. It is doubtful if she overestimated her ability to accomplish all she thought herself capable of. And Virginia—what she had just said smote Rachel with great force because of the similar position in which the two friends found themselves.

Lunch was announced and they went out and were joined by Virginia's grandmother, Madam Page, a handsome, stately woman of sixty-five, and Virginia's brother Rollin, a young man who spent most of his time at one of the clubs and had no ambition for anything but a growing admiration for Rachel Winslow, and whenever she dined or lunched at the Page's, if he knew of it he always planned to be at home.

These three made up the Page family. Virginia's father had been a banker and grain speculator. Her mother had died ten years before, her father within the past year. The grandmother, a Southern woman in birth and training, had all the traditions and feelings that accompany the possession of wealth and social standing that have never been disturbed. She was a shrewd, careful business woman of more than average ability. The family property and wealth were invested, in large measure, under her personal care. Virginia's portion was, without any restriction, her own. She had been trained by her father to understand the ways of the business world, and even the grandmother had been compelled to acknowledge the girl's capacity for taking care of her own money.

Perhaps two persons could not be found anywhere less capable of understanding a girl like Virginia than Madam Page and Rollin. Rachel, who had known the family since she was a girl playmate of Virginia's, could not help thinking of what confronted Virginia in her own home when she once decided on the course which she honestly believed Jesus would take. To-day at lunch, as she recalled Virginia's outbreak in the front room, she tried to picture the scene that would at some time occur between Madam Page and her granddaughter.

"I understand that you are going on the stage, Miss Winslow. We shall all be delighted, I'm sure," said Rollin during the conversation, which had not been very animated.

Rachel colored and felt annoyed. "Who told you?" she asked, while Virginia, who had been very silent and reserved, suddenly roused herself and appeared ready to join in the talk.

"Oh! we hear a thing or two on the street. Besides, every one saw Crandall the manager at church two weeks ago. He doesn't go to church to hear the preaching. In fact, I know other people who don't either, not when there's something better to hear."

Rachel did not color this time, but she answered quietly, "You're mistaken. I'm not going on the stage."

"It's a great pity. You'd make a hit. Everybody is talking about your singing."

This time Rachel flushed with genuine anger. Before she could say anything, Virginia broke in:

"Whom do you mean by 'everybody?'"

"Whom? I mean all the people who hear Miss Winslow on Sundays. What other time do they hear her? It's a great pity, I say, that the general public outside of Raymond cannot hear her voice."

"Let us talk about something else," said Rachel a little sharply. Madam Page glanced at her and spoke with a gentle courtesy.

"My dear, Rollin never could pay an indirect compliment. He is like his father in that. But we are all curious to know something of your plans. We claim the right from old acquaintance, you know; and Virginia has already told us of your concert company offer."

"I supposed of course that was public property," said Virginia, smiling across the table. "I was in the *News* office day before yesterday."

"Yes, yes," replied Rachel hastily. "I understand that, Madam Page. Well, Virginia and I have been talking about it. I have decided not to accept, and that is as far as I have gone at present."

Rachel was conscious of the fact that the conversation had, up to this point, been narrowing her hesitation concerning the concert company's offer down to a decision that would absolutely satisfy her own judgment of Jesus' probable action. It had been the last thing in the world, however, that she had desired, to have her decision made in any way so public as this. Somehow what Rollin Page had said and his manner in saying it had hastened her decision in the matter.

"Would you mind telling us, Rachel, your reasons for refusing the offer? It looks like a great opportunity for a young girl like you. Don't you think the general public ought to hear you? I feel like Rollin about that. A voice like yours belongs to a larger audience than Raymond and the First Church."

Rachel Winslow was naturally a girl of great reserve. She shrank from making her plans or her thoughts public. But with all her repression there was possible in her an occasional sudden breaking out that was simply an impulsive, thoroughly frank, truthful expression of her most inner personal feeling. She spoke now in reply to Madam Page in one of those rare moments of unreserve that added to the attractiveness of her whole character.

"I have no other reason than a conviction that Jesus Christ would do the same thing," she said, looking into Madam Page's eyes with a clear, earnest gaze.

Madam Page turned red and Rollin stared. Before her grandmother could say anything, Virginia spoke. Her rising color showed how she was stirred. Virginia's pale, clear complexion was that of health, but it was generally in marked contrast with Rachel's tropical type of beauty.

"Grandmother, you know we promised to make that the standard of our conduct for a year. Mr. Maxwell's proposition was plain to all who heard it. We have not been able to arrive at our decisions very rapidly. The difficulty in knowing what Jesus would do has perplexed Rachel and me a good deal."

Madam Page looked sharply at Virginia before she added anything.

"Of course I understand Mr. Maxwell's statement. It is perfectly impracticable to put it into practice. I felt confident at the time that those who promised would find it out after a trial and abandon it as visionary and absurd. I have nothing to say about Miss Winslow's affairs, but," she paused and continued with a sharpness that was new to Rachel, "I hope you have no foolish notions in this matter, Virginia."

"I have a great many notions," replied Virginia quietly. "Whether they are foolish or not depends upon my right understanding of what He would do. As soon as I find out I shall do it."

"Excuse me, ladies," said Rollin, rising from the table. "The conversation is getting beyond my depth. I shall retire to the library for a cigar."

He went out of the dining-room and there was silence for a moment. Madam Page waited until the servant had brought in something and then asked her to go out. She was angry and her anger was formidable, although checked in some measure by the presence of Rachel.

"I am older by several years than you, young ladies," she said, and her traditional type of bearing seemed to Rachel to rise up like a great frozen wall between her and every conception of Jesus as a sacrifice. "What you have promised, in a spirit of false emotion I presume, is impossible of performance."

"Do you mean, grandmother, that we cannot possibly act as our Lord would? Or do you mean that, if we try to, we shall offend the customs and prejudices of society?" asked Virginia.

"It is not required! It is not necessary! Besides how can you act with any—" Madam Page paused, broke off her sentence, and then turned to Rachel. "What will your mother say to your decision? My dear, is it not foolish? What do you expect to do with your voice anyway?"

"I don't know what mother will say yet," Rachel answered, with a great shrinking from trying to give her mother's probable answer. If there was a woman in all Raymond with great ambitions for her daughter's success as a singer, Mrs. Winslow was that woman.

"Oh! you will see it in a different light after wiser thought of it. My dear," continued Madam Page rising from the table, "you will live to regret it if you do not accept the concert company's offer or something like it."

Rachel said something that contained a hint of the struggle she was still having. And after a little she went away, feeling that her departure was to be followed by a very painful conversation between Virginia and her grandmother. As she afterward learned, Virginia passed through a crisis of feeling during that scene with her grandmother that hastened her final decision as to the use of her money and her social position.

7

RACHEL WAS GLAD TO ESCAPE AND BE BY HERSELF. A plan was slowly forming in her mind, and she wanted to be alone and think it out carefully. But before she had walked two blocks she was annoyed to find Rollin Page walking beside her.

"Sorry to disturb your thoughts, Miss Winslow, but I happened to be going your way and had an idea you might not object. In fact, I've been walking here for a whole block and you haven't objected."

"I did not see you," said Rachel briefly.

"I wouldn't mind that if you only thought of me once in a while," said Rollin suddenly. He took one last nervous puff on his cigar, tossed it into the street and walked along with a pale look on his face.

Rachel was surprised, but not startled. She had known Rollin as a boy, and there had been a time when they had used each other's first name familiarly. Lately, however, something in Rachel's manner had put an end to that. She was used to his direct attempts at compliments and was sometimes amused by them. To-day she honestly wished him anywhere else.

"Do you ever think of me, Miss Winslow?" asked Rollin after a pause.

"Oh, yes, quite often!" said Rachel with a smile.

"Are you thinking of me now?"

"Yes. That is—yes—I am."

"What?"

"Do you want me to be absolutely truthful?"

"Of course."

"Then I was thinking that I wished you were not here."

Rollin bit his lip and looked gloomy.

"Now look here, Rachel—oh, I know that's forbidden, but I've got to speak some time!—you know how I feel. What makes you treat me so? You used to like me a little, you know."

"Did I? Of course we used to get on very well as boy and girl. But we are older now."

Rachel still spoke in the light, easy way she had used since her first annoyance at seeing him. She was still somewhat preoccupied with her plan, which had been disturbed by Rollin's sudden appearance.

They walked along in silence a little way. The avenue was full of people. Among the persons passing was Jasper Chase. He saw Rachel and Rollin and bowed as they went by. Rollin was watching Rachel closely.

"I wish I was Jasper Chase. Maybe I would stand some chance then," he said moodily.

Rachel colored in spite of herself. She did not say anything and quickened her pace a little. Rollin seemed determined to say something, and Rachel seemed helpless to prevent him. After all, she thought, he might as well know the truth one time as another.

"You know well enough, Rachel, how I feel toward you. Isn't there any hope? I could make you happy. I've loved you a good many years—"

"Why, how old do you think I am?" broke in Rachel with a nervous laugh. She was shaken out of her usual poise of manner.

"You know what I mean," went on Rollin doggedly. "And you have no right to laugh at me just because I want you to marry me."

"I'm not! But it is useless for you to speak, Rollin," said Rachel after a little hesitation, and then using his name in such a frank, simple way that he could attach no meaning to it beyond the familiarity of the old family acquaintance. "It is impossible."

She was still a little agitated by the fact of receiving a proposal of marriage on the avenue. But the noise on the street and sidewalk made the conversation as private as if they were in the house.

"Would—that is—do you think—if you gave me time I would—"

"No!" said Rachel. She spoke firmly; perhaps, she thought afterward, although she did not mean to, she spoke harshly.

They walked on for some time without a word. They were nearing Rachel's home and she was anxious to end the scene.

As they turned off the avenue into one of the quieter streets Rollin spoke suddenly and with more manliness than he had yet shown. There was a distinct note of dignity in his voice that was new to Rachel. "Miss Winslow, I ask you to be my wife. Is there any hope for me that you will ever consent?"

"None in the least." Rachel spoke decidedly.

"Will you tell me why?" He asked the question as if he had a right to a truthful answer.

"Because I do not feel toward you as a woman ought to feel toward the man she marries."

"In other words, you do not love me?"

"I do not and I cannot."

"Why?" That was another question, and Rachel was a little surprised that he should ask it.

"Because—" she hesitated for fear she might say too much in an attempt to speak the exact truth.

"Tell me just why. You can't hurt me more than you have already."

"Well, I do not and I cannot love you because you have no purpose in life. What do you ever do to make the world better? You spend your time in club life, in amusements, in travel, in luxury. What is there in such a life to attract a woman?"

"Not much, I guess," said Rollin with a bitter laugh. "Still, I don't know that I'm any worse than the rest of the men around me. I'm not so bad as some. I'm glad to know your reasons."

He suddenly stopped, took off his hat, bowed gravely and turned back. Rachel went on home and hurried into her room, disturbed in many ways by the event which had so unexpectedly thrust itself into her experience.

When she had time to think it all over she found herself condemned by the very judgment she had passed on Rollin Page. What purpose had she in life? She had been abroad and studied music with one of the famous teachers of Europe. She had come home to Raymond and had been singing in the First Church choir now for a year. She was well paid. Up to that Sunday two weeks ago she had been quite satisfied with herself and with her position. She had shared her mother's ambition, and anticipated growing triumphs in the musical world. What possible career was before her except the regular career of every singer?

She asked the question again and, in the light of her recent reply to Rollin, asked again, if she had any very great purpose in life herself. What would Jesus do? There was a fortune in her voice. She knew it, not necessarily as a matter of personal pride or professional egotism, but simply as a fact. And she was obliged to acknowledge that until two weeks ago she had purposed to use her voice to make money and win admiration and applause. Was that a much higher purpose, after all, than Rollin Page lived for?

She sat in her room a long time and finally went downstairs, resolved to have a frank talk with her mother about the concert company's offer and the new plan which was gradually shaping in her mind. She had already had one talk with her mother and knew that she expected Rachel to accept the offer and enter on a successful career as a public singer.

"Mother," Rachel said, coming at once to the point, much as she dreaded the interview, "I have decided not to go out with the company. I have a good reason for it."

Mrs. Winslow was a large, handsome woman, fond of much company, ambitious for distinction in society and devoted, according to her definitions of success, to the success of her children. Her youngest boy, Louis, two years younger than Rachel, was ready to graduate from a military academy in the summer. Meanwhile she and Rachel were at home together. Rachel's father, like Virginia's, had died while the family was abroad. Like Virginia she found herself, under her present rule of conduct, in complete antagonism with her own immediate home circle. Mrs. Winslow waited for Rachel to go on.

"You know the promise I made two weeks ago, mother?"

"Mr. Maxwell's promise?"

"No, mine. You know what it was, do you not, mother?"

"I suppose I do. Of course all the church members mean to imitate Christ and follow Him, as far as is consistent with our present day surroundings. But what has that to do with your decision in the concert company matter?"

"It has everything to do with it. After asking, 'What would Jesus do?' and going to the source of authority for wisdom, I have been obliged to say that I do not believe He would, in my case, make that use of my voice."

"Why? Is there anything wrong about such a career?"

"No, I don't know that I can say there is."

"Do you presume to sit in judgment on other people who go out to sing in this way? Do you presume to say they are doing what Christ would not do?"

"Mother, I wish you to understand me. I judge no one else; I condemn no other professional singer. I simply decide my own course. As I look at it, I have a conviction that Jesus would do something else."

"What else?" Mrs. Winslow had not yet lost her temper. She did not understand the situation nor Rachel in the midst of it, but she was anxious that her daughter's course should be as distinguished as her natural gifts promised. And she felt confident that when the present unusual religious excitement in the First Church had passed away Rachel would go on with her public life according to the wishes of the family. She was totally unprepared for Rachel's next remark.

"What? Something that will serve mankind where it most needs the service of song. Mother, I have made up my mind to use my voice in some way so as to satisfy my own soul that I am doing something better than pleasing fashionable audiences, or making money, or even gratifying my own love of singing. I am going to do something that will satisfy me when I ask: 'What would Jesus do?' I am not satisfied, and cannot be, when I think of myself as singing myself into the career of a concert company performer."

Rachel spoke with a vigor and earnestness that surprised her mother. But Mrs. Winslow was angry now; and she never tried to conceal her feelings.

"It is simply absurd! Rachel, you are a fanatic! What can you do?"

"The world has been served by men and women who have given it other things that were gifts. Why should I, because I am blessed with a natural gift, at once proceed to put a market price on it and make all the money I can out of it? You know, mother, that you have taught me to think of a musical career always in the light of financial and social success. I have been unable, since I made my promise two weeks ago, to imagine Jesus joining a concert company to do what I should do and live the life I should have to live if I joined it."

Mrs. Winslow rose and then sat down again. With a great effort she composed herself.

"What do you intend to do then? You have not answered my question."

"I shall continue to sing for the time being in the church. I am pledged to sing there through the spring. During the week I am going to sing at the White Cross meetings, down in the Rectangle."

"What! Rachel Winslow! Do you know what you are saying? Do you know what sort of people those are down there?"

Rachel almost quailed before her mother. For a moment she shrank back and was silent. Then she spoke firmly:

"I know very well. That is the reason I am going. Mr. and Mrs. Gray have been working there several weeks. I learned only this morning that they want singers from the churches to help them in their meetings. They use a tent. It is in a part of the city where Christian work is most needed. I shall offer them my help. Mother!" Rachel cried out with the first passionate utterance she had yet used, "I want to do something that will cost me something in the way of sacrifice. I know you will not understand me. But I am hungry to suffer for something. What have we done all our lives for the suffering, sinning side of Raymond? How much have we denied ourselves or given of our personal ease and pleasure to bless the place in which we live or imitate the life of the Saviour of the world? Are we always to go on doing as society selfishly dictates, moving on its little narrow round of pleasures and entertainments, and never knowing the pain of things that cost?"

"Are you preaching at me?" asked Mrs. Winslow slowly. Rachel rose, and understood her mother's words.

"No. I am preaching at myself," she replied gently. She paused a moment as if she thought her mother would say something more, and then went out of the room. When she reached her own room she felt that so far as her own mother was concerned she could expect no sympathy, nor even a fair understanding from her.

She kneeled. It is safe to say that within the two weeks since Henry Maxwell's church had faced that shabby figure with the faded hat more members of his parish had been driven to their knees in prayer than during all the previous term of his pastorate.

She rose, and her face was wet with tears. She sat thoughtfully a little while and then wrote a note to Virginia Page. She sent it to her by a messenger and then went downstairs and told her mother that she and Virginia were going down to the Rectangle that evening to see Mr. and Mrs. Gray, the evangelists.

"Virginia's uncle, Dr. West, will go with us, if she goes. I have asked her to call him up by telephone and go with us. The Doctor is a friend of the Grays, and attended some of their meetings last winter."

Mrs. Winslow did not say anything. Her manner showed her complete disapproval of Rachel's course, and Rachel felt her unspoken bitterness.

About seven o'clock the Doctor and Virginia appeared, and together the three started for the scene of the White Cross meetings.

The Rectangle was the most notorious district in Raymond. It was on the territory close by the railroad shops and the packing houses. The great slum and tenement district of Raymond congested its worst and most wretched elements about the Rectangle. This was a barren field used in the summer by circus companies and wandering showmen. It was shut in by rows of saloons, gambling hells and cheap, dirty boarding and lodging houses.

The First Church of Raymond had never touched the Rectangle problem. It was too dirty, too coarse, too sinful, too awful for close contact. Let us be honest. There had been an attempt to cleanse this sore spot by sending down an occasional committee of singers or Sunday school teachers or gospel visitors from various churches. But the First Church of Raymond, as an institution, had never really done anything to make the Rectangle any less a stronghold of the devil as the years went by.

Into this heart of the coarse part of the sin of Raymond the traveling evangelist and his brave little wife had pitched a good-sized tent and begun meetings. It was the spring of the year and the evenings were beginning to be pleasant. The evangelists had asked for the help of Christian people, and had received more than the usual amount of encouragement. But they felt a great need of more and better music. During the meetings on the Sunday just gone the assistant at the organ had been taken ill. The volunteers from the city were few and the voices were of ordinary quality.

"There will be a small meeting to-night, John," said his wife, as they entered the tent a little after seven o'clock and began to arrange the chairs and light up.

"Yes, I fear so." Mr. Gray was a small, energetic man, with a pleasant voice and the courage of a high-born fighter. He had already made friends in the neighborhood and one of his converts, a heavy-faced man who had just come in, began to help in the arranging of seats.

It was after eight o'clock when Alexander Powers opened the door of his office and started for home. He was going to take a car at the corner of the Rectangle. But he was roused by a voice coming from the tent.

It was the voice of Rachel Winslow. It struck through his consciousness of struggle over his own question that had sent him into the Divine Presence for an answer. He had not yet reached a conclusion. He was tortured with uncertainty. His whole previous course of action as a railroad man was the poorest possible preparation for anything sacrificial. And he could not yet say what he would do in the matter.

Hark! What was she singing? How did Rachel Winslow happen to be down here? Several windows near by went up. Some men quarreling near a saloon stopped and listened. Other figures were walking rapidly in the direction of the Rectangle and the tent. Surely Rachel Winslow had never sung like that in the First Church. It was a marvelous voice. What was it she was singing? Again Alexander Powers, Superintendent of the machine shops, paused and listened.

> *"Where He leads me I will follow,*
> *Where He leads me I will follow,*
> *Where He leads me I will follow,*
> *I'll go with Him, with Him*
> *All the way!"*

The brutal, coarse, impure life of the Rectangle stirred itself into new life as the song, as pure as the surroundings were vile, floated out and into saloon and den and foul lodging. Some one who stumbled hastily by Alexander Powers said in answer to a question:

"De tent's beginning to run over to-night. That's what the talent calls music, eh?"

The Superintendent turned toward the tent. Then he stopped. After a minute of indecision he went on to the corner and took the car for his home. But before he was out of the sound of Rachel's voice he knew he had settled for himself the question of what Jesus would do.

8

"If any man would come after me, let him deny himself and take up his cross daily and follow me."

Henry Maxwell paced his study back and forth. It was Wednesday and he had started to think out the subject of his evening service which fell upon that night. Out of one of his study windows he could see the tall chimney of the railroad shops. The top of the evangelist's tent just showed over the buildings around the Rectangle. He looked out of his window every time he turned in his walk. After a while he sat down at his desk and drew a large piece of paper toward him. After thinking several moments he wrote in large letters the following:

A Number of Things That Jesus Would Probably Do in This Parish

1. Live in a simple, plain manner, without needless luxury on the one hand or undue asceticism on the other.

2. Preach fearlessly to the hypocrites in the church, no matter what their social importance or wealth.

3. Become known as a friend and companion of the sinful people in the Rectangle.

4. Identify Himself with the great causes of humanity in some personal way that would call for self-denial and suffering.

5. Preach against the saloon in Raymond.

6. Show in some practical form His sympathy and love for the common people as well as for the well-to-do, educated, refined people who make up the majority of the parish.

7. Give up the summer trip to Europe this year. (I have been abroad twice and cannot claim any special need of rest. I am well, and could forego this pleasure, using the money for some one who needs a vacation more than I do. There are probably plenty of such people in the city.)

He was conscious, with a humility that was once a stranger to him, that his outline of Jesus' probable action was painfully lacking in depth and power, but he was seeking carefully for concrete shapes into which he might cast his thought of Jesus' conduct. Nearly every point he had put down, meant, for him, a complete overturning of the custom and habit of years in the ministry. In spite of that, he still searched deeper for sources of the Christ-like spirit. He did not attempt to write any more, but sat at his desk absorbed in his effort to catch more and more the spirit of Jesus in his own life. He had forgotten the particular subject for his prayer meeting with which he had begun his morning study.

He was so absorbed over his thought that he did not hear the bell ring; he was roused by the servant who announced a caller. He had sent up his name, Mr. Gray.

Maxwell stepped to the head of the stairs and asked Gray to come up. So Gray came up and stated the reason for his call.

"I want your help, Mr. Maxwell. Of course you have heard what a wonderful meeting we had Monday night and last night. Miss Winslow has done more with her voice than I could do, and the tent won't hold the people."

"I've heard of that. It is the first time the people there have heard her. It is no wonder they are attracted."

"It has been a wonderful revelation to us, and a most encouraging event in our work. But I came to ask if you could not come down tonight and preach. I am suffering from a severe cold. I do not dare trust my voice again. I know it is asking a good deal from such a busy man. But, if you can't come, say so frankly, and I'll try somewhere else."

"I'm sorry, but it's my regular prayer meeting night," began Henry Maxwell. Then he flushed and added, "I shall be able to arrange it in some way so as to come down. You can count on me."

Gray thanked him earnestly and rose to go.

"Won't you stay a minute, Gray, and let us have a prayer together?"

"Yes," said Gray simply.

So the two men kneeled together in the study. Henry Maxwell prayed like a child. Gray was touched to tears as he knelt there. There was something almost pitiful in the way this man who had lived his ministerial life in such a narrow limit of exercise now begged for wisdom and strength to speak a message to the people in the Rectangle.

Gray rose and held out his hand. "God bless you, Mr. Maxwell. I'm sure the Spirit will give you power to-night."

Henry Maxwell made no answer. He did not even trust himself to say that he hoped so. But he thought of his promise and it brought him a certain peace that was refreshing to his heart and mind alike.

So that is how it came about that when the First Church audience came into the lecture room that evening it met with another surprise. There was an unusually large number present. The prayer meetings ever since that remarkable Sunday morning had been attended as never before in the history of the First Church. Mr. Maxwell came at once to the point.

"I feel that I am called to go down to the Rectangle tonight, and I will leave it with you to say whether you will go on with this meeting here. I think perhaps the best plan would be for a few volunteers to go down to the Rectangle with me prepared to help in the after-meeting, if necessary, and the rest to remain here and pray that the Spirit power may go with us."

So half a dozen of the men went with the pastor, and the rest of the audience stayed in the lecture room. Maxwell could not escape the thought as he left the room that probably in his entire church membership there might not be found a score of disciples who were capable of doing work that would successfully lead needy, sinful men into the knowledge of Christ. The thought did not linger in his mind to vex him as he went his way, but it was simply a part of his whole new conception of the meaning of Christian discipleship.

When he and his little company of volunteers reached the Rectangle, the tent was already crowded. They had difficulty in getting to the platform. Rachel was there with Virginia and Jasper Chase who had come instead of the Doctor to-night.

When the meeting began with a song in which Rachel sang the solo and the people were asked to join in the chorus, not a foot of standing room was left in the tent. The night was mild and the sides of the tent were up and a great border of faces stretched around, looking in and forming part of the audience. After the singing, and a prayer by one of the city pastors who was present, Gray stated the reason for his inability to speak, and in his simple manner turned the service over to "Brother Maxwell, of the First Church."

"Who's de bloke?" asked a hoarse voice near the outside of the tent.

"De Fust Church parson. We've got de whole hightone swell outfit to-night."

"Did you say Fust Church? I know him. My landlord's got a front pew up there," said another voice, and there was a laugh, for the speaker was a saloon keeper.

"Trow out de life line 'cross de dark wave!" began a drunken man near by, singing in such an unconscious imitation of a local traveling singer's nasal tone that roars of laughter and jeers of approval rose around him. The people in the tent turned in the direction of the disturbance. There were shouts of "Put him out!" "Give the Fust Church a chance!" "Song! Song! Give us another song!"

Henry Maxwell stood up, and a great wave of actual terror went over him. This was not like preaching to the well-dressed, respectable, good-mannered people up on the boulevard. He began to speak, but the confusion increased. Gray went down into the crowd, but did not seem able to quiet it. Maxwell raised his arm and his voice. The crowd in the tent began to pay some attention, but the noise on the outside increased. In a few minutes the audience was beyond his control. He turned to Rachel with a sad smile.

"Sing something, Miss Winslow. They will listen to you," he said, and then sat down and covered his face with his hands.

It was Rachel's opportunity, and she was fully equal to it. Virginia was at the organ and Rachel asked her to play a few notes of the hymn,

> *"Saviour, I follow on,*
> *Guided by Thee,*
> *Seeing not yet the hand*
> *That leadeth me.*
> *Hushed be my heart and still*
> *Fear I no farther ill,*
> *Only to meet Thy will,*
> *My will shall be."*

Rachel had not sung the first line before the people in the tent were all turned toward her, hushed and reverent. Before she had finished the verse the Rectangle was subdued and tamed. It lay like some wild beast at her feet, and she sang it into harmlessness. Ah! What were the flippant, perfumed, critical audiences in concert halls compared with this dirty, drunken, impure, besotted mass of humanity that trembled and wept and grew strangely, sadly thoughtful under the touch of this divine ministry of this beautiful young woman!

Mr. Maxwell, as he raised his head and saw the transformed mob, had a glimpse of something that Jesus would probably do with a voice like Rachel Winslow's. Jasper Chase sat with his eyes on the singer, and his greatest longing as an ambitious author was swallowed up in his thought of what Rachel Winslow's love might sometimes mean to him. And over in the shadow outside stood the last person any one might have expected to see at a gospel tent service—Rollin Page, who, jostled on every side by rough men and women who stared at the swell in fine clothes, seemed careless of his surroundings and at the same time evidently swayed by the power that Rachel possessed. He had just come over from the club. Neither Rachel nor Virginia saw him that night.

The song was over. Maxwell rose again. This time he felt calmer. What would Jesus do? He spoke as he thought once he never could speak. Who were these people? They were immortal souls. What was Christianity? A calling of sinners, not the righteous, to repentance. How would Jesus speak? What would He say? He could not tell all that His message would include, but he felt sure of a part of it. And in that certainty he spoke on. Never before had he felt "compassion for the multitude." What had the multitude been to him during his ten years in the First Church but a vague, dangerous, dirty, troublesome factor in society, outside of the church and of his reach, an element that caused him occasionally an unpleasant twinge of conscience, a factor in Raymond that was talked about at associations as the "masses," in papers written by the brethren in attempts to show why the "masses" were not being reached. But to-night as he faced the masses he asked himself whether, after all, this was not just about such a multitude as Jesus faced oftenest, and he felt the genuine emotion of love for a crowd which is one of the best indications a preacher ever has that he is living close to the heart of the world's eternal Life. It is easy to love an individual sinner, especially if he is personally picturesque or interesting. To love a multitude of sinners is distinctively a Christ-like quality.

When the meeting closed, there was no special interest shown. No one stayed to the after-meeting. The people rapidly melted away from the tent, and the saloons, which had been experiencing a dull season while the meetings progressed, again drove a thriving trade. The Rectangle, as if to make up for lost time, started in with vigor on its usual night debauch. Maxwell and his little party, including

Virginia, Rachel and Jasper Chase, walked down past the row of saloons and dens until they reached the corner where the cars passed.

"This is a terrible spot," said the minister as he stood waiting for their car. "I never realized that Raymond had such a festering sore. It does not seem possible that this is a city full of Christian disciples."

"Do you think any one can ever remove this great curse of drink?" asked Jasper Chase.

"I have thought lately as never before of what Christian people might do to remove the curse of the saloon. Why don't we all act together against it? Why don't the Christian pastors and the church members of Raymond move as one man against the traffic? What would Jesus do? Would He keep silent? Would He vote to license these causes of crime and death?"

He was talking to himself more than to the others. He remembered that he had always voted for license, and so had nearly all his church members. What would Jesus do? Could he answer that question? Would the Master preach and act against the saloon if He lived to-day? How would He preach and act? Suppose it was not popular to preach against license? Suppose the Christian people thought it was all that could be done to license the evil and so get revenue from the necessary sin? Or suppose the church members themselves owned the property where the saloons stood—what then? He knew that those were the facts in Raymond. What would Jesus do?

He went up into his study the next morning with that question only partly answered. He thought of it all day. He was still thinking of it and recalling certain real conclusions when the *Evening News* came. His wife brought it up and sat down a few minutes while he read to her.

The *Evening News* was at present the most sensational paper in Raymond. That is to say, it was being edited in such a remarkable fashion that its subscribers had never been so excited over a newspaper before. First they had noticed the absence of the prize fight, and gradually it began to dawn upon them that the *News* no longer printed accounts of crime with detailed descriptions, or scandals in private life. Then they noticed that the advertisements of liquor and tobacco were dropped, together with certain others of a questionable character. The discontinuance of the Sunday paper caused the greatest comment of all, and now the character of the editorials was creating the greatest excitement. A quotation from the Monday paper of this week will show what Edward Norman was doing to keep his promise. The editorial was headed:

The Moral Side of Political Questions

The editor of the *News* has always advocated the principles of the great political party at present in power, and has heretofore discussed all political questions from the standpoint of expediency, or of belief in the party as opposed to other political organizations. Hereafter, to be perfectly honest with all our readers, the editor will present and discuss all political questions from the standpoint of right and wrong. In other words, the first question asked in this office about any political question will not be, "Is it in the interests of our party?" or, "Is it according to the principles laid down by our party in its platform," but the question first asked will be, "Is this measure in accordance with the spirit and teachings of Jesus as the author of the greatest standard of life known to men?" That is, to be perfectly plain, the moral side of every political question will be considered its most important side, and the ground will be distinctly taken that nations as well as individuals are under the same law to do all things to the glory of God as the first rule of action.

The same principle will be observed in this office toward candidates for places of responsibility and trust in the republic. Regardless of party politics the editor of the *News* will do all in his power to bring the best men into power, and will not knowingly help to support for office any candidate who is unworthy, no matter how much he may be endorsed by the party. The first question asked about the man and about the measures will be, "Is he the right man for the place?" "Is he a good man with ability?" "Is the measure right?"

There had been more of this, but we have quoted enough to show the character of the editorial. Hundreds of men in Raymond had read it and rubbed their eyes in amazement. A good many of them had promptly written to the *News*, telling the editor to stop their paper.

The paper still came out, however, and was eagerly read all over the city. At the end of a week Edward Norman knew very well that he was fast losing a large number of subscribers. He faced the conditions calmly, although Clark, the managing editor, grimly anticipated ultimate bankruptcy, especially since Monday's editorial.

To-night, as Maxwell read to his wife, he could see in almost every column evidences of Norman's conscientious obedience to his promise. There was an absence of slangy, sensational scare heads. The reading matter under the head lines was in perfect keeping with them. He noticed in two columns that the reporters' name appeared signed at the bottom. And there was a distinct advance in the dignity and style of their contributions.

"So Norman is beginning to get his reporters to sign their work. He has talked with me about that. It is a good thing. It fixes responsibility for items where it belongs and raises the standard of work done. A good thing all around for the public and the writers."

Maxwell suddenly paused. His wife looked up from some work she was doing. He was reading something with the utmost interest. "Listen to this, Mary," he said, after a moment while his lip trembled:

This morning Alexander Powers, Superintendent of the L. and T. R. R. shops in this city, handed in his resignation to the road, and gave as his reason the fact that certain proofs had fallen into his hands of the violation of the Interstate Commerce Law, and also of the state law which has recently been framed to prevent and punish railroad pooling for the benefit of certain favored shippers. Mr. Powers states in his resignation that he can no longer consistently withhold the information he possesses against the road. He will be a witness against it. He has placed his evidence against the company in the hands of the Commission and it is now for them to take action upon it.

The *News* wishes to express itself on this action of Mr. Powers. In the first place he has nothing to gain by it. He has lost a very valuable place voluntarily, when by keeping silent he might have retained it. In the second place, we believe his action ought to receive the approval of all thoughtful, honest citizens who believe in seeing law obeyed and lawbreakers brought to justice. In a case like this, where evidence against a railroad company is generally understood to be almost impossible to obtain, it is the general belief that the officers of the road are often in possession of criminating facts but do not consider it to be any of their business to inform the authorities that the law is being defied. The entire result of this evasion of responsibility on the part of those who are responsible is demoralizing to every young man connected with the road. The editor of the *News* recalls the statement made by a prominent railroad official in this city a little while ago, that nearly every clerk in a certain department of the road understood that large sums of money were made by shrewd violations of the Interstate Commerce Law, was ready to admire the shrewdness with which it was done, and declared that they would all do the same thing if they were high enough in railroad circles to attempt it.*

It is not necessary to say that such a condition of business is destructive to all the nobler and higher standards of conduct, and no young man can live in such an atmosphere of unpunished dishonesty and lawlessness without wrecking his character.

In our judgment, Mr. Powers did the only thing that a Christian man could do. He has rendered brave and useful service to the state and the general public. It is not always an easy matter to determine the relations that exist between the individual citizen and his fixed duty to the public. In this case there is no

---

*This was actually said in one of the General Offices of a great Western railroad, to the author's knowledge.

---

doubt in our minds that the step which Mr. Powers has taken commends itself to every man who believes in law and its enforcement. There are times when the individual must act for the people in ways that will mean sacrifice and loss to him of the gravest character. Mr. Powers will be misunderstood and misrepresented, but there is no question that his course will be approved by every citizen who wishes to see the greatest corporations as well as the weakest individual subject to the same law. Mr. Powers has done all that a loyal, patriotic citizen could do. It now remains for the commission to act upon his evidence which, we understand, is overwhelming proof of the lawlessness of the L. and T. Let the law be enforced, no matter who the persons may be who have been guilty.

9

Henry Maxwell finished reading and dropped the paper.

"I must go and see Powers. This is the result of his promise."

He rose, and as he was going out, his wife said: "Do you think, Henry, that Jesus would have done that ?"

Maxwell paused a moment. Then he answered slowly, "Yes, I think He would. At any rate, Powers has decided so and each one of us who made the promise understands that he is not deciding Jesus' conduct for any one else, only for himself."

"How about his family? How will Mrs. Powers and Celia be likely to take it?"

"Very hard, I've no doubt. That will be Powers' cross in this matter. They will not understand his motive."

Maxwell went out and walked over to the next block where Superintendent Powers lived. To his relief, Powers himself came to the door.

The two men shook hands silently. They instantly understood each other without words. There had never before been such a bond of union between the minister and his parishioner.

"What are you going to do?" Henry Maxwell asked after they had talked over the facts in the case.

"You mean another position? I have no plans yet. I can go back to my old work as a telegraph operator. My family will not suffer, except in a social way."

Powers spoke calmly and sadly. Henry Maxwell did not need to ask him how the wife and daughter felt. He knew well enough that the superintendent had suffered deepest at that point.

"There is one matter I wish you would see to," said Powers after awhile, "and that is, the work begun at the shops. So far as I know, the company will not object to that going on. It is one of the contradictions of the railroad world that Y.M.C.A.'s and other Christian influences are encouraged by the roads, while all the time the most un-Christian and lawless acts may be committed in the official management of the roads themselves. Of course it is well understood that it pays a railroad to have in its employ men who are temperate, honest and Christian. So I have no doubt the master mechanic will have the same courtesy shown him in the use of the room. But what I want you to do, Mr. Maxwell, is to see that my plan is carried out. Will you? You understand what it was in general. You made a very favorable impression on the men. Go down there as often as you can. Get Milton Wright interested to provide something for the furnishing and expense of the coffee plant and reading tables. Will you do it?"

"Yes," replied Henry Maxwell. He stayed a little longer. Before he went away, he and the superintendent had a prayer together, and they parted with that silent hand grasp that seemed to them like a new token of their Christian discipleship and fellowship.

The pastor of the First Church went home stirred deeply by the events of the week. Gradually the truth was growing upon him that the pledge to do as Jesus would was working out a revolution in his parish and throughout the city. Every day added to the serious results of obedience to that pledge. Maxwell did not pretend to see the end. He was, in fact, only now at the very beginning of events that were destined to change the history of hundreds of families not only in Raymond but throughout the entire country. As he thought of Edward Norman and Rachel and Mr. Powers, and of the results that had already come from their actions, he could not help a feeling of intense interest in the probable effect if all the persons in the First Church who had made the pledge, faithfully kept it. Would they all keep it, or would some of them turn back when the cross became too heavy?

He was asking this question the next morning as he sat in his study when the President of the Endeavor Society of his church called to see him.

"I suppose I ought not to trouble you with my case," said young Morris coming at once to his errand, "but I thought, Mr. Maxwell, that you might advise me a little."

"I'm glad you came. Go on, Fred." He had known the young man ever since his first year in the pastorate, and loved and honored him for his consistent, faithful service in the church.

Well, the fact is, I am out of a job. You know I've been doing reporter work on the morning *Sentinel* since I graduated last year. Well, last Saturday Mr. Burr asked me to go down the road Sunday morning and get the details of that train robbery at the Junction, and write the thing up for the extra edition that came out Monday morning, just to get the start of the *News*. I refused to go, and Burr gave me my dismissal. He was in a bad temper, or I think perhaps he would not have done it. He has always treated me well before. Now, do you think Jesus would have done as I did? I ask because the other fellows say I was a fool not to do the work. I want to feel that a Christian acts from motives that may seem strange to others sometimes, but not foolish. What do you think?"

"I think you kept your promise, Fred. I cannot believe Jesus would do newspaper reporting on Sunday as you were asked to do it."

"Thank you, Mr. Maxwell. I felt a little troubled over it, but the I longer I think it over the better I feel."

Morris rose to go, and his pastor rose and laid a loving hand on the young man's shoulder.

"What are you going to do, Fred?"

"I don't know yet. I have thought some of going to Chicago or some large city."

"Why don't you try the *News?*

"They are all supplied. I have not thought of applying there."

Maxwell thought a moment. "Come down to the *News* office with me, and let us see Norman about it."

So a few minutes later Edward Norman received into his room the minister and young Morris, and Maxwell briefly told the cause of the errand.

"I can give you a place on the *News*," said Norman with his keen look softened by a smile that made it winsome. "I want reporters who won't work Sundays. And what is more, I am making plans for a special kind of reporting which I believe you can develop because you are in sympathy with what Jesus would do."

He assigned Morris a definite task, and Maxwell started back to his study, feeling that kind of satisfaction (and it is a very deep kind) which a man feels when he has been even partly instrumental in finding an unemployed person a remunerative position.

He had intended to go right to his study, but on his way home he passed by one of Milton Wright's stores. He thought he would simply step in and shake hands with his parishioner and bid him God-speed in what he had heard he was doing to put Christ into his business. But when he went into the office, Wright insisted on detaining him to talk over some of his new plans. Maxwell asked himself if this was the Milton Wright he used to know, eminently practical, business-like, according to the regular code of the business world, and viewing every thing first and foremost from the standpoint of, "Will it pay?"

"There is no use to disguise the fact, Mr. Maxwell, that I have been compelled to revolutionize the entire method of my business since I made that promise. I have been doing a great many things during the last twenty years in this store that I know Jesus would not do. But that is a small item compared with the number of things I begin to believe Jesus would do. My sins of commission have not been as many as those of omission in business relations."

"What was the first change you made?" He felt as if his sermon could wait for him in his study. As the interview with Milton Wright continued, he was not so sure but that he had found material for a sermon without going back to his study.

"I think the first change I had to make was in my thought of my employees. I came down here Monday morning after that Sunday and asked myself, 'What would Jesus do in His relation to these clerks, bookkeepers, office-boys, draymen, salesmen? Would He try to establish some sort of personal relation to them different from that which I have sustained all these years. I soon answered this by saying, 'Yes.' Then came the question of what that relation would be and what it would lead me to do. I did not see how I could answer it to my satisfaction without getting all my employees together and having a talk with them. So I sent invitations to all of them, and we had a meeting out there in the warehouse Tuesday night.

A good many things came out of that meeting. I can't tell you all. I tried to talk with the men as I imagined Jesus might. It was hard work, for I have not been in the habit of it, and must have made some mistakes. But I can hardly make you believe, Mr. Maxwell, the effect of that meeting on some of the men. Before it closed I saw more than a dozen of them with tears on their faces. I kept asking, 'What would Jesus do?' and the more I asked it the farther along it pushed me into the most intimate and loving relations with the men who have worked for me all these years.

Every day something new is coming up and I am right now in the midst of a reconstruction of the entire business so far as its motive for being conducted is concerned. I am so practically ignorant of all plans for cooperation and its application to business that I am trying to get information from every possible source. I have lately made a special study of the life of Titus Salt, the great mill-owner of Bradford, England, who afterward built that model town on the banks of the Aire. There is a good deal in his plans that will help me. But I have not yet reached definite conclusions in regard to all the details. I am not enough used to Jesus' methods. But see here."

———

Wright eagerly reached up into one of the pigeon holes of his desk and took out a paper.

"I have sketched out what seems to me like a program such as Jesus might go by in a business like mine. I want you to tell me what you think of it:

What Jesus Would Probably Do in Milton Wright's Place as a Business Man

1. He would engage in the business first of all for the purpose of glorifying God, and not for the primary purpose of making money.

2. All money that might be made he would never regard as his own, but as trust funds to be used for the good of humanity.

3. His relations with all the persons in his employ would be the most loving and helpful. He could not help thinking of all of them in the light of souls to be saved. This thought would always be greater than his thought of making money in the business.

4. He would never do a single dishonest or questionable thing or try in any remotest way to get the advantage of any one else in the same business.

5. The principle of unselfishness and helpfulness in the business would direct all its details.

6. Upon this principle he would shape the entire plan of his relations to his employees, to the people who were his customers and to the general business world with which he was connected.

Henry Maxwell read this over slowly. It reminded him of his own attempts the day before to put into a concrete form his thought of Jesus' probable action. He was very thoughtful as he looked up and met Wright's eager gaze.

"Do you believe you can continue to make your business pay on these lines?"

"I do. Intelligent unselfishness ought to be wiser than intelligent selfishness, don't you think? If the men who work as employees begin to feel a personal share in the profits of the business and, more than that, a personal love for themselves on the part of the firm, won't the result be more care, less waste, more diligence, more faithfulness?"

"Yes, I think so. A good many other business men don't, do they? I mean as a general thing. How about your relations to the selfish world that is not trying to make money on Christian principles?"

"That complicates my action, of course."

"Does your plan contemplate what is coming to be known as co-operation?"

"Yes, as far as I have gone, it does. As I told you, I am studying out my details carefully. I am absolutely convinced that Jesus in my place would be absolutely unselfish. He would love all these men in His employ. He would consider the main purpose of all the business to be a mutual helpfulness, and would conduct it all so that God's kingdom would be evidently the first object sought. On those general principles, as I say, I am working. I must have time to complete the details."

When Maxwell finally left he was profoundly impressed with the revolution that was being wrought already in the business. As he passed out of the store he caught something of the new spirit of the place. There was no mistaking the fact that Milton Wright's new relations to his employees were beginning even so soon, after less than two weeks, to transform the entire business. This was apparent in the conduct and faces of the clerks.

"If he keeps on he will be one of the most influential preachers in Raymond," said Maxwell to himself when he reached his study. The question rose as to this continuance in this course when he began to lose money by it, as was possible. He prayed that the Holy Spirit, who had shown Himself with growing power in the company of First Church disciples, might abide long with them all. And with that prayer on his lips and in his heart he began the preparation of a sermon in which he was going to present to his people on Sunday the subject of the saloon in Raymond, as he now believed Jesus would do.

He had never preached against the saloon in this way before. He knew that the things he should say would lead to serious results. Nevertheless, he went on with his work, and every sentence he wrote or shaped was preceded with the question, "Would Jesus say that?" Once in the course of his study, he went down on his knees. No one except himself could know what that meant to him. When had he done that in his preparation of sermons, before the change that had come into his thought of discipleship? As he viewed his ministry now, he did not dare preach without praying long for wisdom. He no longer thought of his dramatic delivery and its effect on his audience. The great question with him now was, "What would Jesus do?"

Saturday night at the Rectangle witnessed some of the most remarkable scenes that Mr. Gray and his wife had ever known. The meetings intensified with each night of Rachel's singing. A stranger passing through the Rectangle in the day-time might have heard a good deal about the meetings in one way and another. It cannot be said that up to that Saturday night there was any appreciable lack of oaths and impurity and heavy drinking. The Rectangle would not have acknowledged that it was growing any better or that even the singing had softened its outward manner. It had too much local pride in being "tough." But in spite of itself there was a yielding to a power it had never measured and did not know well enough to resist beforehand.

Gray had recovered his voice so that by Saturday he was able to speak. The fact that he was obliged to use his voice carefully made it necessary for the people to be very quiet if they wanted to hear. Gradually they had come to understand that this man was talking these many weeks and giving his time and strength to give them a knowledge of a Saviour, all out of a perfectly unselfish love for them. To-night the great crowd was as quiet as Henry Maxwell's decorous audience ever was. The fringe around the tent was deeper and the saloons were practically empty. The Holy Spirit had come at last, and Gray knew that one of the great prayers of his life was going to be answered.

And Rachel—her singing was the best, most wonderful, that Virginia or Jasper Chase had ever known. They came together again to-night, this time with Dr. West, who had spent all his spare time that week in the Rectangle with some charity cases. Virginia was at the organ, Jasper sat on a front seat looking up at Rachel, and the Rectangle swayed as one man towards the platform as she sang:

> *"Just as I am, without one plea,*
> *But that Thy blood was shed for me,*
> *And that Thou bidst me come to Thee,*
> *O Lamb of God, I come, I come."*

Gray hardly said a word. He stretched out his hand with a gesture of invitation. And down the two aisles of the tent, broken, sinful creatures, men and women, stumbled towards the platform. One woman out of the street was near the organ. Virginia caught the look of her face, and for the first time in the life of the rich girl the thought of what Jesus was to the sinful woman came with a suddenness and power that was like nothing but a new birth. Virginia left the organ, went to her, looked into her face and caught her hands in her own. The other girl trembled, then fell on her knees sobbing, with her head down upon the back of the rude bench in front of her, still clinging to Virginia. And Virginia, after a moment's hesitation, kneeled down by her and the two heads were bowed close together.

But when the people had crowded in a double row all about the platform, most of them kneeling and crying, a man in evening dress, different from the others, pushed through the seats and came and kneeled down by the side of the drunken man who had disturbed the meeting when Maxwell spoke. He kneeled within a few feet of Rachel Winslow, who was still singing softly. And as she turned for a moment and looked in his direction, she was amazed to see the face of Rollin Page! For a moment her voice faltered. Then she went on:

> *"Just as I am, thou wilt receive,*
> *Wilt welcome, pardon, cleanse, relieve,*
> *Because Thy promise I believe,*
> *O Lamb of God, I come, I come."*

The voice was as the voice of divine longing, and the Rectangle for the time being was swept into the harbor of redemptive grace.

10

"If any man serve me, let him follow me."

IT WAS NEARLY MIDNIGHT BEFORE THE SERVICES AT THE
Rectangle closed. Gray stayed up long into Sunday morning, praying
and talking with a little group of converts who in the great experiences of their new life, clung to the evangelist with a personal help-
lessness that made it as impossible for him to leave them as if they had
been depending upon him to save them from physical death. Among
these converts was Rollin Page.

Virginia and her uncle had gone home about eleven o'clock, and
Rachel and Jasper Chase had gone with them as far as the avenue
where Virginia lived. Dr. West had walked on a little way with them
to his own home, and Rachel and Jasper had then gone on together
to her mother's.

That was a little after eleven. It was now striking midnight, and
Jasper Chase sat in his room staring at the papers on his desk and going over the last half hour with painful persistence.

He had told Rachel Winslow of his love for her, and she had not
given him her love in return. It would be difficult to know what was
most powerful in the impulse that had moved him to speak to her

to-night. He had yielded to his feelings without any special thought of results to himself, because he had felt so certain that Rachel would respond to his love. He tried to recall the impression she made on him when he first spoke to her.

Never had her beauty and her strength influenced him as tonight. While she was singing he saw and heard no one else. The tent swarmed with a confused crowd of faces and he knew he was sitting there hemmed in by a mob of people, but they had no meaning to him. He felt powerless to avoid speaking to her. He knew he should speak when they were alone.

Now that he had spoken, he felt that he had misjudged either Rachel or the opportunity. He knew, or thought he knew, that she had begun to care something for him. It was no secret between them that the heroine of Jasper's first novel had been his own ideal of Rachel, and the hero in the story was himself and they had loved each other in the book, and Rachel had not objected. No one else knew. The names and characters had been drawn with a subtle skill that revealed to Rachel, when she received a copy of the book from Jasper, the fact of his love for her, and she had not been offended. That was nearly a year ago.

To-night he recalled the scene between them with every inflection and movement unerased from his memory. He even recalled the fact that he began to speak just at that point on the avenue where, a few days before, he had met Rachel walking with Rollin Page. He had wondered at the time what Rollin was saying.

"Rachel," Jasper had said, and it was the first time he had ever spoken her first name, "I never knew till to-night how much I loved you. Why should I try to conceal any longer what you have seen me look? You know I love you as my life. I can no longer hide it from you if I would."

The first intimation he had of a repulse was the trembling of Rachel's arm in his. She had allowed him to speak and had neither turned her face toward him nor away from him. She had looked straight on and her voice was sad but firm and quiet when she spoke.

"Why do you speak to me now? I cannot bear it after what we have seen to-night."

"Why—what—" he had stammered and then was silent.

Rachel withdrew her arm from his but still walked near him. Then he had cried out with the anguish of one who begins to see a great loss facing him where he expected a great joy.

"Rachel! Do you not love me? Is not my love for you as sacred as anything in all of life itself?"

She had walked silent for a few steps after that. They passed a street lamp. Her face was pale and beautiful. He had made a movement to clutch her arm and she had moved a little farther from him.

"No," she had replied. "There was a time—I cannot answer for that—you should not have spoken to me now."

He had seen in these words his answer. He was extremely sensitive. Nothing short of a joyous response to his own love would ever have satisfied him. He could not think of pleading with her.

"Some time—when I am more worthy?" he had asked in a low voice, but she did not seem to hear, and they had parted at her home, and he recalled vividly the fact that no good-night had been said.

Now as he went over the brief but significant scene he lashed himself for his foolish precipitancy. He had not reckoned on Rachel's tense, passionate absorption of all her feeling in the scenes at the tent which were so new in her mind. But he did not know her well enough even yet to understand the meaning of her refusal. When the clock in the First Church struck one he was still sitting at his desk staring at the last page of manuscript of his unfinished novel.

Rachel went up to her room and faced her evening's experience with conflicting emotions. Had she ever loved Jasper Chase? Yes. No. One moment she felt that her life's happiness was at stake over the result of her action. Another, she had a strange feeling of relief that she had spoken as she had.

There was one great, overmastering feeling in her. The response of the wretched creatures in the tent to her singing, the swift, powerful, awesome presence of the Holy Spirit had affected her as never in all her life before. The moment Jasper had spoken her name and she realized that he was telling her of his love she had felt a sudden revulsion for him, as if he should have respected the supernatural events they had just witnessed.

She felt as if it was not the time to be absorbed in anything less than the divine glory of those conversions. The thought that all the time she was singing, with the one passion of her soul to touch the conscience of that tent full of sin, Jasper Chase had been unmoved by it except to love her for herself, gave her a shock as of irreverence on her part as well as on his. She could not tell why she felt as she did, only she knew that if he had not told her to-night she would still have felt the same toward him as she always had. What was that feeling? What had he been to her? Had she made a mistake?

She went to her book case and took out the novel which Jasper had given her. Her face deepened in color as she turned to certain passages which she had read often and which she knew Jasper had written for her. She read them again. Somehow they failed to touch her strongly.

She closed the book and let it lie on the table. She gradually felt that her thought was busy with the sights she had witnessed in the tent. Those faces, men and women, touched for the first time with the Spirit's glory—what a wonderful thing life was after all! The complete regeneration revealed in the sight of drunken, vile, debauched humanity kneeling down to give itself to a life of purity and Christlikeness—oh, it was surely a witness to the superhuman in the world! And the face of Rollin Page by the side of that miserable wreck out of the gutter! She could recall as if she now saw it, Virginia crying with her arms about her brother just before she left the tent, and Mr. Gray kneeling close by, and the girl Virginia had taken into her heart while she whispered something to her before she went out.

All these pictures drawn by the Holy Spirit in the human tragedies brought to a climax there in the most abandoned spot in all Raymond, stood out in Rachel's memory now, a memory so recent that her room seemed for the time being to contain all the actors and their movements.

"No! No!" she said aloud. "He had no right to speak after all that! He should have respected the place where our thoughts should have been. I am sure I do not love him—not enough to give him my life!"

And after she had thus spoken, the evening's experience at the tent came crowding in again, thrusting out all other things. It is perhaps the most striking evidence of the tremendous spiritual factor which had now entered the Rectangle that Rachel felt, even when the great love of a strong man had come very near to her, that the spiritual manifestation moved her with an agitation far greater than anything Jasper had felt for her personally or she for him.

The people of Raymond awoke Sunday morning to a growing knowledge of events which were beginning to revolutionize many of the regular, customary habits of the town. Alexander Powers' action in the matter of the railroad frauds had created a sensation not only in Raymond but throughout the country. Edward Norman's daily changes of policy in the conduct of his paper had startled the community and caused more comment than any recent political event. Rachel Winslow's singing at the Rectangle meetings had made a stir in society and excited the wonder of all her friends.

Virginia's conduct, her presence every night with Rachel, her absence from the usual circle of her wealthy, fashionable acquaintances, had furnished a great deal of material for gossip and question. In addition to these events which centered about these persons who were so well known, there had been all through the city in very many homes and in business and social circles strange happenings.

Nearly one hundred persons in Henry Maxwell's church had made the pledge to do everything after asking: "What would Jesus do?" and the result had been, in many cases, unheard-of actions. The city was stirred as it had never been before. As a climax to the week's events had come the spiritual manifestation at the Rectangle, and the announcement which came to most people before church time of the actual conversion at the tent of nearly fifty of the worst characters in that neighborhood, together with the conversion of Rollin Page, the well-known society and club man.

It is no wonder that under the pressure of all this the First Church of Raymond came to the morning service in a condition that made it quickly sensitive to any large truth. Perhaps nothing had astonished the people more than the great change that had come over the minister, since he had proposed to them the imitation of Jesus in conduct. The dramatic delivery of his sermons no longer impressed them. The self-satisfied, contented, easy attitude of the fine figure and refined face in the pulpit had been displaced by a manner that could not be compared with the old style of his delivery. The sermon had become a message. It was no longer delivered. It was brought to them with a love, an earnestness, a passion, a desire, a humility that poured its enthusiasm about the truth and made the speaker no more prominent than he had to be as the living voice of God.

His prayers were unlike any the people had heard before. They were often broken, even once or twice they had been actually ungrammatical in a phrase or two. When had Henry Maxwell so far forgotten himself in a prayer as to make a mistake of that sort? He knew that he had often taken as much pride in the diction and delivery of his prayers as of his sermons. Was it possible he now so abhorred the elegant refinement of a formal public petition that he purposely chose to rebuke himself for his previous precise manner of prayer? It is more likely that he had no thought of all that. His great longing to voice the needs and wants of his people made him unmindful of an occasional mistake. It is certain that he had never prayed so effectively as he did now.

There are times when a sermon has a value and power due to conditions in the audience rather than to anything new or startling or eloquent in the words said or arguments presented. Such conditions faced Henry Maxwell this morning as he preached against the saloon, according to his purpose determined on the week before. He had no new statements to make about the evil influence of the saloon in Raymond. What new facts were there? He had no startling illustrations of the power of the saloon in business or politics. What could he say that had not been said by temperance orators a great many times?

The effect of his message this morning owed its power to the unusual fact of his preaching about the saloon at all, together with the events that had stirred the people. He had never in the course of his ten years' pastorate mentioned the saloon as something to be regarded in the light of an enemy, not only to the poor and tempted, but to the business life of the place and the church itself. He spoke now with a freedom that seemed to measure his complete sense of conviction that Jesus would speak so.

At the close he pleaded with the people to remember the new life that had begun at the Rectangle. The regular election of city officers was near at hand. The question of license would be an issue in the election. What of the poor creatures surrounded by the hell of drink while just beginning to feel the joy of deliverance from sin? Who could tell what depended on their environment? Was there one word to be said by the Christian disciple, business man, citizen, in favor of continuing the license to crime and shame-producing institutions? Was not the most Christian thing they could do to act as citizens in the matter, fight the saloon at the polls, elect good men to the city offices, and clean the municipality?

How much had prayers helped to make Raymond better while votes and actions had really been on the side of the enemies of Jesus? Would not Jesus do this? What disciple could imagine Him refusing to suffer or to take up His cross in this matter? How much had the members of the First Church ever suffered in an attempt to imitate Jesus? Was Christian discipleship a thing of conscience simply, of custom, of tradition? Where did the suffering come in? Was it necessary in order to follow Jesus' steps to go up Calvary as well as the Mount of Transfiguration?

His appeal was stronger at this point than he knew. It is not too much to say that the spiritual tension of the people reached its highest point right there. The imitation of Jesus which had begun with the volunteers in the church was working like leaven in the organization, and Henry Maxwell would even thus early in his life have been amazed if he could have measured the extent of desire on the part of his people to take up the cross. While he was speaking this morning, before he closed with a loving appeal to the discipleship of two thousand years' knowledge of the Master, many a man and woman in the church was saying as Rachel had said so passionately to her mother: "I want to do something that will cost me something in the way of sacrifice." "I am hungry to suffer something." Truly, Mazzini was right when he said that no appeal is quite so powerful in the end as the call: "Come and suffer."

The service was over, the great audience had gone, and Maxwell again faced the company gathered in the lecture room as on the two previous Sundays. He had asked all to remain who had made the pledge of discipleship, and any others who wished to be included. The after service seemed now to be a necessity. As he went in and faced the people there his heart trembled. There were at least one hundred present. The Holy Spirit was never before so manifest. He missed Jasper Chase. But all the others were present. He asked Milton Wright to pray. The very air was charged with divine possibilities. What could resist such a baptism of power? How had they lived all these years without it?

They counseled together and there were many prayers. Henry Maxwell dated from that meeting some of the serious events that afterward became a part of the history of the First Church and of Raymond. When finally they went home, all of them were impressed with the glory of the Spirit's power.

II

Donald Marsh, President of Lincoln College, walked home with Mr. Maxwell.

"I have reached one conclusion, Maxwell," said Marsh, speaking slowly. "I have found my cross and it is a heavy one, but I shall never be satisfied until I take it up and carry it." Maxwell was silent and the President went on.

"Your sermon to-day made clear to me what I have long been feeling I ought to do. 'What would Jesus do in my place?' I have asked the question repeatedly since I made my promise. I have tried to satisfy myself that He would simply go on as I have done, attending to the duties of my college work, teaching the classes in Ethics and Philosophy. But I have not been able to avoid the feeling that He would do something more. That something is what I do not want to do. It will cause me genuine suffering to do it. I dread it with all my soul. You may be able to guess what it is."

"Yes, I think I know. It is my cross too. I would almost rather do any thing else."

Donald Marsh looked surprised, then relieved. Then he spoke sadly but with great conviction: "Maxwell, you and I belong to a class of professional men who have always avoided the duties of citizenship. We have lived in a little world of literature and scholarly seclusion, doing work we have enjoyed and shrinking from the disagreeable duties that belong to the life of the citizen.

"I confess with shame that I have purposely avoided the responsibility that I owe to this city personally. I understand that our city officials are a corrupt, unprincipled set of men, controlled in large part by the whiskey element and thoroughly selfish so far as the affairs of city government are concerned. Yet all these years I, with nearly every teacher in the college, have been satisfied to let other men run the municipality and have lived in a little world of my own, out of touch and sympathy with the real world of the people. 'What would Jesus do?' I have even tried to avoid an honest answer. I can no longer do so.

"My plain duty is to take a personal part in this coming election, go to the primaries, throw the weight of my influence, whatever it is, toward the nomination and election of good men, and plunge into the very depths of the entire horrible whirlpool of deceit, bribery, political trickery and saloonism as it exists in Raymond today. I would sooner walk up to the mouth of a cannon any time than do this. I dread it because I hate the touch of the whole matter. I would give almost any thing to be able to say, 'I do not believe Jesus would do anything of the sort.' But I am more and more persuaded that He would. This is where the suffering comes for me. It would not hurt me half so much to lose my position or my home. I loathe the contact with this municipal problem. I would so much prefer to remain quietly in my scholastic life with my classes in Ethics and Philosophy. But the call has come to me so plainly that I cannot escape. 'Donald Marsh, follow me. Do your duty as a citizen of Raymond at the point where your citizenship will cost you something. Help to cleanse this municipal stable, even if you do have to soil your aristocratic feelings a little.' Maxwell, this is my cross, I must take it up or deny my Lord."

"You have spoken for me also," replied Maxwell with a sad smile. "Why should I, simply because I am a minister, shelter myself behind my refined, sensitive feelings, and like a coward refuse to touch, except in a sermon possibly, the duty of citizenship? I am unused to the ways of the political life of the city. I have never taken an active part in any nomination of good men. There are hundreds of ministers like me. As a class we do not practice in the municipal life the duties and privileges we preach from the pulpit. 'What would Jesus do?' I am now at a point where, like you, I am driven to answer the question one way. My duty is plain. I must suffer. All my parish work, all my little trials or self-sacrifices are as nothing to me compared with the breaking into my scholarly, intellectual, self-contained habits, of this open, coarse, public fight for a clean city life. I could go and live at the Rectangle the rest of my life and work in the slums for a bare living, and I could enjoy it more than the thought of plunging into a fight for the reform of this whiskey-ridden city. It would cost me less. But, like you, I have been unable to shake off my responsibility. The answer to the question 'What would Jesus do?' in this case leaves me no peace except when I say, Jesus would have me act the part of a Christian citizen. Marsh, as you say, we professional men, ministers, professors, artists, literary men, scholars, have almost invariably been political cowards. We have avoided the sacred duties of citizenship either ignorantly or selfishly. Certainly Jesus in our age would not do that. We can do no less than take up this cross, and follow Him."

The two men walked on in silence for a while. Finally President Marsh said:

"We do not need to act alone in this matter. With all the men who have made the promise we certainly can have companionship, and strength even, of numbers. Let us organize the Christian forces of Raymond for the battle against rum and corruption. We certainly ought to enter the primaries with a force that will be able to do more than enter a protest. It is a fact that the saloon element is cowardly and easily frightened in spite of its lawlessness and corruption. Let us plan a campaign that will mean something because it is organized righteousness. Jesus would use great wisdom in this matter. He would employ means. He would make large plans. Let us do so. If we bear this cross let us do it bravely, like men."

They talked over the matter a long time and met again the next day in Maxwell's study to develop plans. The city primaries were called for Friday. Rumors of strange and unknown events to the average citizen were current that week in political circles throughout Raymond. The Crawford system of balloting for nominations was not in use in the state, and the primary was called for a public meeting at the court house.

The citizens of Raymond will never forget that meeting. It was so unlike any political meeting ever held in Raymond before, that there was no attempt at comparison. The special officers to be nominated were mayor, city council, chief of police, city clerk and city treasurer.

The *Evening News* in its Saturday edition gave a full account of the primaries, and in the editorial columns Edward Norman spoke with a directness and conviction that the Christian people of Raymond were learning to respect deeply, because it was so evidently sincere and unselfish. A part of that editorial is also a part of this history. We quote the following:

> It is safe to say that never before in the history of Raymond was there a primary like the one in the court house last night. It was, first of all, a complete surprise to the city politicians, who have been in the habit of carrying on the affairs of the city as if they owned them, and every one else was simply a tool or a cipher. The overwhelming surprise of the wire pullers last night consisted in the fact that a large number of the citizens of Raymond who have heretofore taken no part in the city's affairs, entered the primary and controlled it, nominating some of the best men for all the offices to be filled at the coming election.

> It was a tremendous lesson in good citizenship. President Marsh of Lincoln College, who never before entered a city primary, and whose face was not even known to the ward politicians, made one of the best speeches ever made in Raymond. It was almost ludicrous to see the faces of the men who for years

have done as they pleased, when President Marsh rose to speak. Many of them asked, 'Who is he?' The consternation deepened as the primary proceeded and it became evident that the old-time ring of city rulers was outnumbered. Rev. Henry Maxwell of the First Church, Milton Wright, Alexander Powers, Professors Brown, Willard and Park of Lincoln College, Dr. West, Rev. George Main of the Pilgrim Church, Dean Ward of the Holy Trinity, and scores of well-known business men and professional men, most of them church members, were present, and it did not take long to see that they had all come with the one direct and definite purpose of nominating the best men possible. Most of those men had never before been seen in a primary. They were complete strangers to the politicians. But they had evidently profited by the politician's methods and were able by organized and united effort to nominate the entire ticket.

As soon as it became plain that the primary was out of their control the regular ring withdrew in disgust and nominated another ticket. The *News* simply calls the attention of all decent citizens to the fact that this last ticket contains the names of whiskey men, and the line is sharply and distinctly drawn between the saloon and corrupt management such as we have known for years, and a clean, honest, capable, business-like city administration, such as every good citizen ought to want. It is not necessary to remind the people of Raymond that the question of local option comes up at the election. That will be the most important question on the ticket. The crisis of our city affairs has been reached. The issue is squarely before us. Shall we continue the rule of rum and boodle and shameless incompetency, or shall we, as President Marsh said in his noble speech, rise as good citizens and begin a new order of things, cleansing our city of the worst enemy known to municipal honesty, and doing what lies in our power to do with the ballot to purify our civic life?

The *News* is positively and without reservation on the side of the new movement. We shall henceforth do all in our power to drive out the saloon and destroy its political strength. We shall advocate the election of the men nominated by the majority of citizens met in the first primary and we call upon all Christians, church members, lovers of right, purity, temperance, and the home, to stand by President Marsh and the rest of the citizens who have thus begun a long-needed reform in our city.

President Marsh read this editorial and thanked God for Edward Norman. At the same time he understood well enough that every other paper in Raymond was on the other side. He did not underestimate the importance and seriousness of the fight which was only just begun. It was no secret that the *News* had lost enormously since it had been governed by the standard of "What would Jesus do?" And the question was, Would the Christian people of Raymond stand by it? Would they make it possible for Norman to conduct a daily Christian paper? Or would the desire for what is called news in the way of crime, scandal, political partisanship of the regular sort, and a dislike to champion so remarkable a reform in journalism, influence them to drop the paper and refuse to give it their financial support? That was, in fact, the question Edward Norman was asking even while he wrote that Saturday editorial. He knew well enough that his action expressed in that editorial would cost him very heavily from the hands of many business men in Raymond. And still, as he drove his pen over the paper, he asked another question, "What would Jesus do?" That question had become a part of his whole life now. It was greater than any other.

But for the first time in its history Raymond had seen the professional men, the teachers, the college professors, the doctors, the ministers, take political action and put themselves definitely and sharply in public antagonism to the evil forces that had so long controlled the machine of the municipal government. The fact itself was astounding. President Marsh acknowledged to himself with a feeling of humiliation, that never before had he known what civic righteousness could accomplish. From that Friday night's work he dated for himself and his college a new definition of the worn phrase, "the scholar in politics." Education for him and those who were under his influence ever after meant some element of suffering. Sacrifice must now enter into the factor of development.

At the Rectangle that week the tide of spiritual life rose high, and as yet showed no signs of flowing back. Rachel and Virginia went every night. Virginia was rapidly reaching a conclusion with respect to a large part of her money. She had talked it over with Rachel and they had been able to agree that if Jesus had a vast amount of money at His disposal He might do with some of it as Virginia planned. At any rate they felt that whatever He might do in such case would have as large an element of variety in it as the differences in persons and circumstances. There could be no one fixed Christian way of using money. The rule that regulated its use was unselfish utility.

But meanwhile the glory of the Spirit's power possessed all their best thought. Night after night that week witnessed miracles as great as walking on the sea or feeding the multitude with a few loaves and fishes. For what greater miracle is there than a regenerate humanity? The transformation of these coarse, brutal, sottish lives into praying, rapturous lovers of Christ, struck Rachel and Virginia every time with the feeling that people may have had when they saw Lazarus walk out of the tomb. It was an experience full of profound excitement for them.

Rollin Page came to all the meetings. There was no doubt of the change that had come over him. Rachel had not yet spoken much with him. He was wonderfully quiet. It seemed as if he was thinking all the time. Certainly he was not the same person. He talked more with Gray than with any one else. He did not avoid Rachel, but he seemed to shrink from any appearance of seeming to wish to renew the acquaintance with her. Rachel found it even difficult to express to him her pleasure at the new life he had begun to know. He seemed to be waiting to adjust himself to his previous relations before this new life began. He had not forgotten those relations. But he was not yet able to fit his consciousness into new ones.

The end of the week found the Rectangle struggling hard between two mighty opposing forces. The Holy Spirit was battling with all

His supernatural strength against the saloon devil which had so long held a jealous grasp on its slaves. If the Christian people of Raymond once could realize what the contest meant to the souls newly awakened to a purer life it did not seem possible that the election could result in the old system of license. But that remained yet to be seen. The horror of the daily surroundings of many of the converts was slowly burning its way into the knowledge of Virginia and Rachel, and every night as they went uptown to their luxurious homes they carried heavy hearts.

"A good many of these poor creatures will go back again," Gray would say with sadness too deep for tears. "The environment does have a good deal to do with the character. It does not stand to reason that these people can always resist the sight and smell of the devilish drink about them. O Lord, how long shall Christian people continue to support by their silence and their ballots the greatest form of slavery known in America?"

He asked the question, and did not have much hope of an immediate answer. There was a ray of hope in the action of Friday night's primary, but what the result would be he did not dare to anticipate. The whiskey forces were organized, alert, aggressive, roused into unusual hatred by the events of the last week at the tent and in the city. Would the Christian forces act as a unit against the saloon? Or would they be divided on account of their business interests or because they were not in the habit of acting all together as the whiskey power always did? That remained to be seen. Meanwhile the saloon reared itself about the Rectangle like some deadly viper hissing and coiling, ready to strike its poison into any unguarded part.

Saturday afternoon as Virginia was just stepping out of her house to go and see Rachel to talk over her new plans, a carriage drove up containing three of her fashionable friends. Virginia went out to the drive-way and stood there talking with them. They had not come to make a formal call but wanted Virginia to go driving with them up on the boulevard. There was a band concert in the park. The day was too pleasant to be spent indoors.

"Where have you been all this time, Virginia?" asked one of the girls, tapping her playfully on the shoulder with a red silk parasol. "We hear that you have gone into the show business. Tell us about it."

Virginia colored, but after a moment's hesitation she frankly told something of her experience at the Rectangle. The girls in the carriage began to be really interested.

"I tell you, girls, let's go 'slumming' with Virginia this afternoon instead of going to the band concert. I've never been down to the Rectangle. I've heard it's an awful wicked place and lots to see. Virginia will act as guide, and it would be"—"real fun" she was going to say, but Virginia's look made her substitute the word "interesting."

Virginia was angry. At first thought she said to herself she would never go under such circumstances. The other girls seemed to be of the same mind with the speaker. They chimed in with earnestness and asked Virginia to take them down there.

Suddenly she saw in the idle curiosity of the girls an opportunity. They had never seen the sin and misery of Raymond. Why should they not see it, even if their motive in going down there was simply to pass away an afternoon.

"Very well, I'll go with you. You must obey my orders and let me take you where you can see the most," she said, as she entered the carriage and took the seat beside the girl who had first suggested the trip to the Rectangle.

12

"For I come to set a man at variance against his father, and the daugh-
ter against her mother, and the daughter-in-law against her
mother-in-law; and a man's foes shall be they of his own household.
Be ye therefore imitators of God, as beloved children; and walk in love,
even as Christ also loved you."

———

"HADN'T WE BETTER TAKE A POLICEMAN ALONG?" SAID one of the girls with a nervous laugh. "It really isn't safe down there, you know."

"There's no danger," said Virginia briefly.

"Is it true that your brother Rollin has been converted?" asked the first speaker, looking at Virginia curiously. It impressed her during the drive to the Rectangle that all three of her friends were regarding her with close attention as if she were peculiar.

"Yes, he certainly is."

"I understand he is going around to the clubs talking with his old friends there, trying to preach to them. Doesn't that seem funny?" said the girl with the red silk parasol.

Virginia did not answer, and the other girls were beginning to feel sober as the carriage turned into a street leading to the Rectangle. As they neared the district they grew more and more nervous. The sights and smells and sounds which had become familiar to Virginia struck the senses of these refined, delicate society girls as something horrible. As they entered farther into the district, the Rectangle

———

seemed to stare as with one great, bleary, beersoaked countenance at this fine carriage with its load of fashionably dressed young women. "Slumming" had never been a fad with Raymond society, and this was perhaps the first time that the two had come together in this way. The girls felt that instead of seeing the Rectangle they were being made the objects of curiosity. They were frightened and disgusted.

"Let's go back. I've seen enough," said the girl who was sitting with Virginia.

They were at that moment just opposite a notorious saloon and gambling house. The street was narrow and the sidewalk crowded. Suddenly, out of the door of this saloon a young woman reeled. She was singing in a broken, drunken sob that seemed to indicate that she partly realized her awful condition, "Just as I am, without one plea"—and as the carriage rolled past she leered at it, raising her face so that Virginia saw it very close to her own. It was the face of the girl who had kneeled sobbing, that night with Virginia kneeling beside her and praying for her.

"Stop!" cried Virginia, motioning to the driver who was looking around. The carriage stopped, and in a moment she was out and had gone up to the girl and taken her by the arm. "Loreen!" she said, and that was all. The girl looked into her face, and her own changed into a look of utter horror. The girls in the carriage were smitten into helpless astonishment. The saloon-keeper had come to the door of the saloon and was standing there looking on with his hands on his hips. And the Rectangle from its windows, its saloon steps, its filthy sidewalk, gutter and roadway, paused, and with undisguised wonder stared at the two girls. Over the scene the warm sun of spring poured its mellow light. A faint breath of music from the band-stand in the park floated into the Rectangle. The concert had begun, and the fashion and wealth of Raymond were displaying themselves up town on the boulevard.

When Virginia left the carriage and went up to Loreen she had no definite idea as to what she would do or what the result of her action would be. She simply saw a soul that had tasted of the joy of a better life slipping back again into its old hell of shame and death. And before she had touched the drunken girl's arm she had asked only one question, "What would Jesus do?" That question was becoming with her, as with many others, a habit of life.

She looked around now as she stood close by Loreen, and the whole scene was cruelly vivid to her. She thought first of the girls in the carriage.

"Drive on; don't wait for me. I am going to see my friend home," she said calmly enough.

The girl with the red parasol seemed to gasp at the word "friend," when Virginia spoke it. She did not say anything. The other girls seemed speechless.

"Go on. I cannot go back with you," said Virginia. The driver started the horses slowly. One of the girls leaned a little out of the carriage.

"Can't we—that is—do you want our help? Couldn't you—"

"No, no!" exclaimed Virginia. "You cannot be of any help to me."

The carriage moved on and Virginia was alone with her charge. She looked up and around. Many faces in the crowd were sympathetic. They were not all cruel or brutal. The Holy Spirit had softened a good deal of the Rectangle.

"Where does she live?" asked Virginia.

No one answered. It occurred to Virginia afterward when she had time to think it over, that the Rectangle showed a delicacy in its sad silence that would have done credit to the boulevard. For the first time it flashed across her that the immortal being who was flung like wreckage upon the shore of this early hell called the saloon, had no place that could be called home. The girl suddenly wrenched her arm from Virginia's grasp. In doing so she nearly threw Virginia down.

"You shall not touch me! Leave me! Let me go to hell! That's where I belong! The devil is waiting for me. See him!" she exclaimed hoarsely. She turned and pointed with a shaking finger at the saloon-keeper. The crowd laughed. Virginia stepped up to her and put her arm about her.

"Loreen," she said firmly, "come with me. You do not belong to hell. You belong to Jesus and He will save you. Come."

The girl suddenly burst into tears. She was only partly sobered by the shock of meeting Virginia.

Virginia looked around again. "Where does Mr. Gray live?" she asked. She knew that the evangelist boarded somewhere near the tent. A number of voices gave the direction.

"Come, Loreen, I want you to go with me to Mr. Gray's," she said, still keeping her hold of the swaying, trembling creature who moaned and sobbed and now clung to her as firmly as before she had repulsed her.

So the two moved on through the Rectangle toward the evangelist's lodging place. The sight seemed to impress the Rectangle seriously. It never took itself seriously when it was drunk, but this was different. The fact that one of the richest, most beautifully-dressed girls in all Raymond was taking care of one of the Rectangle's most noted characters, who reeled along under the influence of liquor, was a fact astounding enough to throw more or less dignity and importance about Loreen herself. The event of Loreen's stumbling through the gutter dead drunk always made the Rectangle laugh and jest. But Loreen staggering along with a young lady from the society circles uptown supporting her, was another thing. The Rectangle viewed it with soberness and more or less wondering admiration.

When they finally reached Mr. Gray's lodging place the woman who answered Virginia's knock said that both Mr. and Mrs. Gray were out somewhere and would not be back until six o'clock.

Virginia had not planned anything farther than a possible appeal to the Grays, either to take charge of Loreen for a while or find some safe place for her until she was sober. She stood now at the door after the woman had spoken, and she was really at a loss to know what to do. Loreen sank down stupidly on the steps and buried her face in her arms. Virginia eyed the miserable figure of the girl with a feeling that she was afraid would grow into disgust.

Finally a thought possessed her that she could not escape. What was to hinder her from taking Loreen home with her? Why should not this homeless, wretched creature, reeking with the fumes of liquor, be cared for in Virginia's own home instead of being consigned to strangers in some hospital or house of charity? Virginia really knew very little about any such places of refuge. As a matter of fact, there were two or three such institutions in Raymond, but it is doubtful if any of them would have taken a person like Loreen in her present condition. But that was not the question with Virginia just now. "What would Jesus do with Loreen?" That was what Virginia faced, and she finally answered it by touching the girl again.

"Loreen, come. You are going home with me. We will take the car here at the corner."

Loreen staggered to her feet and, to Virginia's surprise, made no trouble. She had expected resistance or a stubborn refusal to move. When they reached the corner and took the car it was nearly full of people going uptown. Virginia was painfully conscious of the stare that greeted her and her companion as they entered. But her thought was directed more and more to the approaching scene with her grandmother. What would Madam Page say?

Loreen was nearly sober now. But she was lapsing into a state of stupor. Virginia was obliged to hold fast to her arm. Several times the girl lurched heavily against her, and as the two went up the avenue a curious crowd of so-called civilized people turned and gazed at them. When she mounted the steps of her handsome house Virginia breathed a sigh of relief, even in the face of the interview with the grandmother, and when the door shut and she was in the wide hall with her homeless outcast, she felt equal to anything that might now come.

Madam Page was in the library. Hearing Virginia come in, she came into the hall. Virginia stood there supporting Loreen, who stared stupidly at the rich magnificence of the furnishings around her.

"Grandmother," Virginia spoke without hesitation and very clearly, "I have brought one of my friends from the Rectangle. She is in trouble and has no home. I am going to care for her here a little while."

Madam Page glanced from her granddaughter to Loreen in astonishment.

"Did you say she is one of your friends?" she asked in a cold, sneering voice that hurt Virginia more than anything she had yet felt.

"Yes, I said so." Virginia's face flushed, but she seemed to recall a verse that Mr. Gray had used for one of his recent sermons, "A friend of publicans and sinners." Surely, Jesus would do this that she was doing.

"Do you know what this girl is?" asked Madam Page, in an angry whisper, stepping near Virginia.

"I know very well. She is an outcast. You need not tell me, grandmother. I know it even better than you do. She is drunk at this minute. But she is also a child of God. I have seen her on her knees, repentant. And I have seen hell reach out its horrible fingers after her again. And by the grace of Christ I feel that the least that I can do is to rescue her from such peril. Grandmother, we call ourselves Christians. Here is a poor, lost human creature without a home, slipping back into a life of misery and possibly eternal loss, and we have more than enough. I have brought her here, and I shall keep her."

Madam Page glared at Virginia and clenched her hands. All this was contrary to her social code of conduct. How could society excuse familiarity with the scum of the streets? What would Virginia's action cost the family in the way of criticism and loss of standing, and all that long list of necessary relations which people of wealth and position must sustain to the leaders of society? To Madam Page society represented more than the church or any other institution. It was a power to be feared and obeyed. The loss of its good-will was a loss more to be dreaded than anything except the loss of wealth itself.

She stood erect and stern and confronted Virginia, fully roused and determined. Virginia placed her arm about Loreen and calmly looked her grandmother in the face.

"You shall not do this, Virginia! You can send her to the asylum for helpless women. We can pay all the expenses. We cannot afford for the sake of our reputations to shelter such a person."

"Grandmother, I do not wish to do anything that is displeasing to you, but I must keep Loreen here to-night, and longer if it seems best."

"Then you can answer for the consequences! I do not stay in the same house with a miserable—" Madam Page lost her self-control. Virginia stopped her before she could speak the next word.

"Grandmother, this house is mine. It is your home with me as long as you choose to remain. But in this matter I must act as I fully believe Jesus would in my place. I am willing to bear all that society may say or do. Society is not my God. By the side of this poor soul I do not count the verdict of society as of any value."

"I shall not stay here, then!" said Madam Page. She turned suddenly and walked to the end of the hall. She then came back, and going up to Virginia said, with an emphasis that revealed her intense excitement of passion:

"You can always remember that you have driven your grandmother out of your house in favor of a drunken woman"; then, without waiting for Virginia to reply, she turned again and went upstairs. Virginia called a servant and soon had Loreen cared for. She was fast lapsing into a wretched condition. During the brief scene in the hall she had clung to Virginia so hard that her arm was sore from the clutch of the girl's fingers.

Virginia did not know whether her grandmother would leave the house or not. She had abundant means of her own, was perfectly well and vigorous and capable of caring for herself. She had sisters and brothers living in the South and was in the habit of spending several weeks in the year with them. Virginia was not anxious about her welfare as far as that went. But the interview had been a painful one. Going over it, as she did in her room before she went down to tea, she found little cause for regret. "What would Jesus do?" There was no question in her mind that she had done the right thing. If she had made a mistake, it was one of judgment, not of heart.

13

WHEN THE BELL RANG FOR TEA SHE WENT DOWN AND her grandmother did not appear. She sent a servant to her room who brought back word that Madam Page was not there. A few minutes later Rollin came in. He brought word that his grandmother had taken the evening train for the South. He had been at the station to see some friends off, and had by chance met his grandmother as he was coming out. She had told him her reason for going.

Virginia and Rollin comforted each other at the tea table, looking at each other with earnest, sad faces.

"Rollin," said Virginia, and for the first time, almost, since his conversion she realized what a wonderful thing her brother's changed life meant to her, "do you blame me? Am I wrong?"

"No, dear, I cannot believe you are. This is very painful for us. But if you think this poor creature owes her safety and salvation to your personal care, it was the only thing for you to do. O Virginia, to think that we have all these years enjoyed our beautiful home and all these luxuries selfishly, forgetful of the multitudes like this woman! Surely Jesus in our places would do what you have done."

And so Rollin comforted Virginia and counseled with her that evening. And of all the wonderful changes that she henceforth was to know on account of her great pledge, nothing affected her so powerfully as the thought of Rollin's change of life. Truly, this man in Christ was a new creature. Old things were passed away. Behold, all things in him had become new.

Dr. West came that evening at Virginia's summons and did everything necessary for the outcast. She had drunk herself almost into delirium. The best that could be done for her now was quiet nursing and careful watching and personal love. So, in a beautiful room, with a picture of Christ walking by the Sea hanging on the wall, where her bewildered eyes caught daily something more of its hidden meaning, Loreen lay, tossed she hardly knew how into this haven, and Virginia crept nearer the Master than she had ever been, as her heart went out towards this wreck which had thus been flung torn and beaten at her feet.

Meanwhile the Rectangle awaited the issue of the election with more than usual interest; and Mr. Gray and his wife wept over the poor, pitiful creatures who, after a struggle with surroundings that daily tempted them, too often wearied of the struggle and, like Loreen, threw up their arms and went whirling over the cataract into the boiling abyss of their previous condition.

The after-meeting at the First Church was now eagerly established. Henry Maxwell went into the lecture-room on the Sunday succeeding the week of the primary, and was greeted with an enthusiasm that made him tremble at first for its reality. He noted again the absence of Jasper Chase, but all the others were present, and they seemed drawn very close together by a bond of common fellowship that demanded and enjoyed mutual confidences. It was the general feeling that the spirit of Jesus was the spirit of very open, frank confession of experience. It seemed the most natural thing in the world, therefore, for Edward Norman to be telling all the rest of the company about the details of his newspaper.

"The fact is, I have lost a great deal of money during the last three weeks. I cannot tell just how much. I am losing a great many subscribers every day."

"What do the subscribers give as their reason for dropping the paper?" asked Mr. Maxwell. All the rest were listening eagerly.

"There are a good many different reasons. Some say they want a paper that prints all the news; meaning, by that, the crime details, sensations like prize fights, scandals and horrors of various kinds. Others object to the discontinuance of the Sunday edition. I have lost hundreds of subscribers by that action, although I have made satisfactory arrangements with many of the old subscribers by giving them even more in the extra Saturday edition than they formerly had in the Sunday issue. My greatest loss has come from a falling off in advertisements, and from the attitude I have felt obliged to take on political questions. The last action has really cost me more than any other. The bulk of my subscribers are intensely partisan. I may as well tell you all frankly that if I continue to pursue the plan which I honestly believe Jesus would pursue in the matter of political issues and their treatment from a non-partisan and moral standpoint, the *News* will not be able to pay its operating expenses unless one factor in Raymond can be depended on."

He paused a moment and the room was very quiet. Virginia seemed specially interested. Her face glowed with interest. It was like the interest of a person who had been thinking hard of the same thing which Norman went on to mention.

"That one factor is the Christian element in Raymond. Say the *News* has lost heavily from the dropping off of people who do not care for a Christian daily, and from others who simply look upon a newspaper as a purveyor of all sorts of material to amuse or interest them, are there enough genuine Christian people in Raymond who will rally to the support of a paper such as Jesus would probably edit? Or are the habits of the church people so firmly established in their demand for the regular type of journalism that they will not take a paper unless it is stripped largely of the Christian and moral purpose? I may say in this fellowship gathering that owing to recent complications in my business affairs outside of my paper I have been obliged to lose a large part of my fortune. I had to apply the same rule of Jesus' probable conduct to certain transactions with other men who did not apply it to their conduct, and the result has been the loss of a great deal of money. As I understand the promise we made, we were not to ask any question about 'Will it pay?' but all our action was to be based on the one question, 'What would Jesus do?' Acting on that rule of conduct, I have been obliged to lose nearly all the money I have accumulated in my paper. It is not necessary for me to go into details. There is no question with me now, after the three weeks' experience I have had, that a great many men would lose vast sums of money under the present system of business if this rule of Jesus was honestly applied. I mention my loss here because I have the fullest faith in the final success of a daily paper conducted on the lines I have recently laid down, and I had planned to put into it my entire fortune in order to win final success. As it is now, unless, as I said, the Christian people of Raymond, the church members and professing disciples, will support the paper with subscriptions and advertisements, I cannot continue its publication on the present basis."

Virginia asked a question. She had followed Mr. Norman's confession with the most intense eagerness.

"Do you mean that a Christian daily ought to be endowed with a large sum like a Christian college in order to make it pay?"

"That is exactly what I mean. I had laid out plans for putting into the *News* such a variety of material in such a strong and truly interesting way that it would more than make up for whatever was absent from its columns in the way of un-Christian matter. But my plans called for a very large output of money. I am very confident that a Christian daily such as Jesus would approve, containing only what He would print, can be made to succeed financially if it is planned on the right lines. But it will take a large sum of money to work out the plans."

"How much, do you think?" asked Virginia quietly.

Edward Norman looked at her keenly, and his face flushed a moment as an idea of her purpose crossed his mind. He had known her when she was a little girl in the Sunday-school, and he had been on intimate business relations with her father.

"I should say half a million dollars in a town like Raymond could be well spent in the establishment of a paper such as we have in mind," he answered. His voice trembled a little. The keen look on his grizzled face flashed out with a stern but thoroughly Christian anticipation of great achievements in the world of newspaper life, as it had opened up to him within the last few seconds.

"Then," said Virginia, speaking as if the thought was fully considered, "I am ready to put that amount of money into the paper on the one condition, of course, that it be carried on as it has been begun."

"Thank God!" exclaimed Mr. Maxwell softly. Norman was pale. The rest were looking at Virginia. She had more to say.

"Dear friends," she went on, and there was a sadness in her voice that made an impression on the rest that deepened when they thought it over afterwards, "I do not want any of you to credit me with an act of great generosity. I have come to know lately that the money which I have called my own is not mine, but God's. If I, as steward of His, see some wise way to invest His money, it is not an occasion for vainglory or thanks from any one simply because I have proved honest in my administration of the funds He has asked me to use for His glory.

"I have been thinking of this very plan for some time. The fact is, dear friends, that in our coming fight with the whiskey power in Raymond—and it has only just begun—we shall need the *News* to champion the Christian side. You all know that all the other papers are for the saloon. As long as the saloon exists, the work of rescuing dying souls at the Rectangle is carried on at a terrible disadvantage. What can Mr. Gray do with his gospel meetings when half his converts are drinking people, daily tempted and enticed by the saloon on every corner? It would be giving up to the enemy to allow the *News* to fail. I have great confidence in Mr. Norman's ability. I have not seen his plans, but I have the same confidence that he has in making the paper succeed if it is carried forward on a large enough scale. I cannot believe that Christian intelligence in journalism will be inferior to un-Christian intelligence, even when it comes to making the paper pay financially. So that is my reason for putting this money—God's, not mine—into this powerful agent for doing as Jesus would do. If we can keep such a paper going for one year, I shall be willing to see that amount of money used in that experiment. Do not thank me. Do not consider my doing it a wonderful thing. What have I done with God's money all these years but gratify my own selfish personal desires? What can I do with the rest of it but try to make some reparation for what I have stolen from God? That is the way I look at it now. I believe it is what Jesus would do."

Over the lecture-room swept that unseen yet distinctly felt wave of Divine Presence. No one spoke for a while. Mr. Maxwell standing there, where the faces lifted their intense gaze into his, felt what he had already felt—a strange setting back out of the nineteenth century into the first, when the disciples had all things in common, and a spirit of fellowship must have flowed freely between them such as the First Church of Raymond had never before known. How much had his church membership known of this fellowship in daily interests before this little company had begun to do as they believed Jesus would do? It was with difficulty that he thought of his present age and surroundings. The same thought was present with all the rest, also. There was an unspoken comradeship such as they had never known. It was present with them while Virginia was speaking, and during the silence that followed. If it had been defined by any of them it would perhaps have taken some such shape as this: "If I shall, in the course of my obedience to my promise, meet with loss or trouble in the world, I can depend upon the genuine, practical sympathy and fellowship of any other Christian in this room who has, with me, made the pledge to do all things by the rule, 'What would Jesus do?'"

All this, the distinct wave of spiritual power emphasized. It had the effect that a physical miracle may have had on the early disciples in giving them a feeling of confidence in the Lord that helped them to face loss and martyrdom with courage and even joy.

Before they went away this time there were several confidences like those of Edward Norman's. Some of the young men told of loss of places owing to their honest obedience to their promise. Alexander Powers spoke briefly of the fact that the Commission had promised to take action on his evidence at the earliest date possible.

He was engaged at his old work of telegraphy. It was a significant fact that, since his action in resigning his position, neither his wife nor daughter had appeared in public. No one but himself knew the bitterness of that family estrangement and misunderstanding of the higher motive. Yet many of the disciples present in the meeting carried similar burdens. These were things which they would not talk about. Henry Maxwell, from his knowledge of his people, could almost certainly know that obedience to their pledge had produced in the heart of families separation of sympathy and even the introduction of enmity and hatred. Truly, a man's foes are they of his own household when the rule of Jesus is obeyed by some and disobeyed by others. Jesus is a great divider of life. One must walk parallel with Him or directly across His way.

14

BUT MORE THAN ANY OTHER FEELING AT THIS MEET-
ing rose the tide of fellowship for one another. Maxwell watched it,
trembling for its climax which he knew was not yet reached. When it
was, where would it lead them? He did not know, but he was not un-
duly alarmed about it. Only he watched with growing wonder the results of that simple promise as it was being obeyed in these various
lives. Those results were already being felt all over the city. Who
could measure their influence at the end of a year?

One practical form of this fellowship showed itself in the assurances which Edward Norman received of support for his paper.
There was a general flocking toward him when the meeting closed,
and the response to his appeal for help from the Christian disciples
in Raymond was fully understood by this little company. The value
of such a paper in the homes and in behalf of good citizenship, especially at the present crisis in the city, could not be measured. It remained to be seen what could be done now that the paper was
endowed so liberally. But it still was true, as Norman insisted, that
money alone could not make the paper a power. It must receive the

support and sympathy of the Christians in Raymond before it could be counted as one of the great forces of the city.

The week that followed this Sunday meeting was one of great excitement in Raymond. It was the week of the election. President Marsh, true to his promise, took up his cross and bore it manfully, but with shuddering, with groans and even tears, for his deepest conviction was touched, and he tore himself out of the scholarly seclusion of years with a pain and anguish that cost him more than anything he had ever done as a follower of Christ. With him were a few of the college professors who had made the pledge in the First Church. Their experience and suffering were the same as his; for their isolation from all the duties of citizenship had been the same. The same was also true of Henry Maxwell, who plunged into the horror of this fight against whiskey and its allies with a sickening dread of each day's new encounter with it. For never before had he borne such a cross. He staggered under it, and in the brief intervals when he came in from the work and sought the quiet of his study for rest, the sweat broke out on his forehead, and he felt the actual terror of one who marches into unseen, unknown horrors. Looking back on it afterwards he was amazed at his experience. He was not a coward, but he felt the dread that any man of his habits feels when confronted suddenly with a duty which carries with it the doing of certain things so unfamiliar that the actual details connected with it betray his ignorance and fill him with the shame of humiliation.

When Saturday, the election day, came, the excitement rose to its height. An attempt was made to close all the saloons. It was only partly successful. There was a great deal of drinking going on all day. The Rectangle boiled and heaved and cursed and turned its worst side out to the gaze of the city. Gray had continued his meetings during the week, and the results had been even greater than he had dared to hope. When Saturday came, it seemed to him that the crisis in his work had been reached. The Holy Spirit and the Satan of rum seemed to rouse up to a desperate conflict. The more interest in the meetings, the more ferocity and vileness outside. The saloon men no longer concealed their feelings. Open threats of violence were made.

Once during the week Gray and his little company of helpers were assailed with missiles of various kinds as they left the tent late at night. The police sent down a special force, and Virginia and Rachel were always under the protection of either Rollin or Dr. West. Rachel's power in song had not diminished. Rather, with each night, it seemed to add to the intensity and reality of the Spirit's presence.

Gray had at first hesitated about having a meeting that night. But he had a simple rule of action, and was always guided by it. The Spirit seemed to lead him to continue the meeting, and so Saturday night he went on as usual.

The excitement all over the city had reached its climax when the polls closed at six o'clock. Never before had there been such a contest in Raymond. The issue of license or no-license had never been an issue under such circumstances. Never before had such elements in the city been arrayed against each other. It was an unheard-of thing that the President of Lincoln College, the pastor of the First Church, the Dean of the Cathedral, the professional men living in fine houses on the boulevard, should come personally into the wards, and by their presence and their example represent the Christian conscience of the place. The ward politicians were astonished at the sight. However, their astonishment did not prevent their activity. The fight grew hotter every hour, and when six o'clock came neither side could have guessed at the result with any certainty. Every one agreed that never before had there been such an election in Raymond, and both sides awaited the announcement of the result with the greatest interest.

It was after ten o'clock when the meeting at the tent was closed. It had been a strange and, in some respects, a remarkable meeting. Maxwell had come down again at Gray's request. He was completely worn out by the day's work, but the appeal from Gray came to him in such a form that he did not feel able to resist it. President Marsh was also present. He had never been to the Rectangle, and his curiosity was aroused from what he had noticed of the influence of the evangelist in the worst part of the city. Dr. West and Rollin had come with Rachel and Virginia; and Loreen, who still stayed with Virginia, was present near the organ, in her right mind, sober, with a humility and dread of herself that kept her as close to Virginia as a faithful dog. All through the service she sat with bowed head, weeping a part of the time, sobbing when Rachel sang the song, "I was a wandering sheep," clinging with almost visible, tangible yearning to the one hope she had found, listening to prayer and appeal and confession all about her like one who was a part of a new creation, yet fearful of her right to share in it fully.

The tent had been crowded. As on some other occasions, there was more or less disturbance on the outside. This had increased as the night advanced, and Gray thought it wise not to prolong the service.

Once in a while a shout as from a large crowd swept into the tent. The returns from the election were beginning to come in, and the Rectangle had emptied every lodging house, den and hovel into the streets.

In spite of these distractions Rachel's singing kept the crowd in the tent from dissolving. There were a dozen or more conversions. Finally the people became restless and Gray closed the service, remaining a little while with the converts.

Rachel, Virginia, Loreen, Rollin and the Doctor, President Marsh, Mr. Maxwell and Dr. West went out together, intending to go down to the usual waiting place for their car. As they came out of the tent they were at once aware that the Rectangle was trembling on the verge of a drunken riot, and as they pushed through the gathering mobs in the narrow streets they began to realize that they themselves were objects of great attention.

"There he is the bloke in the tall hat! He's the leader!" shouted a rough voice. President Marsh, with his erect, commanding figure, was conspicuous in the little company.

"How has the election gone? It is too early to know the result yet, isn't it?" He asked the question aloud, and a man answered:

"They say second and third wards have gone almost solid for no-license. If that is so, the whiskey men have been beaten."

"Thank God! I hope it is true!" exclaimed Maxwell. "Marsh, we are in danger here. Do you realize our situation? We ought to get the ladies to a place of safety."

"That is true," said Marsh gravely. At that moment a shower of stones and other missiles fell over them. The narrow street and sidewalk in front of them was completely choked with the worst elements of the Rectangle.

"This looks serious," said Maxwell. With Marsh and Rollin and Dr. West he started to go forward through a small opening, Virginia, Rachel, and Loreen following close and sheltered by the men, who now realized something of their danger. The Rectangle was drunk and enraged. It saw in Marsh and Maxwell two of the leaders in the election contest which had perhaps robbed them of their beloved saloon.

"Down with the aristocrats!" shouted a shrill voice, more like a woman's than a man's. A shower of mud and stones followed. Rachel remembered afterwards that Rollin jumped directly in front of her and received on his head and chest a number of blows that would probably have struck her if he had not shielded her from them.

And just then, before the police reached them, Loreen started forward in front of Virginia and pushed her aside, looking up and screaming. It was so sudden that no one had time to catch the face of the one who did it. But out of the upper window of a room, over the very saloon where Loreen had come out a week before, some one had thrown a heavy bottle. It struck Loreen on the head and she fell to the ground. Virginia turned and instantly kneeled down by her.

The police officers by that time had reached the little company.

President Marsh raised his arm and shouted over the howl that was beginning to rise from the wild beast in the mob.

"Stop! You've killed a woman!" The announcement partly sobered the crowd.

"Is it true?" Maxwell asked it, as Dr. West kneeled on the other side of Loreen, supporting her.

"She's dying!" said Dr. West briefly.

Loreen opened her eyes and smiled at Virginia, who wiped the blood from her face and then bent over and kissed her. Loreen smiled again, and the next minute her soul was in Paradise.

And yet this is only one woman out of thousands killed by this drink evil. Crowd back, now, ye sinful men and women in this filthy street! Let this august dead form be borne through your stupefied, sobered ranks! She was one of your own children. The Rectangle had stamped the image of the beast on her. Thank Him who died for sinners that the other image of a new soul now shines out of her pale clay. Crowd back! Give them room! Let her pass reverently, followed and surrounded by the weeping, awestruck company of Christians. Ye killed her, ye drunken murderers! And yet—and yet—O Christian America, who killed this woman? Stand back! Silence, there! A woman has been killed. Who? Loreen. Child of the streets. Poor, drunken, vile sinner. O Lord God, how long, how long? Yes. The saloon killed her; that is, the Christians of America, who license the saloon. And the Judgment Day only shall declare who was the murderer of Loreen.

15

"He that followeth me shall not walk in darkness."

THE BODY OF LOREEN LAY IN STATE AT THE PAGE MAN-
sion on the avenue. It was Sunday morning and the clear sweet
spring air, just beginning to breathe over the city the perfume of
early blossoms in the woods and fields, swept over the casket from
one of the open windows at the end of the grand hall. The church
bells were ringing and people on the avenue going by to service
turned curious, inquiring looks up at the great house and then went
on, talking of the recent events which had so strangely entered into
and made history in the city.

At the First Church, Mr. Maxwell, bearing on his face marks of
the scene he had been through, confronted an immense congregation, and spoke to it with a passion and a power that came so
naturally out of the profound experiences of the day before that
his people felt for him something of the old feeling of pride they
once had in his dramatic delivery. Only this was with a different
attitude. And all through his impassioned appeal this morning,
there was a note of sadness and rebuke and stern condemnation

that made many of the members pale with self-accusation or with inward anger.

For Raymond had awakened that morning to the fact that the city had gone for license after all. The rumor at the Rectangle that the second and third wards had gone no-license proved to be false. It was true that the victory was won by a very meager majority. But the result was the same as if it had been overwhelming. Raymond had voted to continue for another year the saloon. The Christians of Raymond stood condemned by the result. More than a hundred professing Christian disciples had failed to go to the polls, and many more than that number had voted with the whiskey men. If all the church members of Raymond had voted against the saloon, it would today be outlawed instead of crowned king of the municipality. For that had been the fact in Raymond for years. The saloon ruled. No one denied that. What would Jesus do? And this woman who had been brutally struck down by the very hand that had assisted so eagerly to work her earthly ruin—what of her? Was it anything more than the logical sequence of the whole horrible system of license, that for another year the very saloon that received her so often and compassed her degradation, from whose very spot the weapon had been hurled that struck her dead, would, by the law which the Christian people of Raymond voted to support, perhaps open its doors to-morrow and damn a hundred Loreens before the year had drawn to its bloody close?

All this, with a voice that rang and trembled and broke in sobs of anguish for the result, did Henry Maxwell pour out upon his people that Sunday morning. And men and women wept as he spoke. President Marsh sat there, his usual erect, handsome, firm, bright self-confident bearing all gone; his head bowed upon his breast, the great tears rolling down his cheeks, unmindful of the fact that never before had he shown outward emotion in a public service. Edward Norman near by sat with his clearcut, keen face erect, but his lip trembled and he clutched the end of the pew with a feeling of emotion that struck deep into his knowledge of the truth as Maxwell spoke it. No man had given or suffered more to influence public opinion that week than Norman. The thought that the Christian conscience had been aroused too late or too feebly, lay with a weight of accusation upon the heart of the editor. What if he had begun to do as Jesus would have done, long ago? Who could tell what might have been accomplished by this time! And up in the choir, Rachel Winslow, with her face bowed on the railing of the oak screen, gave way to a feeling which she had not allowed yet to master her, but it so unfitted her for her part that when Mr. Maxwell finished and she tried to sing the closing solo after the prayer, her voice broke, and for the first time in her life she was obliged to sit down, sobbing, and unable to go on.

Over the church, in the silence that followed this strange scene, sobs and the noise of weeping arose. When had the First Church yielded to such a baptism of tears? What had become of its regular, precise, conventional order of service, undisturbed by any vulgar emotion and unmoved by any foolish excitement? But the people had lately had their deepest convictions touched. They had been living so long on their surface feelings that they had almost forgotten the deeper wells of life. Now that they had broken the surface, the people were convicted of the meaning of their discipleship.

Mr. Maxwell did not ask, this morning, for volunteers to join those who had already pledged to do as Jesus would. But when the congregation had finally gone, and he had entered the lecture-room, it needed but a glance to show him that the original company of followers had been largely increased. The meeting was tender; it glowed with the Spirit's presence; it was alive with strong and lasting resolve to begin a war on the whiskey power in Raymond that would break its reign forever. Since the first Sunday when the first company of volunteers had pledged themselves to do as Jesus would do, the different meetings had been characterized by distinct impulses or impressions. To-day, the entire force of the gathering seemed to be directed to this one large purpose. It was a meeting full of broken prayers of contrition, of confession, of strong yearning for a new and better city life. And all through it ran one general cry for deliverance from the saloon and its awful curse.

But if the First Church was deeply stirred by the events of the last week, the Rectangle also felt moved strangely in its own way. The death of Loreen was not in itself so remarkable a fact. It was her recent acquaintance with the people from the city that lifted her into special prominence and surrounded her death with more than ordinary importance. Every one in the Rectangle knew that Loreen was at this moment lying in the Page mansion up on the avenue. Exaggerated reports of the magnificence of the casket had already furnished material for eager gossip. The Rectangle was excited to know the details of the funeral. Would it be public? What did Miss Page intend to do? The Rectangle had never before mingled even in this distant personal manner with the aristocracy on the boulevard. The opportunities for doing so were not frequent. Gray and his wife were besieged by inquirers who wanted to know what Loreen's friends and acquaintances were expected to do in paying their last respects to her. For her acquaintance was large and many of the recent converts were among her friends.

So that is how it happened that Monday afternoon, at the tent, the funeral service of Loreen was held before an immense audience that choked the tent and overflowed beyond all previous bounds. Gray had gone up to Virginia's and, after talking it over with her and Maxwell, the arrangement had been made.

"I am and always have been opposed to large public funerals," said Gray, whose complete wholesome simplicity of character was one of its great sources of strength; "but the cry of the poor creatures who knew Loreen is so earnest that I do not know how to refuse this desire to see her and pay her poor body some last little honor. What do you think, Mr. Maxwell? I will be guided by your judgment in the matter. I am sure that whatever you and Miss Page think best, will be right."

"I feel as you do," replied Mr. Maxwell. "Under the circumstances I have a great distaste for what seems like display at such times. But this seems different. The people at the Rectangle will not come here to service. I think the most Christian thing will be to let them have the service at the tent. Do you think so, Miss Virginia?"

"Yes," said Virginia. "Poor soul! I do not know but that some time I shall know she gave her life for mine. We certainly cannot and will not use the occasion for vulgar display. Let her friends be allowed the gratification of their wishes. I see no harm in it."

So the arrangements were made, with some difficulty, for the service at the tent; and Virginia with her uncle and Rollin, accompanied by Maxwell, Rachel and President Marsh, and the quartet from the First Church, went down and witnessed one of the strange things of their lives.

It happened that that afternoon a somewhat noted newspaper correspondent was passing through Raymond on his way to an editorial convention in a neighboring city. He heard of the contemplated service at the tent and went down. His description of it was written in a graphic style that caught the attention of very many readers the next day. A fragment of his account belongs to this part of the history of Raymond:

There was a very unique and unusual funeral service held here this afternoon at the tent of an evangelist, Rev. John Gray, down in the slum district known as the Rectangle. The occasion was caused by the killing of a woman during an election riot last Saturday night. It seems she had been recently converted during the evangelist's meetings, and was killed while returning from one of the meetings in company with other converts and some of her friends. She was a common street drunkard, and yet the services at the tent were as impressive as any I ever witnessed in a metropolitan church over the most distinguished citizen.

In the first place, a most exquisite anthem was sung by a trained choir. It struck me, of course—being a stranger in the place—with considerable astonishment to hear voices like those one naturally expects to hear only in great churches or concerts, at such a meeting as this. But the most remarkable part of the music was a solo sung by a strikingly beautiful young woman, a Miss Winslow who, if I remember right, is the young singer who was sought for by Crandall the manager of National Opera, and who for some reason refused to accept his offer to go on the stage. She had a most wonderful manner in singing, and everybody was weeping before she had sung a dozen words. That, of course, is not so strange an effect to be produced at a funeral service, but the voice itself was one of thousands. I understand Miss Winslow sings in the First Church of Raymond and could probably command almost any salary as a public singer. She will probably be heard from soon. Such a voice could win its way anywhere.

The service aside from the singing was peculiar. The evangelist, a man of apparently very simple, unassuming style, spoke a few words, and he was followed by a fine looking man, the Rev. Henry Maxwell, pastor of the First Church of Raymond. Mr. Maxwell spoke of the fact that the dead woman had been fully prepared to go, but he spoke in a peculiarly sensitive manner of the effect of the liquor business on the lives of men and women like this one. Raymond, of course, being a railroad town and the centre of the great packing interests for this region, is full of saloons. I caught from the minister's remarks that he had only recently changed his views in regard to license. He certainly made a very striking address, and yet it was in no sense inappropriate for a funeral.

Then followed what was perhaps the queer part of this strange service. The women in the tent, at least a large part of them up near the coffin, began to sing in a soft, tearful way, "I was a wandering sheep." Then while the singing was going on, one row of women stood up and walked slowly past the casket, and as they went by, each one placed a flower of some kind upon it. Then they sat down and another row filed past, leaving their flowers. All the time the singing continued softly like rain on a tent cover when the wind is gentle. It was one of the simplest and at the same time one of the most impressive sights I ever witnessed. The sides of the tent were up, and hundreds of people who could not get in stood outside, all as still as death itself, with wonderful sadness and solemnity for such rough looking people. There must have been a hundred of these women, and I was told many of them had been converted at the meetings just recently. I cannot describe the effect of that singing. Not a man sang a note. All women's voices, and so soft, and yet so distinct, that the effect was startling.

The service closed with another solo by Miss Winslow, who sang, "There were ninety and nine." And then the evangelist asked them all to bow their heads while he prayed. I was obliged in order to catch my train to leave during the prayer, and the last view I caught of the service as the train went by the shops was a sight of the great crowd pouring out of the tent and forming in open ranks while the coffin was borne out by six of the women. It is a long time since I have seen such a picture in this unpoetic Republic.

If Loreen's funeral impressed a passing stranger like this, it is not difficult to imagine the profound feelings of those who had been so intimately connected with her life and death. Nothing had ever entered the Rectangle that had moved it so deeply as Loreen's body in that coffin. And the Holy Spirit seemed to bless with special power the use of this senseless clay. For that night He swept more than a score of lost souls, mostly women, into the fold of the Good Shepherd.

It should be said here that Mr. Maxwell's statements concerning the opening of the saloon from whose windows Loreen had been killed, proved nearly exactly true. It was formally closed Monday and Tuesday while the authorities made arrests of the proprietors charged with the murder. But nothing could be proved against any one, and before Saturday of that week the saloon was running as regularly as ever. No one on the earth was ever punished by earthly courts for the murder of Loreen.

16

No one in all Raymond, including the Rectangle, felt Loreen's death more keenly than Virginia. It came like a distinct personal loss to her. That short week while the girl had been in her home had opened Virginia's heart to a new life. She was talking it over with Rachel the day after the funeral. They were sitting in the hall of the Page mansion.

"I am going to do something with my money to help those women to a better life." Virginia looked over to the end of the hall where, the day before, Loreen's body had lain. "I have decided on a good plan, as it seems to me. I have talked it over with Rollin. He will devote a large part of his money also to the same plan."

"How much money have you, Virginia, to give in this way?" asked Rachel. Once, she would never have asked such a personal question. Now, it seemed as natural to talk frankly about money as about anything else that belonged to God.

"I have available for use at least four hundred and fifty thousand dollars. Rollin has as much more. It is one of his bitter regrets now that his extravagant habits of life before his conversion practically

---

threw away half that father left him. We are both eager to make all the reparation in our power. 'What would Jesus do with this money?' We want to answer that question honestly and wisely. The money I shall put into the *News* is, I am confident, in a line with His probable action. It is as necessary that we have a Christian daily paper in Raymond, especially now that we have the saloon influence to meet, as it is to have a church or a college. So I am satisfied that the five hundred thousand dollars that Mr. Norman will know how to use so well will be a powerful factor in Raymond to do as Jesus would.

"About my other plan, Rachel, I want you to work with me. Rollin and I are going to buy up a large part of the property in the Rectangle. The field where the tent now is has been in litigation for years. We mean to secure the entire tract as soon as the courts have settled the title.

"For some time I have been making a special study of the various forms of college settlements and residence methods of Christian work and Institutional church work in the heart of great city slums. I do not know that I have yet been able to tell just what is the wisest and most effective kind of work that can be done in Raymond. But I do know this much. My money—I mean God's, which he wants me to use—can build wholesome lodging-houses, refuges for poor women, asylums for shop girls, safety for many and many a lost girl like Loreen.

"And I do not want to be simply a dispenser of this money. God help me! I do want to put myself into the problem. But you know, Rachel, I have a feeling all the time that all that limitless money and limitless personal sacrifice can possibly do, will not really lessen very much the awful condition at the Rectangle as long as the saloon is legally established there. I think that is true of any Christian work now being carried on in any great city. The saloon furnishes material to be saved faster than the settlement or residence or rescue mission work can save it."

Virginia suddenly rose and paced the hall. Rachel answered sadly, and yet with a note of hope in her voice:

"It is true. But, Virginia, a wonderful amount of good can be done with this money! And the saloon cannot always remain here. The time must come when the Christian forces in the city will triumph."

Virginia paused near Rachel, and her pale, earnest face lighted up. "I believe that too. The number of those who have promised to do as Jesus would is increasing. If we once have, say, five hundred such disciples in Raymond, the saloon is doomed. But now, dear, I want you to look at your part in this plan for capturing and saving the Rectangle. Your voice is a power.

"I have had many ideas lately. Here is one of them. You could organize among the girls a Musical Institute; give them the benefit of your training. There are some splendid voices in the rough there. Did any one ever hear such singing as that yesterday by those women? Rachel, what a beautiful opportunity! You shall have the best of material in the way of organs and orchestras that money can provide, and what cannot be done with music to win souls there into higher and purer and better living?"

Before Virginia had ceased speaking Rachel's face was perfectly transformed with the thought of her life work. It flowed into her heart and mind like a flood, and the torrent of her feeling overflowed in tears that could not be restrained. It was what she had dreamed of doing herself. It represented to her something that she felt was in keeping with a right use of her talent.

"Yes," she said, as she rose and put her arm about Virginia, while both girls in the excitement of their enthusiasm paced the hall. "Yes, I will gladly put my life into that kind of service. I do believe that Jesus would have me use my life in this way. Virginia, what miracles can we not accomplish in humanity if we have such a lever as consecrated money to move things with!"

"Add to it consecrated personal enthusiasm like yours, and it certainly can accomplish great things," said Virginia smiling. And before Rachel could reply, Rollin came in.

He hesitated a moment, and then was passing out of the hall into the library when Virginia called him back and asked some questions about his work.

Rollin came back and sat down, and together the three discussed their future plans. Rollin was apparently entirely free from embarrassment in Rachel's presence while Virginia was with them, only his manner with her was almost precise, if not cold. The past seemed to have been entirely absorbed in his wonderful conversion. He had not forgotten it, but he seemed to be completely caught up for this present time in the purpose of his new life. After a while Rollin was called out, and Rachel and Virginia began to talk of other things.

"By the way, what has become of Jasper Chase?" Virginia asked the question innocently, but Rachel flushed and Virginia added with a smile, "I suppose he is writing another book. Is he going to put you into this one, Rachel? You know I always suspected Jasper Chase of doing that very thing in his first story."

"Virginia," Rachel spoke with the frankness that had always existed between the two friends, "Jasper Chase told me the other night that he—in fact—he proposed to me—or he would, if—"

Rachel stopped and sat with her hands clasped on her lap, and there were tears in her eyes.

"Virginia, I thought a little while ago I loved him, as he said he loved me. But when he spoke, my heart felt repelled, and I said what I ought to say. I told him no. I have not seen him since. That was the night of the first conversions at the Rectangle."

"I am glad for you," said Virginia quietly.

"Why?" asked Rachel a little startled.

"Because, I never really liked Jasper Chase. He is too cold and—I do not like to judge him, but I have always distrusted his sincerity in taking the pledge at the church with the rest."

Rachel looked at Virginia thoughtfully.

"I have never given my heart to him I am sure. He touched my emotions, and I admired his skill as a writer. I have thought at times that I cared a good deal for him. I think perhaps if he had spoken to me at any other time than the one he chose, I could easily have persuaded myself that I loved him. But not now."

Again Rachel paused suddenly, and when she looked up at Virginia again there were tears on her face. Virginia came to her and put her arm about her tenderly.

When Rachel had left the house, Virginia sat in the hall thinking over the confidence her friend had just shown her. There was something still to be told, Virginia felt sure from Rachel's manner, but she did not feel hurt that Rachel had kept back something. She was simply conscious of more on Rachel's mind than she had revealed.

Very soon Rollin came back, and he and Virginia, arm in arm as they had lately been in the habit of doing, walked up and down the long hall. It was easy for their talk to settle finally upon Rachel because of the place she was to occupy in the plans which were being made for the purchase of property at the Rectangle.

"Did you ever know of a girl of such gifted powers in vocal music who was willing to give her life to the people as Rachel is going to do? She is going to give music lessons in the city, have private pupils to make her living, and then give the people in the Rectangle the benefit of her culture and her voice."

"It is certainly a very good example of self-sacrifice," replied Rollin a little stiffly.

Virginia looked at him a little sharply. "But don't you think it is a very unusual example? Can you imagine—" here Virginia named half a dozen famous opera singers—doing anything of this sort?"

"No, I cannot," Rollin answered briefly. "Neither can I imagine Miss—" he spoke the name of the girl with the red parasol who had begged Virginia to take the girls to the Rectangle—"doing what you are doing, Virginia."

"Any more than I can imagine Mr.—" Virginia spoke the name of a young society leader—"going about to the clubs doing your work, Rollin." The two walked on in silence for the length of the hall.

"Coming back to Rachel," began Virginia, "Rollin, why do you treat her with such a distinct, precise manner? I think, Rollin—pardon me if I hurt you—that she is annoyed by it. You need to be on easy terms. I don't think Rachel likes this change."

Rollin suddenly stopped. He seemed deeply agitated. He took his arm from Virginia's and walked alone to the end of the hall. Then he returned, with his hands behind him, and stopped near his sister and said, "Virginia, have you not learned my secret?"

Virginia looked bewildered, then over her face the unusual color crept, showing that she understood.

"I have never loved any one but Rachel Winslow." Rollin spoke calmly enough. "That day she was here when you talked about her refusal to join the concert company, I asked her to be my wife; out there on the avenue. She refused me, as I knew she would. And she gave as her reason the fact that I had no purpose in life, which was true enough. Now that I have a purpose, now that I am a new man, don't you see, Virginia, how impossible it is for me to say anything? I owe my very conversion to Rachel's singing. And yet that night while she sang I can honestly say that, for the time being, I never thought of her voice except as God's message. I believe that all my personal love for her was for the time merged into a personal love to my God and my Saviour." Rollin was silent, then he went on with more emotion. "I still love her, Virginia. But I do not think she ever could love me." He stopped and looked his sister in the face with a sad smile.

"I don't know about that," said Virginia to herself. She was noting Rollin's handsome face, his marks of dissipation nearly all gone now, the firm lips showing manhood and courage, the clear eyes looking into hers frankly, the form strong and graceful. Rollin was a man now. Why should not Rachel come to love him in time? Surely the two were well fitted for each other, especially now that their purpose in life was moved by the same Christian force.

She said something of all this to Rollin, but he did not find much comfort. When they closed the interview, Virginia carried away the impression that Rollin meant to go his way with his chosen work, trying to reach the fashionable men at the clubs, and while not avoiding Rachel, seeking no occasions for meeting her. He was distrustful of his power to control his feeling. And Virginia could see that he dreaded even the thought of a second refusal in case he did let Rachel know that his love was still the same.

17

THE NEXT DAY SHE WENT DOWN TO THE *News* OFFICE TO
see Edward Norman and arrange the details of her part in the establishment of the paper on its new foundation. Mr. Maxwell was present
at this conference, and the three agreed that whatever Jesus would do
in detail as editor of a daily paper, He would be guided by the same
general principles that directed His conduct as the Saviour of the
world.

"I have tried to put down here in concrete form some of the
things that it has seemed to me Jesus would do," said Edward Norman.

He read from a paper lying on his desk, and Maxwell was reminded again of his own effort to put into written form his own
conception of Jesus' probable action, and also of Milton Wright's
same attempt in his business.

"I have headed this, 'What would Jesus do as Edward Norman,
editor of a daily newspaper in Raymond?'

1. He would never allow a sentence or a picture in his paper
that could be called bad or coarse or impure in any way.

2. He would probably conduct the political part of the paper from the standpoint of non-partisan patriotism, always looking upon all political questions in the light of their relation to the Kingdom of God, and advocating measures from the standpoint of their relation to the welfare of the people, always on the basis of "What is right?" never on the basis of "What is for the best interests of this or that party?" In other words, He would treat all political questions as he would treat every other subject, from the standpoint of the advancement of the Kingdom of God on earth.

Edward Norman looked up from the reading a moment. "You understand that is my opinion of Jesus' probable action on political matters in a daily paper. I am not passing judgment on other newspaper men who may have a different conception of Jesus' probable action from mine. I am simply trying to answer honestly, 'What would Jesus do as Edward Norman?' And the answer I find is what I have put down."

3. The end and aim of a daily paper conducted by Jesus would be to do the will of God. That is, His main purpose in carrying on a newspaper would not be to make money, or gain political influence; but His first and ruling purpose would be to so conduct His paper that it would be evident to all His subscribers that He was trying to seek first the Kingdom of God by means of His paper. This purpose would be as distinct and unquestioned as the purpose of a minister or a missionary or any unselfish martyr in Christian work anywhere.

4. All questionable advertisements would be impossible.

5. The relations of Jesus to the employees on the paper would be of the most loving character.

"So far as I have gone," said Norman again looking up, "I am of opinion that Jesus would employ practically some form of co-operation that would represent the idea of a mutual interest in a business where all were to move together for the same great end. I am working out such a plan, and I am confident it will be successful. At any rate, once the element of personal love is introduced into a business like this, and the selfish principle of doing it for personal profits to a man or company is taken out, I do not see any way except the most loving personal interest between editors, reporters, pressmen, and all who contribute anything to the life of the paper. And that interest would be expressed not only in the personal love and sympathy but in a sharing with the profits of the business."

6. As editor of a daily paper to-day, Jesus would give large space to the work of the Christian world. He would devote a page possibly to the facts of Reform, of sociological problems, of institutional church work and similar movements.

7. He would do all in His power in His paper to fight the saloon as an enemy of the human race and an unnecessary part of our civilization. He would do this regardless of public sentiment in the matter and, of course, always regardless of its effect upon His subscription list.

Again Edward Norman looked up. "I state my honest conviction on this point. Of course, I do not pass judgment on the Christian men who are editing other kinds of papers to-day. But as I interpret Jesus, I believe He would use the influence of His paper to remove the saloon entirely from the political and social life of the nation."

8. Jesus would not issue a Sunday edition.

9. He would print the news of the world that people ought to know. Among the things they do not need to know, and which would not be published, would be accounts of brutal prize-fights, long accounts of crimes, scandals in private families, or any other human events which in any way would conflict with the first point mentioned in this outline.

10. If Jesus had the amount of money to use on a paper which we have, He would probably secure the best and strongest Christian men and women to co-operate with him in the mat-

ter of contributions. That will be my purpose, as I shall be able to show you in a few days.

11. Whatever the details of the paper might demand as the paper developed along its definite plan, the main principle that guided it would always be the establishment of the Kingdom of God in the world. This large general principle would necessarily shape all the detail.

Edward Norman finished reading the plan. He was very thoughtful. "I have merely sketched a faint outline. I have a hundred ideas for making the paper powerful that I have not thought out fully as yet. This is simply suggestive. I have talked it over with other newspaper men. Some of them say I will have a weak, namby-pamby Sunday school sheet. If I get out something as good as a Sunday school it will be pretty good.

"Why do men, when they want to characterize something as particularly feeble, always use a Sunday-school as a comparison, when they ought to know that the Sunday-school is one of the strongest, most powerful influences in our civilization in this country to-day? But the paper will not necessarily be weak because it is good. Good things are more powerful than bad.

The question with me is largely one of support from the Christian people of Raymond. There are over twenty thousand church members here in this city. If half of them will stand by the *News* its life is assured. What do you think, Maxwell, of the probability of such support?"

"I don't know enough about it to give an intelligent answer. I believe in the paper with all my heart. If it lives a year, as Miss Virginia said, there is no telling what it can do. The great thing will be to issue such a paper, as near as we can judge, as Jesus probably would, and put into it all the elements of Christian brains, strength, intelligence and sense; and command respect for freedom from bigotry, fanaticism, narrowness and anything else that is contrary to the spirit of Jesus. Such a paper will call for the best that human thought and action is capable of giving. The greatest minds in the world would have their powers taxed to the utmost to issue a Christian daily."

"Yes," Edward Norman spoke humbly. "I shall make a great many mistakes, no doubt. I need a great deal of wisdom. But I want to do as Jesus would. 'What would He do?' I have asked it, and shall continue to do so, and abide by the results."

"I think we are beginning to understand," said Virginia, "the meaning of that command, 'Grow in the grace and knowledge of our Lord and Saviour Jesus Christ.' I am sure I do not know all that He would do in detail until I know Him better."

"That is very true," said Henry Maxwell. "I am beginning to understand that I cannot interpret the probable action of Jesus until I know better what His spirit is. The greatest question in all of human life is summed up when we ask, 'What would Jesus do?' if, as we ask it, we also try to answer it from a growth in knowledge of Jesus himself. We must know Jesus before we can imitate Him."

When the arrangement had been made between Virginia and Edward Norman, he found himself in possession of the sum of five hundred thousand dollars to use for the establishment of a Christian daily paper. When Virginia and Maxwell had gone, Norman closed his door and, alone with the Divine Presence, asked like a child for help from his all-powerful Father. All through his prayer as he knelt before his desk ran the promise, "If any man lack wisdom, let him ask of God who giveth to all men liberally and upbraideth not, and it shall be given him." Surely his prayer would be answered, and the kingdom advanced through this instrument of God's power, this mighty press, which had become so largely degraded to the base uses of man's avarice and ambition.

Two months went by. They were full of action and of results in the city of Raymond and especially in the First Church. In spite of the approaching heat of the summer season, the after-meeting of the disciples who had made the pledge to do as Jesus would do, continued with enthusiasm and power. Gray had finished his work at the Rectangle, and an outward observer going through the place could not have seen any difference in the old conditions, although there was an actual change in hundreds of lives. But the saloons, dens, hovels, gambling houses, still ran, overflowing their vileness into the lives of fresh victims to take the place of those rescued by the evangelist. And the devil recruited his ranks very fast.

Henry Maxwell did not go abroad. Instead of that, he took the money he had been saving for the trip and quietly arranged for a summer vacation for a whole family living down in the Rectangle, who had never gone outside of the foul district of the tenements. The pastor of the First Church will never forget the week he spent with this family making the arrangements. He went down into the Rectangle one hot day when something of the terrible heat in the horrible tenements was beginning to be felt, and helped the family to the station, and then went with them to a beautiful spot on the coast where, in the home of a Christian woman, the bewildered city tenants breathed for the first time in years the cool salt air, and felt blow about them the pine-scented fragrance of a new lease of life.

There was a sickly babe with the mother, and three other children, one a cripple. The father, who had been out of work until he had been, as he afterwards confessed to Maxwell, several times on the edge of suicide, sat with the baby in his arms during the journey, and when Maxwell started back to Raymond, after seeing the family settled, the man held his hand at parting, and choked with his utterance, and finally broke down, to Maxwell's great confusion. The mother, a wearied, worn-out woman who had lost three children the year before from a fever scourge in the Rectangle, sat by the car window all the way and drank in the delights of sea and sky and field. It all seemed a miracle to her. And Maxwell, coming back into Raymond at the end of that week, feeling the scorching, sickening heat all the more because of his little taste of the ocean breezes, thanked God for the joy he had witnessed, and entered upon his discipleship with a humble heart, knowing for almost the first time in his life this special kind of sacrifice. For never before had he denied himself his regular summer trip away from the heat of Raymond, whether he felt in any great need of rest or not.

"It is a fact," he said in reply to several inquiries on the part of his church, "I do not feel in need of a vacation this year. I am very well and prefer to stay here." It was with a feeling of relief that he succeeded in concealing from every one but his wife what he had done with this other family. He felt the need of doing anything of that sort without display or approval from others.

So the summer came on, and Maxwell grew into a large knowledge of his Lord. The First Church was still swayed by the power of the Spirit. Maxwell marveled at the continuance of His stay. He knew very well that from the beginning nothing but the Spirit's presence had kept the church from being torn asunder by the remarkable testing it had received of its discipleship. Even now there were many of the members among those who had not taken the pledge, who regarded the whole movement as Mr. Winslow did, in the nature of a fanatical interpretation of Christian duty, and looked for the return of the old normal condition. Meanwhile the whole body of disciples was under the influence of the Spirit, and the pastor went his way that summer, doing his parish work in great joy, keeping up his meetings with the railroad men as he had promised Alexander Powers, and daily growing into a better knowledge of the Master.

Early one afternoon in August, after a day of refreshing coolness following a long period of heat, Jasper Chase walked to his window in the apartment house on the avenue and looked out.

On his desk lay a pile of manuscript. Since that evening when he had spoken to Rachel Winslow he had not met her. His singularly sensitive nature—sensitive to the point of extreme irritability when he was thwarted—served to thrust him into an isolation that was intensified by his habits as an author.

All through the heat of summer he had been writing. His book was nearly done now. He had thrown himself into its construction with a feverish strength that threatened at any moment to desert him and leave him helpless. He had not forgotten his pledge made with the other church members at the First Church. It had forced itself upon his notice all through his writing, and ever since Rachel had said no to him, he had asked a thousand times, "Would Jesus do this? Would He write this story?" It was a social novel, written in a style that had proved popular. It had no purpose except to amuse. Its moral teaching was not bad, but neither was it Christian in any positive way. Jasper Chase knew that such a story would probably sell. He was conscious of powers in this way that the social world petted and admired. "What would Jesus do?" He felt that Jesus would never write such a book. The question obtruded on him at the most inopportune times. He became irascible over it. The standard of Jesus for an author was too ideal. Of course, Jesus would use His powers to produce something useful or helpful, or with a purpose. What was he, Jasper Chase, writing this novel for? Why, what nearly every writer wrote for—money, money, and fame as a writer. There was no secret with him that he was writing this new story with that object. He was not poor, and so had no great temptation to write for money. But he was urged on by his desire for fame as much as anything. He must write this kind of matter. But what would Jesus do? The question plagued him even more than Rachel's refusal. Was he going to break his promise? "Did the promise mean much after all?" he asked.

As he stood at the window, Rollin Page came out of the club house just opposite. Jasper noted his handsome face and noble figure as he started down the street. He went back to his desk and turned over some papers there. Then he came back to the window. Rollin was walking down past the block and Rachel Winslow was walking beside him. Rollin must have overtaken her as she was coming from Virginia's that afternoon.

Jasper watched the two figures until they disappeared in the crowd on the walk. Then he turned to his desk and began to write. When he had finished the last page of the last chapter of his book it was nearly dark. "What would Jesus do?" He had finally answered the question by denying his Lord. It grew darker in his room. He had deliberately chosen his course, urged on by his disappointment and loss.

"But Jesus said unto him, no man having put his hand to the plow, and looking back, is fit for the Kingdom of God."

18

What is that to thee? Follow thou me.

WHEN ROLLIN STARTED DOWN THE STREET THE AFTER-
noon that Jasper stood looking out of his window he was not thinking of Rachel Winslow and did not expect to see her anywhere. He
had come suddenly upon her as he turned into the avenue and his
heart had leaped up at the sight of her. He walked along by her now,
rejoicing after all in a little moment of this earthly love he could not
drive out of his life.

"I have just been over to see Virginia," said Rachel. "She tells me
the arrangements are nearly completed for the transfer of the Rectangle property."

"Yes. It has been a tedious case in the courts. Did Virginia show
you all the plans and specifications for building?"

"We looked over a good many. It is astonishing to me where Virginia has managed to get all her ideas about this work."

"Virginia knows more now about Arnold Toynbee and East End
London and Institutional Church work in America than a good
many professional slum workers. She has been spending nearly all
summer in getting information." Rollin was beginning to feel more

at ease as they talked over this coming work of humanity. It was safe, common ground.

"What have you been doing all summer? I have not seen much of you," Rachel suddenly asked, and then her face warmed with its quick flush of tropical color as if she might have implied too much interest in Rollin or too much regret at not seeing him oftener.

"I have been busy," replied Rollin briefly.

"Tell me something about it," persisted Rachel. "You say so little. Have I a right to ask?"

She put the question very frankly, turning toward Rollin in real earnest.

"Yes, certainly," he replied, with a graceful smile. "I am not so certain that I can tell you much. I have been trying to find some way to reach the men I once knew and win them into more useful lives."

He stopped suddenly as if he were almost afraid to go on. Rachel did not venture to suggest anything.

"I have been a member of the same company to which you and Virginia belong," continued Rollin, beginning again. "I have made the pledge to do as I believe Jesus would do, and it is in trying to answer this question that I have been doing my work."

"That is what I do not understand. Virginia told me about the other. It seems wonderful to think that you are trying to keep that pledge with us. But what can you do with the club men?"

"You have asked me a direct question and I shall have to answer it now," replied Rollin, smiling again. "You see, I asked myself after that night at the tent, you remember" (he spoke hurriedly and his voice trembled a little), "what purpose I could now have in my life to redeem it, to satisfy my thought of Christian discipleship? And the more I thought of it, the more I was driven to a place where I knew I must take up the cross.

"Did you ever think that of all the neglected beings in our social system none are quite so completely left alone as the fast young men who fill the clubs and waste their time and money as I used to? The churches look after the poor, miserable creatures like those in the Rectangle; they make some effort to reach the working man, they have a large constituency among the average salary-earning people, they send money and missionaries to the foreign heathen, but the fashionable, dissipated young men around town, the club men, are left out of all plans for reaching and Christianizing. And yet no class of people need it more.

"I said to myself : 'I know these men, their good and their bad qualities. I have been one of them. I am not fitted to reach the Rectangle people. I do not know how. But I think I could possibly reach some of the young men and boys who have money and time to spend.' So that is what I have been trying to do. When I asked as you did, 'What would Jesus do?' that was my answer. It has been also my cross."

Rollin's voice was so low on this last sentence that Rachel had difficulty in hearing him above the noise around them. But she knew what he had said. She wanted to ask what his methods were. But she did not know how to ask him. Her interest in his plan was larger than mere curiosity. Rollin Page was so different now from the fashionable young man who had asked her to be his wife that she could not help thinking of him and talking with him as if he were an entirely new acquaintance.

They had turned off the avenue and were going up the street to Rachel's home. It was the same street where Rollin had asked Rachel why she could not love him. They were both stricken with a sudden shyness as they went on. Rachel had not forgotten that day and Rollin could not. She finally broke a long silence by asking what she had not found words for before.

"In your work with the club men, with your old acquaintances, what sort of reception do they give you? How do you approach them? What do they say?"

Rollin was relieved when Rachel spoke. He answered quickly:

"Oh, it depends on the man. A good many of them think I am a crank. I have kept my membership up and am in good standing in that way. I try to be wise and not provoke any unnecessary criticism. But you would be surprised to know how many of the men have responded to my appeal. I could hardly make you believe that only a few nights ago a dozen men became honestly and earnestly engaged in a conversation over religious matters. I have had the great joy of seeing some of the men give up bad habits and begin a new life. 'What would Jesus do?' I keep asking it. The answer comes slowly, for I am feeling my way slowly. One thing I have found out. The men are not fighting shy of me. I think that is a good sign. Another thing: I have actually interested some of them in the Rectangle work, and when it is started up they will give something to help make it more powerful. And in addition to all the rest, I have found a way to save several of the young fellows from going to the bad in gambling."

Rollin spoke with enthusiasm. His face was transformed by his interest in the subject which had now become a part of his real life. Rachel again noted the strong, manly tone of his speech. With it all she knew there was a deep, underlying seriousness which felt the burden of the cross even while carrying it with joy. The next time she spoke it was with a swift feeling of justice due to Rollin and his new life.

"Do you remember I reproached you once for not having any purpose worth living for?" she asked, while her beautiful face seemed to Rollin more beautiful than ever when he had won sufficient self-control to look up. "I want to say, I feel the need of saying, in justice to you now, that I honor you for your courage and your obedience to the promise you have made as you interpret the promise. The life you are living is a noble one."

Rollin trembled. His agitation was greater than he could control. Rachel could not help seeing it. They walked along in silence. At last Rollin said:

"I thank you. It has been worth more to me than I can tell you to hear you say that." He looked into her face for one moment. She read his love for her in that look, but he did not speak.

When they separated Rachel went into the house and, sitting down in her room, she put her face in her hands and said to herself: "I am beginning to know what it means to be loved by a noble man. I shall love Rollin Page after all. What am I saying! Rachel Winslow, have you forgotten—"

She rose and walked back and forth. She was deeply moved. Nevertheless, it was evident to herself that her emotion was not that of regret or sorrow. Somehow a glad new joy had come to her. She had entered another circle of experience, and later in the day she rejoiced with a very strong and sincere gladness that her Christian discipleship found room in this crisis for her feeling. It was indeed a part of it, for if she was beginning to love Rollin Page it was the Christian man she had begun to love; the other never would have moved her to this great change.

And Rollin, as he went back, treasured a hope that had been a stranger to him since Rachel had said no that day. In that hope he went on with his work as the days sped on, and at no time was he more successful in reaching and saving his old acquaintances than in the time that followed that chance meeting with Rachel Winslow.

The summer had gone and Raymond was once more facing the rigor of her winter season. Virginia had been able to accomplish a part of her plan for "capturing the Rectangle," as she called it. But the building of houses in the field, the transforming of its bleak, bare aspect into an attractive park, all of which was included in her plan, was a work too large to be completed that fall after she had secured the property. But a million dollars in the hands of a person who truly wants to do with it as Jesus would, ought to accomplish wonders for humanity in a short time, and Henry Maxwell, going over to the scene of the new work one day after a noon hour with the shop men, was amazed to see how much had been done outwardly.

Yet he walked home thoughtfully, and on his way he could not avoid the question of the continual problem thrust upon his notice by the saloon. How much had been done for the Rectangle after all? Even counting Virginia's and Rachel's work and Mr. Gray's, where had it actually counted in any visible quantity? Of course, he said to himself, the redemptive work begun and carried on by the Holy Spirit in His wonderful displays of power in the First Church and in the tent meetings had had its effect upon the life of Raymond. But as he walked past saloon after saloon and noted the crowds going in and coming out of them, as he saw the wretched dens, as many as ever apparently, as he caught the brutality and squalor and open misery and degradation on countless faces of men and women and children, he sickened at the sight. He found himself asking how much cleansing could a million dollars poured into this cesspool accomplish? Was not the living source of nearly all the human misery they sought to relieve untouched as long as the saloons did their deadly but legitimate work? What could even such unselfish Christian discipleship as Virginia's and Rachel's do to lessen the stream of vice and crime so long as the great spring of vice and crime flowed as deep and strong as ever? Was it not a practical waste of beautiful lives for these young women to throw themselves into this earthly hell, when for every soul rescued by their sacrifice the saloon made two more that needed rescue?

He could not escape the question. It was the same that Virginia had put to Rachel in her statement that, in her opinion, nothing really permanent would ever be done until the saloon was taken out of the Rectangle. Henry Maxwell went back to his parish work that afternoon with added convictions on the license business.

But if the saloon was a factor in the problem of the life of Raymond, no less was the First Church and its little company of disciples who had pledged to do as Jesus would do. Henry Maxwell, standing at the very centre of the movement, was not in a position to judge of its power as some one from the outside might have done. But Raymond itself felt the touch in very many ways, not knowing all the reasons for the change.

The winter was gone and the year was ended, the year which Henry Maxwell had fixed as the time during which the pledge should be kept to do as Jesus would do. Sunday, the anniversary of that one a year ago, was in many ways the most remarkable day that the First Church ever knew. It was more important than the disciples in the First Church realized. The year had made history so fast and so serious that the people were not yet able to grasp its significance. And the day itself which marked the completion of a whole year of such discipleship was characterized by such revelations and confessions that the immediate actors in the events themselves could not understand the value of what had been done, or the relation of their trial to the rest of the churches and cities of the country.

It happened that the week before that anniversary Sunday the Rev. Calvin Bruce, D.D., of the Nazareth Avenue Church, Chicago, was in Raymond, where he had come on a visit to some old friends, and incidentally to see his old seminary classmate, Henry Maxwell. He was present at the First Church and was an exceedingly attentive and interested spectator. His account of the events in Raymond, and especially of that Sunday, may throw more light on the entire situation than any description or record from other sources.

19

[Letter from Rev. Calvin Bruce, D. D., of the Nazareth Avenue Church, Chicago, to Rev. Philip A. Caxton, D. D., New York City.]

"My Dear Caxton:

"It is late Sunday night, but I am so intensely awake and so overflowing with what I have seen and heard that I feel driven to write you now some account of the situation in Raymond as I have been studying it, and as it has apparently come to a climax to-day. So this is my only excuse for writing so extended a letter at this time.

"You remember Henry Maxwell in the Seminary. I think you said the last time I visited you in New York that you had not seen him since we graduated. He was a refined, scholarly fellow, you remember, and when he was called to the First Church of Raymond within a year after leaving the Seminary, I said to my wife, 'Raymond has made a good choice. Maxwell will satisfy them as a sermonizer.' He has been here eleven years, and I understand that up to a year ago he had gone on in the regular course of the ministry, giving good satisfaction and drawing good congregations. His church was counted the largest and wealthiest church in Raymond. All the best people attended it, and most of them belonged. The quartet choir was famous for its music, especially for its soprano, Miss Winslow, of whom I shall have more to say; and, on the whole, as I understand the facts, Maxwell was in a comfortable berth, with a very good salary, pleasant surroundings, a not very exacting parish of refined, rich, respectable people—such a church and parish as nearly all the young men of the seminary in our time looked forward to as very desirable.

"But a year ago to-day Maxwell came into his church on Sunday morning, and at the close of the service made the astounding proposition that the members of his church volunteer for a year not to do anything without first asking the question, 'What would Jesus do?' and, after answering it, to do what in their honest judgment He would do, regardless of what the result might be to them.

"The effect of this proposition, as it has been met and obeyed by a number of members of the church, has been so remarkable that, as you know, the attention of the whole country has been directed to the movement. I call it a 'movement' because from the action taken to-day, it seems probable that what has been tried here will reach out into the other churches and cause a revolution in methods, but more especially in a new definition of Christian discipleship.

"In the first place, Maxwell tells me he was astonished at the response to his proposition. Some of the most prominent members in the church made the promise to do as Jesus would. Among them were Edward Norman, editor of the *Daily News*, which has made such a sensation in the newspaper world; Milton Wright, one of the leading merchants in Raymond; Alexander Powers, whose action in the matter of the railroads against the interstate commerce laws made such a stir about a year ago; Miss Page, one of Raymond's leading society heiresses, who has lately dedicated her entire fortune, as I understand, to the Christian daily paper and the work of reform in the slum district known as the Rectangle; and Miss Winslow, whose reputation as a singer is now national, but who in obedience to what she has decided to be Jesus' probable action, has devoted her talent to volunteer work among the girls and women who make up a large part of the city's worst and most abandoned population.

"In addition to these well-known people has been a gradually increasing number of Christians from the First Church and lately from other churches of Raymond. A large proportion of these volunteers who pledged themselves to do as Jesus would do comes from the Endeavor societies. The young people say that they have already embodied in their society pledge the same principle in the words, 'I promise Him that I will strive to do whatever He would have me do.' This is not exactly what is included in Maxwell's proposition, which is that the disciple shall try to do what Jesus would probably do in the disciple's place. But the result of an honest obedience to either pledge, he claims, will be practically the same, and he is not surprised that the largest numbers have joined the new discipleship from the Endeavor Society.

"I am sure the first question you will ask is, 'What has been the result of this attempt? What has it accomplished or how has it changed in any way the regular life of the church or the community?'

"You already know something, from reports of Raymond that have gone over the country, what the events have been. But one needs to come here and learn something of the changes in individual lives, and especially the change in the church life, to realize all that is meant by this following of Jesus' steps so literally. To tell all that would be to write a long story or series of stories. I am not in a position to do that, but I can give you some idea perhaps of what has been done as told me by friends here and by Maxwell himself.

"The result of the pledge upon the First Church has been twofold. It has brought about a spirit of Christian fellowship which Maxwell tells me never before existed, and which now impresses him as being very nearly what the Christian fellowship of the apostolic churches must have been; and it has divided the church into two distinct groups of members. Those who have not taken the pledge regard the others as foolishly literal in their attempt to imitate the example of Jesus. Some of them have drawn out of the church and no longer attend, or they have removed their membership entirely to other churches. Some are an element of internal strife, and I heard rumors of an attempt on their part to force Maxwell's resignation. I do not know that this element is very strong in the church. It has been held in check by a wonderful continuance of spiritual power, which dates from the first Sunday the pledge was taken a year ago, and also by the fact that so many of the most prominent members have been identified with the movement.

"The effect on Maxwell is very marked. I heard him preach in our State Association four years ago. He impressed me at the time as having considerable power in dramatic delivery, of which he himself was somewhat conscious. His sermon was well written and abounded in what the Seminary students used to call 'fine passages.' The effect of it was what an average congregation would call 'pleasing.' This morning I heard Maxwell preach again, for the first time since then. I shall speak of that farther on. He is not the same man. He gives me the impression of one who has passed through a crisis of revolution. He tells me this revolution is simply a new definition of Christian discipleship. He certainly has changed many of his old habits and many of his old views. His attitude on the saloon question is radically opposite to the one he entertained a year ago. And in his entire thought of the ministry, his pulpit and parish work, I find he has made a complete change. So far as I can understand, the idea that is moving him on now is the idea that the Christianity of our times must represent a more literal imitation of Jesus, and especially in the element of suffering. He quoted to me in the course of our conversation several times the verses in Peter: 'For even hereunto were ye called, because Christ also suffered for you, leaving you an example, that ye would follow His steps'; and he seems filled with the conviction that what our churches need today more than anything else is this factor of joyful suffering for Jesus in some form. I do not know as I agree with him, altogether; but, my dear Caxton, it is certainly astonishing to note the results of this idea as they have impressed themselves upon this city and this church.

"You ask how about the results on the individuals who have made this pledge and honestly tried to be true to it. Those results are, as I have said, a part of individual history and cannot be told in detail. Some of them I can give you so that you may see that this form of discipleship is not merely sentiment or fine posing for effect.

"For instance, take the case of Mr. Powers, who was superintendent of the machine shops of the L. and T. R. R. here. When he acted upon the evidence which incriminated the road he lost his position, and more than that, I learn from my friends here, his family and social relations have become so changed that he and his family no longer appear in public. They have dropped out of the social circle where once they were so prominent. By the way, Caxton, I understand in this connection that the Commission, for one reason or another, postponed action on this case, and it is now rumored that the L. and T. R. R. will pass into a receiver's hands very soon. The president of the road who, according to the evidence submitted by Powers, was the principal offender, has resigned, and complications which have risen since point to the receivership. Meanwhile, the superintendent has gone back to his old work as a telegraph operator. I met him at the church yesterday. He impressed me as a man who had, like Maxwell, gone through a crisis in character. I could not help thinking of him as being good material for the church of the first century when the disciples had all things in common.

"Or take the case of Mr. Norman, editor of the *Daily News*. He risked his entire fortune in obedience to what he believed was Jesus' action, and revolutionized his entire conduct of the paper at the risk of a failure. I send you a copy of yesterday's paper. I want you to read it carefully. To my mind it is one of the most interesting and remarkable papers ever printed in the United States. It is open to criticism, but what could any mere man attempt in this line that would be free from criticism. Take it all in all, it is so far above the ordinary conception of a daily paper that I am amazed at the result. He tells me that the paper is beginning to be read more and more by the Christian people of the city. He was very confident of its final success. Read his editorial on the money questions, also the one on the coming election in Raymond when the question of license will again be an issue. Both articles are of the best from his point of view. He says he never begins an editorial or, in fact, any part of his newspaper work, without first asking, 'What would Jesus do?' The result is certainly apparent.

"Then there is Milton Wright, the merchant. He has, I am told, so revolutionized his business that no man is more beloved to-day in Raymond. His own clerks and employees have an affection for him that is very touching. During the winter, while he was lying dangerously ill at his home, scores of clerks volunteered to watch and help in any way possible, and his return to his store was greeted with marked demonstrations. All this has been brought about by the element of personal love introduced into the business. This love is not mere words, but the business itself is carried on under a system of cooperation that is not a patronizing recognition of inferiors, but a real sharing in the whole business. Other men on the street look upon Milton Wright as odd. It is a fact, however, that while be has lost heavily in some directions, he has increased his business, and is to-day respected and honored as one of the best and most successful merchants in Raymond.

"And there is Miss Winslow. She has chosen to give her great talent to the poor of the city.

"Her plans include a Musical Institute where choruses and classes in vocal music shall be a feature. She is enthusiastic over her life work. In connection with her friend Miss Page she has planned a course in music which, if carried out, will certainly do much to lift up the lives of the people down there. I am not too old, dear Caxton, to be interested in the romantic side of much that has also been tragic here in Raymond, and I must tell you that it is well understood here that Miss Winslow expects to be married this spring to a brother of Miss Page who was once a society leader and club man, and who was converted in a tent where his wife-that-is-to-be took an active part in the service. I don't know all the details of this little romance, but I imagine there is a story wrapped up in it, and it would make interesting reading if we only knew it all.

"These are only a few illustrations of results in individual lives owing to obedience to the pledge. I meant to have spoken of President

Marsh of Lincoln College. He is a graduate of my alma mater and I knew him slightly when I was in the senior year. He has taken an active part in the recent municipal campaign, and his influence in the city is regarded as a very large factor in the coming election. He impressed me, as did all the other disciples in this movement, as having fought out some hard questions, and as having taken up some real burdens that have caused and still do cause that suffering of which Henry Maxwell speaks, a suffering that does not eliminate, but does appear to intensify, a positive and practical joy.

20

"BUT I AM PROLONGING THIS LETTER, POSSIBLY TO YOUR weariness. I am unable to avoid the feeling of fascination which my entire stay here has increased. I want to tell you something of the meeting in the First Church to-day.

"As I said, I heard Maxwell preach. At his earnest request I had preached for him the Sunday before, and this was the first time I had heard him since the Association meeting four years ago. His sermon this morning was as different from his sermon then as if it had been thought out and preached by some one living on another planet. I was profoundly touched. I believe I actually shed tears once. Others in the congregation were moved like myself. His text was: 'What is that to thee?' Follow thou Me.' It was a most unusually impressive appeal to the Christians of Raymond to obey Jesus' teachings and follow in His steps regardless of what others might do. I cannot give you even the plan of the sermon. It would take too long. At the close of the service there was the usual after meeting that has become a regular feature of the First Church. Into this meeting have come all those who made the pledge to do as Jesus would do, and the time is

---

spent in mutual fellowship, confession, question as to what Jesus would do in special cases, and prayer that the one great guide of every disciple's conduct may be the Holy Spirit.

"Maxwell asked me to come into this meeting. Nothing in all my ministerial life, Caxton, has so moved me as that meeting. I never felt the Spirit's presence so powerfully. It was a meeting of reminiscenses and of the most loving fellowship. I was irresistibly driven in thought back to the first years of Christianity. There was something about all this that was apostolic in its simplicity and Christ imitation.

"I asked questions. One that seemed to arouse more interest than any other was in regard to the extent of the Christian disciple's sacrifice of personal property. Maxwell tells me that so far no one has interpreted the spirit of Jesus in such a way as to abandon his earthly possessions, give away of his wealth, or in any literal way imitate the Christians of the order, for example, of St. Francis of Assisi. It was the unanimous consent, however, that if any disciple should feel that Jesus in his own particular case would do that, there could be only one answer to the question.

"Maxwell admitted that he was still to a certain degree uncertain as to Jesus' probable action when it came to the details of household living, the possession of wealth, the holding of certain luxuries. It is, however, very evident that many of these disciples have repeatedly carried their obedience to Jesus to the extreme limit, regardless of financial loss. There is no lack of courage or consistency at this point.

"It is also true that some of the business men who took the pledge have lost great sums of money in this imitation of Jesus, and many have, like Alexander Powers, lost valuable positions owing to the impossibility of doing what they had been accustomed to do and at the same time what they felt Jesus would do in the same place. In connection with these cases it is pleasant to record the fact that many who have suffered in this way have been at once helped financially by those who still have means. In this respect I think it is true that these disciples have all things in common. Certainly such scenes as I witnessed at the First Church at that after service this morning I never saw in my church or in any other. I never dreamed that such Christian fellowship could exist in this age of the world. I was almost incredulous as to the witness of my own senses. I still seem to be asking myself if this is the close of the nineteenth century in America.

"But now, dear friend, I come to the real cause of this letter, the real heart of the whole question as the First Church of Raymond has forced it upon me. Before the meeting closed to-day steps were taken to secure the cooperation of all other Christian disciples in this country. I think Maxwell took this step after long deliberation. He said as much to me one day when we were discussing the effect of this movement upon the church in general.

"'Why,' he said, 'suppose that the church membership generally in this country made this pledge and lived up to it! What a revolution it would cause in Christendom! But why not? Is it any more than the disciple ought to do? Has he followed Jesus, unless he is willing to do this? Is the test of discipleship any less to-day than it was in Jesus' time?'

"I do not know all that preceded or followed his thought of what ought to be done outside of Raymond, but the idea crystallized to-day in a plan to secure the fellowship of all the Christians in America. The churches, through their pastors, will be asked to form disciple gatherings like the one in the First Church. Volunteers will be called for in the great body of church members in the United States, who will promise to do as Jesus would do. Maxwell spoke particularly of the result of such general action on the saloon question. He is terribly in earnest over this. He told me that there was no question in his mind that the saloon would be beaten in Raymond at the election now near at hand. If so, they could go on with some courage to do the redemptive work begun by the evangelist and now taken up by the disciples in his own church. If the saloon triumphs again there will be a terrible and, as he thinks, unnecessary waste of Christian sacrifice. But, however we differ on that point, he convinced his church that the time had come for a fellowship with other Christians. Surely, if the First Church could work such changes in society and its surroundings, the church in general if combining such a fellowship, not of creed but of conduct, ought to stir the entire nation to a higher life and a new conception of Christian following.

"This is a grand idea, Caxton, but right here is where I find my self hesitating. I do not deny that the Christian disciple ought to follow Christ's steps as closely as these here in Raymond have tried to do. But I cannot avoid asking what the result would be if I ask my church in Chicago to do it.

"I am writing this after feeling the solemn, profound touch of the Spirit's presence, and I confess to you, old friend, that I cannot call up in my church a dozen prominent business or professional men who would make this trial at the risk of all they hold dear. Can you do any better in your church? What are we to say? That the churches would not respond to the call: 'Come and suffer?' Is our standard of Christian discipleship a wrong one? Or are we possibly deceiving ourselves, and would we be agreeably disappointed if we once asked our people to take such a pledge faithfully?

"The actual results of the pledge as obeyed here in Raymond are enough to make any pastor tremble, and at the same time long with yearning that they might occur in his own parish. Certainly never have I seen a church so signally blessed by the Spirit as this one. But—am I myself ready to take this pledge? I ask the question honestly, and I dread to face an honest answer. I know well enough that I should have to change very much in my life if I undertook to follow His steps so closely.

"I have called myself a Christian for many years. For the past ten years I have enjoyed a life that has had comparatively little suffering in it. I am, honestly I say it, living at a long distance from municipal problems and the life of the poor, the degraded, and the abandoned. What would the obedience to this pledge demand of me? I hesitate to answer.

"My church is wealthy, full of well-to-do, satisfied people. The standard of their discipleship is, I am aware, not of a nature to respond to the call of suffering or personal loss. I say: 'I am aware.' I may be mistaken. I may have erred in not stirring their deeper life.

"Caxton, my friend, I have spoken my inmost thought to you. Shall I go back to my people next Sunday and stand up before them in my large city church and say: 'Let us follow Jesus closer; let us walk in His steps where it will cost us something more than it is costing us now; let us pledge not to do anything without first asking: What would Jesus do?' If I should go before them with that message, it would be a strange and startling one to them. But why? Are we not ready to follow Him all the way? What is it to be a follower of Jesus? What does it mean to imitate Him? What does it mean to walk in His steps?"

The Rev. Calvin Bruce, D. D., of the Nazareth Avenue Church, Chicago, let his pen fall on the table. He had come to the parting of the ways, and his question, he felt sure, was the question of many and many a man in the ministry and in the church. He went to his window and opened it. He was oppressed with the weight of his convictions and he felt almost suffocated with the air in the room. He wanted to see the stars and feel the breath of the world.

The night was very still. The clock in the First Church was just striking midnight. As it finished a clear, strong voice down in the direction of the Rectangle came floating up to him as if borne on radiant pinions.

It was a voice of one of Gray's old converts, a night watchman at the packing houses, who sometimes solaced his lonesome hours by a verse or two of some familiar hymn:

> *"Must Jesus bear the cross alone*
> *And all the world go free?*
> *No, there's a cross for every one,*
> *And there's a cross for me."*

The Rev. Calvin Bruce turned away from the window and, after a little hesitation, he kneeled. "What would Jesus do?" That was the burden of his prayer. Never had he yielded himself so completely to the Spirit's searching revealing of Jesus. He was on his knees a long time. He retired and slept fitfully with many awakenings. He rose before it was clear dawn, and threw open his window again. As the light in the east grew stronger he repeated to himself: "What would Jesus do? Shall I follow His steps?"

The sun rose and flooded the city with its power. When shall the dawn of a new discipleship usher in the conquering triumph of a closer walk with Jesus? When shall Christendom tread more closely the path he made?

> *"It is the way the Master trod;*
> *Shall not the servant tread it still?"*

With this question throbbing through his whole being the Rev. Calvin Bruce, D. D., went back to Chicago, and the great crisis in his Christian life in the ministry suddenly broke irresistibly upon him.

21

"Master, I will follow Thee whithersoever Thou goest."

THE SATURDAY AFTERNOON MATINEE AT THE AUDITO-
rium in Chicago was just over and the usual crowd was struggling to
get to its carriage before any one else. The Auditorium attendant was
shouting out the numbers of different carriages and the carriage doors
were slamming as the horses were driven rapidly up to the curb, held
there impatiently by the drivers who had shivered long in the raw east
wind, and then let go to plunge for a few minutes into the river of ve-
hicles that tossed under the elevated railway and finally went whirling
off up the avenue.

"Now then, 624," shouted the Auditorium attendant; "624!" he
repeated, and there dashed up to the curb a splendid span of black
horses attached to a carriage having the monogram, "C. R. S." in gilt
letters on the panel of the door.

Two girls stepped out of the crowd towards the carriage. The older
one had entered and taken her seat and the attendant was still holding the door open for the younger, who stood hesitating on the curb.

"Come, Felicia! What are you waiting for! I shall freeze to death!"
called the voice from the carriage.

The girl outside of the carriage hastily unpinned a bunch of English violets from her dress and handed them to a small boy who was standing shivering on the edge of the sidewalk almost under the horses' feet.

He took them, with a look of astonishment and a "Thank ye, lady!" and instantly buried a very grimy face in the bunch of perfume.

The girl stepped into the carriage, the door shut with the incisive bang peculiar to well-made carriages of this sort, and in a few moments the coachman was speeding the horses rapidly up one of the boulevards.

"You are always doing some queer thing or other, Felicia," said the older girl as the carriage whirled on past the great residences already brilliantly lighted.

"Am I? What have I done that is queer now, Rose?" asked the other, looking up suddenly and turning her head towards her sister.

'Oh, giving those violets to that boy! He looked as if he needed a good hot supper more than a bunch of violets. It's a wonder you didn't invite him home with us. I shouldn't have been surprised if you had. You are always doing such queer things."

"Would it be queer to invite a boy like that to come to the house and get a hot supper?" Felicia asked the question softly and almost as if she were alone.

"'Queer' isn't just the word, of course," replied Rose indifferently. "It would be what Madam Blanc calls 'outre.' Decidedly. Therefore you will please not invite him or others like him to hot suppers because I suggested it. Oh, dear! I'm awfully tired."

She yawned, and Felicia silently looked out of the window in the door.

"The concert was stupid and the violinist was simply a bore. I don't see how you could sit so still through it all," Rose exclaimed a little impatiently.

"I liked the music," answered Felicia quietly.

"You like anything. I never saw a girl with so little critical taste."

Felicia colored slightly, but would not answer. Rose yawned again, and then hummed a fragment of a popular song. Then she exclaimed abruptly:

"I'm sick of 'most everything. I hope the 'Shadows of London' will be exciting to-night."

"The 'Shadows of Chicago,'" murmured Felicia.

"The 'Shadows of Chicago!' The 'Shadows of London,' the play, the great drama with its wonderful scenery, the sensation of New York for two months. You know we have a box with the Delanos to-night."

Felicia turned her face towards her sister. Her great brown eyes were very expressive and not altogether free from a sparkle of luminous heat.

"And yet we never weep over the real thing on the actual stage of life. What are the 'Shadows of London' on the stage to the shadows of London or Chicago as they really exist? Why don't we get excited over the facts as they are?"

"Because the actual people are dirty and disagreeable and it's too much bother, I suppose," replied Rose carelessly. "Felicia, you can never reform the world. What's the use? We're not to blame for the poverty and misery. There have always been rich and poor; and there always will be. We ought to be thankful we're rich."

"Suppose Christ had gone on that principle," replied Felicia, with unusual persistence. "Do you remember Dr. Bruce's sermon on that verse a few Sundays ago: 'For ye know the grace of our Lord Jesus Christ, that though he was rich yet for our sakes he became poor, that ye through his poverty might become rich'?"

"I remember it well enough," said Rose with some petulance, "and didn't Dr. Bruce go on to say that there is no blame attached to people who have wealth if they are kind and give to the needs of the poor? And I am sure that he himself is pretty comfortably settled. He never gives up his luxuries just because some people go hungry. What good would it do if he did? I tell you, Felicia, there will always be poor and rich in spite of all we can do. Ever since Rachel Winslow has written about those queer doings in Raymond you have upset the whole family. People can't live at that concert pitch all the time. You see if Rachel doesn't give it up soon. It's a great pity, she doesn't come to Chicago and sing in the Auditorium concerts. I heard to-day that she had received an offer. I'm going to write and urge her to come. I'm just dying to hear her sing."

Felicia looked out of the window and was silent. The carriage rolled on past two blocks of magnificent private residences and turned into a wide driveway under a covered passage, and the sisters hurried into the house. It was an elegant mansion of gray stone furnished like a palace, every corner of it warm with the luxury of paintings, sculpture, art and modern refinement.

The owner of it all, Mr. Charles R. Sterling, stood before an open grate fire smoking a cigar. He had made his money in grain speculation and railroad ventures, and was reputed to be worth something over two millions. His wife was a sister of Mrs. Winslow of Raymond. She had been an invalid for several years. The two girls, Rose and Felicia, were the only children. Rose was twenty-one years old, fair, vivacious, educated in a fashionable college, just entering society and already somewhat cynical and indifferent. A very hard young lady to please, her father said, sometimes playfully, sometimes sternly. Felicia was nineteen, with a tropical beauty somewhat like her cousin, Rachel Winslow, with warm, generous impulses just waking into Christian feeling, capable of all sorts of expression, a puzzle to her father, a source of irritation to her mother and with a great unsurveyed territory of thought and action in herself, of which she was more than dimly conscious. There was that in Felicia that would easily endure any condition in life if only the liberty to act fully on her conscientious convictions were granted her.

"Here's a letter for you, Felicia," said Mr. Sterling, handing it to her.

Felicia sat down and instantly opened the letter, saying as she did so: "It's from Rachel."

"Well, what's the latest news from Raymond?" asked Mr. Sterling, taking his cigar out of his mouth and looking at Felicia as he often did with half-shut eyes, as if he were studying her.

"Rachel says Dr. Bruce has been staying in Raymond for two Sundays and has seemed very much interested in Mr. Maxwell's pledge in the First Church."

"What does Rachel say about herself?" asked Rose, who was lying on a couch almost buried under a half dozen elegant cushions.

"She is still singing at the Rectangle. Since the tent meetings closed she sings in an old hall until the new buildings which her friend, Virginia Page, is putting up are completed."

"I must write Rachel to come to Chicago and visit us. She ought not to throw away her voice in that railroad town upon all those people who don't appreciate her."

Mr. Sterling lighted a new cigar and Rose exclaimed: "Rachel is so queer. She might set Chicago wild with her voice if she sang in the Auditorium. And there she goes on throwing it away on people who don't know what they are hearing."

"Rachel won't come here unless she can do it and keep her pledge at the same time," said Felicia, after a pause.

"What pledge?" Mr. Sterling asked the question and then added hastily: "Oh, I know, yes! A very peculiar thing that. Alexander Powers used to be a friend of mine. We learned telegraphy in the same office. Made a great sensation when he resigned and handed over that evidence to the Interstate Commerce Commission. And he's back at his telegraph again. There have been queer doings in Raymond during the past year. I wonder what Dr. Bruce thinks of it on the whole. I must have a talk with him about it."

"He is at home and will preach to-morrow," said Felicia. "Perhaps he will tell us something about it."

There was silence for a minute. Then Felicia said abruptly, as if she had gone on with a spoken thought to some invisible hearer: "And what if he should propose the same pledge to the Nazareth Avenue Church?"

"Who? What are you talking about?" asked her father a little sharply.

"About Dr. Bruce. I say, what if he should propose to our church what Mr. Maxwell proposed to his, and ask for volunteers who would pledge themselves to do everything after asking the question, 'What would Jesus do?' "

"There's no danger of it," said Rose, rising suddenly from the couch as the tea-bell rang.

"It's a very impracticable movement, to my mind," said Mr. Sterling shortly.

"I understand from Rachel's letter that the Raymond church is going to make an attempt to extend the idea of the pledge to other churches. If it succeeds it will certainly make great changes in the churches and in people's lives," said Felicia.

"Oh, well, let's have some tea first!" said Rose, walking into the dining-room. Her father and Felicia followed, and the meal proceeded in silence. Mrs. Sterling had her meals served in her room. Mr. Sterling was preoccupied. He ate very little and excused himself early, and although it was Saturday night, he remarked as he went out that he should be down town late on some special business.

"Don't you think father looks very much disturbed lately?" asked Felicia a little while after he had gone out.

"Oh, I don't know! I hadn't noticed anything unusual," replied Rose. After a silence she said: "Are you going to the play to-night, Felicia? Mrs. Delano will be here at half past seven. I think you ought to go. She will feel hurt if you refuse."

"I'll go. I don't care about it. I can see shadows enough without going to the play."

"That's a doleful remark for a girl nineteen years old to make," replied Rose. "But then you're queer in your ideas anyhow, Felicia. If you are going up to see mother, tell her I'll run in after the play if she is still awake."

Felicia went up to see her mother and remained with her until the Delano carriage came. Mrs. Sterling was worried about her husband. She talked incessantly, and was irritated by every remark Felicia made. She would not listen to Felicia's attempts to read even a part of Rachel's letter, and when Felicia offered to stay with her for the evening, she refused the offer with a good deal of positive sharpness.

22

FELICIA STARTED OFF TO THE PLAY NOT VERY HAPPY, BUT she was familiar with that feeling, only sometimes she was more unhappy than at others. Her feeling expressed itself to-night by a withdrawal into herself. When the company was seated in the box and the curtain had gone up Felicia was back of the others and remained for the evening by herself. Mrs. Delano, as chaperon for half a dozen young ladies, understood Felicia well enough to know that she was "queer," as Rose so often said, and she made no attempt to draw her out of her corner. And so the girl really experienced that night by herself one of the feelings that added to the momentum that was increasing the coming on of her great crisis.

The play was an English melodrama, full of startling situations, realistic scenery and unexpected climaxes. There was one scene in the third act that impressed even Rose Sterling.

It was midnight on Blackfriars Bridge. The Thames flowed dark and forbidding below. St. Paul's rose through the dim light imposing, its dome seeming to float above the buildings surrounding it. The figure of a child came upon the bridge and stood there for a moment

peering about as if looking for some one. Several persons were cross-
ing the bridge, but in one of the recesses about midway of the river a
woman stood, leaning out over the parapet, with a strained agony of
face and figure that told plainly of her intention. Just as she was
stealthily mounting the parapet to throw herself into the river, the
child caught sight of her, ran forward with a shrill cry more animal
than human, and seizing the woman's dress dragged back upon it
with all her little strength. Then there came suddenly upon the scene
two other characters who had already figured in the play, a tall,
handsome, athletic gentleman dressed in the fashion, attended by a
slim-figured lad who was as refined in dress and appearance as the
little girl clinging to her mother, who was mournfully hideous in her
rags and repulsive poverty. These two, the gentleman and the lad,
prevented the attempted suicide, and after a tableau on the bridge
where the audience learned that the man and woman were brother
and sister, the scene was transferred to the interior of one of the slum
tenements in the East Side of London. Here the scene painter and
carpenter had done their utmost to produce an exact copy of a famous court and alley well known to the poor creatures who make up
a part of the outcast London humanity. The rags, the crowding, the
vileness, the broken furniture, the horrible animal existence forced
upon creatures made in God's image were so skillfully shown in this
scene that more than one elegant woman in the theatre, seated like
Rose Sterling in a sumptuous box surrounded with silk hangings and
velvet covered railing, caught herself shrinking back a little as if con-
tamination were possible from the nearness of this piece of scenery. It
was almost too realistic, and yet it had a horrible fascination for Felicia as she sat there alone, buried back in a cushioned seat and absorbed in thoughts that went far beyond the dialogue on the stage.

From the tenement scene the play shifted to the interior of a no-
bleman's palace, and almost a sigh of relief went up all over the house
at the sight of the accustomed luxury of the upper classes. The contrast was startling. It was brought about by a clever piece of staging
that allowed only a few moments to elapse between the slum and the
palace scene. The dialogue went on, the actors came and went in

their various roles, but upon Felicia the play made but one distinct impression. In reality the scenes on the bridge and in the slums were only incidents in the story of the play, but Felicia found herself living those scenes over and over. She had never philosophized about the causes of human misery, she was not old enough, she had not the temperament that philosophizes. But she felt intensely, and this was not the first time she had felt the contrast thrust into her feeling between the upper and the lower conditions of human life. It had been growing upon her until it had made her what Rose called "queer," and other people in her circle of wealthy acquaintances called very unusual. It was simply the human problem in its extreme of riches and poverty, its refinement and its vileness, that was, in spite of her unconscious attempts to struggle against the facts, burning into her life the impression that would in the end either transform her into a woman of rare love and self-sacrifice for the world, or a miserable enigma to herself and all who knew her.

"Come, Felicia, aren't you going home?" said Rose. The play was over, the curtain down, and people were going noisily out, laughing and gossiping as if "The Shadows of London" were simply good diversion, as they were, put on the stage so effectively.

Felicia rose and went out with the rest quietly, and with the absorbed feeling that had actually left her in her seat oblivious of the play's ending. She was never absent-minded, but often thought herself into a condition that left her alone in the midst of a crowd.

"Well, what did you think of it?" asked Rose when the sisters had reached home and were in the drawing-room. Rose really had considerable respect for Felicia's judgment of a play.

"I thought it was a pretty fair picture of real life."

"I mean the acting," said Rose, annoyed.

"The bridge scene was well acted, especially the woman's part. I thought the man overdid the sentiment a little."

"Did you? I enjoyed that. And wasn't the scene between the two cousins funny when they first learned they were related? But the slum scene was horrible. I think they ought not to show such things in a play. They are too painful."

"They must be painful in real life, too," replied Felicia.

"Yes, but we don't have to look at the real thing. It's bad enough at the theatre where we pay for it."

Rose went into the dining-room and began to eat from a plate of fruit and cakes on the sideboard.

"Are you going up to see mother?" asked Felicia after a while. She had remained in front of the drawing-room fire.

"No," replied Rose from the other room. "I won't trouble her to-night. If you go in tell her I am too tired to be agreeable."

So Felicia turned into her mother's room, as she went up the great staircase and down the upper hall. The light was burning there, and the servant who always waited on Mrs. Sterling was beckoning Felicia to come in.

"Tell Clara to go out," exclaimed Mrs. Sterling as Felicia came up to the bed.

Felicia was surprised, but she did as her mother bade her, and then inquired how she was feeling.

"Felicia," said her mother, "can you pray?"

The question was so unlike any her mother had ever asked before that she was startled. But she answered:

"Why, yes, mother. Why do you ask such a question?"

"Felicia, I am frightened. Your father—I have had such strange fears about him all day. Something is wrong with him. I want you to pray."

"Now, here, mother?"

"Yes. Pray, Felicia."

Felicia reached out her hand and took her mother's. It was trembling. Mrs. Sterling had never shown such tenderness for her younger daughter, and her strange demand now was the first real sign of any confidence in Felicia's character.

The girl kneeled, still holding her mother's trembling hand, and prayed. It is doubtful if she had ever prayed aloud before. She must have said in her prayer the words that her mother needed, for when it was silent in the room the invalid was weeping softly and her nervous tension was over.

Felicia stayed some time. When she was assured that her mother would not need her any longer she rose to go.

"Good night, mother. You must let Clara call me if you feel badly in the night."

"I feel better now." Then as Felicia was moving away, Mrs. Sterling said: "Won't you kiss me, Felicia?"

Felicia went back and bent over her mother. The kiss was almost as strange to her as the prayer had been. When Felicia went out of the room her cheeks were wet with tears. She had not often cried since she was a little child.

Sunday morning at the Sterling mansion was generally very quiet. The girls usually went to church at eleven o'clock service. Mr. Sterling was not a member but a heavy contributor, and he generally went to church in the morning. This time he did not come down to breakfast, and finally sent word by a servant that he did not feel well enough to go out. So Rose and Felicia drove up to the door of the Nazareth Avenue Church and entered the family pew alone.

When Dr. Bruce walked out of the room at the rear of the platform and went up to the pulpit to open the Bible as his custom was, those who knew him best did not detect anything unusual in his manner or his expression. He proceeded with the service as usual. He was calm and his voice was steady and firm. His prayer was the first intimation the people had of anything new or strange in the service. It is safe to say that the Nazareth Avenue Church had not heard Dr. Bruce offer such a prayer before during the twelve years he had been pastor there. How would a minister be likely to pray who had come out of a revolution in Christian feeling that had completely changed his definition of what was meant by following Jesus? No one in Nazareth Avenue Church had any idea that the Rev. Calvin Bruce, D. D., the dignified, cultured, refined Doctor of Divinity, had within a few days been crying like a little child on his knees, asking for strength and courage, and Christlikeness to speak his Sunday message; and yet the prayer was an unconscious involuntary disclosure of his soul's experience such as the Nazareth Avenue people had seldom heard, and never before from that pulpit.

In the hush that succeeded the prayer a distinct wave of spiritual power moved over the congregation. The most careless persons in the church felt it. Felicia, whose sensitive religious nature responded swiftly to every touch of emotion, quivered under the passing of that supernatural pressure, and when she lifted her head and looked up at the minister there was a look in her eyes that announced her intense, eager anticipation of the scene that was to follow. And she was not alone in her attitude. There was something in the prayer and the result of it that stirred many and many a disciple in that church. All over the house men and women leaned forward, and when Dr. Bruce began to speak of his visit to Raymond, in the opening sentence of his address which this morning preceded his sermon, there was an answering response in the people that came back to him as he spoke, and thrilled him with the hope of a spiritual baptism such as he had never during all his ministry experienced.

23

"I AM JUST BACK FROM A VISIT TO RAYMOND," DR.
Bruce began, "and I want to tell you something of my impressions of
the movement there."

He paused and his look went out over his people with yearning
for them and at the same time with a great uncertainty at his heart.
How many of his rich, fashionable, refined, luxury-loving members
would understand the nature of the appeal he was soon to make to
them? He was altogether in the dark as to that. Nevertheless he had
been through his desert, and had come out of it ready to suffer. He
went on now after that brief pause and told them the story of his stay
in Raymond. The people already knew something of that experiment
in the First Church. The whole country had watched the progress of
the pledge as it had become history in so many lives. Mr. Maxwell
had at last decided that the time had come to seek the fellowship of
other churches throughout the country. The new discipleship in Raymond had proved to be so valuable in its results that he wished the
churches in general to share with the disciples in Raymond. Already
there had begun a volunteer movement in many churches through-

out the country, acting on their own desire to walk closer in the steps of Jesus. The Christian Endeavor Society had, with enthusiasm, in many churches taken the pledge to do as Jesus would do, and the result was already marked in a deeper spiritual life and a power in church influence that was like a new birth for the members.

All this Dr. Bruce told his people simply and with a personal interest that evidently led the way to the announcement which now followed. Felicia had listened to every word with strained attention. She sat there by the side of Rose, in contrast like fire beside snow, although even Rose was alert and as excited as she could be.

"Dear friends," he said, and for the first time since his prayer the emotion of the occasion was revealed in his voice and gesture, "I am going to ask that Nazareth Avenue Church take the same pledge that Raymond Church has taken. I know what this will mean to you and me. It will mean the complete change of very many habits. It will mean, possibly, social loss. It will mean very probably, in many cases, loss of money. It will mean suffering. It will mean what following Jesus meant in the first century, and then it meant suffering, loss, hardship, separation, from everything un-Christian. But what does following Jesus mean? The test of discipleship is the same now as then. Those of us who volunteer in this church to do as Jesus would do, simply promise to walk in His steps as He gave us commandment."

Again he paused, and now the result of his announcement was plainly visible in the stir that went up over the congregation. He added in a quiet voice that all who volunteered to make the pledge to do as Jesus would do, were asked to remain after the morning service.

Instantly he proceeded with his sermon. His text was, "Master, I will follow Thee whithersoever Thou goest." It was a sermon that touched the deep springs of conduct; it was a revelation to the people of the definition their pastor had been learning; it took them back to the first century of Christianity; above all, it stirred them below the conventional thought of years as to the meaning and purpose of church membership. It was such a sermon as a man can preach once in a lifetime, and with enough in it for people to live on all through the rest of their lifetime.

The service closed in a hush that was slowly broken. People rose here and there, a few at a time. There was a reluctance in the movements of some that was very striking. Rose, however, walked straight out of the pew, and as she reached the aisle she turned her head and beckoned to Felicia. By that time the congregation was rising all over the church. "I am going to stay," she said, and Rose had heard her speak in the same manner on other occasions, and knew that her resolve could not be changed. Nevertheless she went back into the pew two or three steps and faced her.

"Felicia," she whispered, and there was a flush of anger on her cheeks, "this is folly. What can you do? You will bring some disgrace on the family. What will father say? Come!"

Felicia looked at her but did not answer at once. Her lips were moving with a petition that came from the depth of feeling that measured a new life for her. She shook her head.

"No, I am going to stay. I shall take the pledge. I am ready to obey it. You do not know why I am doing this."

Rose gave her one look and then turned and went out of the pew, and down the aisle. She did not even stop to talk with her acquaintances. Mrs. Delano was going out of the church just as Rose stepped into the vestibule.

"So you are not going to join Dr. Bruce's volunteer company?" Mrs. Delano asked, in a queer tone that made Rose redden.

"No, are you? It is simply absurd. I have always regarded that Raymond movement as fanatical. You know cousin Rachel keeps us posted about it."

"Yes, I understand it is resulting in a great deal of hardship in many cases. For my part, I believe Dr. Bruce has simply provoked disturbance here. It will result in splitting our church. You see if it isn't so. There are scores of people in the church who are so situated that they can't take such a pledge and keep it. I am one of them," added Mrs. Delano as she went out with Rose.

———

When Rose reached home, her father was standing in his usual attitude before the open fireplace, smoking a cigar.

"Where is Felicia?" he asked as Rose came in.

"She stayed to an after-meeting," replied Rose shortly. She threw off her wraps and was going upstairs when Mr. Sterling called after her.

"An after-meeting? What do you mean?"

"Dr. Bruce asked the church to take the Raymond pledge."

Mr. Sterling took his cigar out of his mouth and twirled it nervously between his fingers.

"I didn't expect that of Dr. Bruce. Did many of the members stay?"

"I don't know. I didn't," replied Rose, and she went upstairs leaving her father standing in the drawing-room.

After a few moments he went to the window and stood there looking out at the people driving on the boulevard. His cigar had gone out, but he still fingered it nervously. Then he turned from the window and walked up and down the room. A servant stepped across the hall and announced dinner and he told her to wait for Felicia. Rose came downstairs and went into the library. And still Mr. Sterling paced the drawing-room restlessly.

He had finally wearied of the walking apparently, and throwing himself into a chair was brooding over something deeply when Felicia came in.

He rose and faced her. Felicia was evidently very much moved by the meeting from which she had just come. At the same time she did not wish to talk too much about it. Just as she entered the drawing-room, Rose came in from the library.

"How many stayed?" she asked. Rose was curious. At the same time she was skeptical of the whole movement in Raymond.

"About a hundred," replied Felicia gravely. Mr. Sterling looked surprised. Felicia was going out of the room, but he called to her:

"Do you really mean to keep the pledge?" he asked.

Felicia colored. Over her face and neck the warm blood flowed and she answered, "You would not ask such a question, father, if you had been at the meeting." She lingered a moment in the room, then asked to be excused from dinner for a while and went up to see her mother.

No one but they two ever knew what that interview between Felicia and her mother was. It is certain that she must have told her mother something of the spiritual power that had awed every person present in the company of disciples who faced Dr. Bruce in that meeting after the morning service. It is also certain that Felicia had never before known such an experience, and would never have thought of sharing it with her mother if it had not been for the prayer the evening before. Another fact is also known of Felicia's experience at this time. When she finally joined her father and Rose at the table she seemed unable to tell them much about the meeting. There was a reluctance to speak of it as one might hesitate to attempt a description of a wonderful sunset to a person who never talked about anything but the weather.

When that Sunday in the Sterling mansion was drawing to a close and the soft, warm lights throughout the dwelling were glowing through the great windows, in a corner of her room, where the light was obscure, Felicia kneeled, and when she raised her face and turned it towards the light, it was the face of a woman who had already defined for herself the greatest issues of earthly life.

That same evening, after the Sunday evening service, Dr. Bruce was talking over the events of the day with his wife. They were of one heart and mind in the matter, and faced their new future with all the faith and courage of new disciples. Neither was deceived as to the probable results of the pledge to themselves or to the church.

They had been talking but a little while when the bell rang and Dr. Bruce going to the door exclaimed, as he opened it:

"It is you, Edward! Come in."

There came into the hall a commanding figure. The Bishop was of extraordinary height and breadth of shoulder, but of such good proportions that there was no thought of ungainly or even of unusual size. The impression the Bishop made on strangers was, first, that of great health, and then of great affection.

He came into the parlor and greeted Mrs. Bruce, who after a few moments was called out of the room, leaving the two men together. The Bishop sat in a deep, easy chair before the open fire. There was just enough dampness in the early spring of the year to make an open fire pleasant.

"Calvin, you have taken a very serious step today," he finally said, lifting his large dark eyes to his old college classmate's face. "I heard of it this afternoon. I could not resist the desire to see you about it to-night."

"I'm glad you came." Dr. Bruce laid a hand on the Bishop's shoulder. "You understand what this means, Edward?"

"I think I do. Yes, I am sure." The Bishop spoke very slowly and thoughtfully. He sat with his hands clasped together. Over his face, marked with lines of consecration and service and the love of men, a shadow crept, a shadow not caused by the firelight. Again he lifted his eyes toward his old friend.

"Calvin, we have always understood each other. Ever since our paths led us in different ways in church life we have walked together in Christian fellowship."

"It is true," replied Dr. Bruce with an emotion he made no attempt to conceal or subdue. "Thank God for it. I prize your fellowship more than any other man's. I have always known what it meant, though it has always been more than I deserve."

The Bishop looked affectionately at his friend. But the shadow still rested on his face. After a pause he spoke again:

"The new discipleship means a crisis for you in your work. If you keep this pledge to do all things as Jesus would do—as I know you will—it requires no prophet to predict some remarkable changes in your parish." The Bishop looked wistfully at his friend and then continued: "In fact, I do not see how a perfect upheaval of Christianity, as we now know it, can be prevented if the ministers and churches generally take the Raymond pledge and live it out." He paused as if he were waiting for his friend to say something, to ask some question. But Bruce did not know of the fire that was burning in the

Bishop's heart over the very question that Maxwell and himself had fought out.

"Now, in my church, for instance," continued the Bishop, "it would be rather a difficult matter, I fear, to find very many people who would take a pledge like that and live up to it. Martyrdom is a lost art with us. Our Christianity loves its ease and comfort too well to take up anything so rough and heavy as a cross. And yet what does following Jesus mean? What is it to walk in His steps?"

The Bishop was soliloquizing now and it is doubtful if he thought, for the moment, of his friend's presence. For the first time there flashed into Dr. Bruce's mind a suspicion of the truth. What if the Bishop would throw the weight of his great influence on the side of the Raymond movement? He had the following of the most aristocratic, wealthy, fashionable people, not only in Chicago, but in several large cities. What if the Bishop should join this new discipleship!

The thought was about to be followed by the word. Dr. Bruce had reached out his hand and with the familiarity of lifelong friendship had placed it on the Bishop's shoulder and was about to ask a very important question, when they were both startled by the violent ringing of the bell. Mrs. Bruce had gone to the door and was talking with some one in the hall. There was a loud exclamation and then, as the Bishop rose and Bruce was stepping toward the curtain that hung before the entrance to the parlor, Mrs. Bruce pushed it aside. Her face was white and she was trembling.

"O Calvin! Such terrible news! Mr. Sterling—oh, I cannot tell it! What a blow to those girls!"

"What is it?" Mr. Bruce advanced with the Bishop into the hall and confronted the messenger, a servant from the Sterlings. The man was without his hat and had evidently run over with the news, as Dr. Bruce lived nearest of any intimate friends of the family.

"Mr. Sterling shot himself, sir, a few minutes ago. He killed himself in his bed-room. Mrs. Sterling—"

"I will go right over, Edward. Will you go with me? The Sterlings are old friends of yours."

The Bishop was very pale, but calm as always. He looked his friend in the face and answered:

"Aye, Calvin, I will go with you not only to this house of death, but also the whole way of human sin and sorrow, please God."

And even in that moment of horror at the unexpected news, Dr. Bruce understood what the Bishop had promised to do.

24

These are they which follow the Lamb whithersoever He goeth.

WHEN DR. BRUCE AND THE BISHOP ENTERED THE STER-ling mansion everything in the usually well appointed household was in the greatest confusion and terror. The great rooms downstairs were empty, but overhead were hurried footsteps and confused noises.

One of the servants ran down the grand staircase with a look of horror on her face just as the Bishop and Dr. Bruce were starting to go up. "Miss Felicia is with Mrs. Sterling," the servant stammered in answer to a question, and then burst into a hysterical cry and ran through the drawing-room and out of doors.

At the top of the staircase the two men were met by Felicia. She walked up to Dr. Bruce at once and put both hands in his. The Bishop then laid his hand on her head and the three stood there a moment in perfect silence. The Bishop had known Felicia since she was a little child. He was the first to break the silence.

"The God of all mercy be with you, Felicia, in this dark hour. Your mother—"

The Bishop hesitated. Out of the buried past he had, during his hurried passage from his friend's to this house of death, irresistibly drawn the one tender romance of his young manhood. Not even Bruce knew that. But there had been a time when the Bishop had offered the incense of a singularly undivided affection upon the altar of his youth to the beautiful Camilla Rolfe, and she had chosen between him and the millionaire. The Bishop carried no bitterness with his memory; but it was still a memory.

For answer to the Bishop's unfinished query, Felicia turned and went back into her mother's room. She had not said a word yet, but both men were struck with her wonderful calm. She returned to the hall door and beckoned to them, and the two ministers, with a feeling that they were about to behold something very unusual, entered.

Rose lay with her arms outstretched upon the bed. Clara, the nurse, sat with her head covered, sobbing in spasms of terror. And Mrs. Sterling with "the light that never was on sea or land" luminous on her face, lay there so still that even the Bishop was deceived at first. Then, as the great truth broke upon him and Dr. Bruce, he staggered, and the sharp agony of the old wound shot through him. It passed, and left him standing there in that chamber of death with the eternal calmness and strength that the children of God have a right to possess. And right well he used that calmness and strength in the days that followed.

The next moment the house below was in a tumult. Almost at the same time the doctor who had been sent for at once, but lived some distance away, came in, together with police officers, who had been summoned by frightened servants. With them were four or five newspaper correspondents and several neighbors. Dr. Bruce and the Bishop met this miscellaneous crowd at the head of the stairs and succeeded in excluding all except those whose presence was necessary. With these the two friends learned all the facts ever known about the "Sterling tragedy," as the papers in their sensational accounts next day called it.

Mr. Sterling had gone into his room that evening about nine o'clock and that was the last seen of him until, in half an hour, a shot was heard in the room, and a servant who was in the hall ran into the room and found him dead on the floor, killed by his own hand. Felicia at the time was sitting by her mother. Rose was reading in the library. She ran upstairs, saw her father as he was being lifted upon the couch by the servants, and then ran screaming into her mother's room, where she flung herself down at the foot of the bed in a swoon. Mrs. Sterling had at first fainted at the shock, then rallied with a wonderful swiftness and sent for Dr. Bruce. She had then insisted on seeing her husband. In spite of Felicia's efforts, she had compelled Clara to support her while she crossed the hall and entered the room where her husband lay. She had looked upon him with a tearless face, had gone back to her own room, was laid on her bed, and as Dr. Bruce and the Bishop entered the house she, with a prayer of forgiveness for herself and for her husband on her quivering lips, had died, with Felicia bending over her and Rose still lying senseless at her feet.

So great and swift had been the entrance of grim Death into that palace of luxury that Sunday night! But the full cause of his coming was not learned until the facts in regard to Mr. Sterling's business affairs were finally disclosed.

Then it was learned that for some time he had been facing financial ruin owing to certain speculations that had in a month's time swept his supposed wealth into complete destruction. With the cunning and desperation of a man who battles for his very life when he saw his money, which was all the life he ever valued, slipping from him, he had put off the evil day to the last moment. Sunday afternoon, however, he had received news that proved to him beyond a doubt the fact of his utter ruin. The very house that he called his, the chairs in which he sat, his carriage, the dishes from which he ate, had all been bought with money for which he himself had never really done an honest stroke of pure labor.

It had all rested on a tissue of deceit and speculation that had no foundation in real values. He knew that fact better than any one else, but he had hoped, with the hope such men always have, that the same methods that brought him the money would also prevent the loss. He had been deceived in this as many others have been. As soon as the truth that he was practically a beggar had dawned upon him, he saw no escape from suicide. It was the irresistible result of such a life as he had lived. He had made money his god. As soon as that god was gone out of his little world there was nothing more to worship; and when a man's object of worship is gone he has no more to live for. Thus died the great millionaire, Charles R. Sterling. And, verily, he died as the fool dieth, for what is the gain or the loss of money compared with the unsearchable riches of eternal life which are beyond the reach of speculation, loss or change?

Mrs. Sterling's death was the result of the shock. She had not been taken into her husband's confidence for years, but she knew that the source of his wealth was precarious. Her life for several years had been a death in life. The Rolfes always gave an impression that they could endure more disaster unmoved than any one else. Mrs. Sterling illustrated the old family tradition when she was carried into the room where her husband lay. But the feeble tenement could not hold the spirit and it gave up the ghost, torn and weakened by long years of suffering and disappointment.

The effect of this triple blow, the death of father and mother, and the loss of property, was instantly apparent in the sisters. The horror of events stupefied Rose for weeks. She lay unmoved by sympathy or any effort to rally. She did not seem yet to realize that the money which had been so large a part of her very existence was gone. Even when she was told that she and Felicia must leave the house and be dependent on relatives and friends, she did not seem to understand what it meant.

Felicia, however, was fully conscious of the facts. She knew just what had happened and why. She was talking over her future plans with her cousin Rachel a few days after the funerals. Mrs. Winslow and Rachel had left Raymond and come to Chicago at once as soon as the terrible news had reached them, and with other friends of the family were planning for the future of Rose and Felicia.

"Felicia, you and Rose must come to Raymond with us. That is settled. Mother will not hear to any other plan at present," Rachel had said, while her beautiful face glowed with love for her cousin, a love that had deepened day by day, and was intensified by the knowledge that they both belonged to the new discipleship.

"Unless I can find something to do here," answered Felicia. She looked wistfully at Rachel, and Rachel said gently:

"What could you do, dear?"

"Nothing. I was never taught to do anything except a little music, and I do not know enough about it to teach it or earn my living at it. I have learned to cook a little," Felicia added with a slight smile.

"Then you can cook for us. Mother is always having trouble with her kitchen," said Rachel, understanding well enough she was now dependent for her very food and shelter upon the kindness of family friends. It is true the girls received a little something out of the wreck of their father's fortune, but with a speculator's mad folly he had managed to involve both his wife's and his children's portion in the common ruin.

"Can I? Can I?" Felicia responded to Rachel's proposition as if it were to be considered seriously. "I am ready to do anything honorable to make my living and that of Rose. Poor Rose! She will never be able to get over the shock of our trouble."

"We will arrange the details when we get to Raymond," Rachel said, smiling through her tears at Felicia's eager willingness to care for herself.

So in a few weeks Rose and Felicia found themselves a part of the Winslow family in Raymond. It was a bitter experience for Rose, but there was nothing else for her to do and she accepted the inevitable, brooding over the great change in her life and in many ways adding to the burden of Felicia and her cousin Rachel.

Felicia at once found herself in an atmosphere of discipleship that was like heaven to her in its revelation of companionship. It is true that Mrs. Winslow was not in sympathy with the course that Rachel was taking, but the remarkable events in Raymond since the pledge was taken were too powerful in their results not to impress even such a woman as Mrs. Winslow. With Rachel, Felicia found a perfect fellowship. She at once found a part to take in the new work at the

Rectangle. In the spirit of her new life she insisted upon helping in the housework at her aunt's, and in a short time demonstrated her ability as a cook so clearly that Virginia suggested that she take charge of the cooking at the Rectangle.

Felicia entered upon this work with the keenest pleasure. For the first time in her life she had the delight of doing something of value for the happiness of others. Her resolve to do everything after asking, "What would Jesus do?" touched her deepest nature. She began to develop and strengthen wonderfully. Even Mrs. Winslow was obliged to acknowledge the great usefulness and beauty of Felicia's character. The aunt looked with astonishment upon her niece, this city-bred girl, reared in the greatest luxury, the daughter of a millionaire, now walking around in her kitchen, her arms covered with flour and occasionally a streak of it on her nose, for Felicia at first had a habit of rubbing her nose forgetfully when she was trying to remember some recipe, mixing various dishes with the greatest interest in their results, washing up pans and kettles and doing the ordinary work of a servant in the Winslow kitchen and at the rooms at the Rectangle Settlement. At first Mrs. Winslow remonstrated.

"Felicia, it is not your place to be out here doing this common work. I cannot allow it."

"Why, Aunt? Don't you like the muffins I made this morning?" Felicia would ask meekly, but with a hidden smile, knowing her aunt's weakness for that kind of muffin.

"They were beautiful, Felicia. But it does not seem right for you to be doing such work for us."

"Why not? What else can I do?"

Her aunt looked at her thoughtfully, noting her remarkable beauty of face and expression.

"You do not always intend to do this kind of work Felicia?"

"Maybe I shall. I have had a dream of opening an ideal cook shop in Chicago or some large city and going around to the poor families in some slum district like the Rectangle, teaching the mothers how to prepare food properly. I remember hearing Dr. Bruce say once that he believed one of the great miseries of comparative poverty consisted in poor food. He even went so far as to say that he thought some kinds of crime could be traced to soggy biscuit and tough beefsteak. I'm sure I would be able to make a living for Rose and myself and at the same time help others."

Felicia brooded over this dream until it became a reality. Meanwhile she grew into the affections of the Raymond people and the Rectangle folks, among whom she was known as the "angel cook." Underneath the structure of the beautiful character she was growing, always rested her promise made in Nazareth Avenue Church. "What would Jesus do?" She prayed and hoped and worked and regulated her life by the answer to that question. It was the inspiration of her conduct and the answer to all her ambition.

25

THREE MONTHS HAD GONE BY SINCE THE SUNDAY morning when Dr. Bruce came into his pulpit with the message of the new discipleship. They were three months of great excitement in Nazareth Avenue Church. Never before had Rev. Calvin Bruce realized how deep the feeling of his members flowed. He humbly confessed that the appeal he had made met with an unexpected response from men and women who, like Felicia, were hungry for something in their lives that the conventional type of church membership and fellowship had failed to give them.

But Dr. Bruce was not yet satisfied for himself. He cannot tell what his feeling was or what led to the movement he finally made, to the great astonishment of all who knew him, better than by relating a conversation between him and the Bishop at this time in the history of the pledge in Nazareth Avenue Church. The two friends were as before in Dr. Bruce's house, seated in his study.

"You know what I have come in this evening for?" the Bishop was saying after the friends had been talking some time about the results of the pledge with the Nazareth Avenue people.

Dr. Bruce looked over at the Bishop and shook his head.

"I have come to confess that I have not yet kept my promise to walk in His steps in the way that I believe I shall be obliged to if I satisfy my thought of what it means to walk in His steps."

Dr. Bruce had risen and was pacing his study. The Bishop remained in the deep easy chair with his hands clasped, but his eye burned with the glow that belonged to him before he made some great resolve.

"Edward," Dr. Bruce spoke abruptly, "I have not yet been able to satisfy myself, either, in obeying my promise. But I have at last decided on my course. In order to follow it I shall be obliged to resign from Nazareth Avenue Church."

"I knew you would," replied the Bishop quietly. "And I came in this evening to say that I shall be obliged to do the same thing with my charge."

Dr. Bruce turned and walked up to his friend. They were both laboring under a repressed excitement.

"Is it necessary in your case?" asked Bruce.

"Yes. Let me state my reasons. Probably they are the same as yours. In fact, I am sure they are." The Bishop paused a moment, then went on with increasing feeling:

"Calvin, you know how many years I have been doing the work of my position, and you know something of the responsibility and care of it. I do not mean to say that my life has been free from burden-bearing or sorrow. But I have certainly led what the poor and desperate of this sinful city would call a very comfortable, yes, a very luxurious life. I have had a beautiful house to live in, the most expensive food, clothing and physical pleasures. I have been able to go abroad at least a dozen times, and have enjoyed for years the beautiful companionship of art and letters and music and all the rest, of the very best. I have never known what it meant to be without money or its equivalent. And I have been unable to silence the question of late: 'What have I suffered for the sake of Christ?' Paul was told what great things he must suffer for the sake of his Lord. Maxwell's position at Raymond is well taken when he insists that to walk in the steps of Christ means to suffer. Where has my suffering come in? The petty trials and annoyances of my clerical life are not worth mentioning as sorrows or sufferings. Compared with Paul or any of the Christian martyrs or early disciples I have lived a luxurious, sinful life, full of ease and pleasure. I cannot endure this any longer. I have that within me which of late rises in overwhelming condemnation of such a following of Jesus. I have not been walking in His steps. Under the present system of church and social life I see no escape from this condemnation except to give the most of my life personally to the actual physical and soul needs of the wretched people in the worst part of this city."

The Bishop had risen now and walked over to the window. The street in front of the house was as light as day, and he looked out at the crowds passing, then turned and with a passionate utterance that showed how deep the volcanic fire in him burned, he exclaimed:

"Calvin, this is a terrible city in which we live! Its misery, its sin, its selfishness, appall my heart. And I have struggled for years with the sickening dread of the time when I should be forced to leave the pleasant luxury of my official position to put my life into contact with the modern paganism of this century. The awful condition of the girls in some great business places, the brutal selfishness of the insolent society fashion and wealth that ignores all the sorrow of the city, the fearful curse of the drink and gambling hell, the wail of the unemployed, the hatred of the church by countless men who see in it only great piles of costly stone and upholstered furniture and the minister as a luxurious idler, all the vast tumult of this vast torrent of humanity with its false and its true ideas, its exaggeration of evils in the church and its bitterness and shame that are the result of many complex causes, all this as a total fact in its contrast with the easy, comfortable life I have lived, fills me more and more with a sense of mingled terror and self accusation. I have heard the words of Jesus many times lately: 'Inasmuch as ye did it not unto one of these least My brethren, ye did it not unto Me.' And when have I personally visited the prisoner or the desperate or the sinful in any way that has actually caused me suffering? Rather, I have followed the conventional soft habits of my position and have lived in the society of the rich, refined, aristocratic members of my congregations. Where has the suffering come in? What have I suffered for Jesus' sake? Do you know, Calvin," he turned abruptly toward his friend, "I have been tempted of late to lash myself with a scourge. If I had lived in Martin Luther's time I should have bared my back to a self-inflicted torture."

Dr. Bruce was very pale. Never had he seen the Bishop or heard him when under the influence of such a passion. There was a sudden silence in the room. The Bishop sat down again and bowed his head.

Dr. Bruce spoke at last:

"Edward, I do not need to say that you have expressed my feelings also. I have been in a similar position for years. My life has been one of comparative luxury. I do not, of course, mean to say that I have not had trials and discouragements and burdens in my church ministry. But I cannot say that I have suffered any for Jesus. That verse in Peter constantly haunts me: 'Christ also suffered for you, leaving you an example that ye should follow His steps.' I have lived in luxury. I do not know what it means to want. I also have had my leisure for travel and beautiful companionship. I have been surrounded by the soft, easy comforts of civilization. The sin and misery of this great city have beaten like waves against the stone walls of my church and of this house in which I live, and I have hardly heeded them, the walls have been so thick. I have reached a point where I cannot endure this any longer. I am not condemning the Church. I love her.

"I am not forsaking the Church. I believe in her mission and have no desire to destroy. Least of all, in the step I am about to take do I desire to be charged with abandoning the Christian fellowship. But I feel that I must resign my place as pastor of Nazareth Church in order to satisfy myself that I am walking as I ought to walk in His steps. In this action I judge no other minister and pass no criticism on others' discipleship. But I feel as you do. Into a close contact with the sin and shame and degradation of this great city I must come personally. And I know that to do that I must sever my immediate connection with Nazareth Avenue Church. I do not see any other way for myself to suffer for His sake as I feel that I ought to suffer."

Again that sudden silence fell over those two men. It was no ordinary action they were deciding. They had both reached the same conclusion by the same reasoning, and they were too thoughtful, too well accustomed to the measuring of conduct, to underestimate the seriousness of their position.

"What is your plan?" The Bishop at last spoke gently, looking with the smile that always beautified his face. The Bishop's face grew in glory now every day.

"My plan," replied Dr. Bruce slowly, "is, in brief, the putting of myself into the centre of the greatest human need I can find in this city and living there. My wife is fully in accord with me. We have already decided to find a residence in that part of the city where we can make our personal lives count for the most."

"Let me suggest a place." The Bishop was on fire now. His fine face actually glowed with the enthusiasm of the movement in which he and his friend were inevitably embarked. He went on and unfolded a plan of such far-reaching power and possibility that Dr. Bruce, capable and experienced as he was, felt amazed at the vision of a greater soul than his own.

They sat up late, and were as eager and even glad as if they were planning for a trip together to some rare land of unexplored travel. Indeed, the Bishop said many times afterward that the moment his decision was reached to live the life of personal sacrifice he had chosen he suddenly felt an uplifting as if a great burden were taken from him. He was exultant. So was Dr. Bruce from the same cause.

Their plan as it finally grew into a workable fact was in reality nothing more than the renting of a large building formerly used as a warehouse for a brewery, reconstructing it and living in it themselves in the very heart of a territory where the saloon ruled with power, where the tenement was its filthiest, where vice and ignorance and shame and poverty were congested into hideous forms. It was not a new idea. It was an idea started by Jesus Christ when He left His Father's House and forsook the riches that were His in order to get nearer humanity and, by becoming a part of its sin, helping to draw humanity apart from its sin. The University Settlement idea is not modern. It is as old as Bethlehem and Nazareth. And in this particular case it was the nearest approach to anything that would satisfy the hunger of these two men to suffer for Christ.

There had sprung up in them at the same time a longing that amounted to a passion, to get nearer the great physical poverty and spiritual destitution of the mighty city that throbbed around them. How could they do this except as they became a part of it as nearly as one man can become a part of another's misery? Where was the suffering to come in unless there was an actual self-denial of some sort? And what was to make that self-denial apparent to themselves or any one else, unless it took this concrete, actual, personal form of trying to share the deepest suffering and sin of the city?

So they reasoned for themselves, not judging others. They were simply keeping their own pledge to do as Jesus would do, as they honestly judged He would do. That was what they had promised. How could they quarrel with the result if they were irresistibly compelled to do what they were planning to do?

The Bishop had money of his own. Every one in Chicago knew that he had a handsome fortune. Dr. Bruce had acquired and saved by literary work carried on in connection with his parish duties more than a comfortable competence. This money, a large part of it, the two friends agreed to put at once into the work, most of it into the furnishing of the Settlement House.

26

MEANWHILE, NAZARETH AVENUE CHURCH WAS EXPE-
riencing something never known before in all its history. The simple
appeal on the part of its pastor to his members to do as Jesus would
do had created a sensation that still continued. The result of that appeal was very much the same as in Henry Maxwell's church in Raymond, only this church was far more aristocratic, wealthy and
conventional.

Nevertheless when, one Sunday morning in early summer, Dr.
Bruce came into his pulpit and announced his resignation, the sensation deepened all over the city, although he had advised with his
board of trustees, and the movement he intended was not a matter
of surprise to them. But when it became publicly known that the
Bishop had also announced his resignation and retirement from the
position he had held so long, in order to go and live himself in the
centre of the worst part of Chicago, the public astonishment
reached its height.

"But why?" the Bishop replied to one valued friend who had almost with tears tried to dissuade him from his purpose. "Why

should what Dr. Bruce and I propose to do seem so remarkable a thing, as if it were unheard of that a Doctor of Divinity and a Bishop should want to save lost souls in this particular manner?

"If we were to resign our charge for the purpose of going to Bombay or Hong Kong or any place in Africa, the churches and the people would exclaim at the heroism of missions. Why should it seem so great a thing if we have been led to give our lives to help rescue the heathen and the lost of our own city in the way we are going to try it? Is it then such a tremendous event that two Christian ministers should be not only willing but eager to live close to the misery of the world in order to know it and realize it? Is it such a rare thing that love of humanity should find this particular form of expression in the rescue of souls?"

And however the Bishop may have satisfied himself that there ought to be nothing so remarkable about it at all, the public continued to talk and the churches to record their astonishment that two such men, so prominent in the ministry, should leave their comfortable homes, voluntarily resign their pleasant social positions and enter upon a life of hardship, of self-denial and actual suffering. Christian America! Is it a reproach on the form of our discipleship that the exhibition of actual suffering for Jesus on the part of those who walk in His steps always provokes astonishment at the sight of something very unusual?

Nazareth Avenue Church parted from its pastor with regret for the most part, although the regret was modified with a feeling of relief on the part of those who had refused to take the pledge. Dr. Bruce carried with him the respect of men who, entangled in business in such a way that obedience to the pledge would have ruined them, still held in their deeper, better natures a genuine admiration for courage and consistency. They had known Dr. Bruce many years as a kindly, conservative, safe man, but the thought of him in the light of sacrifice of this sort was not familiar to them. As fast as they understood it, they gave their pastor the credit of being absolutely true to his recent convictions as to what following Jesus meant. Nazareth Avenue Church never lost the impulse of that movement started by Dr. Bruce. Those who went with him in making the promise breathed into the church the very breath of divine life, and are continuing that lifegiving work at this present time.

It was fall again, and the city faced another hard winter. The Bishop one afternoon came out of the Settlement and walked around the block, intending to go on a visit to one of his new friends in the district. He had walked about four blocks when he was attracted by a shop that looked different from the others. The neighborhood was still quite new to him, and every day he discovered some strange spot or stumbled upon some unexpected humanity.

The place that attracted his notice was a small house close by a Chinese laundry. There were two windows in the front, very clean, and that was remarkable to begin with. Then, inside the widow, was a tempting display of cookery, with prices attached to the various articles that made him wonder somewhat, for he was familiar by this time with many facts in the life of the people once unknown to him. As he stood looking at the windows, the door between them opened and Felicia Sterling came out.

"Felicia!" exclaimed the Bishop. "When did you move into my parish without my knowledge?"

"How did you find me so soon?" inquired Felicia.

"Why, don't you know? These are the only clean windows in the block."

"I believe they are," replied Felicia with a laugh that did the Bishop good to hear.

"But why have you dared to come to Chicago without telling me, and how have you entered my diocese without my knowledge?" asked the Bishop. And Felicia looked so like that beautiful, clean, educated, refined world he once knew, that he might be pardoned for seeing in her something of the old Paradise. Although, to speak truth for him, he had no desire to go back to it.

"Well, dear Bishop," said Felicia, who had always called him so, "I knew how overwhelmed you were with your work. I did not want to burden you with my plans. And besides, I am going to offer you my services. Indeed, I was just on my way to see you and ask your advice. I am settled here for the present with Mrs. Bascom, a saleswoman who rents our three rooms, and with one of Rachel's music pupils who is being helped to a course in violin by Virginia Page. She is from the people," continued Felicia, using the words "from the people" so gravely and unconsciously that her hearer smiled, "and I am keeping house for her and at the same time beginning an experiment in pure food for the masses. I am an expert and I have a plan I want you to admire and develop. Will you, dear Bishop?"

"Indeed I will," he replied. The sight of Felicia and her remarkable vitality, enthusiasm and evident purpose almost bewildered him.

"Martha can help at the Settlement with her violin and I will help with my messes. You see, I thought I would get settled first and work out something, and then come with some real thing to offer. I'm able to earn my own living now."

"You are?" the Bishop said a little incredulously. "How? Making those things?"

"Those things!" said Felicia with a show of indignation. "I would have you know, sir, that 'those things' are the best-cooked, purest food products in this whole city."

"I don't doubt it," he replied hastily, while his eyes twinkled. "Still, 'the proof of the pudding'—you know the rest."

"Come in and try some!" she exclaimed. "You poor Bishop! You look as if you hadn't had a good meal for a month."

She insisted on his entering the little front room where Martha, a wide-awake girl with short, curly hair, and an unmistakable air of music about her, was busy with practice.

"Go right on, Martha. This is the Bishop. You have heard me speak of him so often. Sit down there and let me give you a taste of the fleshpots of Egypt, for I believe you have been actually fasting."

So they had an improvised lunch, and the Bishop who, to tell the truth, had not taken time for weeks to enjoy his meals, feasted on the delight of his unexpected discovery and was able to express his astonishment and gratification at the quality of the cookery.

"I thought you would at least say it is as good as the meals you used to get at the Auditorium at the big banquets," said Felicia slyly.

"As good as! The Auditorium banquets were simply husks compared with this one, Felicia. But you must come to the Settlement. I want you to see what we are doing. And I am simply astonished to find you here earning your living this way. I begin to see what your plan is. You can be of infinite help to us. You don't really mean that you will live here and help these people to know the value of good food?"

"Indeed I do," she answered gravely. "That is my gospel. Shall I not follow it?"

"Aye, Aye! You're right. Bless God for sense like yours! When I left the world," the Bishop smiled at the phrase, "they were talking a good deal about the 'new woman.' If you are one of them, I am a convert right now and here."

"Flattery! Still is there no escape from it, even in the slums of Chicago?" Felicia laughed again. And the man's heart, heavy though it had grown during several months of vast sin-bearing, rejoiced to hear it! It sounded good. It was good. It belonged to God.

Felicia wanted to visit the Settlement, and went back with him. She was amazed at the results of what considerable money and a good deal of consecrated brains had done. As they walked through the building they talked incessantly. She was the incarnation of vital enthusiasm, and he wondered at the exhibition of it as it bubbled up and sparkled over.

They went down into the basement and the Bishop pushed open a door from behind which came the sound of a carpenter's plane. It was a small but well equipped carpenter's shop. A young man with a paper cap on his head and clad in blouse and overalls was whistling and driving the plane as he whistled. He looked up as the two entered, and took off his cap. As he did so, his little finger carried a small curling shaving up to his hair and it caught there.

"Miss Sterling, Mr. Stephen Clyde," said the Bishop. "Clyde is one of our helpers here two afternoons in the week."

Just then the bishop was called upstairs and he excused himself a moment, leaving Felicia and the young carpenter together.

"We have met before," said Felicia looking at Clyde frankly.

"Yes, 'back in the world,' as the Bishop says," replied the young man, and his fingers trembled a little as they lay on the board he had been planing.

"Yes." Felicia hesitated. "I am very glad to see you."

"Are you?" The flush of pleasure mounted to the young carpenter's forehead. "You have had a great deal of trouble since—since—then," he said, and then he was afraid he had wounded her, or called up painful memories. But she had lived over all that.

"Yes, and you also. How is it that you're working here?"

"It is a long story, Miss Sterling. My father lost his money and I was obliged to go to work. A very good thing for me. The Bishop says I ought to be very grateful. I am. I am very happy now. I learned the trade, hoping some time to be of use. I am night clerk at one of the hotels. That Sunday morning when you took the pledge at Nazareth Avenue Church, I took it with the others."

"Did you?" said Felicia slowly. "I am glad."

Just then the Bishop came back, and very soon he and Felicia went away leaving the young carpenter at his work. Some one noticed that he whistled louder than ever as he planed.

"Felicia," said the Bishop, "did you know Stephen Clyde before?"

"Yes, 'back in the world,' dear Bishop. He was one of my acquaintances in Nazareth Avenue Church."

"Ah!" said the Bishop.

"We were very good friends," added Felicia.

"But nothing more?" the Bishop ventured to ask.

Felicia's face glowed for an instant. Then she looked her companion in the eyes frankly and answered:

"Truly and truly, nothing more."

"It would be just the way of the world for those two people to come to like each other though," thought the man to himself, and somehow the thought made him grave. It was almost like the old pang over Camilla. But it passed, leaving him afterwards, when Felicia had gone back, with tears in his eyes and a feeling that was almost hope that Felicia and Stephen would like each other. "After all," he said, like the sensible, good man that he was, "is not romance a part of humanity? Love is older than I am, and wiser."

The week following, the Bishop had an experience that belongs to this part of the Settlement history. He was coming back to the Settlement very late from some gathering of the striking tailors, and was walking along with his hands behind him, when two men jumped out from behind an old fence that shut off an abandoned factory from the street, and faced him. One of the men thrust a pistol in his face, and the other threatened him with a ragged stake that had evidently been torn from the fence.

"Hold up your hands, and be quick about it!" said the man with the pistol.

The place was solitary and the Bishop had no thought of resistance. He did as he was commanded, and the man with the stake began to go through his pockets. He was calm. His nerves did not quiver. As he stood there with his hands uplifted, an ignorant spectator might have thought that he was praying for the souls of these two men. And he was. And his prayer was singularly answered that very night.

27

*"Righteousness shall go before him
and shall set us in the way of his steps."*

THE BISHOP WAS NOT IN THE HABIT OF CARRYING much money with him, and the man with the stake who was searching him uttered an oath at the small amount of change he found. As he uttered it, the man with the pistol savagely said, "Jerk out his watch! We might as well get all we can out of the job!"

The man with the stake was on the point of laying hold of the chain when there was a sound of footsteps coming towards him.

"Get behind the fence! We haven't half searched him yet! Mind you keep shut now, if you don't want—"

The man with the pistol made a significant gesture with it and, with his companion, pulled and pushed the Bishop down the alley and through a ragged, broken opening in the fence. The three stood still there in the shadow until the footsteps passed.

"Now, then, have you got the watch?" asked the man with the pistol.

"No, the chain is caught somewhere!" and the other man swore again.

"Break it then!"

"No, don't break it," the Bishop said, and it was the first time he had spoken. "The chain is the gift of a very dear friend. I should be sorry to have it broken."

At the sound of the Bishop's voice the man with the pistol started as if he had been suddenly shot by his own weapon. With a quick movement of his other hand he turned the Bishop's head toward's what little light was shining from the alleyway, at the same time taking a step nearer.

Then, to the amazement of his companion, he said roughly: "Leave the watch alone! We've got the money. That's enough!"

"Enough! Fifty cents! You don't reckon—"

Before the man with the stake could say another word he was confronted with the muzzle of the pistol turned from the Bishop's head towards his own.

"Leave that watch be! And put back the money too. This is the Bishop we've held up—the Bishop—do you hear?"

"And what of it! The President of the United States wouldn't be too good to hold up, if—"

"I say, you put the money back, or in five seconds I'll blow a hole through your head that'll let in more sense than you have to spare now!" said the other.

For a second the man with the stake seemed to hesitate at this strange turn in events, as if measuring his companion's intention. Then he hastily dropped the money back into the rifled pocket.

"You can take your hands down, sir." The man lowered his weapon slowly, still keeping an eye on the other man, and speaking with rough respect. The Bishop slowly brought his arms to his side, and looked earnestly at the two men. In the dim light it was difficult to distinguish features. He was free to go his way now, but he stood there making no movement.

"You can go on. You needn't stay any longer on our account." The man who had acted as spokesman turned and sat down on a stone. The other man stood viciously digging his stake into the ground.

"That's just what I am staying for," replied the Bishop. He sat down on a board that projected from the broken fence.

"You must like our company. It is hard sometimes for people to tear themselves away from us," and the man standing up laughed coarsely.

"Shut up!" exclaimed the other. "We're on the road to hell, though, that's sure enough. We need better company than ourselves and the devil."

"If you would only allow me to be of any help," the Bishop spoke gently, even lovingly. The man on the stone stared at the Bishop through the darkness. After a moment of silence he spoke slowly like one who had finally decided upon a course he had at first rejected. "Do you remember ever seeing me before?"

"No," said the Bishop. "The light is not very good and I have really not had a good look at you."

"Do you know me now?" The man suddenly took off his hat and getting up from the stone walked over to the Bishop until they were near enough to touch each other.

The man's hair was coal black except one spot on the top of his head about as large as the palm of the hand, which was white.

The minute the Bishop saw that, he started. The memory of fifteen years ago began to stir in him. The man helped him.

"Don't you remember one day back in '81 or '82 a man came to your house and told a story about his wife and child having been burned to death in a tenement fire in New York?"

"Yes, I begin to remember now." The other man seemed to be interested. He ceased digging his stake in the ground and stood still listening.

"Do you remember how you took me into your own house that night and spent all next day trying to find me a job? And how when you succeeded in getting me a place in a warehouse as foreman, I promised to quit drinking because you asked me to?"

"I remember it now. I hope you have kept your promise."

The man laughed savagely. Then he struck his hand against the fence with such sudden passion that he drew blood.

"Kept it! I was drunk inside of a week! I've been drinking ever since. But I've never forgotten you nor your prayer. Do you remember the morning after I came to your house, after breakfast you had prayers and asked me to come in and sit with the rest? That got me! But my mother used to pray! I can see her now kneeling down by my bed when I was a lad. Father came in one night and kicked her while she was kneeling there by me. But I never forgot that prayer of yours that morning. You prayed for me just as mother used to, and you didn't seem to take 'count of the fact that I was ragged and tough-looking and more than half drunk when I rang your door bell.

"Oh, what a life I've lived! The saloon has housed me and homed me and made hell on earth for me. But that prayer stuck to me all the time. My promise not to drink was broken into a thousand pieces inside of two Sundays, and I lost the job you found for me and landed in a police station two days later, but I never forgot you nor your prayer. I don't know what good it has done me, but I never forgot it. And I won't do any harm to you nor let any one else. So you're free to go. That's why."

The Bishop did not stir. Somewhere a church clock struck one. The man had put on his hat and gone back to his seat on the stone. The Bishop was thinking hard.

"How long is it since you had work?" he asked, and the man standing up answered for the other.

"More'n six months since either of us did anything to tell of; unless you count 'holding up' work. I call it pretty wearing kind of a job myself, especially when we put in a night like this and don't make nothin'."

"Suppose I found good jobs for both of you? Would you quit this and begin all over?"

"What's the use?" the man on the stone spoke sullenly. "I've reformed a hundred times. Every time I go down deeper. The devil's begun to foreclose on me already. It's too late."

"No!" said the Bishop. And never before the most entranced audience had he felt the desire for souls burn up in him so strongly. All the time he sat there during the remarkable scene he prayed, "O Lord Jesus, give me the souls of these two for Thee! I am hungry for them. Give them to me!"

"No!" the Bishop repeated. "What does God want of you two men? It doesn't so much matter what I want. But He wants just what I do in this case. You two men are of infinite value to Him." And then his wonderful memory came to his aid in an appeal such as no one on earth among men could make under such circumstances. He had remembered the man's name in spite of the wonderfully busy years that lay between his coming to the house and the present moment.

"Burns," he said, and he yearned over the men with an unspeakable longing for them both, "if you and your friend here will go home with me to-night I will find you both places of honorable employment. I will believe in you and trust you. You are both comparatively young men. Why should God lose you?

"It is a great thing to win the love of the Great Father. It is a small thing that I should love you. But if you need to feel again that there is love in the world, you will believe me when I say, my brothers, that I love you, and in the name of Him who was crucified for our sins I cannot bear to see you miss the glory of the human life. Come, be men! Make another try for it, God helping you. No one but God and you and myself need ever know anything of this to-night. He has forgiven it the minute you ask Him to. You will find that true. Come! We'll fight it out together, you two and I. It's worth fighting for, everlasting life is. It was the sinner that Christ came to help. I'll do what I can for you. O God, give me the souls of these two men!" and he broke into a prayer to God that was a continuation of his appeal to the men.

His pent-up feeling had no other outlet. Before he had prayed many moments Burns was sitting with his face buried in his hands, sobbing. Where were his mother's prayers now? They were adding to the power of the Bishop's. And the other man, harder, less moved, without a previous knowledge of the Bishop, leaned back against the fence, stolid at first. But as the prayer went on, he was moved by it. What force of the Holy Spirit swept over his dulled, brutal, coarsened life, nothing but the eternal records of the recording angel can ever disclose. But the same supernatural Presence that smote Paul on the road to Damascus, and poured through Henry Maxwell's church the morning he asked disciples to follow in Jesus' steps, and had again, broken irresistibly over the Nazareth Avenue congregation, now manifested Himself in this foul corner of the mighty city and over the natures of these two sinful sunken men, apparently lost to all the pleadings of conscience and memory and God. The prayer seemed to break open the crust that for years had surrounded them and shut them off from divine communication. And they themselves were thoroughly startled by it.

The Bishop ceased, and at first he himself did not realize what had happened. Neither did they. Burns still sat with his head bowed between his knees. The man leaning against the fence looked at the Bishop with a face in which new emotions of awe, repentance, astonishment and a broken gleam of joy struggled for expression.

The Bishop rose. "Come, my brothers. God is good. You shall stay at the Settlement tonight, and I will make good my promise as to the work."

The two men followed him in silence. When they reached the Settlement it was after two o'clock. He let them in and led them to a room. At the door he paused a moment. His tall, commanding figure stood in the doorway and his pale face, worn with his recent experience, was illuminated with the divine glory.

"God bless you, my brothers!" he said, and leaving them his benediction he went away.

In the morning he almost dreaded to face the men. But the impression of the night had not worn away. True to his promise he secured work for them. The janitor at the Settlement needed an assistant, owing to the growth of the work there. So Burns was given the place. The Bishop succeeded in getting his companion a position as driver for a firm of warehouse dray manufacturers not far from the Settlement. And the Holy Spirit, struggling in these two darkened sinful men, began His marvelous work of regeneration.

28

It was the afternoon of that morning when Burns was installed in his new position as assistant janitor that he was cleaning off the front steps of the Settlement, when he paused a moment and stood up to look about him. The first thing he noticed was a beer sign just across the alley. He could almost touch it with his broom, from where he stood. Over the street immediately opposite were two large saloons, and a little farther down were three more.

Suddenly the door of the nearest saloon opened and a man came out. At the same time two more went in. A strong odor of beer floated up to Burns as he stood on the steps. He clutched his broom handle tightly and began to sweep again. He had one foot on the porch and another on the steps just below. He took another step down, still sweeping. The sweat stood on his forehead although the day was frosty and the air chill. The saloon door opened again and three or four men came out. A child went in with a pail, and came out a moment later with a quart of beer. The child went by on the sidewalk just below him, and the odor of the beer came up to him.

He took another step down, still sweeping desperately. His fingers were purple as he clutched the handle of the broom.

Then suddenly he pulled himself up one step and swept over the spot he had just cleaned. He then dragged himself by a tremendous effort back to the floor of the porch and went over into the corner of it farthest from the saloon and began to sweep there. "O God!" he cried, "if the Bishop would only come back!" The Bishop had gone out with Dr. Bruce somewhere, and there was no one about that he knew.

He swept in the corner for two or three minutes. His face was drawn with the agony of his conflict. Gradually he edged out again towards the steps and began to go down them. He looked towards the sidewalk and saw that he had left one step unswept. The sight seemed to give him a reasonable excuse for going down there to finish his sweeping.

He was on the sidewalk now, sweeping the last step, with his face towards the Settlement and his back turned partly on the saloon across the alley. He swept the step a dozen times. The sweat rolled over his face and dropped down at his feet. By degrees he felt that he was drawn over towards that end of the step nearest the saloon. He could smell the beer and rum now as the fumes rose around him. It was like the infernal sulphur of the lowest hell, and yet it dragged him as by a giant's hand nearer its source.

He was down in the middle of the sidewalk now, still sweeping. He cleared the space in front of the Settlement and even went out into the gutter and swept that. He took off his hat and rubbed his sleeve over his face. His lips were pallid and his teeth chattered. He trembled all over like a palsied man and staggered back and forth as if he was already drunk. His soul shook within him.

He had crossed over the little piece of stone flagging that measured the width of the alley, and now he stood in front of the saloon, looking at the sign, and staring into the window at the pile of whiskey and beer bottles arranged in a great pyramid inside. He moistened his lips with his tongue and took a step forward, looking around him stealthily. The door suddenly opened again and some one came out. Again the hot, penetrating smell of liquor swept out into the cold air, and he took another step towards the saloon door which had shut behind the customer. As he laid his fingers on the door handle, a tall figure came around the corner. It was the Bishop.

He seized Burns by the arm and dragged him back upon the sidewalk. The frenzied man, now mad for a drink, shrieked out a curse and struck at his friend savagely. It is doubtful if he really knew at first who was snatching him away from his ruin. The blow fell upon the Bishop's face and cut a gash in his cheek. He never uttered a word. But over his face a look of majestic sorrow swept. He picked Burns up as if he had been a child and actually carried him up the steps and into the house. He put him down in the hall and then shut the door and put his back against it.

Burns fell on his knees sobbing and praying. The Bishop stood there panting with his exertion, although Burns was a slightly-built man and had not been a great weight for a man of his strength to carry. He was moved with unspeakable pity.

"Pray, Burns—pray as you never prayed before! Nothing else will save you!"

"O God! Pray with me. Save me! Oh, save me from my hell!" cried Burns. And the Bishop knelt by him in the hall and prayed as only he could pray.

After that they rose and Burns went to his room. He came out of it that evening like a humble child. And the Bishop went his way older from that experience, bearing on his body the marks of the Lord Jesus. Truly he was learning something of what it means to walk in His steps.

But the saloon! It stood there, and all the others lined the street like so many traps set for Burns. How long would the man be able to resist the smell of the damnable stuff? The Bishop went out on the porch. The air of the whole city seemed to be impregnated with the odor of beer. "How long, O Lord, how long?" be prayed. Dr. Bruce came out, and the two friends talked about Burns and his temptation.

"Did you ever make any inquiries about the ownership of this property adjoining us?" the Bishop asked.

"No, I haven't taken time for it. I will now if you think it would be worth while. But what can we do, Edward, against the saloon in this great city? It is as firmly established as the churches or politics. What power can ever remove it?"

"God will do it in time, as He has removed slavery," was the grave reply. "Meanwhile I think we have a right to know who controls this saloon so near the Settlement."

"I'll find out," said Dr. Bruce.

Two days later he walked into the business office of one of the members of Nazareth Avenue Church and asked to see him a few moments. He was cordially received by his old parishioner, who welcomed him into his room and urged him to take all the time he wanted.

"I called to see you about that property next the Settlement where the Bishop and myself now are, you know. I am going to speak plainly, because life is too short and too serious for us both to have any foolish hesitation about this matter. Clayton, do you think it is right to rent that property for a saloon?"

Dr. Bruce's question was as direct and uncompromising as he had meant it to be. The effect of it on his old parishioner was instantaneous.

The hot blood mounted to the face of the man who sat there a picture of business activity in a great city. Then he grew pale, dropped his head on his hands, and when he raised it again Dr. Bruce was amazed to see a tear roll over his face.

"Doctor, did you know that I took the pledge that morning with the others?"

"Yes, I remember."

"But you never knew how I have been tormented over my failure to keep it in this instance. That saloon property has been the temptation of the devil to me. It is the best paying investment at present that I have. And yet it was only a minute before you came in here that I was in an agony of remorse to think how I was letting a little earthly gain tempt me into a denial of the very Christ I had promised to follow. I knew well enough that He would never rent property for such a purpose. There is no need, Dr. Bruce, for you to say a word more."

Clayton held out his hand and Dr. Bruce grasped it and shook it hard. After a little he went away. But it was a long time afterwards that he learned all the truth about the struggle that Clayton had known. It was only a part of the history that belonged to Nazareth Avenue Church since that memorable morning when the Holy Spirit sanctioned the Christ-like pledge. Not even the Bishop and Dr. Bruce, moving as they now did in the very presence itself of divine impulses, knew yet that over the whole sinful city the Spirit was brooding with mighty eagerness, waiting for the disciples to arise to the call of sacrifice and suffering, touching hearts long dull and cold, making business men and money-makers uneasy in their absorption by the one great struggle for more wealth, and stirring through the church as never in all the city's history the church had been moved. The Bishop and Dr. Bruce had already seen some wonderful things in their brief life at the Settlement. They were to see far greater soon, more astonishing revelations of the divine power than they had supposed possible in this age of the world.

Within a month the saloon next to the Settlement was closed. The saloon-keeper's lease had expired, and Clayton not only closed the property to the whiskey men, but offered the building to the Bishop and Dr. Bruce to use for the Settlement work, which had now grown so large that the building they had first rented was not sufficient for the different industries that were planned.

One of the most important of these was the pure-food department suggested by Felicia. It was not a month after Clayton turned the saloon property over to the Settlement that Felicia found herself installed in the very room where souls had been lost, as head of the department not only of cooking but of a course of housekeeping for girls who wished to go out to service. She was now a resident of the Settlement, and found a home with Mrs. Bruce and the other young women from the city who were residents. Martha, the violinist, remained at the place where the Bishop had first discovered the two girls, and came over to the Settlement certain evenings to give lessons in music.

"Felicia, tell us your plan in full now," said the Bishop one evening when, in a rare interval of rest from the great pressure of work, he was with Dr. Bruce, and Felicia had come in from the other building.

"Well, I have long thought of the hired girl problem," said Felicia with an air of wisdom that made Mrs. Bruce smile as she looked at the enthusiastic, vital beauty of this young girl, transformed into a new creature by the promise she had made to live the Christ-like life. "And I have reached certain conclusions in regard to it that you men are not yet able to fathom, but Mrs. Bruce will understand me."

"We acknowledge our infancy, Felicia. Go on," said the Bishop humbly.

"Then this is what I propose to do. The old saloon building is large enough to arrange into a suite of rooms that will represent an ordinary house. My plan is to have it so arranged, and then teach housekeeping and cooking to girls who will afterwards go out to service. The course will be six months' long; in that time I will teach plain cooking, neatness, quickness, and a love of good work."

"Hold on, Felicia!" the Bishop interrupted, "this is not an age of miracles!"

"Then we will make it one," replied Felicia. "I know this seems like an impossibility, but I want to try it. I know a score of girls already who will take the course, and if we can once establish something like an esprit de corps among the girls themselves, I am sure it will be of great value to them. I know already that the pure food is working a revolution in many families."

"Felicia, if you can accomplish half what you propose it will bless this community," said Mrs. Bruce. "I don't see how you can do it, but I say, God bless you, as you try."

"So say we all!" cried Dr. Bruce and the Bishop, and Felicia plunged into the working out of her plan with the enthusiasm of her discipleship which every day grew more and more practical and serviceable.

It must be said here that Felicia's plan succeeded beyond all expectations. She developed wonderful powers of persuasion, and taught her girls with astonishing rapidity to do all sorts of housework. In time, the graduates of Felicia's cooking school came to be prized by housekeepers all over the city. But that is anticipating our story. The history of the Settlement has never yet been written. When it is Felicia's part will be found of very great importance.

The depth of winter found Chicago presenting, as every great city of the world presents to the eyes of Christendom the marked contrast between riches and poverty, between refinement, luxury, ease, and ignorance, depravity, destitution and the bitter struggle for bread. It was a hard winter but a gay winter. Never had there been such a succession of parties, receptions, balls, dinners, banquets, fetes, gayeties. Never had the opera and the theatre been so crowded with fashionable audiences. Never had there been such a lavish display of jewels and fine dresses and equipages. And on the other hand, never had the deep want and suffering been so cruel, so sharp, so murderous. Never had the winds blown so chilling over the lake and through the thin shells of tenements in the neighborhood of the Settlement. Never had the pressure for food and fuel and clothes been so urgently thrust up against the people of the city in their most importunate and ghastly form. Night after night the Bishop and Dr. Bruce with their helpers went out and helped save men and women and children from the torture of physical privation. Vast quantities of food and clothing and large sums of money were donated by the churches, the charitable societies, the civic authorities and the benevolent associations. But the personal touch of the Christian disciple was very hard to secure for personal work. Where was the discipleship that was obeying the Master's command to go itself to the suffering and give itself with its gift in order to make the gift of value in time to come? The Bishop found his heart sink within him as he faced this fact more than any other. Men would give money who would not think of giving themselves. And the money they gave did not represent any real sacrifice because they did not miss it. They gave what was the easiest to give, what hurt them the least. Where did the sacrifice come in? Was this following Jesus? Was this going with Him all the way? He had been to members of his own aristocratic, splendidly wealthy congregations, and was appalled to find how few men and women of that luxurious class in the churches would really suffer any genuine inconvenience for the sake of suffering humanity. Is charity the giving of worn-out garments? Is it a ten dollar bill given to a paid visitor or secretary of some benevolent organization in the church? Shall the man never go and give his gift himself? Shall the woman never deny herself her reception or her party or her musicale, and go and actually touch, herself, the foul, sinful sore of diseased humanity as it festers in the great metropolis? Shall charity be conveniently and easily done through some organization? Is it possible to organize the affections so that love shall work disagreeable things by proxy?

All this the Bishop asked as he plunged deeper into the sin and sorrow of that bitter winter. He was bearing his cross with joy. But he burned and fought within over the shifting of personal love by the many upon the hearts of the few. And still, silently, powerfully, resistlessly, the Holy Spirit was moving through the churches, even the aristocratic, wealthy, ease-loving members who shunned the terrors of the social problem as they would shun a contagious disease.

This fact was impressed upon the Settlement workers in a startling way one morning. Perhaps no incident of that winter shows more plainly how much of a momentum had already grown out of the movement of Nazareth Avenue Church and the action of Dr. Bruce and the Bishop that followed the pledge to do as Jesus would do.

29

THE BREAKFAST HOUR AT THE SETTLEMENT WAS THE ONE hour in the day when the whole family found a little breathing space to fellowship together. It was an hour of relaxation. There was a great deal of good-natured repartee and much real wit and enjoyable fun at this hour. The Bishop told his best stories. Dr. Bruce was at his best in anecdote. This company of disciples was healthily humorous in spite of the atmosphere of sorrow that constantly surrounded them. In fact, the Bishop often said the faculty of humor was as God-given as any other and in his own case it was the only safety valve he had for the tremendous pressure put upon him.

This particular morning he was reading extracts from a morning paper for the benefit of the others. Suddenly he paused and his face instantly grew stern and sad. The rest looked up and a hush fell over the table.

"Shot and killed while taking a lump of coal from a car! His family was freezing and he had had no work for six months. Six children and a wife all packed into a cabin with three rooms, on the West Side. One child wrapped in rags in a closet!"

These were headlines that he read slowly. He then went on and read the detailed account of the shooting and the visit of the reporter to the tenement where the family lived. He finished, and there was silence around the table. The humor of the hour was swept out of existence by this bit of human tragedy. The great city roared about the Settlement. The awful current of human life was flowing in a great stream past the Settlement House, and those who had work were hurrying to it in a vast throng. But thousands were going down in the midst of that current, clutching at last hopes, dying literally in a land of plenty because the boon of physical toil was denied them.

There were various comments on the part of the residents. One of the new-comers, a young man preparing for the ministry, said:

"Why don't the man apply to one of the charity organizations for help? Or to the city? It certainly is not true that even at its worst this city full of Christian people would knowingly allow any one to go without food or fuel."

"No, I don't believe it would," replied Dr. Bruce. "But we don't know the history of this man's case. He may have asked for help so often before that, finally, in a moment of desperation he determined to help himself. I have known such cases this winter."

"That is not the terrible fact in this case," said the Bishop. "The awful thing about it is the fact that the man had not had any work for six months."

"Why don't such people go out into the country?" asked the divinity student.

Some one at the table who had made a special study of the opportunities for work in the country answered the question. According to the investigator the places that were possible for work in the country were exceedingly few for steady employment, and in almost every case they were offered only to men without families. Suppose a man's wife or children were ill. How would he move or get into the country? How could he pay even the meager sum necessary to move his few goods? There were a thousand reasons probably why this particular man did not go elsewhere.

"Meanwhile there are the wife and children," said Mrs. Bruce. "How awful! Where is the place, did you say?"

"Why, it is only three blocks from here. This is the 'Penrose district.' I believe Penrose himself owns half of the houses in that block. They are among the worst houses in this part of the city. And Penrose is a church member."

"Yes, he belongs to the Nazareth Avenue Church," replied Dr. Bruce in a low voice.

The Bishop rose from the table the very figure of divine wrath. He had opened his lips to say what seldom came from him in the way of denunciation, when the bell rang and one of the residents went to the door.

"Tell Dr. Bruce and the Bishop I want to see them. Penrose is the name—Clarence Penrose. Dr. Bruce knows me."

The family at the breakfast table heard every word. The Bishop exchanged a significant look with Dr. Bruce and the two men instantly left the table and went out into the hall.

"Come in here, Penrose," said Dr. Bruce, and they ushered the visitor into the reception room, closed the door and were alone.

Clarence Penrose was one of the most elegant looking men in Chicago. He came from an aristocratic family of great wealth and social distinction. He was exceedingly wealthy and had large property holdings in different parts of the city. He had been a member of Dr. Bruce's church many years. He faced the two ministers with a look of agitation on his face that showed plainly the mark of some unusual experience. He was very pale and his lips trembled as he spoke. When had Clarence Penrose ever before yielded to such a strange emotion?

"This affair of the shooting! You understand? You have read it? The family lived in one of my houses. It is a terrible event. But that is not the primary cause of my visit." He stammered and looked anxiously into the faces of the two men. The Bishop still looked stern. He could not help feeling that this elegant man of leisure could have done a great deal to alleviate the horrors in his tenements, possibly have prevented this tragedy if he had sacrificed some of his personal ease and luxury to better the conditions of the people in his district.

Penrose turned toward Dr. Bruce. "Doctor!" he exclaimed, and there was almost a child's terror in his voice. "I came to say that I have had an experience so unusual that nothing but the supernatural can explain it. You remember I was one of those who took the pledge to do as Jesus would do. I thought at the time, poor fool that I was, that I had all along been doing the Christian thing. I gave liberally out of my abundance to the church and charity. I never gave myself to cost me any suffering. I have been living in a perfect hell of contradictions ever since I took that pledge. My little girl, Diana you remember, also took the pledge with me. She has been asking me a great many questions lately about the poor people and where they live. I was obliged to answer her. One of her questions last night touched my sore! 'Do you own any houses where these poor people live? Are they nice and warm like ours?' You know how a child will ask questions like these. I went to bed tormented with what I now know to be the divine arrows of conscience. I could not sleep. I seemed to see the judgment day. I was placed before the Judge. I was asked to give an account of my deeds done in the body. 'How many sinful souls had I visited in prison? What had I done with my stewardship? How about those tenements where people froze in winter and stifled in summer? Did I give any thought to them except to receive the rentals from them? Where did my suffering come in? Would Jesus have done as I had done and was doing? Had I broken my pledge? How had I used the money and the culture and the social influence I possessed? Had I used it to bless humanity, to relieve the suffering, to bring joy to the distressed and hope to the desponding? I had received much. How much had I given?'

"All this came to me in a waking vision as distinctly as I see you two men and myself now. I was unable to see the end of the vision. I had a confused picture in my mind of the suffering Christ pointing a condemning finger at me, and the rest was shut out by mist and darkness. I have not slept for twenty-four hours. The first thing I saw this morning was the account of the shooting at the coal yards. I read the account with a feeling of horror I have not been able to shake off. I am a guilty creature before God."

Penrose paused suddenly. The two men looked at him solemnly. What power of the Holy Spirit moved the soul of this hitherto self-satisfied, elegant, cultured man who belonged to the social life that was accustomed to go its way placidly, unmindful of the great sorrows of a great city and practically ignorant of what it means to suffer for Jesus' sake? Into that room came a breath such as before swept over Henry Maxwell's church and through Nazareth avenue. The Bishop laid his hand on the shoulder of Penrose and said: "My brother, God has been very near to you. Let us thank Him."

"Yes! Yes!" sobbed Penrose. He sat down on a chair and covered his face. The Bishop prayed. Then Penrose quietly said: "Will you go with me to that house?"

For answer the two men put on their overcoats and went with him to the home of the dead man's family.

That was the beginning of a new and strange life for Clarence Penrose. From the moment he stepped into that wretched hovel of a home and faced for the first time in his life a despair and suffering such as he had read of but did not know by personal contact, he dated a new life.

It would be another long story to tell how, in obedience to his pledge he began to do with his tenement property as he knew Jesus would do. What would Jesus do with tenement property if He owned it in Chicago or any other great city of the world? Any man who can imagine any true answers to this question can easily tell what Clarence Penrose began to do.

Now before that winter reached its bitter climax many things occurred in the city which concerned the lives of all the characters in this history of the disciples who promised to walk in His steps.

It chanced by one of those coincidences that seem to occur preternaturally that one afternoon just as Felicia came out of the Settlement with a basket of food which she was going to leave as a sample with a baker in the Penrose district, Stephen Clyde opened the door of the carpenter shop in the basement and came out in time to meet her as she reached the sidewalk.

"Let me carry your basket, please," he said.

"Why do you say 'please'?" asked Felicia, handing over the basket while they walked along.

"I would like to say something else," replied Stephen, glancing at her shyly and yet with a boldness that frightened him, for he had been loving Felicia more every day since he first saw her and especially since he stepped into the shop that day with the Bishop, and for weeks now they had been thrown in each other's company.

"What else?" asked Felicia, innocently falling into the trap.

"Why—" said Stephen, turning his fair, noble face full toward her and eyeing her with the look of one who would have the best of all things in the universe, "I would like to say: 'Let me carry your basket, dear Felicia'."

Felicia never looked so beautiful in her life. She walked on a little way without even turning her face toward him. It was no secret with her own heart that she had given it to Stephen some time ago. Finally she turned and said shyly, while her face grew rosy and her eyes tender:

"Why don't you say it, then?"

"May I?" cried Stephen, and he was so careless for a minute of the way he held the basket, that Felicia exclaimed:

"Yes! But oh, don't drop my goodies!"

"Why, I wouldn't drop anything so precious for all the world, dear Felicia," said Stephen, who now walked on air for several blocks, and what was said during that walk is private correspondence that we have no right to read. Only it is a matter of history that day that the basket never reached its destination, and that over in the other direction, late in the afternoon, the Bishop, walking along quietly from the Penrose district, in rather a secluded spot near the outlying part of the Settlement district, heard a familiar voice say:

"But tell me, Felicia, when did you begin to love me?"

"I fell in love with a little pine shaving just above your ear that day when I saw you in the shop!" said the other voice with a laugh so clear, so pure, so sweet that it did one good to hear it.

"Where are you going with that basket?" he tried to say sternly.

"We are taking it to—where are we taking it, Felicia?" "Dear Bishop, we are taking it home to begin—" "To begin housekeeping with," finished Stephen, coming to the rescue.

"Are you?" said the Bishop. "I hope you will invite me to share. I know what Felicia's cooking is."

"Bishop, dear Bishop!" said Felicia, and she did not pretend to hide her happiness; "indeed, you shall be the most honored guest. Are you glad?"

"Yes, I am," he replied, interpreting Felicia's words as she wished. Then he paused a moment and said gently:

"God bless you both!" and went his way with a tear in his eye and a prayer in his heart, and left them to their joy.

Yes. Shall not the same divine power of love that belongs to earth be lived and sung by the disciples of the Man of Sorrows and the Burden-bearer of sins? Yea, verily! And this man and woman shall walk hand in hand through this great desert of human woe in this city, strengthening each other, growing more loving with the experience of the world's sorrows, walking in His steps even closer yet because of their love for each other, bringing added blessing to thousands of wretched creatures because they are to have a home of their own to share with the homeless.

"For this cause," said our Lord Jesus Christ, "shall a man leave his father and mother and cleave unto his wife." And Felicia and Stephen, following the Master, love him with a deeper, truer service and devotion because of the earthly affection which Heaven itself sanctions with its solemn blessing.

But it was a little after the love story of the Settlement became a part of its glory that Henry Maxwell of Raymond came to Chicago with Rachel Winslow and Virginia Page and Rollin and Alexander Powers and President Marsh, and the occasion was a remarkable gathering at the hall of the Settlement arranged by the Bishop and

Dr. Bruce, who had finally persuaded Mr. Maxwell and his fellow disciples in Raymond to come on to be present at this meeting.

There were invited into the Settlement Hall, meeting for that night men out of work, wretched creatures who had lost faith in God and man, anarchists and infidels, free-thinkers and no-thinkers. The representation of all the city's worst, most hopeless, most dangerous, depraved elements faced Henry Maxwell and the other disciples when the meeting began. And still the Holy Spirit moved over the great, selfish, pleasure-loving, sin-stained city, and it lay in God's hand, not knowing all that awaited it.

Every man and woman at the meeting that night had seen the Settlement motto over the door blazing through the transparency set up by the divinity student: "What would Jesus do?"

And Henry Maxwell, as for the first time he stepped under the doorway, was touched with a deeper emotion than he had felt in a long time as he thought of the first time that question had come to him in the piteous appeal of the shabby young man who had appeared in the First Church of Raymond at the morning service.

Was his great desire for fellowship going to be granted? Would the movement begun in Raymond actually spread over the country? He had come to Chicago with his friends partly to see if the answer to that question would be found in the heart of the great city life. In a few minutes he would face the people. He had grown very strong and calm since he first spoke with trembling to that company of workingmen in the railroad shops, but now as then he breathed a deeper prayer for help. Then he went in, and with the rest of the disciples he experienced one of the great and important events of the earthly life. Somehow he felt as if this meeting would indicate something of an answer to his constant query: "What would Jesus do?"

And to-night as he looked into the faces of men and women who had for years been strangers and enemies to the Church, his heart cried out: "O, my Master, teach the Church, Thy Church, how to follow Thy steps better!" Is that prayer of Henry Maxwell's to be answered? Will the Church in the city respond to the call to follow Him? Will it choose to walk in His steps of pain and suffering? And still, over all the city broods the Spirit. Grieve Him not, O city! For He was never more ready to revolutionize this world than now!

30

"Now, when Jesus heard these things, He said unto him,
Yet lackest thou one thing: sell all that thou hast,
and distribute unto the poor, and thou shalt have treasure in
heaven: and come, follow Me."

WHEN HENRY MAXWELL BEGAN TO SPEAK TO THE SOULS crowded into the Settlement Hall that night it is doubtful if he ever faced such an audience in his life. It is quite certain that the city of Raymond did contain such a variety of humanity. Not even the Rectangle at its worst could furnish so many men and women who had fallen entirely out of the reach of the church and of all religious and even Christian influences.

What did he talk about? He had already decided that point. He told in the simplest language he could command some of the results of obedience to the pledge as it had been taken in Raymond. Every man and woman in that audience knew something about Jesus Christ. They all had some idea of His character, and however much they had grown bitter toward the forms of Christian ecclesiasticism or the social system, they preserved some standard of right and truth, and what little some of them still retained was taken from the person of the Peasant of Galilee.

So they were interested in what Maxwell said. "What would Jesus do?" He began to apply the question to the social problem in gen-

---

eral, after finishing the story of Raymond. The audience was respectfully attentive. It was more than that. It was genuinely interested.

As Mr. Maxwell went on, faces all over the hall leaned forward in a way seldom seen in church audiences or anywhere except among workingmen or the people of the street when once they are thoroughly aroused. "What would Jesus do?" Suppose that were the motto not only of the churches but of the business men, the politicians, the newspapers, the workingmen, the society people—how long would it take under such a standard of conduct to revolutionize the world? What was the trouble with the world? It was suffering from selfishness. No one ever lived who had succeeded in overcoming selfishness like Jesus. If men followed Him regardless of results the world would at once begin to enjoy a new life.

Maxwell never knew how much it meant to hold the respectful attention of that hall full of diseased and sinful humanity. The Bishop and Dr. Bruce, sitting there, looking on, seeing many faces that represented scorn of creeds, hatred of the social order, desperate narrowness and selfishness, marveled that even so soon under the influence of the Settlement life, the softening process had begun already to lessen the bitterness of hearts, many of which had grown bitter from neglect and indifference.

And still, in spite of the outward show of respect to the speaker, no one, not even the Bishop, had any true conception of the feeling pent up in that room that night. Among those who had heard of the meeting and had responded to the invitation were twenty or thirty men out of work who had strolled past the Settlement that afternoon, read the notice of the meeting, and had come in out of curiosity and to escape the chill east wind. It was a bitter night and the saloons were full. But in that whole district of over thirty thousand souls, with the exception of the saloons, there was not a door open except the clean, pure Christian door of the Settlement. Where would a man without a home or without work or without friends naturally go unless to the saloon?

It had been the custom at the Settlement for a free discussion to follow any open meeting of this kind, and when Mr. Maxwell finished and sat down, the Bishop, who presided that night, rose and made the announcement that any man in the hall was at liberty to ask questions, to speak out his feelings or declare his convictions, always with the understanding that whoever took part was to observe the simple rules that governed parliamentary bodies and obey the three-minute rule which, by common consent, would be enforced on account of the numbers present.

Instantly a number of voices from men who had been at previous meetings of this kind exclaimed, "Consent! consent!"

The Bishop sat down, and immediately a man near the middle of the hall rose and began to speak.

"I want to say that what Mr. Maxwell has said tonight comes pretty close to me. I knew Jack Manning, the fellow he told about who died at his house. I worked on the next case to his in a printer's shop in Philadelphia for two years. Jack was a good fellow. He loaned me five dollars once when I was in a hole and I never got a chance to pay him back. He moved to New York, owing to a change in the management of the office that threw him out, and I never saw him again. When the linotype machines came in I was one of the men to go out, just as he did. I have been out most of the time since. They say inventions are a good thing. I don't always see it myself; but I suppose I'm prejudiced. A man naturally is when he loses a steady job because a machine takes his place.

"About this Christianity he tells about, it's all right. But I never expect to see any such sacrifices on the part of the church people. So far as my observation goes they're just as selfish and as greedy for money and worldly success as anybody. I except the Bishop and Dr. Bruce and a few others. But I never found much difference between men of the world, as they are called, and church members when it came to business and money making. One class is just as bad as another there."

Cries of "That's so!" "You're right!" "Of course!" interrupted the speaker, and the minute he sat down two men who were on the floor for several seconds before the first speaker was through began to talk at once.

The Bishop called them to order and indicated which was entitled to the floor. The man who remained standing began eagerly:

"This is the first time I was ever in here, and may be it'll be the last. Fact is, I am about at the end of my string. I've tramped this city for work till I'm sick. I'm in plenty of company. Say! I'd like to ask a question of the minister, if it's fair. May I?"

"That's for Mr. Maxwell to say," said the Bishop.

"By all means," replied Mr. Maxwell quickly. "Of course, I will not promise to answer it to the gentleman's satisfaction."

"This is my question." The man leaned forward and stretched out a long arm with a certain dramatic force that grew naturally enough out of his condition as a human being. "I want to know what Jesus would do in my case. I haven't had a stroke of work for two months.

"I've got a wife and three children, and I love them as much as if I was worth a million dollars. I've been living off a little earnings I saved up during the World's Fair jobs I got. I'm a carpenter by trade, and I've tried every way I know to get a job. You say we ought to take for our motto, 'What would Jesus do?' What would He do if He was out of work like me?

"I can't be somebody else and ask the question. I want to work. I'd give anything to grow tired of working ten hours a day the way I used to. Am I to blame because I can't manufacture a job for myself? I've got to live, and my wife and my children have got to live. But how? What would Jesus do? You say that's the question we ought to ask."

Mr. Maxwell sat there staring at the great sea of faces all intent on his, and no answer to this man's question seemed for the time being to be possible. "O God!" his heart prayed; "this is a question that brings up the entire social problem in all its perplexing entanglement of human wrongs and its present condition contrary to every desire of God for a human being's welfare. Is there any condition more awful than for a man in good health, able and eager to work, with no means of honest livelihood unless he does work, actually unable to get anything to do, and driven to one of three things: begging or charity at the hands of friends or strangers, suicide or starvation?

'What would Jesus do?'" It was a fair question for the man to ask. It was the only question he could ask, supposing him to be a disciple of Jesus. But what a question for any man to be obliged to answer under such conditions?

All this and more did Henry Maxwell ponder. All the others were thinking in the same way. The Bishop sat there with a look so stern and sad that it was not hard to tell how the question moved him. Dr. Bruce had his head bowed. The human problem had never seemed to him so tragic as since he had taken the pledge and left his church to enter the Settlement. What would Jesus do? It was a terrible question. And still the man stood there, tall and gaunt and almost terrible, with his arm stretched out in an appeal which grew every second in meaning. At length Mr. Maxwell spoke.

"Is there any man in the room, who is a Christian disciple, who has been in this condition and has tried to do as Jesus would do? If so, such a man can answer this question better than I can."

There was a moment's hush over the room and then a man near the front of the hall slowly rose. He was an old man, and the hand he laid on the back of the bench in front of him trembled as he spoke.

"I think I can safely say that I have many times been in just such a condition, and I have always tried to be a Christian under all conditions. I don't know as I have always asked this question, 'What would Jesus do?' when I have been out of work, but I do know I have tried to be His disciple at all times. Yes," the man went on, with a sad smile that was more pathetic to the Bishop and Mr. Maxwell than the younger man's grim despair; "yes, I have begged, and I have been to charity institutions, and I have done everything when out of a job except steal and lie in order to get food and fuel. I don't know as Jesus would have done some of the things I have been obliged to do for a living, but I know I have never knowingly done wrong when out of work. Sometimes I think maybe He would have starved sooner than beg. I don't know."

The old man's voice trembled and he looked around the room timidly. A silence followed, broken by a fierce voice from a large, black-haired, heavily-bearded man who sat three seats from the

Bishop. The minute he spoke nearly every man in the hall leaned forward eagerly. The man who had asked the question, "What would Jesus do in my case?" slowly sat down and whispered to the man next to him: "Who's that?"

"That's Carlsen, the Socialist leader. Now you'll hear something."

"This is all bosh, to my mind," began Carlsen, while his great bristling beard shook with the deep inward anger of the man. "The whole of our system is at fault. What we call civilization is rotten to the core. There is no use trying to hide it or cover it up. We live in an age of trusts and combines and capitalistic greed that means simply death to thousands of innocent men, women and children. I thank God, if there is a God—which I very much doubt—that I, for one, have never dared to marry and make a home. Home! Talk of hell! Is there any bigger one than this man and his three children has on his hands right this minute? And he's only one out of thousands. And yet this city, and every other big city in this country, has its thousands of professed Christians who have all the luxuries and comforts, and who go to church Sundays and sing their hymns about giving all to Jesus and bearing the cross and following Him all the way and being saved! I don't say that there aren't good men and women among them, but let the minister who has spoken to us here to-night go into any one of a dozen aristocratic churches I could name and propose to the members to take any such pledge as the one he's mentioned here to-night, and see how quick the people would laugh at him for a fool or a crank or a fanatic. Oh, no! That's not the remedy. That can't ever amount to anything. We've got to have a new start in the way of government. The whole thing needs reconstructing. I don't look for any reform worth anything to come out of the churches. They are not with the people. They are with the aristocrats, with the men of money. The trusts and monopolies have their greatest men in the churches. The ministers as a class are their slaves. What we need is a system that shall start from the common basis of socialism, founded on the rights of the common people—"

Carlsen had evidently forgotten all about the three-minutes rule and was launching himself into a regular oration that meant, in his usual surroundings before his usual audience, an hour at least, when the man just behind him pulled him down unceremoniously and arose. Carlsen was angry at first and threatened a little disturbance, but the Bishop reminded him of the rule, and he subsided with several mutterings in his beard, while the next speaker began with a very strong eulogy on the value of the single tax as a genuine remedy for all the social ills. He was followed by a man who made a bitter attack on the churches and ministers, and declared that the two great obstacles in the way of all true reform were the courts and the ecclesiastical machines.

When he sat down a man who bore every mark of being a street laborer sprang to his feet and poured a perfect torrent of abuse against the corporations, especially the railroads. The minute his time was up a big, brawny fellow, who said he was a metal worker by trade, claimed the floor and declared that the remedy for the social wrongs was Trades Unionism. This, he said, would bring on the millennium for labor more surely than anything else. The next man endeavored to give some reasons why so many persons were out of employment, and condemned inventions as works of the devil. He was loudly applauded by the rest.

Finally the Bishop called time on the "free for all," and asked Rachel to sing.

Rachel Winslow had grown into a very strong, healthful, humble Christian during that wonderful year in Raymond dating from the Sunday when she first took the pledge to do as Jesus would do, and her great talent for song had been fully consecrated to the service of the Master. When she began to sing to-night at this Settlement meeting, she had never prayed more deeply for results to come from her voice, the voice which she now regarded as the Master's, to be used for Him.

Certainly her prayer was being answered as she sang. She had chosen the words,

"Hark! The voice of Jesus calling,
Follow me, follow me!"

Again Henry Maxwell, sitting there, was reminded of his first night at the Rectangle in the tent when Rachel sang the people into quiet. The effect was the same here. What wonderful power a good voice consecrated to the Master's service always is! Rachel's great natural ability would have made her one of the foremost opera singers of the age. Surely this audience had never heard such a melody. How could it? The men who had drifted in from the street sat entranced by a voice which "back in the world," as the Bishop said, never could be heard by the common people because the owner of it would charge two or three dollars for the privilege. The song poured out through the hall as free and glad as if it were a foretaste of salvation itself. Carlsen, with his great, black-bearded face uplifted, absorbed the music with the deep love of it peculiar to his nationality, and a tear ran over his cheek and glistened in his beard as his face softened and became almost noble in its aspect. The man out of work who had wanted to know what Jesus would do in his place sat with one grimy hand on the back of the bench in front of him, with his mouth partly open, his great tragedy for the moment forgotten. The song, while it lasted, was food and work and warmth and union with his wife and babies once more. The man who had spoken so fiercely against the churches and ministers sat with his head erect, at first with a look of stolid resistance, as if he stubbornly resisted the introduction into the exercises of anything that was even remotely connected with the church or its forms of worship. But gradually he yielded to the power that was swaying the hearts of all the persons in that room, and a look of sad thoughtfulness crept over his face.

The Bishop said that night while Rachel was singing that if the world of sinful, diseased, depraved, lost humanity could only have the gospel preached to it by consecrated prima donnas and professional tenors and altos and basses, he believed it would hasten the coming of the Kingdom quicker than any other one force. "Why, oh why," he cried in his heart as he listened, "has the world's great treasure of song been so often held far from the poor because the personal possessor of voice or fingers, capable of stirring divinest melody, has so often regarded the gift as something with which to make money? Shall there be no martyrs among the gifted ones of the earth? Shall there be no giving of this great gift as well as of others ?"

And Henry Maxwell, again as before, called up that other audience at the Rectangle with increasing longing for a larger spread of the new discipleship. What he had seen and heard at the Settlement burned into him deeper than the belief that the problem of the city would be solved if the Christians in it should once follow Jesus as He gave commandment. But what of this great mass of humanity, neglected and sinful, the very kind of humanity the Saviour came to save, with all its mistakes and narrowness, its wretchedness and loss of hope, above all its unqualified bitterness towards the church? That was what smote him deepest. Was the church then so far from the Master that the people no longer found Him in the church? Was it true that the church had lost its power over the very kind of humanity which in the early ages of Christianity it reached in the greatest numbers? How much was true in what the Socialist leader said about the uselessness of looking to the church for reform or redemption, because of the selfishness and seclusion and aristocracy of its members?

He was more and more impressed with the appalling fact that the comparatively few men in that hall, now being held quiet for a while by Rachel's voice, represented thousands of others just like them, to whom a church and a minister stood for less than a saloon or a beer garden as a source of comfort or happiness. Ought it to be so? If the church members were all doing as Jesus would do could it remain true that armies of men would walk the streets for jobs and hundreds of them curse the church and thousands of them find in the saloon their best friend? How far were the Christians responsible for this human problem that was personally illustrated right in this hall to-night? Was it true that the great city churches would as a rule refuse to walk in Jesus' steps so closely as to suffer—actually suffer for His sake?

Henry Maxwell kept asking this question even after Rachel had finished singing and the meeting had come to an end after a social gathering which was very informal. He asked it while the little company of residents with the Raymond visitors were having a devotional service, as the custom in the Settlement was. He asked it during a conference with the Bishop and Dr. Bruce which lasted until one o'clock. He asked it as he knelt again before sleeping and poured out his soul in a petition for spiritual baptism on the church in America such as it had never known. He asked it the first thing in the morning and all through the day as he went over the Settlement district and saw the life of the people so far removed from the Life abundant. Would the church members, would the Christians, not only in the churches of Chicago, but throughout the country, refuse to walk in His steps if, in order to do so, they must actually take up a cross and follow Him? This was the one question that continually demanded answer.

31

HE HAD PLANNED WHEN HE CAME TO THE CITY TO RE-turn to Raymond and be in his own pulpit on Sunday. But Friday morning he had received at the Settlement a call from the pastor of one of the largest churches in Chicago, and had been invited to fill the pulpit for both morning and evening service.

At first he hesitated, but finally accepted, seeing in it the hand of the Spirit's guiding power. He would test his own question. He would prove the truth or falsity of the charge made against the church at the Settlement meeting. How far would it go in its self-denial for Jesus' sake? How closely would it walk in His steps? Was the church willing to suffer for its Master?

Saturday night he spent in prayer, nearly the whole night. There had never been so great a wrestling in his soul, even during his strongest experiences in Raymond. He had entered upon another new experience. The definition of his own discipleship was receiving an added test at this time, and he was being led into a larger truth of the Lord.

Sunday morning the great church was filled to its utmost. Henry Maxwell, coming into the pulpit from that all-night vigil, felt the pressure of a great curiosity on the part of the people. They had heard of the Raymond movement, as all the churches had, and the recent action of Dr. Bruce had added to the general interest in the pledge. With this curiosity was something deeper, more serious. Mr. Maxwell felt that also. And in the knowledge that the Spirit's presence was his living strength, he brought his message and gave it to that church that day.

He had never been what would be called a great preacher. He had not the force nor the quality that makes remarkable preachers. But ever since he had promised to do as Jesus would do, he had grown in a certain quality of persuasiveness that had all the essentials of true eloquence. This morning the people felt the complete sincerity and humility of a man who had gone deep into the heart of a great truth.

After telling briefly of some results in his own church in Raymond since the pledge was taken, he went on to ask the question he had been asking since the Settlement meeting. He had taken for his theme the story of the young man who came to Jesus asking what he must do to obtain eternal life. Jesus had tested him. "Sell all that thou hast and give to the poor, and thou shalt have treasure in heaven; and come follow me." But the young man was not willing to suffer to that extent. If following Jesus meant suffering in that way, he was not willing. He would like to follow Jesus, but not if he had to give so much.

"Is it true," continued Henry Maxwell, and his fine, thoughtful face glowed with a passion of appeal that stirred the people as they had seldom been stirred, "is it true that the church of to-day, the church that is called after Christ's own name, would refuse to follow Him at the expense of suffering, of physical loss, of temporary gain? The statement was made at a large gathering in the Settlement last week by a leader of workingmen that it was hopeless to look to the church for any reform or redemption of society. On what was that statement based? Plainly on the assumption that the church contains for the most part men and women who think more of their own ease and luxury than of the sufferings and needs and sins of humanity. How far is that true? Are the Christians of America ready to have their discipleship tested? How about the men who possess large wealth? Are they ready to take that wealth and use it as Jesus would? How about the men and women of great talent? Are they ready to consecrate that talent to humanity as Jesus undoubtedly would do?

"Is it not true that the call has come in this age for a new exhibition of Christian discipleship? You who live in this great sinful city must know that better than I do. Is it possible you can go your ways careless or thoughtless of the awful condition of men and women and children who are dying, body and soul, for need of Christian help? Is it not a matter of concern to you personally that the saloon kills its thousands more surely than war? Is it not a matter of personal suffering in some form for you that thousands of able-bodied, willing men tramp the streets of this city and all cities, crying for work and drifting into crime and suicide because they cannot find it? Can you say that this is none of your business? Let each man look after himself? Would it not be true, think you, that if every Christian in America did as Jesus would do, society itself, the business world, yes, the very political system under which our commercial and governmental activity is carried on, would be so changed that human suffering would be reduced to a minimum?

"What would be the result if all the church members of this city tried to do as Jesus would do? It is not possible to say in detail what the effect would be. But it is easy to say, and it is true, that instantly the human problem would begin to find an adequate answer.

"What is the test of Christian discipleship? Is it not the same as in Christ's own time? Have our surroundings modified or changed the test? If Jesus were here today would He not call some of the members of this very church to do just what He commanded the young man, and ask them to give up their wealth and literally follow Him? I believe He would do that if He felt certain that any church member thought more of his possessions than of the Saviour. The test would be the same to-day as then. I believe Jesus would demand—He does demand now—as close a following, as much suffering, as great self-denial as when He lived in person on the earth and said, 'Except a man renounce all that he hath he cannot be my disciple.' That is, unless he is willing to do it for my sake, he cannot be my disciple.

"What would be the result if in this city every church member should begin to do as Jesus would do? It is not easy to go into details of the result. But we all know that certain things would be impossible that are now practiced by church members. What would Jesus do in the matter of wealth? How would He spend it? What principle would regulate His use of money? Would He be likely to live in great luxury and spend ten times as much on personal adornment and entertainment as He spent to relieve the needs of suffering humanity? How would Jesus be governed in the making of money? Would He take rentals from saloons and other disreputable property, or even from tenement property that was so constructed that the inmates had no such things as a home and no such possibility as privacy or cleanliness?

"What would Jesus do about the great army of unemployed and desperate who tramp the streets and curse the church, or are indifferent to it, lost in the bitter struggle for the bread that tastes bitter when it is earned on account of the desperate conflict to get it? Would Jesus care nothing for them? Would He go His way in comparative ease and comfort? Would He say that it was none of His business? Would He excuse Himself from all responsibility to remove the causes of, such a condition?

"What would Jesus do in the center of a civilization that hurries so fast after money that the very girls employed in great business houses are not paid enough to keep soul and body together without fearful temptations so great that scores of them fall and are swept over the great boiling abyss; where the demands of trade sacrifice hundreds of lads in a business that ignores all Christian duties toward them in the way of education and moral training and personal affection? Would Jesus, if He were here to-day as a part of our age and commercial industry, feel nothing, do nothing, say nothing, in the face of these facts which every business man knows?

"What would Jesus do? Is not that what the disciple ought to do? Is he not commanded to follow in His steps? How much is the Christianity of the age suffering for Him? Is it denying itself at the cost of ease, comfort, luxury, elegance of living? What does the age need more than personal sacrifice? Does the church do its duty in following Jesus when it gives a little money to establish missions or relieve extreme cases of want? Is it any sacrifice for a man who is worth ten million dollars simply to give ten thousand dollars for some benevolent work? Is he not giving something that cost him practically nothing so far as any personal suffering goes? Is it true that the Christian disciples to-day in most of our churches are living soft, easy, selfish lives, very far from any sacrifice that can be called sacrifice? What would Jesus do?

"It is the personal element that Christian discipleship needs to emphasize. 'The gift without the giver is bare.' The Christianity that attempts to suffer by proxy is not the Christianity of Christ. Each individual Christian business man, citizen, needs to follow in His steps along the path of personal sacrifice to Him. There is not a different path to-day from that of Jesus' own times. It is the same path. The call of this dying century and of the new one soon to be, is a call for a new discipleship, a new following of Jesus, more like the early, simple, apostolic Christianity, when the disciples left all and literally followed the Master. Nothing but a discipleship of this kind can face the destructive selfishness of the age with any hope of overcoming it. There is a great quantity of nominal Christianity to-day. There is need of more of the real kind. We need revival of the Christianity of Christ. We have, unconsciously, lazily, selfishly, formally grown into a discipleship that Jesus himself would not acknowledge. He would say to many of us when we cry, 'Lord, Lord,' 'I never knew you!' Are we ready to take up the cross? Is it possible for this church to sing with exact truth,

'Jesus, I my cross have taken,
All to leave and follow Thee?'

"If we can sing that truly, then we may claim discipleship. But if our definition of being a Christian is simply to enjoy the privileges of worship, be generous at no expense to ourselves, have a good, easy time surrounded by pleasant friends and by comfortable things, live respectably and at the same time avoid the world's great stress of sin and trouble because it is too much pain to bear it—if this is our definition of Christianity, surely we are a long way from following the steps of Him who trod the way with groans and tears and sobs of anguish for a lost humanity; who sweat, as it were, great drops of blood, who cried out on the upreared cross, 'My God, my God, why hast thou forsaken me?'

"Are we ready to make and live a new discipleship? Are we ready to reconsider our definition of a Christian? What is it to be a Christian? It is to imitate Jesus. It is to do as He would do. It is to walk in His steps."

When Henry Maxwell finished his sermon, he paused and looked at the people with a look they never forgot and, at the moment, did not understand. Crowded into that fashionable church that day were hundreds of men and women who had for years lived the easy, satisfied life of a nominal Christianity. A great silence fell over the congregation. Through the silence there came to the consciousness of all the souls there present a knowledge, stranger to them now for years, of a Divine Power. Every one expected the preacher to call for volunteers who would do as Jesus would do. But Maxwell had been led by the Spirit to deliver his message this time and wait for results to come.

He closed the service with a tender prayer that kept the Divine Presence lingering very near every hearer, and the people slowly rose to go out. Then followed a scene that would have been impossible if any mere man had been alone in his striving for results.

Men and women in great numbers crowded around the platform to see Mr. Maxwell and to bring him the promise of their consecration to the pledge to do as Jesus would do. It was a voluntary, spontaneous movement that broke upon his soul with a result he could not measure. But had he not been praying for this very thing? It was an answer that more than met his desires.

There followed this movement a prayer service that in its impressions repeated the Raymond experience. In the evening, to Mr. Maxwell's joy, the Endeavor Society almost to a member came forward, as so many of the church members had done in the morning, and seriously, solemnly, tenderly, took the pledge to do as Jesus would do. A deep wave of spiritual baptism broke over the meeting near its close that was indescribable in its tender, joyful, sympathetic results.

That was a remarkable day in the history of that church, but even more so in the history of Henry Maxwell. He left the meeting very late. He went to his room at the Settlement where he was still stopping, and after an hour with the Bishop and Dr. Bruce, spent in a joyful rehearsal of the wonderful events of the day, he sat down to think over again by himself all the experience he was having as a Christian disciple.

He had kneeled to pray, as he always did before going to sleep, and it was while he was on his knees that he had a waking vision of what might be in the world when once the new discipleship had made its way into the conscience and conscientiousness of Christendom. He was fully conscious of being awake, but no less certainly did it seem to him that he saw certain results with great distinctiveness, partly as realities of the future, partly great longings that they might be realities. And this is what Henry Maxwell saw in this waking vision:

He saw himself, first, going back to the First Church in Raymond, living there in a simpler, more self-denying fashion than he had yet been willing to live, because he saw ways in which he could help others who were really dependent on him for help. He also saw, more dimly, that the time would come when his position as pastor of the church would cause him to suffer more on account of growing opposition to his interpretation of Jesus and His conduct. But this was vaguely outlined. Through it all he heard the words, "My grace is sufficient for thee."

He saw Rachel Winslow and Virginia Page going on with their work of service at the Rectangle, and reaching out loving hands of helpfulness far beyond the limits of Raymond. Rachel he saw married to Rollin Page, both fully consecrated to the Master's use, both following His steps with an eagerness intensified and purified by their love for each other. And Rachel's voice sang on, in slums and dark places of despair and sin, and drew lost souls back to God and heaven once more.

He saw President Marsh of the college using his great learning and his great influence to purify the city, to ennoble its patriotism, to inspire the young men and women who loved as well as admired him to lives of Christian service, always teaching them that education means great responsibility for the weak and the ignorant.

He saw Alexander Powers meeting with sore trials in his family life, with a constant sorrow in the estrangement of wife and friends, but still going his way in all honor, serving in all his strength the Master whom he had obeyed, even unto the loss of social distinction and wealth.

He saw Milton Wright, the merchant, meeting with great reverses. Thrown upon the future by a combination of circumstances, with vast business interests involved in ruin through no fault of his own, but coming out of his reverses with clean Christian honor, to begin again and work up to a position where he could again be to hundreds of young men an example of what Jesus would do in business.

He saw Edward Norman, editor of the *News,* by means of the money given by Virginia, creating a force in journalism that in time came to be recognized as one of the real factors of the nation to mold its principles and actually shape its policy, a daily illustration of the might of a Christian press, and the first of a series of such papers begun and carried on by other disciples who had also taken the pledge.

He saw Jasper Chase, who had denied his Master, growing into a cold, cynical, formal life, writing novels that were social successes, but each one with a sting in it, the reminder of his denial, the bitter remorse that, do what he would, no social success could remove.

He saw Rose Sterling, dependent for some years upon her aunt and Felicia, finally married to a man far older than herself, accepting the burden of a relation that had no love in it on her part, because of her desire to be the wife of a rich man and enjoy the physical luxuries that were all of life to her. Over this life also the vision cast certain dark and awful shadows but they were not shown in detail.

He saw Felicia and Stephen Clyde happily married, living a beautiful life together, enthusiastic, joyful in suffering, pouring out their great, strong, fragrant service into the dull, dark, terrible places of the great city, and redeeming souls through the personal touch of their home, dedicated to the Human Homesickness all about them.

He saw Dr. Bruce and the Bishop going on with the Settlement work. He seemed to see the great blazing motto over the door enlarged, "What would Jesus do?" and by this motto every one who entered the Settlement walked in the steps of the Master.

He saw Burns and his companion and a great company of men like them, redeemed and giving in turn to others, conquering their passions by the divine grace, and proving by their daily lives the reality of the new birth even in the lowest and most abandoned.

And now the vision was troubled. It seemed to him that as he knelt he began to pray, and the vision was more of a longing for a future than a reality in the future. The church of Jesus in the city and throughout the country! Would it follow Jesus?

Was the movement begun in Raymond to spend itself in a few churches like Nazareth Avenue and the one where he had preached to-day, and then die away as a local movement, a stirring on the surface but not to extend deep and far? He felt with agony after the vision again. He thought he saw the church of Jesus in America open its heart to the moving of the Spirit and rise to the sacrifice of its case and self-satisfaction in the name of Jesus. He thought he saw the motto, "What would Jesus do?" inscribed over every church door, and written on every church member's heart.

The vision vanished. It came back clearer than before, and he saw the Endeavor Societies all over the world carrying in their great processions at some mighty convention a banner on which was written,

"What would Jesus do?" And he thought in the faces of the young men and women he saw future joy of suffering, loss, self-denial, martyrdom. And when this part of the vision slowly faded, he saw the figure of the Son of God beckoning to him and to all the other actors in his life history. An Angel Choir somewhere was singing. There was a sound as of many voices and a shout as of a great victory. And the figure of Jesus grew more and more splendid. He stood at the end of a long flight of steps. "Yes! Yes! O my Master, has not the time come for this dawn of the millenium of Christian history? Oh, break upon the Christendom of this age with the light and the truth. Help us to follow Thee all the way!"

He rose at last with the awe of one who has looked at heavenly things. He felt the human forces and the human sins of the world as never before. And with a hope that walks hand in hand with faith and love Henry Maxwell, disciple of Jesus, laid him down to sleep and dreamed of the regeneration of Christendom, and saw in his dream a church of Jesus without spot or wrinkle or any such thing, following Him all the way, walking obediently in His steps.

THE END

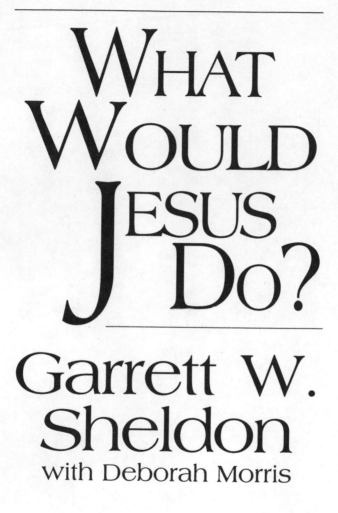

WHAT WOULD JESUS DO?

Garrett W. Sheldon

with Deborah Morris

Preface

WHEN I WAS GROWING UP, MY FAMILY FREQUENTLY
spoke of my great-grandfather, Rev. Charles M. Sheldon, and
that he had written a religious book called *In His Steps*. I was told
this book had sold more copies than any other religious book
except the Bible, an estimated thirty million copies in fifteen
languages worldwide. It was also something of a family joke that
because of a faulty copyright my great-grandfather earned almost
no money from this best-selling book, but that he didn't mind
because he rejoiced that the message was so popular.

In His Steps was originally published in 1896, and it told the
story of a group of people in a church that took a pledge to follow
in Christ's steps by asking themselves in their daily lives, "What
would Jesus do?"

The effects of that new discipleship are told through characters: a newspaper publisher, a woman singer, a businessman,
young people. Each story emphasizes the vital importance of
immediate, personal Christian action in our daily choices and
decisions. It represents behavior informed by God's Word and the
Holy Spirit toward family members, friends, co-workers, acquaintances, and strangers. They reveal a daily walk with our

Savior's ways of reverence, love, peace, patience, humility, forbearance, reproachment, and forgiveness. The individuals in this story show the dramatic transformation in people's lives as they seek God's will in their lives and allow the Holy Spirit to live Christ's life through them.

I felt called to write an updated version of my great-grandfather's book for several reasons. One was a writer asking himself, *What would Jesus do in my place?* Another was my personal experience with the problems of the contemporary church and the realization that the question "What would Jesus do?" provided many solutions. The lifelong deepening of my Christian faith and life experiences that proved to me its truth fueled a desire to share its joys with others.

Many sources fed the awakening of that faith, including the writings of C. S. Lewis, the preaching of Charles Stanley, and the fellowship of many brothers and sisters in Christ. The realization came to me that after almost one hundred years, *In His Steps* could be updated with stories of contemporary Christians following obediently in Christ's footsteps.

My prayer is that it will bring something of God's saving grace to its readers and bless them with a hint of His glory.

Like the original book, *What Would Jesus Do?* is based on many actual events in the lives of believers but may not always represent specific living persons. My great-grandfather found inspiration for many of the stories in actual Christian endeavors in nineteenth-century America, and I have likewise instilled many of the characters in this book with real events of actual people following in the steps of Jesus. I know personally of hundreds of people who have turned their lives around, replacing joy for sorrow, peace for anxiety, love for hatred, fulfillment for emptiness, and service for bondage through a faithful walk with Jesus, indwelled by the Holy Spirit, obedient to our heavenly Father. To walk "in the steps" of Jesus is not only possible; it is a wonderful life-transforming reality for millions of Spirit-filled Christians around the world! Only recently, I heard from a lawyer and businessman on the West Coast whose life was enriched by applying the standard "What would Jesus do?" to his own business life. This new life of joyful Christian discipleship can be real for anyone who accepts Jesus as his or her Lord and Savior, seeks God's loving will through the knowledge of His Scriptures, the comfort and guidance of His Holy Spirit, and the love and support of true Christian fellowship in His church.

My mother's simple Baptist faith introduced me to God's saving grace early in my life. I am also grateful to my father, Charles M. Sheldon II, for his Christian witness and love, which have given me a taste of the heavenly Father's love for me. My wife Elaine's faith and witness have blessed my own Christian walk and contributed greatly to this book. My church family at Trinity Life Center Church in Coeburn, Virginia, and its pastors John and Martha McCarroll, have shown that a Spirit-filled, loving Christian fellowship can give one a taste of heaven. The Reverend Jim Collie, a dedicated Baptist Student Union campus minister and dear friend, gave unending encouragement and love. I felt that the Lord led me to publish this volume with Broadman & Holman and that has been confirmed by the wonderful care I have received by its staff, especially my editor Vicki Crumpton, whose kindness and skill have been a real blessing to this author.

To God be the glory.

GWS (Wise, Virginia; Spring 1993)

Acknowledgment

MANY THANKS TO THOSE PEOPLE WHO WENT "THE EX-
tra mile" to contribute to this book by providing valuable
glimpses into their professional lives, including Terry Mitchell,
airport operations manager at Dallas's Love Field, and Ray Khalil,
owner of the Southwest's popular "Swift-T" convenience store
chain.

Also many thanks to pastor Keith Stewart, who contributed
his prayers, insights, sermon notes, and fondness for alliterative
message headings with unfailing good humor.

I

MICHAEL MAXWELL DREW A DEEP BREATH AND, GLANC-ing at the computer screen, read aloud the catchy sentence he'd just written: "Remember, the road to success is marked with many tempting parking places!" Even to his own ears, his rich baritone sounded convincing, warm, and personal with exactly the right touch of humor.

Then the phone rang—again. Although it was barely ten o'clock that overcast Friday morning, the busy minister's attempts to finish that week's sermon outline had been interrupted repeatedly.

Must be the weather, he thought in exasperation, wishing he'd remembered to turn on the answering machine. *I'll never finish if this keeps up.* When he answered the phone, however, he managed to keep the irritation out of his voice. "This is Michael Maxwell," he said. "What can I do for you?"

"Pastor Maxwell?" It was the breathless drawl of Lauren Woods, the attractive singles group coordinator at church. She'd recently volunteered to help with the mail ministry, an offer Michael suspected was motivated more by a desire to spend time with him than to see the church expand.

In his high-profile position at the prestigious First Church of Ashton, the handsome thirty-five-year-old had learned to take such displays of misplaced devotion in stride.

"Yes, Lauren?" he said shortly.

"I was working this morning on the advertising mailers for our next church concert," she began, "and I was wondering if . . ." Only half-listening, Michael fingered the ornate letter opener he'd bought in Spain the previous year, then narrowed his eyes to peer absently at the ceiling. This year, he and Sharon planned to vacation in Italy.

We both need a break, he thought. *Between our church schedule and fund-raising for the building committee, there's not been much time for anything else.*

Suddenly, he realized Lauren had asked him a question—something about ordering new mailing labels. "Uh, sure, that'll be fine," he replied hastily. "Keep up the good work." He put down the phone with relief, then switched on the answering machine before anyone else could call.

"That," he muttered, "is absolutely the last interruption I can stand this morning."

Sharon Maxwell, dark haired and stylishly dressed, had quietly entered the study. "I'm leaving now, so you'll have the house to yourself for a few hours. I have to go to the church to look at the fall curriculum for the preschool department." She smiled and bent to kiss her husband's cheek. "Need anything while I'm out?"

"Not that I can think of," Michael replied wearily, running his hand through his sandy brown hair. "I'm just going to sit here and try to finish my message notes for Sunday. If anybody else in the church has a crisis before lunch, they'll just have to call Dial-a-Prayer." They both laughed.

A few minutes later, in the soothing quiet of the empty house, Michael once again focused his attention on Sunday's sermon. He was on the next-to-last message of his latest series, "God's Steps to Success." His text for this week was 1 Peter 2:21:

To this you were called, because Christ suffered for you,
leaving you an example,
that you should follow in his steps.

His usual technique was to organize the message into an easy-to-follow outline, preferably with catchy subheadings. Today he had settled on "Discovery, Development, and Determination," drawing illustrations from the life of Christ to underscore the first two points. Now, with renewed enthusiasm, he started on the final point: "Determining to follow in Jesus' steps." He had just typed, "Three obstacles—Pride, Pain, Prejudice" when the door-bell pealed loudly.

Distracted, the minister shifted in his seat but didn't move to answer the door. When the bell rang a second time, however, he made an exasperated sound under his breath and stood up. Whoever it was, they weren't going away.

He was surprised to find a young, weary-looking black woman on his front step. Obviously pregnant, she appeared to be in her mid-twenties. She was gripping the hand of a well-scrubbed, but shabbily dressed, toddler.

"Are you the pastor of First Church?" she asked nervously. "Somebody told me he lived here."

"I'm Pastor Maxwell," Michael said slowly. "Is there something I can help you with?"

The woman stared up at him, taking in his rugged tanned features, his expensive shirt, his sharp green eyes. "I'm not really sure," she answered warily. "I need someone to watch my little girl."

Puzzled, the minister shook his head. "I'm sorry, but I don't know any baby-sitters. My wife and I don't have any children yet. Our church daycare center is just down the street; you might want to try there." He started to ease the door closed.

"Please," the woman said, a note of desperation in her voice. "You don't understand. I don't have any money to pay for day-care, and I already went to the church. They're the ones who sent me here."

Seeing his doubtful expression, she hurried on, "It would just be for a few weeks, until I got my first paycheck. I just got a job as a waitress downtown, but I can't take Hallie with me. I don't have anyone else to watch her."

Maxwell hesitated, unaccountably touched by the young woman's plight. But what could *he* do? "I really am sorry," he said sympathetically. "I wish I could help, but I don't know anybody who could do something like that. Would you like to leave your phone number in case I think of someone?"

She hesitated, but finally shook her head. She and the little girl turned away and started back toward the sidewalk. Michael gently closed the door and headed back to his study. The young mother's face lingered in his mind for a moment, but once he started working again, his absorption in the sermon quickly crowded everything else from his thoughts.

When Sharon returned home two hours later, she found her husband sitting on the edge of their bed, clad in gym shorts and pulling on tennis shoes. "Hi there," she greeted him. "I guess you finished your sermon. How did it turn out?"

"Pretty good," he replied. "I just hope we have better weather on Sunday than we've had the last few weeks. It's always easier to preach to big crowds."

He pulled his gym bag from the closet and tossed it onto the bed. "I'm going to the health club to work out for a few hours." He shifted his shoulders gingerly. "This sermon took a lot more work than it should have. I'm stiff all over!"

At dinner that evening, Sharon brought up the preschool's new plans for the fall. "They'll be using audio and video tapes to teach math and reading," she said. "It's all set to music. The smaller kids will just love it."

She suddenly paused. "Oh, that reminds me. I meant to tell you earlier, but while I was at the church a woman came in with a little girl, looking for child care. She was pregnant and seemed—I don't know—kind of distraught. Apparently she didn't have any money, so they couldn't help her. I felt really bad for her."

Michael glanced up. "I bet it was the same one who showed up here this morning. I guess she didn't have a husband, but I wonder where her family is? Surely they could help her out."

"You'd think so," Sharon said thoughtfully.

Sunday morning dawned bright and clear in Ashton. A warm, gentle breeze had swept up from the south, clearing away the last of the dark clouds and bringing with it the first hint of spring. As eleven o'clock approached, the enormous parking lot of First Church of Ashton was packed.

Inside, Daniel Marshall, the tall, graying president of Lincoln Christian College, greeted Dr. Patricia West, a tall, thirtyish trauma surgeon quoted as an authority on several new emergency procedures. Jenny Paige, a fashionably dressed real estate developer in her late fifties, swept into the sanctuary with her son, Roger, who at twenty-four had inherited both her piercing blue eyes and her business acumen. Ted Newton, the wiry general manager of WFBB-TV, paused to shake hands with Alex Powell, a portly black man of military bearing who managed operations at Vickers Field Regional Airport. The First Church membership roster read like a "Who's Who" list of the most intellectual and affluent people in the city. The worship team at the front was just starting the pre-service performance, a contemporary instrumental version of "I Surrender All," including drums, piano, saxophone, synthesizer, and two electric guitars. It was a recognized signal for everyone to make their way to their seats.

The music at First Church rivaled many top professional Christian performances and was heavily advertised in the glossy brochures mailed to the community each month. The church held frequent concerts and had purchased a marquee-style billboard to place along the highway. It featured a tall picture of Michael and boldly proclaimed: *"Pastor Michael Maxwell Presents: Jesus!"* followed by that month's concert schedule.

Michael was aware that some people were drawn to First Church because of its sophisticated image, while others were offended by the church's contemporary thrust and slick advertising. He wasn't disturbed by the criticism.

"We have to get people in the door if we want them to hear the gospel," he insisted. "We're competing with the sports and entertainment industries and all their gimmicks. If it takes billboards or TV ads to get people's attention, that's okay." To keep the music top quality, the church had recently invested in a sound system that would make most concert halls envious.

At precisely eleven o'clock the worship team opened the service with prayer and led the congregation in several short choruses. Then the two lead vocalists, Rachel Wingate and Jason Clark, stepped forward to perform the morning's special.

The church instantly grew still. Rachel, twenty-two, could be a top magazine model with her curly, auburn hair and striking, gray-green eyes. Jason, two years older, was her perfect counterpart, tall and muscular with stylishly long, blond hair. Together they exuded an almost electric stage presence that left the congregation quivering with anticipation.

As the first strains of music started, Rachel spoke into her cordless microphone, "Pastor Maxwell will be delivering a message this morning about following Jesus. Jason and I would like to sing a song for you now about that subject, a remake of the old hymn 'Where He Leads Me I Will Follow.'"

Her comments ended at precisely the right moment in the musical introduction. After only the briefest of pauses she nodded at Jason, and with bright smiles they swept into the song:

> *I can hear my Savior calling,*
> *I can hear my Savior calling,*
> *I can hear my Savior calling,*
> *"Take thy cross and follow,*
> *follow me!"*

As usual, the sweetness of their harmony literally drew gasps from the audience. Some people wiped their eyes and murmured, "Beautiful, just beautiful," while others, sensing the almost palpable link between the striking young couple, speculated about a future fairy-tale wedding. Rachel and Jason continued into the chorus:

> *Where He leads me I will follow,*
> *Where He leads me I will follow,*
> *Where He leads me I will follow,*
> *I'll go with him, with him,*
> *all the way.*

When the last note tapered away, there was a thunderous round of applause, joined by Michael Maxwell as he took the pulpit. "Thank you, Rachel and Jason," he said warmly as the applause subsided. "After music like that, I'm not even sure I *need* to preach." The audience laughed appreciatively. After a few initial comments, Michael opened his Bible and began his sermon. He was exhilarated by the crowd's easy response that morning; as usual, the combination of music, comfortable seating and soothing surroundings had paved the way for his message. Although he avoided thinking of it in such terms, the careful staging of the Sunday morning services had played a large part in his ministerial success.

His sermon that morning was, as always, both stimulating and entertaining. Michael Maxwell loved standing in the pulpit, loved preaching the Word of God in ringing terms and observing the reaction of his widely-varied audience. He always included humorous stories and true anecdotes to keep his message lively and was usually rewarded with comments like, "Excellent job, Pastor. The service just flew by." All in all, Michael was deeply satisfied with his life, his church, and his future.

Now, concluding the message, he closed his Bible and motioned for the worship team to proceed with the final chorus.

As he stepped out from behind the pulpit, however, he was startled by the sound of a shout from the audience. The shocked congregation turned to stare as a young black woman in the last row stepped out into the aisle and walked slowly toward the front, leading a small child by the hand.

With a jolt, Michael recognized his visitors from Friday. Before he could react they were standing at the front of the church. The woman's eyes looked red and tear-swollen, and as she turned to face the crowd she seemed to be moving in a feverish dream.

"I know you're not supposed to speak out in church," she said unevenly, "I'm sorry for interrupting, but I've reached the end of my rope. I don't have anywhere else to turn." Michael waved off two deacons who were striding purposefully toward the woman. He listened in dumb astonishment as she went on, "Six months ago when I found out I was pregnant again, my husband disappeared. I guess he didn't want to be bothered. I'd been taking computer programming classes at night, but after Jim left I had to drop out and go to work at a convenience store. My boss let me keep my daughter there with me, but then I got sick and they had to let me go. I got evicted from our apartment two weeks ago. Hallie and I have been living in my car ever since."

When she paused to take a shaky breath, Michael stole a glance at the silent congregation. Cliff Bright, the plump and balding owner of the "Mr. B Food Stores" chain, looked bewildered, his wife slightly irritated. Lauren Woods appeared horrified. Jason Clark and Rachel Wingate, seated on the front row, seemed riveted by the scene. Jason, embarrassed, suddenly shifted his eyes to the floor, but Rachel gazed on steadily at the woman with a deeply troubled expression. In the midst of the motionless crowd, her pale, intense face stood out as distinctly as if it had been framed in fire.

"The thing is," the woman continued, almost as if talking to herself, "I've been desperate these last few days. I didn't want charity, just someone to watch my daughter until I got my first paycheck. I called my parents, but they said God was punishing me for marrying someone like Jim. That's okay, I guess, but is He punishing my little girl too? Then I tried all the daycares, hoping I could work something out, but they just shook their heads. I guess I can't blame them; they've probably heard the same story before." She shut her eyes for a long moment, then opened them slowly. "I'm really sorry," she said wearily. "I shouldn't be bothering you people with my problems. But all this just doesn't make sense to me. What does it mean when people sing about 'surrendering all' and 'following Jesus'? I mean, I went to six different churches this last week looking for help, and your pastor here was one of the only people who'd even talk to me. He offered to take my phone number. That would have been great if I'd just had a phone. I thought—I always thought church people were supposed to act like Jesus—you know, 'doing unto others' and all that stuff. Isn't that right? But now it's too late, and I've lost the job—," she broke off in a sob, her lower lip trembling as she gazed down at her small daughter.

When she lifted her head again, her dark brown eyes were filled with despair. "I don't know what I'm going to do now. Where else can I go? I just wish—I really thought somebody would watch Hallie for just a few days, or at least give her a hot meal, so I could work. Isn't that what Jesus would do? *What would Jesus do?* I—I—" The woman lifted one trembling hand to her forehead, then, without warning, uttered a sharp exclamation of pain and doubled over, her face twisted with agony. When Michael leaped forward to steady her, she stared up at him without recognition, then with another gasping cry went limp in his arms.

A horrified murmur swept through the church. "Somebody call an ambulance!" Michael shouted.

The audience rose and crowded the aisles. Rachel Wingate impulsively stepped forward to help Michael lower the woman to the floor, then turned to comfort the frightened little girl. She was still cradling the child in her arms when Dr. Patricia West broke through the crowd and knelt beside the prostrate figure.

After a moment the tall surgeon looked up, her face grim.

"She's hemorrhaging," she said. "She needs to get to the hospital *fast.*"

2

THE AMBULANCE LEFT FOR ASHTON MEMORIAL HOSPItal with the woman, tentatively identified as twenty-five-year-old Brenda Collier. Michael, more shaken than he was willing to admit, stood on the church steps talking with Alex Powell, Jason Clark, Jenny and Roger Paige, and several others who had lingered after the abruptly dismissed service. The child had remained behind with them, still clinging tearfully to Rachel.

"So what happens now?" asked Jason, glancing over at Rachel. He was more than a little surprised at her protective manner toward the little girl. She hadn't even seemed to notice the unsightly tear stains the sobbing child had left on the front of her jade silk dress.

Michael answered slowly, "Sharon and I are going to the hospital to see what we can do for her. It's the least we can do, since—" His voice trailed away, causing the others to look at him in surprise. They'd never seen their popular, well-spoken minister at a loss for words.

Rachel quietly stepped into the gap. "Pastor Maxwell, why don't I take the little girl home with me for now? I've got plenty of room in my apartment, and I'm on spring break from college right now." She paused, then added firmly, "I really wouldn't mind at all."

Jason looked surpised, and Roger Paige raised a questioning eyebrow. Rachel Wingate had never struck any of them as the motherly type. But Michael didn't question the young singer's offer. "Thanks, Rachel," he said. "That would be a big help."

At the hospital the Maxwells learned that Brenda Collier was in critical condition—and that due to the large amount of blood she'd lost, the child she'd carried had been stillborn. She hadn't awakened since her collapse at the church. They went to the waiting room and huddled together on the hard couch, distraught.

"If only I'd stepped in when she asked for help at the church," Sharon said brokenly. "Michael, how could I have ignored someone dying right in front of my eyes?"

But he was struggling with his own burden of guilt. "I was just as bad, or even worse. She practically begged me for help, but I turned her away because I was too busy preparing a sermon!" He laughed bitterly. "I can't believe this. Every time I think of her asking, 'What would Jesus do?' I'm condemned by my own words about following in His steps."

Deeply shaken, they began a prayerful vigil for the near-stranger lying in the Critical Care Unit.

Monday morning dawned with no change in Brenda's condition. Michael and Sharon had remained at the hospital throughout the long night; now they wearily walked downstairs to the cafeteria and bought cups of coffee. They had just sat down when they heard a familiar voice.

"Pastor Maxwell? Mrs. Maxwell?" It was Rachel, with little Hallie. She slipped into a chair beside them and lifted the child onto her lap. "I brought her to see her mommy. How is she?"

Sharon shook her head tiredly. "Not good, I'm afraid. She lost a lot of blood. They've given her transfusions, but she still isn't responding. The doctors aren't very encouraging."

Rachel was silent for a moment, taking in the information. Sharon studied the singer's pale face, suddenly realizing how odd it was that she had come to the hospital to check on the woman.

Rachel had always avoided unpleasant situations, preferring to serve the church with her musical talents. Had she also been affected by the woman's desperate words, "What would Jesus do?"

Rachel leaned down to gently rest her cheek against Hallie's, her long, auburn hair vivid against the child's short, dark braids. "Can I help somehow? Have you already notified her family about what's happened?"

Michael shook his head. "We're still trying to find them. Yesterday we called the apartments where she used to live, but her neighbors didn't know much about her. The apartment manager said Brenda and her husband had moved from somewhere in the Southwest, but he didn't have any names or addresses. He thought Jim Collier had gotten into drugs in the last six months. He thinks he's probably still around here somewhere."

"But if he's taking drugs," Rachel murmured, looking down at Hallie, "we wouldn't let him take her, would we? I mean, if something happens to her mother?"

Sharon met her eyes. "Not if we can help it."

For the next twenty-four hours, the minister and his wife rarely left Ashton Memorial. Dr. West kept them posted on Brenda's condition and occasionally let them visit the unconscious woman. Hoping she might somehow be able to hear them, Michael and Sharon repeatedly assured her that little Hallie was being cared for.

Rachel had, in fact, been acting with surprising skill as a surrogate mother. After leaving the hospital the day before, she had taken Hallie shopping for some much-needed clothes and shoes at the nearby Ashton Square Mall. Strolling along hand in hand with the child, Rachel was mildly amused by the stares they drew from several matrons. She helped Hallie try on several new spring dresses at one store, then at another selected socks and underwear, a sunny yellow nightgown, a pair of flowered shoes, and after a moment's thought, a wide plastic hair pick, baby shampoo, and hair conditioner specially made for coarse black hair.

"Now all I have to do is figure out how to fix your hair back in all those little braids once I wash it," she told Hallie as they waited to check out.

"I have a feeling it's harder than it looks." The little girl, understanding Rachel's warm tone if not her words, bounced up and down and said appealingly, "Up!" Rachel smiled and picked her up, leaning her forehead against Hallie's for a moment.

"I love you, little one," she whispered, her eyes glistening with tears as she thought of the young woman silently fighting for her life at Ashton Memorial.

What would become of her daughter if she died?

It was late that Tuesday afternoon, as Michael and Sharon sat in the hospital waiting room, that Dr. West looked around the corner. A moment later the trauma surgeon entered the room with a staff physician, Dr. Kenneth Bender.

The Maxwells looked up, correctly interpreting their solemn expressions. Sharon said softly, "She's gone, isn't she?"

Dr. West nodded, seeming unable to speak. Dr. Bender cleared his throat. "Has anyone located her family yet?"

Michael shook his head. "We're still trying. But if we can't find them quickly, the church will take responsibility for the arrangements."

Over the next few days, as word spread of the tragedy, the church office was flooded with calls. In Michael Maxwell's ten years at First Church of Ashton, he had never witnessed such an outpouring of concern for a stranger. It was as if the church had suddenly awakened from a numbing sleep.

On Thursday, Jim Collier was finally located in a Chicago suburb, living with a seventeen-year-old girl. Although he claimed to be shocked at the death of his wife and child, he balked at making the two-hour drive to Ashton to make funeral arrangements—or even to provide for his daughter's care.

"No man in his right mind could be that callous. I have to believe it was drugs talking," Michael told Sharon afterwards. "But at least I got a phone number from him for Brenda's parents in Arizona."

Mr. and Mrs. Anderson took the news of their daughter's death much harder than their son-in-law had.

"Brenda didn't tell us she was pregnant," Mrs. Anderson said tearfully, "or that she'd been evicted from her apartment. She just said Jim had left her again and she needed to drop out of school and go back to work. We'd helped her out before, but each time she got back on her feet, Jim showed up again, and she took him back. This time I was furious with her. I told her she was getting what she deserved for marrying a man like that!"

Michael tried to comfort them, but it was a distressing conversation. They said they would fly into Ashton the next day to arrange for their daughter's body to be brought back to Arizona, and also to pick up their small granddaughter.

"Thank you, pastor, for calling us," Mr. Anderson said brokenly. "So few people are willing to become involved these days, even so-called Christians. That's one reason my wife and I quit going to church years ago." He drew a shaky breath. "I think now maybe that was a mistake."

Over the days that followed, Michael faced an agonizing time of prayer and self-examination. How, he asked himself miserably, had he drifted so far from his beginnings in the ministry? He had started out earnestly wanting to touch people's lives, but as his success had grown, so had his responsibilities. For the last five years his "job description" at First Church had more closely resembled that of a corporate CEO than a pastor.

Dear Lord, he prayed, *please take me back to the basics. Teach me what it truly means to be Your disciple.*

That Sunday morning dawned on the city of Ashton exactly as the Sunday before. The air was fresh and clean, scented with the first spring flowers. Michael Maxwell entered his pulpit to face one of the largest congregations that had ever crowded into First Church.

The service started quietly that morning. The worship team led a few simple songs but omitted the usual musical special. The subdued feeling among those in the service resulted in only a half-hearted attempt at applause as the musicians took their seats. Rachel Wingate had noticeable dark circles under her eyes.

Now, as Michael gazed out over the congregation, he seemed curiously hesitant. His usual quick smile was missing, and there was an uncomfortable silence as he laid out his notes and opened his Bible. Several church members exchanged glances; their handsome young pastor looked almost ill.

Michael cleared his throat. "We'll conclude our series on 'God's Steps to Success' this morning with the message, 'Believing and Achieving,' " he said slowly. "But before we begin, please join with me in prayer."

As he closed his eyes and began to ask God's blessing on the service, Brenda Collier's face suddenly rose to his mind with vivid clarity. A painful lump constricted his throat as he heard again her desperate challenge, "What would Jesus do?"

His voice abruptly faltered. "Above all, heavenly Father," he prayed, "show us this morning what it really means to follow in Your steps. In Jesus' name we pray, amen."

The sermon that followed was far from eloquent. Twice Michael lost his place in his notes and had to go back over a point to make it clear. It was evident that some idea which had little to do with that morning's message struggled in his thoughts for expression.

Finally, toward the end of the service, the minister seemed to make a decision. Closing his Bible, he stepped out from behind the pulpit to face the congregation.

"Last week," he said with a sudden strength painfully absent from his earlier message, "a young woman named Brenda Collier stood up in our morning service to tell how she'd gone to various churches and businesses here in Ashton asking for help but each time had been turned away. She wondered what we Christians mean when we sing songs like 'I Surrender All,' when in fact, we seem to surrender very little. Then she posed a very simple question: 'What would Jesus do?' For those of you who haven't yet heard, she passed away Tuesday afternoon at Ashton Memorial Hospital. The child she was carrying at that time was stillborn."

Michael paused and looked out over the congregation; he'd never seen so many earnest faces. Jenny Paige fixed her sharp blue eyes on him, her expression unreadable; beside her, even cynical young Roger was unusually attentive. *How can I adequately express what I am feeling?* Michael thought. "Jesus made it clear that we demonstrate our love for Him by how we treat those around us in need. Most of us know the passage in Matthew:

'I was hungry and you gave me something to eat,
I was thirsty and you gave me something to drink,
I was a stranger and you invited me in,
I needed clothes and you clothed me,
I was sick and you looked after me,
I was in prison and you came to visit me.'

Then the righteous will answer him,
'Lord, when did we see you hungry and feed you,
or thirsty and give you something to drink?
When did we see you a stranger and invite you in,
or needing clothes and clothe you?
When did we see you sick or in prison and go to visit you?'

The King will reply,
'I tell you the truth, whatever you did for one of the least
of these brothers of mine, you did for me.'

Then he will say to those on his left,
'Depart from me, you who are cursed,
into the eternal fire prepared for the devil and his angels.

For I was hungry and you gave me nothing to eat,
I was thirsty and you gave me nothing to drink,
I was a stranger and you did not invite me in,
I needed clothes and you did not clothe me,
I was sick and in prison and you did not look after me.'

They will also answer
'Lord, when did we see you hungry or thirsty
or a stranger or needing clothes or sick or in prison,
and did not help you?'

He will reply,
'I tell you the truth, whatever you did not do for one of
the least of these, you did not do for me.' "
         Matthew 25:35–45

Pain was apparent in the strained lines of Michael's face. "Few of you know this, but Brenda Collier actually came to my door asking for help. She was a stranger—and I didn't invite her in. She was hungry—I didn't feed her. She needed clothes—but I didn't offer any. I didn't realize it at the time, but in turning her away, I turned away my Lord."

He stopped, groping for the right words. "I've done a lot of praying and soul-searching these last few days, and I've come to some difficult conclusions. No church program, no matter how well done, can touch other people as powerfully as individual acts of compassion.

"I wasn't planning to do this today, but I can't think of any better time than now to share an idea that's gradually been forming in my mind."

In the audience Alex Powell suddenly sat up straighter, his square features projecting a determined attentiveness. Across the church Ted Newton nervously ran his fingers through his thick, wavy hair, looking puzzled but alert. Cliff Bright leaned slightly forward, his plump face expectant. When his wife frowned and touched his arm, he settled back but kept his eyes on the pastor.

Michael wondered, as he studied their faces, how many would respond to the proposal he was about to make. He plunged on, choosing his words carefully.

"What I'm going to suggest now shouldn't seem strange or fanatical, but I'm sure that at least some of you will see it in that light. I'll put it to you bluntly: I want volunteers from First Church who will, along with me, commit for one full year to take no action without first asking the question, 'What would Jesus do?' "

Michael paused, half expecting some audible reaction from the audience. But they sat frozen, every eye fixed intently on his face.

"After asking yourself that question, those of you who take this pledge will attempt to follow Jesus as best you know how, no matter what the consequences. After the service today, I will be in the lecture room to talk with everyone willing to join me in taking such a pledge."

He took a deep breath and let it out slowly. The paralyzed congregation began to stir, some members glancing at each other in astonishment. It wasn't like Michael Maxwell to suggest such a radical idea.

Three rows back, a secretary named Terri Bannister stared sightlessly at her burgundy leather Bible, considering the minister's challenge. She'd been attending First Church for two years now with her three children, despite her husband's scornful disapproval of "religious brainwashing." How would he react if she took such a pledge?

Directly behind her, Lauren Woods was also looking thoughtful. Deep in her heart there was a sudden stirring, an almost forgotten longing for—what? Was it possible the emptiness in her life was actually a yearning to walk with God Himself?

Michael closed the service in prayer, and then the worship team began to play softly. Rachel Wingate was noticeably missing from the front, as was Jason Clark. As the sanctuary began to empty, animated groups stood around talking about the pastor's radical proposition. Michael said good-bye to several visitors, then headed toward the lecture room.

He paused just outside the door, wondering who, if anyone, had responded to the challenge. Out of all the affluent and sophisticated members of First Church, he could think of less than a dozen men and women whose Christian commitment might lend itself to such a dramatic move. Uttering a silent prayer, he entered the room.

He was startled to find perhaps fifty people waiting. He glanced around, noting with some astonishment that along with Sharon and several dedicated members like Alex Powell and Daniel Marshall were some others he'd consider extremely unlikely to participate under the circumstances: Ted Newton, Jenny Paige, Rachel Wingate, Dr. West, and Jason Clark.

When the minister walked to the front, a hush fell over the crowd. He turned to face them, his strong face plainly revealing the depth of emotion he felt. Michael hadn't realized until that very moment what an overwhelming love he had for these earnest-faced men and women. His eyesight momentarily blurred, and he was forced to bow his head to regain control before he spoke. "Will you please pray with me?" he asked quietly.

"Lord, we are gathered here today to begin a great adventure with You. We don't know where it will take us, and we feel a little uncertain about the future, but we trust You to guide us in this endeavor step by step."

From the very first word he uttered, the almost tangible presence of the Holy Spirit filled the room, touching them all. As the prayer went on, this Presence grew in power, bringing tears to many people's eyes. If an audible voice had spoken from heaven to bless the bold step they were taking, not one person present would have felt any more certain of God's approval.

When the prayer ended there was a silence that lasted several minutes. Michael slowly looked up, seeing his own sense of wonder reflected in Sharon's eyes, as well as in the faces of many of the others. For a moment he couldn't speak.

"As you know," he finally said with difficulty, "I've been forced this past week to face some very unpleasant truths about myself. Somewhere along the line, I started substituting programs and church activities for personal involvement with people. I could make up excuses for it, but the fact is, *it's not what Jesus would do*.

"So, as I announced this morning, I have determined for the next year, starting today, to live every day by asking myself, 'What would Jesus do?' Once I decide to the best of my ability what action He would take in a specific situation, I will try to follow through, regardless of the consequences.

"This is the pledge I'm making before you and before God. I'm glad many of you decided to join me."

There was a quiet but unanimous murmur of assent. Michael asked, "Are there any questions?"

Rachel Wingate raised her hand. "Pastor Maxwell," she said hesitantly, "I'm not really sure how I'm supposed to figure out what He would do in my place. I mean, life today is nothing like it was in Bible times."

Michael nodded. "I don't have a quick answer to that," he admitted, "but I know that if we pray and ask for guidance from the Holy Spirit, we'll have it. Remember what Jesus said?

'But when he, the Spirit of truth, comes,
he will guide you into all truth.
He will not speak on his own;
he will speak only what he hears,
and he will tell you what is yet to come.' "

John 16:13–15

"But what if someone else thinks Jesus would do something differently than you're doing it?" asked Daniel Marshall, thinking of the differing opinions expressed among the professors and theologians at Lincoln Christian College.

"You can't help that. But as long as we all do our best to follow Jesus' example as closely as possible, I can't believe there'll be too much confusion. The important thing is, once we ask the Spirit to tell us what Jesus would do and receive an answer, we have to act on it, regardless of the consequences to ourselves. Are we agreed?"

Everyone nodded, and Michael felt a growing sense of joy. *I don't know where all this will take us,* he thought in excitement, *but I'm certain this is the right thing to do.* After talking for a few more minutes, they agreed to meet in the lecture room again the following Sunday.

Alex Powell closed in prayer, and again the Spirit manifested Himself in power and love. Heads remained bowed a long time, and when the group slowly stood up to leave, there was a feeling of awe that prevented speech. Sharon walked outside with Rachel Wingate and Lauren Woods.

After the room cleared, Michael retreated to his office and knelt beside the couch to pray. He remained there by himself for almost an hour, unaware that he and First Church would soon witness the most remarkable series of events the city of Ashton had ever known.

3

Ted Newton walked through the doors of Channel 5, WFBB-TV, on Monday morning with a new, but still unformed, resolve. Although the tall, energetic station manager had stayed after church Sunday largely on impulse, he had been firm in taking the pledge to make decisions only after asking, "What would Jesus do?" Now, as he considered what that might mean in the days and weeks ahead, he felt both excited and apprehensive.

Arriving a few minutes early, he sat down at his desk and automatically glanced at his appointment calendar. As usual, it was packed solid. But this time, instead of immediately plunging into the day's tasks, Ted got up and closed his door. Feeling distinctly awkward, he knelt beside his desk on the plush carpet and silently asked the Holy Spirit to direct him that day.

Then he got up, switched on the TV monitor bank that stretched along one wall of his office, and settled back in his comfortable leather chair to read the "overnights," the area-wide ratings from the previous day's programming. Every few minutes, he glanced up to scan the TV screens which simultaneously monitored Channel 5 and four of its biggest Chicago competitors. As president and general manager of the local network affiliate, it was his responsibility to make sure their station consistently captured a major share of the market.

This morning the overnights looked good; their prime-time programming the previous evening had drawn an 18 rating and 31 percent share, and they'd shown a healthy profit. In a gesture familiar to those who worked with him, Ted ran his fingers nervously through his hair and bent closer to compare their performance with the competition's. With another "sweeps" period on the horizon, it was crucial that advertisers saw Channel 5 as *the* place to buy air time.

He was still studying the ratings sheet when the program director tapped on the door and stuck his head inside.

"Do you have time to talk about that 'Wednesday's Child' special for next week?" Keith Walton asked. "I need to know if we're going to preempt the network programming to air it."

Ted smiled and waved him in. "This is probably as good a time as any. Have a seat."

Keith settled himself comfortably into a chair, admiring the office's expensive decor. Lush green plants were positioned near the plate glass window, and the textured walls were adorned with various impressionist paintings and plaques. A small, framed picture of Newton's smiling, blond wife and twelve-year-old daughter was propped by his appointment calendar. His mahogany desk was scattered with engraved paperweights and mementos presented to him for years of community service.

"Looking at our lineup for next Wednesday," Keith said, "I think it would be a major mistake to bump 'Lexa' to air a show about abused children who need homes. We're already struggling in that time slot, and a depressing show like that might send us down even farther."

Ted considered it briefly. "I think you're right. Let's stay with the scheduled programming."

"Sounds good."

The program director was almost to the door when Ted suddenly said, "Keith? Just a minute."

It had struck him belatedly that he'd made the decision without any thought to the pledge he had taken. Now, with a conscious effort, he silently asked himself, *What would Jesus do in this situation?*

"On second thought," he said slowly, "I think maybe we should run 'Wednesday's Child' after all. We'll preempt 'Lexa' this time and hope for the best."

"But why?" Keith asked, puzzled.

"That's my decision. Let production know, will you?"

"But—," the program director stared at his boss in astonishment. "But Ted, that's just—"

The general manager cut him off with a placatory gesture. "I guess I owe you an explanation," he said. "Come back in and close the door."

When Keith sat back down, Newton looked at him appraisingly. The program director attended a small fellowship on the outskirts of Ashton's south side, a blighted residential area generally avoided by the larger churches. Although the two men had worked together at the station for over three years and enjoyed a comfortable relationship, they had never discussed religious issues.

That was about to change.

"Keith," Ted said, "if Jesus Christ were the general manager of Channel 5, do you think He would run a talk show about—," he flipped through several papers and continued, " 'Older Women, Younger Men,' in place of a special that might help needy children find adoptive homes?"

Keith laughed. "You're kidding, right?"

"No, I'm really not," Ted responded mildly. "What do you think He would do?"

"Probably run 'Wednesday's Child.' But—"

"There are no 'buts.' I made a commitment yesterday not to make any decisions for the next year without first asking myself, 'What would Jesus do?' That's the reason for my decision."

Keith slumped in his chair, looking a little dazed. "If this gets back to the Broadcast Division, they're going to explode. I mean, I'm all for it, but do you honestly think this station can operate successfully like that? People want to be entertained, not preached at. In an ideal world, doing the right thing would always pay off—but this isn't an ideal world. We'll lose viewers, and advertisers will pull their accounts." He gave Ted a sharp look. "You'll lose your contract."

Ted nodded slowly. "If we start losing viewers, that's exactly what will happen. But," he added, "I can't help but think that at least some people will appreciate an attempt on our part to show increased integrity in what we air. We might do better than ever!"

Keith, still skeptical, muttered darkly, "I hope you're right."

Leaving Newton's office, the program director wore a bewildered look, like a man who'd stumbled by accident into a stranger's house. He was both impressed and shaken by his boss's unlikely decision to run the station by a higher standard. It was risky—but what an incredible adventure it could be if it succeeded!

As he made his way back to his own department, however, he shook his head. *It won't work,* he thought glumly. *I just hope he doesn't take the rest of us down with him.*

Ted was struggling with the same thought. Having made the decision, he was willing to bear the personal consequences of his actions. But was it fair to involve station employees like Keith in a venture that might prove to be disastrous?

What would Jesus do?

He pulled out a sheet of paper and, after a moment's hesitation, wrote neatly across the top:

WHAT JESUS MIGHT DO IN TED NEWTON'S POSITION

1. He wouldn't pressure subordinates to support His decisions, only to comply with them. He would make it clear that any protests they voiced would not jeopardize their positions in any way.

2. If the public reacted negatively to the programming changes, He would openly take the blame.

I could let the Ashton Herald *television critic know I'd made the changes over my program director's protests,* Ted thought wryly. *That would get the word out quickly enough.* He paused, his eyes straying to the picture of his small family. Kim and Ashley had left right after church to go shopping for Ashley's school orchestra dress and had missed the meeting about the First Church pledge. How would they react if his actions cost him his job? After a moment he continued, his face grave:

3. If it became apparent that the attempt to profitably run Channel 5 by the standard of asking, "What would Jesus do?" was failing, and that the company was losing money due to His personal commitment, He would offer to voluntarily terminate His two-year contract and resign as president and general manager.

Ted sighed. Now, if Keith Walton was proved right in his gloomy assessment, no one but Ted himself would suffer.

4

THE PRE-DAWN AIR WAS DAMP AND CHILLY, THE SKY gray, as Alex Powell strode briskly through the airport employee parking garage. Reaching the elevator, he pressed the call button, straightening his sports coat and tie as he waited. This crisp Wednesday morning already held the promise of turning into a long and difficult day.

Powell, a broad-shouldered black man in his late fifties, managed the Vickers Field Operations Division. He stepped through the elevator doors, pressed "2," then waited as the mechanism creaked and groaned its way slowly upward. The regional airport, built almost forty years earlier, was definitely feeling its age.

And so am I, thought Alex ruefully, rubbing one graying temple as he thought of the day ahead. *Until we decide how to fix the noise problem out at the runup building, I'm going to do nothing but sit in meetings.*

Still musing, Powell stepped out onto the second floor, waving at Maggie, a young woman on the custodial crew. She shyly returned his wave before bending back to her task of cleaning a water fountain.

Entering the airport operations department, Alex paused to

pour himself a cup of coffee before heading back to his own rather small office. Vickers Field, although far larger than many regional airports, was still modest by comparison to Chicago's O'Hare International, only forty-five minutes away by commuter flight. But the advantages of working at Vickers—less bureaucracy and more ability to have a personal impact—more than compensated for the cramped office space.

Powell lowered himself into his desk chair and, coffee mug in hand, picked up the daily report: two stapled pages detailing weather conditions, maintenance or custodial problems, airport activities and an inspection checklist. Scanning down the pages, he was relieved to see that no "139s"—serious problems requiring immediate action—had occurred since he'd left the previous evening.

The few problems listed were simple ones: (1) Light out above Grey Aero Tech hangar; (2) Clocks in main terminal not reset for daylight saving time. Chuck Finley, Powell's managerial counterpart in Facilities, had probably already dispatched workers to correct those items.

Finley, a licensed engineer, managed the airport's maintenance, repair, and custodial crews, while Powell was in charge of overall operations: inspections, security, emergency rescue crews, and ground transport. There were times, however, when their responsibilities overlapped, causing tension between them. It was part of Powell's job to make frequent inspection tours of the airport operations areas, noting repair or maintenance problems like pitted taxiways or peeling paint. The facilities manager often took his meticulous reports personally.

"Do you have to pick on *every* tiny detail?" Finley frequently demanded. "Are you just trying to make me look bad?" He was only slightly mollified by Alex's assurances that he was just doing his job.

Now, as Alex prepared to work his way down the list of noise and security issues he needed to discuss with the airport board, he paused, as he did most mornings, to silently commit his day to the Lord. It was a habit he had formed years before during a difficult recovery from alcoholism. That experience had taught him, far more effectively than any sermon, how to rely on God's presence in his daily life. He credited it with holding his marriage together during those painful months.

Despite his strong commitment, however, Alex had been intrigued by Michael Maxwell's challenge. Was it possible, he wondered, that he had fallen into comfortable Christian routines that had left him blind to the needs of those around him? Was he truly living as Jesus would in his place?

Open my eyes, he now prayed simply, *and show me how to imitate You today.*

The morning passed quickly. Powell and Finley met briefly to discuss several minor maintenance problems, and then they decided to break for lunch.

A surprisingly good Italian restaurant, "Ciccio's," was located in the airport. Standing in the cafeteria line, Powell spotted Maggie and an older woman on the custodial crew sitting down at a corner table. As he watched they started spreading out home-packed lunches. Almost instantly, the restaurant manager swooped down on their table. His deep voice carried across the small room.

"I'm sorry," he said icily, "but you can't bring your lunches in here. You need to go to the employee break room."

Maggie looked embarrased. "But we bought drinks here, and I bought a salad. I'd rather skip lunch than eat in that break room. It's so gloomy and filthy it makes me lose my appetite."

The man gave her a haughty look. "Then why don't you clean it? Aren't you good at that job?"

Maggie hastily began to gather her lunch and help her friend with hers. She jumped when Alex Powell suddenly appeared and towered over the table.

"Have a seat," he told Maggie firmly, then turned to the manager. "These two ladies will be my guests for lunch today."

Finley, just behind him, took in the scene with thinly-veiled astonishment. What was Alex thinking to invite two *janitors* to sit with them?

Powell took a seat, noting Finley's disapproval with wry amusement. "You don't have to sit with us," he said dryly. "I see

Roger in line; he'll probably be looking for a table in just a minute."

"Actually, I had something I needed to discuss with him anyway, and this *would* be the perfect time. Sure you don't mind?"

"Not at all. Good talking to you, Chuck."

Alex watched the facilities manager retreat to the safety of the other table, then turned to smile encouragingly at Maggie and her friend. In their weary faces he found all the assurance he needed that he'd done the right thing.

You acted on My behalf, a still, small voice seemed to whisper. *Well done, My good and faithful servant.*

That afternoon, before he left for home, Alex Powell made an unaccustomed diversion to the employee break room in the basement. Walking in slowly, he noted the peeling linoleum, the dirty green walls devoid of any decoration, and the water-stained ceiling tiles. The metal table legs were rusted and the vinyl seat cushions were cracked with age. The only "luxury" in the room—a single soda machine—had an Out of Order sign taped across it. He stood there for several minutes, lost in thought. It was only gradually that an exciting idea began to stir at the back of his mind.

5

IT WAS SUNDAY MORNING, AND FIRST CHURCH OF ASH-
ton was crowded once again. There was excitement in the air, a
kind of breathless anticipation as the time drew near for the
service to begin. Even the worship team seemed to feel it. As they
started playing the morning prelude, several instrumentalists
closed their eyes, focusing their attention on the Lord rather than
the audience. A sweet spirit seemed to fill the church and the
hearts of those gathered there.

Ted and Kim Newton were talking quietly when Dr. Patricia
West came in and looked around the sanctuary. Recognizing the
station manager from the after-church meeting the previous Sunday, she smiled and extended her hand.

"How has your week been?" she asked, broadening her smile
to include Kim. "For me, it's definitely been a strange seven
days."

Ted returned her handshake, then introduced Kim. "I know
what you mean," he said excitedly. "I felt like I woke up Monday
morning in a whole new country where I had to rethink even my
simplest decisions. It's odd, though; I feel better, less stressed,

than I have in years. It's nice to know that if I follow Jesus, it's *His* job to worry about the future."

Kim reacted to her husband's words by shooting a sharp glance in his direction. After fourteen years of marriage, she thought she knew Ted well. He'd always been outgoing and impulsive, a "workaholic" who wasn't happy unless he had several projects going at one time. He was usually miserable on vacations, anxious to get back to the station.

For the past week, though, he'd been acting—well, strange. He kept talking about this "pledge" he had taken and trying to convince her to stay after church this week with him to hear about it. They'd been discussing it—arguing, really—when the doctor interrupted. Kim wanted to understand, but she was deeply disturbed. What if this new idea of Ted's compromised his position at Channel 5?

Across the sanctuary, Jenny Paige, Alex Powell, and his wife, Cheryl, were also talking about their experiences. Jenny, her silver hair loosely gathered in an elegant knot, had chosen a seat beside the Powells near the front of the church. Roger also sat with them, but appeared more interested in scanning the congregation for potential business contacts than in his mother's conversation.

The Powells were both animated, so obviously excited about something, that Jenny finally asked in amusement, "What's happening that I don't know about?"

Alex laughed. "It's probably not all that exciting, but it looks like an idea I had this last week is going to work out." He went on to explain, "I just talked with Pastor Maxwell, and he's agreed to come to Vickers Field to lead a twice-weekly Bible study before hours in the employee break room. I cleared it with the director of Aviation, and I also talked him into having the break room refurbished to make it a decent place for the work crews to relax."

Jenny looked thoughtful. "Do you think any of the workers will actually show up for a Bible study?"

"Eight people already said they'd come, and that they'd bring others."

Cheryl smiled. "He hasn't been this excited about work in a

long time. I think he'd be out at Vickers Field today if I'd let him!"

Just then the service started.

After the opening prayer and choruses, Michael Maxwell stepped up and laid his Bible on the pulpit, but he didn't immediately start into the message. Instead, he looked out over the congregation with a sudden, deep stirring of compassion, the feeling of a loving shepherd for his flock. The wrenching intensity of his emotions left him momentarily unsettled.

"Today," he finally began, "I'll be preaching a message titled 'God's Wake-Up Call.' For some of you it will only reinforce what you've experienced this past week; for others, it will probably seem overly blunt or even offensive. All I can tell you is that I honestly believe, in keeping with the pledge I made last week, that this is what Jesus would preach in my place."

The sermon that followed was dramatically different from those he had preached in the past. Rather than using clever phrases to appeal to his listeners' intellects or delivering a calculated "feel-good" message, he wielded God's Word to strip away systematically all the sophisticated excuses for lives ruled by lust, greed, or selfish ambition.

"Jesus was known as a friend of sinners," he said. "He offered mercy and forgiveness to thieves, adulterers, even murderers. He reserved His harshest words for 'religious' people: self-righteous churchgoers who lived by their own rules, who often painlessly gave to noble causes but turned a deaf ear to the poor and helpless on their own doorsteps. He had a name for those people. He called them 'hypocrites.' "

There was a long moment of silence as the full implication of his words swept across the congregation. Some faces showed shock and indignation. Just who was Pastor Maxwell accusing of hypocrisy? The very people who paid his salary every week? Several exchanged glances, already planning their irate comments once the service ended.

Others' faces, however, held a solemn acknowledgment of the truth—and even more, a hunger for guidance. Like the young man who cried, "What must I do to be saved?" they waited to hear what they should do to be counted worthy of the name "Christian."

Michael continued, "In the Gospel of Mark, Jesus said this:

'If anyone would come after me, he must deny himself
and take up his cross and follow me.
For whoever wants to save his life will lose it, but whoever loses his life for me and for the gospel will save it.

'What good is it for a man to gain the whole world,
yet forfeit his own soul?
Or what can a man give in exchange for his soul?

'If anyone is ashamed of me and my words
in this adulterous and sinful generation,
the Son of Man will be ashamed of him
when he comes in his Father's glory with the holy angels.'
        Mark 8:34–38

"I believe the time has come for us to ask ourselves some hard questions. In this self-serving age when most of us are reluctant to forgo any luxury or desire, what, on a practical level, have we denied ourselves? What cross have we borne for Christ's sake? What suffering have we willingly endured?" He looked out over the congregation, vaguely aware of Alex Powell's slight nod and Cliff Bright's thoughtful gaze. There was a hushed stillness across the sanctuary, an almost holy sense of reflection. *Please, Lord,* Maxwell prayed, *let this message reach their hearts.*

"God's wake-up call for some of us might be to put aside an expensive vacation or new car and follow Him in giving to those in need; for others it might be to sacrifice our social standing in order to speak out against moral compromise. The 'cross' you are called to bear will probably be different from mine and from that of your neighbor's.

"But the fact is, if you're a Christian, you have been called by God to embark on an incredible adventure, an 'abundant life' that involves both joy and sacrifice. How many are willing to accept that calling? How many would rather stay comfortably asleep, untouched by the world that's dying around us?"

His ringing words hung in the air, reverberating as a living sword of truth that pierced the very hearts and souls of those who listened. When he led in prayer, some who had never before wept in church found their faces wet with tears.

To close the service, Rachel Wingate stood up to sing. Her voice rose, strong and sweet, in a quiet hymn of praise, but this time something was different. She wasn't "performing"; she was rejoicing in God's goodness. Her lovely face was transformed, all traces of her former vanity gone. The audience instinctively sensed the change without fully understanding it.

Michael asked those who had remained after the service the previous week to briefly meet again in the lecture room and also invited any others willing to take the pledge to join them. After speaking with a few visitors, he hurried back to the lecture room. He noted without comment that some long-standing members—including Martha Robinson, the church treasurer—had formed a small, unhappy group in the lobby. Several of them, seeing his glance, quickly looked away.

The crowd in the lecture room had almost doubled this time. Michael moved among them murmuring joyful greetings. He saw that Kim Newton had come with Ted this time, although she appeared uncomfortable. In the far back he spotted Cliff Bright, without his wife's company. The plump store owner looked both miserable and determined.

Michael made his way over to him and clasped his hand warmly. "Glad to see you, Cliff," he said quietly. "I guess Elizabeth didn't want to come?" Cliff shook his head. "She didn't want *me* to come either. I wanted to last week, but—" His round face bore a look of pain and sorrow that brought to Michael's mind Jesus' words:

"I did not come to bring peace, but a sword. . . . 'A man's enemies will be the members of his own household.'

"Anyone who loves his father or mother more than me is not worthy of me;
anyone who loves his son or daughter more than me is not worthy of me;

and anyone who does not take his cross and follow me is not worthy of me."
  Matthew 10:34, 36–38

As before, Michael opened with prayer. And as before, the Holy Spirit swept through the room. Afterward, the group talked informally, asking questions and comparing experiences.

Alex Powell shared his news about the employee Bible study beginning at the airport. "I believe that in my place Jesus would be concerned about the employees, both spiritually and physically. It'll be easier for them to believe that God cares for them if they see that *I* care for them."

Terri Bannister nodded. "I wish more Christians thought like that. My boss goes to church every Sunday and talks about God all the time, but he always cuts my lunch break short or expects me to work overtime without pay. When I mention it he acts surprised, but nothing ever changes. If I didn't already know the Lord, I'd have a bad attitude toward God because of him." Several others agreed.

Then Ted Newton revealed that he had declined to purchase another year's programming of "Lexa."

"I went through a list of Lexa's shows this past year, and it made me sick. She did interviews like, 'Mothers and Daughters Who Share the Same Lover' and 'Men Who've Killed Their Wives—and Gone Free.' 'Lexa' is one of our most popular daytime shows, but I can't justify it any longer. We're replacing it with a new interactive talk show, 'On Call,' that'll have a changing panel of child psychologists, marriage counselors, drug and alcohol addiction experts, and so forth. They'll take calls and answer questions, then use a computerized list of free counseling services to refer viewers to local help."

"How do you think most people will react to the change?" asked Jason Clark.

"At first, probably like the president of the Broadcast Division," Ted said wryly. "He thought I was crazy. But after I showed him some demographic studies of who our viewers are and surveys showing they're asking for more 'family fare,' he finally agreed to try it. If it doesn't work, though—" Ted raised one dark eyebrow and shrugged. "He's taking a big risk on my word."

A few others shared their experiences at home or on the job and received support and encouragement in turn. When they finally adjourned after silent prayer, many in the group seemed reluctant to leave.

That night, Michael and Sharon stayed up late talking about what they had seen and heard that day. Sharon had spent almost an hour after the evening service talking with Jenny Paige.

"I've never really had the chance before to get to know her," she told Michael, "but she's really serious about this pledge. Did you know that she's the one who just bought the old Jeffers Building downtown?"

"No, but it doesn't surprise me. She and her son own half the commercial property in Ashton's south side."

Sharon looked thoughtful. "She said she was having a hard time deciding what Jesus would do in her place. He never had money or owned property, so the Bible doesn't give her a direct example to follow. She asked us to pray with her about that." She hesitated. "She also asked us to pray for Roger. He hasn't come to either of the pledge meetings, has he?"

"No, and I don't think he's going to. To tell the truth, I think he just comes to church out of habit or maybe to establish business contacts. He's got a pretty wild reputation, the typical 'too much, too soon' scenario. I wouldn't be surprised if he's into some pretty exotic 'recreational' drugs." He added thoughtfully, "I wonder if things would've been different if his father hadn't died when he did. Fourteen is a tough age to be left fatherless."

Before bed, they kneeled together to pray for Jenny, Roger, and many of the others. For the first time in years they both felt connected, closely linked to the lives, joys, and sorrows of their First Church "family."

6

CLIFF BRIGHT PERCHED UNCOMFORTABLY ON THE kitchen barstool in his posh north Ashton home, drinking coffee and pretending to read the morning paper. The small color television nestled on the counter beneath the polished oak spice cabinets was tuned to Channel 5 News. Although it was barely 8:30 that Monday morning, there had already been a three-car accident on the freeway and a domestic shooting on the south side which left two people dead.

Elizabeth walked in and set her coffee cup down by the sink with unnecessary force. When Cliff flinched, she whirled on him.

"So you're going ahead anyway?" she demanded, her eyes hard behind her glasses. "You're going to ignore my feelings about this silly pledge business and go along with those religious fanatics at First Church? I can't believe it. I just can't believe it!"

"Liz, it's not like that at all," he protested. "I told you; there were about a hundred people there. Even Jenny Paige took the pledge, and *she's* sure no religious fanatic. It's just—it's just something I feel like I should do."

When she didn't respond, Cliff added with unaccustomed

firmness, "I'm sorry you're upset. But I already took the pledge, and I'm not going to back out now."

The Brights, to most casual observers, appeared to live an almost storybook existence. They had married straight out of college, when Cliff was a handsome, easygoing accountant and Elizabeth was a popular and cheerful beauty queen. For a wedding present Elizabeth's father, owner of a successful grocery chain in the Southwest, had set Cliff up in his own business by buying him a small corner grocery store in Ashton.

"With a lot of hard work, you'll build this one store into a whole string of stores," he'd told his young son-in-law. "That's how I started, and look at me now!" Elizabeth was thrilled.

Both father and daughter failed to notice that Cliff wasn't interested in owning a string of retail stores. It was a position utterly unsuited to his retiring personality. But what could he do? He thanked his father-in-law and set about the business of being a store owner.

Now, years later, he had succeeded beyond expectations. From that first store, Cliff had built a chain of eighteen thriving Mr. B Food Stores. He was a rich and busy man, and if he ever recalled with regret his early dreams of owning and operating his own small accounting firm, he never mentioned it.

"So what do you plan to do," Elizabeth asked scathingly, "hang pictures of Jesus in all our stores? That'll be great for business."

"No," Cliff said slowly. "I really don't know yet what I'm going to do. I need time to think about it." Elizabeth stormed out of the kitchen, leaving Cliff to stare disconsolately at the paper.

I wonder if it would've been different if we'd been able to have kids, he thought for the millionth time. *Maybe Liz wouldn't be so bitter and pushy. She wanted a baby so badly.*

Three miles away, in the Newton's brightly wallpapered kitchen, Ted and Kim were bustling around getting ready to leave. Kim worked three mornings a week at Holden Jeweler's in the Ashton Square Mall appraising, cleaning, and repairing jewelry. Her boss had called the previous afternoon to say there were already two rings and a broken bracelet awaiting her attention.

She was rinsing her coffee cup when Ted suddenly stepped up behind her, wrapped her in his arms, and leaned down to quickly kiss her. She laughed, smoothing her wavy, blond hair back into place.

"What's that for?"

"For being such a nice little wife," Ted quipped, then ducked as she slapped playfully at him. "No, really, I'm just glad to be married to you. I feel very lucky."

Kim giggled. "You know, I'm still not sure about this pledge thing at church, but I have to admit you've been a lot nicer to live with lately."

Ted grinned. "In that case, how about meeting me for lunch today? We haven't done that in a long time."

"Sounds good. See you at noon?"

In a modest brick home in the Ashlake subdivision, Terri Bannister had just sent the last of her kids off to the school bus stop. Like so many mornings, Ray had been so rushed that he'd barely taken time to speak to her and the children before he left. It was like he no longer cared that he had a family.

Now, with just fifteen minutes to spare before she had to leave for work, she sat down at the kitchen table and bowed her head.

"Father," she said quietly, "please guide me today in Your ways. And please, Lord, help Ray come to know You."

In an attractively furnished off-campus apartment, Rachel Wingate was just getting up, squinting against the bright sunlight shafting in through her bedroom window. Spring break was over, time once again to hit the books. Her first class started at ten o'clock. Pushing her heavy auburn hair back from her face, she walked, yawning, to the kitchen, and put a cup of water in the microwave. While she waited, she inserted a disc into the CD player in the living room. She liked starting the morning out with music.

A few minutes later, as she sipped hot tea, she wondered—

again—how Hallie Collier was doing. It was odd how, in just five short days, the child had become such an important part of her life. The apartment had seemed empty ever since the little girl left for Arizona with her grandparents.

Rachel was momentarily startled when the wall phone rang loudly a few feet away. Still holding her tea, she picked up the receiver.

It was Jason. "Hi, beautiful," he said. "What're you doing?"

Rachel realized that, because of her thoughts, she'd been half expecting it to be the Andersons, Hallie's grandparents. Unfairly, she found Jason's smooth voice suddenly irritating.

"Waking up," she said shortly. "Look, Jason, I've got class this morning, and I'm running a little behind. Can I call you later."

"Sure. Talk to you then."

Rachel hung up, a little confused by her feelings. She and Jason had been dating steadily for over a year, and lately they'd started talking seriously of marriage. They both loved music and dancing, and there was no question that they found each other attractive. Everyone said they were perfect for each other. *So what's my problem?* Rachel wondered. *Just because he griped about my keeping Hallie is no reason to feel this way. It just bothered me that he kept making snide comments about her being black.*

Still musing, she got dressed and went into the bathroom to put on her makeup. It was then that she spotted the yellow note she'd stuck on the mirror the night before: What Would Jesus Do? *Maybe that's it,* Rachel thought. *Jason took the pledge with me, but it doesn't seem to have meant nearly as much to him. That really bothers me.*

Cheryl Powell looked out her kitchen window, admiring the new green leaves on the towering maple tree in the backyard. She loved the ranch-style home she and Alex had saved for and had built on five wooded acres.

After seeing Alex off several hours earlier, she had enjoyed a few minutes of peace and quiet before her one-year-old grand-daughter arrived. She baby-sat little Cara from 7:00 a.m. until noon every day while her daughter worked part time as a nurse's aide.

Now, with the baby contentedly playing with blocks on the living room floor, Cheryl settled down on the couch and opened her Bible. She read for a few minutes, then bowed her head.

Please let Your Spirit lead me today, she prayed. *And show Alex how to be Your representative at the airport.*

At a graceful mansion on Harmony Creek, Jenny Paige paused to pray before she left for her office. . . . Daniel Marshall kneeled in his study to ask for guidance that day at Lincoln Christian College. . . . Dr. West, preparing for an early surgery, silently committed both herself and her patient to the great Physician. . . . Across the city, in various ways, those touched by the First Church pledge prepared for a new day and week of faithfully following in Jesus' steps.

7

MICHAEL MAXWELL ROSE FROM HIS KNEES, THEN slowly walked over to the window. The sky was bright and cloudless.

In the distance, an airplane began its approach toward Vickers Field. Michael saw it sparkle as it circled downward and caught the morning's sunlight. It made him think of Alex Powell. *I still don't know what I'm going to say out there at the Bible study tomorrow morning,* he thought. *I wish I knew more about the problems those people face.*

He'd spent most of the morning praying about that and many other things. His path, in so many ways, was unclear. He needed a concrete plan, some definite course of action for his pastorate of First Church.

With sudden determination, he went back to his desk, turned on his computer, and typed in a centered heading: Things Jesus Probably Would Do as Pastor of First Church. At first all his conflicting ideas made it difficult to sort out his thoughts. But finally he began:

1. He would preach fearlessly against hypocrisy, even if it offended powerful people in His congregation.

2. He would, without hesitation, befriend people of all kinds, disregarding His "image" and not considering Himself above them in any way.

3. He would make sure that all church advertising glorified God instead of people or institutions.

Michael paused, aware of his hesitation to go on. The first three items already meant, for him, some fairly radical changes. But as he'd prayed, he had become increasingly convinced that he needed to ask himself some hard questions—and face the answers.

He continued:

4. He would live in a simple manner, without needless luxury on one hand or undue asceticism on the other.

5. He would work tirelessly to reach and restore those entangled in drug and alcohol abuse and other worldly traps.

6. He would give up the summer trip to Italy and use the money for something less self-indulgent.

He was so absorbed in his thoughts that at first he didn't hear Sharon saying, "Michael? Someone is here to see you."

Behind her stood a sharply-dressed young man who looked vaguely familiar. Michael shook his hand and asked him to be seated. "I don't want to take up too much of your time, Reverend," the man said, "but my partner and I had heard about your church band, and on Sunday we came to hear it for ourselves. It was absolutely incredible!"

Surprised at Michael's lack of response, he continued, "Anyway, I'm here because our company, V. C. Productions, has been looking everywhere for a female singer to play a supporting role in a movie we'll be shooting in Chicago. Your female vocalist—Rachel Wingate, is it?—looks like she'd be perfect."

"What kind of movie is it?" Michael asked slowly.

"It's fantastic, a psychological thriller about a young man with multiple personalities. We'd like to audition Rachel for the role of his girlfriend, a nightclub singer. This guy ends up killing both his parents and almost killing her."

Michael felt sick. "Look, I'll give your card to Ms. Wingate, but I don't know if she'll be interested. If she wants to talk to you, she'll call you back direct. Okay?"

"Fine, fine. But I'll need to hear from her by next week, one way or the other. There's a lot of money involved and plenty of other women who'd kill for a part like this."

After the man left, Maxwell stared unseeingly at the business card in his hand, then went back to his knees. For the next hour he interceded on Rachel's behalf, knowing that the young singer would soon face a difficult decision which could easily change the entire course of her life.

It was a rainy Thursday morning in downtown Ashton. Cliff Bright sat in his sixth floor office at the Ashton Towers going over the previous day's sales reports from his stores. He made notes on a few and set them aside.

A slow and careful thinker, Bright had spent the last three days considering how to apply practically his pledge to ask, "What would Jesus do?" Although some matters still weren't clear, one thing he'd quickly determined—the soft porn magazines stocked in his stores would have to go.

He buzzed his secretary. "Rebecca? Can you come in here please?"

After dictating a company-wide memo ordering that effective immediately all pornographic magazines should be pulled from the shelves, he returned to his scrutiny of the sales reports.

Most of the stores were thriving, but there were one or two serious problems. Store #16 had a continuing pattern of inventory shortage, most likely due to either shoplifting or employee theft. Unfortunately, it was an all-too-common problem. *I'll put security on it,* he thought. *If we don't stop the problem, I'll have to bring in a new manager.*

Another troubled store was #12. Bright noted that sales had dropped over 25 percent in the last six weeks. The accounting department had also attached a note saying that several customers had called to complain that the manager, Connie Garza, had snapped at them.

Bright frowned. Connie had always been one of his best managers: bright, cheerful, popular with customers. It didn't sound like her. He made a note to pay a visit that afternoon to her store.

At WFBB-TV, Ted Newton was dealing with a different kind of problem. Seated across from his desk were two well-dressed salesmen from Adray Brothers, a major distributor of syndicated programming. They were pushing hard to convince him to buy a package of three shows.

One salesman leaned forward in his chair with an earnest look. "I'm really trying to do you a favor here, Mr. Newton. We've already got a strong bid on this package from another station, but I'd like to see you get it. What do you say?"

Ted studied him for a moment, then replied with steel in his voice, "I already told you I'd take the children's science program and 'Movie Reviewers,' but I definitely don't want 'Exposé.' You know as well as I do that tying programs together like that is illegal."

The salesman looked offended. "Look, Mr. Newton, business is business, and anyway, it's no secret that the top shows are only available in packages."

Ted didn't immediately reply. It was true, of course, and in the past he had often bought packages in order to get what he wanted. But now . . .

He abruptly stood up and faced the startled men.

"Then I guess that ends our conversation, gentlemen. I won't participate in unethical practices, and if this is the only way you'll deal with me, you won't be selling to this station anymore at all. I'll see you to the door."

On the way back to his office, Ted wondered grimly how much of an impact the loss of "Movie Reviewers" and "Kid Whiz" would have on Channel 5. He would have to quickly find replacements to run in several sensitive time slots.

But it was the right thing to do, he thought. *Going along with an underhanded deal would make me just as guilty as them.*

His thoughts were interrupted by a tap on the door. Keith Walton entered the office with a broad smile.

"Have you heard the news yet about yesterday's 'Wednesday's Child' show?" he asked.

"No. What happened?"

"We just got a call a few minutes ago from a supervisor with the Child Protective Services. You know the five children who were featured? Since we aired the show, CPS has had over *twenty* calls from families interested in adopting them! She asked if there was any way we would consider running a weekly 'Wednesday's Child' program to help some of the other children find homes."

The news instantly dispelled Ted's earlier gloom. "That's fantastic!" he exclaimed. "What do you think about the idea, Keith?"

The program director grinned sheepishly. "I know I gave you a hard time about it last week, but the more I thought about it, the more convinced I was that you were right. I think we ought to try a weekly show, at least as an experiment."

Keith paused. "Oh, and Ted—," he said, "I want you to know that what you said about your pledge and everything has really made me start thinking. I respect the stand you took." The two men shook hands, grinning, aware of a new bond between them.

Despite the gray drizzle falling steadily on Vickers Field, Alex Powell was having a great day. Sixteen employees had shown up for this morning's Bible study in the break room with Pastor Maxwell. He'd been a little surprised at how quickly the mostly black work crews had accepted the affluent white minister, but his eagerness to learn more about the problems they faced seemed to smooth the way for him to share the gospel.

And the break room looked terrific. The gloomy green walls had been painted a cheerful yellow and the stained ceiling tiles replaced. New tables and chairs had been installed atop gleaming new linoleum, and framed photographs of vintage airplanes graced the walls. The one broken soda machine had been replaced with four snack vending machines, along with a coffeepot, a small refrigerator, and a microwave.

Alex had just returned from lunch. He was in his office reviewing his latest "to do" list on the computer when Corey Snyder, one of five operations officers at the airport, politely knocked on the open door. He had attended the Bible study that morning.

"Alex?" he said. "Can I talk to you for a minute?"

Powell swiveled away from the computer and motioned for him to enter. Snyder dragged a straight chair closer to the desk and sat down.

"You said this morning that if anyone had any ideas about how to improve working conditions around here to tell you about it. I ate lunch in the break room with a bunch of the guys from the electrical shop, and they came up with some good suggestions. Do you have time to listen?"

"Just let me get something to write on." Powell fished out a legal pad from an untidy stack of papers on his desk, pulled a pen from his drawer, then said, "Okay, I'm ready."

"First of all, fixing up the break room was a great idea. When I was down there today there must have been fifteen or twenty people in there eating, and they all think you're a hero." Snyder grinned. "They're talking about hanging your picture in a place of honor over the microwave."

Powell chuckled, flattered. "That would make them all lose their appetites. I think they'd better stick with airplanes."

Snyder smiled. "Anyway, several of the older guys brought up the fact that they'd like to learn to use the computers in their departments instead of always having to depend on the younger workers. They wondered if some kind of in-house training program might be possible."

Powell was impressed. "I don't know why not. I actually think it's a great idea, and that's a skill they could transfer to other jobs too. I'll see what I can do." He made a note on the pad.

"Several others mentioned that in the city their same jobs involve both more responsibility and more money. They wondered if, at some point, they could have their positions redefined to get them more personally involved in how the airport is run. A lot of them have worked here for years, and they feel they could be used more efficiently—and paid more fairly."

Powell nodded slowly. "That sounds reasonable. You know, I wonder—what do you think about setting up some kind of monthly brainstorming session where employees can share ideas like this directly with management?"

"I think it would work. There are a lot of good people here who'd like to feel they can make a difference. Their satisfaction with their jobs would definitely go up if they felt someone was seriously listening to them."

"That's understandable. Thanks for taking the time, Corey. I'll see what I can do about these things."

After the operations officer left, Alex studied the notes he'd made on the legal pad. The effect of the pledge he'd taken was already spreading to an ever-widening group of people, some whose names he didn't even know. The realization left him both grateful and excited.

Cliff Bright eased his bulk with some difficulty from behind the steering wheel of his expensive car, now parked in front of Store #12. Through the glass storefront he could see Connie Garza waiting on a customer, a heavyset man in construction clothes.

When Cliff opened the door, an electronic chime sounded. Garza looked up, her eyes widening when she saw it was "Mr. B" himself.

He tried to ease her discomfort with a friendly smile, but the strain in her face was unmistakable. What had happened to etch those anxious lines into the bubbly young store manager's face?

"I just dropped by to check in with you, Connie," Bright said casually. "How's everything going?"

"Okay I guess, Mr. Bright," she replied with a soft Hispanic accent. When she turned to wait on another customer, Bright studied her profile. Although her thick dark hair was pulled neatly back into a ponytail, her uniform shirt had several stains. One button was missing, clumsily replaced with a safety pin. Her name tag was askew.

The store was also in less than immaculate condition. The floor needed sweeping, and many of the shelves were poorly stocked and in disarray. The glass doors of the refrigerated section were thickly fingerprinted.

When the store was empty again, Cliff said gently, "Connie, I think we need to talk."

To his dismay, her eyes instantly brimmed with tears. She sank onto the tall stool behind the counter and covered her face with both hands. Cliff watched helplessly as her shoulders began to shake with silent sobs.

Just then the bell sounded announcing the entrance of a customer. Cliff quickly moved behind the counter and spoke to the shaken manager. "Connie, go to the back and relax for a few minutes. I'll watch the counter."

The next time the store emptied, Bright hand-lettered a Closed for One Hour sign and taped it to the front door. Then he went back to the employee area where Garza waited.

She looked up. "I'm sorry, Mr. Bright," she said desperately. "I don't usually act like this; I really don't. It's just—"

Cliff held both palms up in a calming gesture. "It's okay. Let's just talk for a few minutes, all right?"

From the moment he'd seen the store's condition, Bright had realized the logical solution was to replace Garza. Although firing managers was one of his least favorite tasks, it was often necessary. He normally didn't hesitate.

But now, seeing Connie's condition, he didn't want to act hastily. Part of it was because of her past work record, but another part was due, oddly enough, to Brenda Collier. After her death, Bright had quietly inquired to see if the convenience store that had fired her when she got sick was one of his. As it turned out, it wasn't—but it easily could have been.

"Has something been going on with your family, Connie?" he asked. "You don't seem your usual self."

She didn't meet his eyes. "Yes, sir," she said. "Four months ago, my husband started having bad coughing fits. He's smoked since he was fourteen so he's always coughed a lot, but when he started coughing up blood I made him go to the doctor. They sent him in for a chest X-ray—he has lung cancer."

Cliff shook his head in sympathy but didn't say anything.

She went on, "He went in for surgery three weeks ago, and they took out part of one lung. He's been going through chemotherapy since then, but we don't really know how much good it's doing. He can't work, and he's sick all the time. It's taken every dime just to meet our part of the insurance."

She finally met Bright's eyes. "I know I've been letting things here slip," she said pleadingly. "I'll try to do better. I really will. I—I don't know what I'd do if I lost my job on top of everything else right now."

Bright quickly put her mind at ease. "You're not going to lose your job, Connie. You've been a good manager for a long time, and I know you'll work through this. What can I do to help you?"

Unexpectedly, the young manager once again burst into tears. "I don't know what to say," she sobbed in relief. "I'm so tired and irritable these days, and I barely have enough energy to get up in the morning, much less to stock shelves. I know my sales have gone down."

"Would it help if I temporarily assigned an extra clerk here to help you get everything back in order?"

"Yes, I think it would. Could you do that?"

Bright smiled. "I'm the boss, remember? I can do whatever I want." His words brought a faint smile to the harried manager's face.

Before he left, Bright called and arranged for a clerk to be transferred from one of the other stores to #12. He also invited Connie to church the following Sunday. "You need to be around people who care about you and your husband," he told her. "It can make a big difference to know you're not facing it all alone." She said she would try to come.

Cliff found himself humming as he drove back to his office. *Maybe,* he thought, *having to run a chain of convenience stores isn't so bad after all.*

8

RACHEL WINGATE STARED INCREDULOUSLY AT PASTOR Maxwell. Earlier, when she received the message from him requesting that she drop by the church office, she'd gone expecting to hear about a change in the music program for Sunday. Instead, Michael told her of the offer from V. C. Productions.

"You mean they actually want to give me a part where I'd get to sing?" she asked excitedly. "I can't believe it!"

Maxwell handed her the man's business card, then looked at her steadily. "He'll explain about the movie and part when you call him. But Rachel, why don't we pray about it now and ask for the Holy Spirit's guidance?" She quickly agreed.

Back at home, Rachel dialed the number for V. C. Productions and was soon put through to Mark Downs, one of the producers. He quickly described the movie, *Secret Rage,* and her part as a nightclub singer.

"This is a large role for a newcomer," he said, "but my partner and I heard you sing at First Church, and we think you'll be perfect. Can you come to our Chicago office Monday morning to read for us?"

"I'd love to," Rachel said, "but I'd like to ask a few questions first. Will this role require me—" she paused, then plunged on in embarrassment—"will it require me to curse or to appear in any—in any compromising scenes?"

Downs laughed. "Honey, give me a break. For God's sake, you'll be a *nightclub singer!* You'll have to swear, of course, and there's one love scene. But you don't have to get naked or anything; you can wear a flesh-colored body suit if you want. We'll manage the rest with camera angles."

Rachel was silent for a moment. "I'd like to have time to think this over. Can I call you back on Monday?"

Downs was irritated. "Sure, sure, honey. But I hope you have better sense than to let some moralistic ideas keep you from the chance of a lifetime. Talk to you then."

The phone clicked in Rachel's ear. Chewing her lip, she slowly replaced the receiver. She thought for a moment, then picked up the phone again and called Jason.

A few minutes later her doorbell rang. As always, Rachel was struck by Jason's physical presence, his muscular physique, and clear blue eyes. He took her in his arms briefly, then she invited him to sit down.

She quickly explained the offer from V. C. Productions. She told him everything, including the amount of money involved and the role requirements. Then she looked him in the face.

"What do you think I should do, Jason? It's a great opportunity, but I'm still not sure about it, especially in view of our First Church pledge. I mean, it's not *all* that bad, and I guess it might actually lead to other roles where I could be more selective, but still—"

Jason, excited, waved aside her concerns. "Hey, you can't expect your first role to be just what you want. But later on, who knows? You might be able to do a lot of good once you're established in the industry. Maybe this is God's plan for you."

His soothing words and reassurances slowly erased the troubled lines on Rachel's forehead. "Maybe you're right," she said, her eyes suddenly sparkling. "Oh, Jason, can you believe it? I'm going to be a *movie star!*"

It was only later, after he left, that she walked into her bathroom to see the small yellow note stuck on the mirror: What Would Jesus Do?

The simple words sent a wave of doubt washing over her again, leaving her torn and agitated. Irritated, she jerked the note off and crumpled it in her hand—then stood frozen, staring at her image in the mirror. Slowly, tears welled in her eyes and spilled down her cheeks.

What am I doing? she thought. Carefully smoothing the note, she stuck it back on the mirror, then went into her bedroom and sank to her knees on the white carpet.

Father, she prayed, *You know how much I'd like to do a movie. But if that's not what You want for me, I'll obey and follow You.*

At about that same time, Alex Powell was walking back into his office with a fresh cup of coffee, hoping to get some paperwork done. He had just set the cup down next to his computer when the phone rang.

"Alex?" said Chuck Finley. "Do you have a minute to talk about Jet-Rep?" Jet-Rep was an aircraft repair and maintenance company that was building a large new facility at Vickers Field.

"Sure. What's the problem?"

"No problem, really. We just need to speed things up. When do you think we'll get the board's approval for the security system we need?"

Alex grinned into the receiver. "You know how fast they move, Chuck. It could be next week, or it could be three weeks from now. Is there a rush?"

There was a slight pause. "Well," Finley said casually, "you know we've already got the runway extension under construction, and by next week the new building will be far enough along for us to start installing the security system. We can't afford any delays on this project."

Alex frowned, puzzled. "How can it possibly be that far along already? We only signed the agreement with Jet-Rep three months ago."

There was another significant pause. Four months before, when Jet-Rep had approached the airport about building a new facility on its grounds, it had caused a great deal of excitement. A lease agreement with the aircraft repair company would not only benefit the airport, it would also create almost five hundred new jobs in the area.

There was only one major problem: Vickers' runways weren't sufficient to handle the larger commercial aircraft Jet-Rep maintained and serviced. Although the location was ideal, Jet-Rep was considering two other regional airports as well.

"Alex," Finley finally said. "The only way we got Jet-Rep to commit to the lease agreement was by promising to have the facility *and* a runway extension finished in six months."

Alex was stunned. "How could you promise them that? It sometimes takes the board that long just to *approve* a big contract like that!"

"We didn't go through the board." Finley sighed. "Look, I know you're not going to like this, but going through normal channels would've made it impossible. Stokes and I talked to the director about it, and we found a way around all the red tape. Instead of presenting it as one major contract and going through the normal bidding and approval process, we divided it up into a number of smaller contracts, all under the per-item cost limits. We've had construction crews out there working around the clock for weeks."

Alex gripped the phone receiver tightly, a sick feeling deep in his stomach. "Did you talk to *any* of the board members about this?"

Finley laughed. "Are you kidding? Most of those guys are political appointees who don't know one end of an airplane from the other. They wouldn't care that it might cost Vickers the lease agreement with Jet-Rep. They'd insist on business as usual."

Now it was Alex's turn to be silent. Vickers Field was regulated by the city of Ashton with rigid standards and procedures for all airport expansion or improvements. What Finley had just described to him was borderline fraud, a deliberate flaunting of the regulatory board's authority.

Why did he have to tell me? he thought. *I'd rather not know anything about it.*

But like it or not, he did know—and he was now faced with a wrenching decision. What, if anything, should he do with his knowledge?

That Saturday, the *Ashton Herald* contained a feature article about Ted Newton. The Child Protective Services worker who had called Channel 5 to report the exciting results of the "Wednesday's Child" broadcast had also called the newspaper, hoping to apply public pressure to the station to air similar programs in the future. A reporter had been dispatched to WFBB-TV. The article started by detailing the happy results of the Wednesday broadcast, then continued:

> According to at least one Channel 5 employee, the decision to preempt the hit talk show "Lexa" in order to air the "Wednesday's Child" special was made by Ted Newton, president and general manager of WFBB-TV. But apparently it was just one of many controversial decisions Newton has recently made, including dropping "Lexa" entirely for the next season in favor of a "healthier" talk show, "On Call." Newton is also said to be considering dropping several major clothing and perfume advertisers' commercial spots unless they "clean them up."
>
> Why the sudden change? Newton says he "no longer feels comfortable airing shows [he] perceives as damaging to families.
>
> "I hope to see Channel 5 gain a reputation in our community as a leader in responsible programming and reporting," Newton says. "I'd like concerned parents to know that their children can safely watch Channel 5 without being exposed to vulgar shows or commercials, or to movies that subtly undermine their values."

Many people might say that Ted Newton's ideas are unrealistic in this day and age, but after seeing the joy on the faces of the five youngsters tentatively placed for adoption this last week thanks to Channel 5, I'm not so sure.

Only time—and the ratings—will tell.

9

THE AFTER-CHURCH MEETING THAT SUNDAY HAD TO BE
moved out of the lecture room when more than a hundred people
showed up.

As they filed back into the sanctuary they'd just left, there
seemed to be an unusual amount of excitement in the air. Rachel
Wingate, trailed by a sulky Jason Clark, was talking animatedly
with Jenny Paige. A small group was clustered around Ted Newton talking to him about the *Herald* article. Kim, at his side,
looked positively radiant.

Alex and Cheryl Powell, on the other hand, were abnormally
quiet. Before the service that morning, Alex had drawn Michael
aside and asked to speak with him privately after the meeting.
The minister had quickly agreed.

After opening with prayer, Michael asked if anyone wanted to
share a testimony. Several people laughed when Ted immediately
jumped to his feet.

"Sorry, but I'm about to burst," he said with a sheepish grin.
"This has been an incredible week. I don't know how many of
you saw the 'Wednesday's Child' special we ran a few days ago,
but it was about five 'hard to place' children in the area who

needed adoptive homes. You might have already read it in the *Ashton Herald*, but after our show, Child Protective Services got calls from more than twenty couples interested in adopting!

"The thing is, I almost didn't allow the show to air. If it weren't for the pledge I'd taken here, 'Lexa' would've run like usual—and five kids would still be homeless."

As he sat back down there was a spontaneous burst of applause, not for Ted but for the Lord who had led him so faithfully. Then Jenny Paige stood up, ignoring an attempt by Rachel Wingate to stop her.

"Rachel's not going to tell you about this, so I'm going to instead," she said briskly. "This last week, a production company offered her a part as a nightclub singer in a television movie being filmed in Chicago. The part involved a lot of money, but it also involved a sex scene and a fair amount of cursing.

"But in keeping with her pledge, Rachel asked herself honestly what Jesus would do—then did it."

Jenny looked down at the young woman fondly. "She turned down the offer, and I, for one, am extremely proud of her."

A murmur of agreement ran through the crowd.

An elderly man leaned forward to pat Rachel's shoulder. "Young lady," he said softly, "God will give you something a hundred times better than what you gave up; you wait and see." She smiled wanly, the pain of the decision still evident on her face.

Several people were surprised when Cliff Bright spoke up after a moment. Although he and Elizabeth had been First Church members for more than six years, few people knew them well. Cliff usually seemed withdrawn and a little sad. Now, though, his round face was positively beaming.

"I had an interesting week," he said. "I began my pledge later than some of you, so I'm really just getting started.

"There are lots of things I haven't thought through yet, but one thing I quickly decided is that Jesus wouldn't sell or distribute 'girlie' magazines in any store He owned. As of several days ago, none of my stores carry them anymore."

This time there was no hesitation; everyone cheered. "You did the right thing," Terri Bannister told him. "I've always hated taking my kids into convenience stores because of that." Others also chimed in to express their support and encouragement.

But Cliff wasn't finished. "What's really exciting, though, is that I saw one of my store managers here in church this morning. In all the years I've thought of myself as a 'Christian employer,' I've never even considered inviting an employee to church. Taking this pledge is changing my whole attitude toward them, and even toward the job itself."

Several other stories were shared, then the group prayed together, this time taking turns praying for one another. An intense feeling of love swept over the room as the Spirit once again demonstrated His presence, bringing a strong sense of family to those gathered in Jesus' name.

When the meeting was finally dismissed, Alex and Cheryl Powell lingered behind in the quiet sanctuary. "Come on back to my office," Michael told them.

The three talked long and earnestly, then solemnly knelt together to seek God's face. If anyone had chanced to look into the church office at that moment, they might have caught a glimpse of an intense spiritual battle being waged.

Two weeks later, the *Ashton Herald* carried another front-page story about a First Church member.

ASHTON

—Yesterday, long-time Vickers Field Operations Manager Alex Powell turned in his resignation after appearing before the airport regulatory board to expose unethical contract practices used in recent new construction on airport property. His revelations have caused a formal investigation to be launched into the multi-million-dollar Jet-Rep project.

In a statement televised last night on Channel 5, WFBB-TV, Powell, visibly shaken, expressed deep regret over having to expose the scandal at the airport where he's worked for almost fifteen years, but said his silence would have made him as "morally responsible" as those who participated in the fraudulent practices. Although he wasn't required to resign, he said he felt it best since he will be called to testify against several highly placed airport officials, including his own direct superior, the director of Aviation.

He offered his full support to Richard Olds, the new operations manager at Vickers Field.

IO

MICHAEL AND SHARON ATE A QUIET BREAKFAST, SOBERED
by the morning paper's announcement of Alex Powell's resignation.

"I need to go see him tonight," Michael said. "He did this
because of his pledge. He told me weeks ago about this whole
situation, and we prayed together for guidance. I guess he got his
answer."

Sharon looked up, troubled. "The paper says this will probably
kill the Jet-Rep project and cause over five hundred jobs that were
coming into Ashton to be moved to Norville. Michael, do you
really think Jesus would've done that?"

He considered. "I think," he said thoughtfully, "that, given
the same circumstances, He probably would. But the point is,
Alex believes that's what He would do, and it's his responsibility
to follow through with it."

He added, "It was no easy decision for him, Sharon. In less
than a year he would have been eligible for full retirement bene-
fits. Now his and Cheryl's future looks pretty uncertain. They're
still making payments on their new house, you know."

Although Powell's action had created a sensation in Ashton,

other strange events involving First Church members had also drawn a lot of attention. The reforms Cliff Bright had made in his stores had inspired many favorable comments, as had Ted Newton's ongoing changes at Channel 5. All through the city— in homes, businesses, and social circles—people were starting to ask, "What's getting into these Christians?"

One instantly noticeable change was in the First Church bill-board along the highway.

Soon after Michael had written his list of things Jesus might do as pastor of First Church, he had called the deacons together to talk about the church advertising. Several of them were aston-ished at the abrupt turnaround in the minister's attitude, but they agreed to modify the mail-out fliers, and also to have the bill-board repainted. Michael's photograph was replaced with a pic-ture of a rough-hewn wooden cross, and the billboard now read:

If Anyone Would Come After Me,
He Must Deny Himself and Take Up His Cross
And Follow Me.
Matthew 16:24

Although many both in and out of the church welcomed the changes, there were a few who found the harsh cross image dis-tasteful. One was Martha Robinson, the church treasurer.

"I don't know what Pastor Maxwell is thinking," she com-plained to members of the building committee. "First this pledge thing, and now shoving a *cross* in people's faces—as if that will make them want to join our church! And I'll tell you another thing; our attendance *and* collections have steadily gone down over the last six weeks. If he keeps this up, he's going to run this church into the ground."

Michael heard about the conversation when one of the older building committee members came to him, troubled about the growing division in the church.

"Pastor, I've been attending First Church since it began over thirty-five years ago, and in that time I've outlasted six preach-ers," he said. "Each time, it started like this, with little complaints and grumblings. I wouldn't want to see that happen to you."

Michael smiled. "I'm afraid I've been so busy I haven't even noticed, but I appreciate your concern. I'm not going to change what I'm doing, though, because I honestly believe it's what Jesus would do."

That evening Michael went out to the Powell's house to talk and pray with them. After he got home, he sank wearily into a chair.

"Alex and Cheryl are both really broken up over this, Sharon," he said. "Not only over Alex's job, but because he was just starting to see some really good things happen out there at Vickers. He's hoping that Richard Olds, the man who's replacing him, will continue a lot of the things he started."

Sharon moved behind him and began to gently massage his neck and shoulders as he continued. "I'll call Cheryl in the morning. She probably needs some moral support about now, too."

She moved around to perch on the arm of his chair, suddenly aware of several new lines in Michael's face. Less than two months into his pledge, he was already starting to show the physical strain of bearing the burdens of those who, with him, had promised to "take up their crosses" and follow Christ.

Letters to the Editor of the *Ashton Herald*:

Dear Sir:

Regarding the recent action of Alex Powell, former operations manager at Vickers Field Regional Airport, I'd like to say that I'm astonished and outraged that, for the sake of his rather vague "principles" over a minor point, he would throw away five hundred new jobs for Ashton.

Harry Chandler, Director
Ashton Community Affairs Center

To the Editor:

Since I'm one of the unemployed people who had hoped to be hired at Jet-Rep, I'd like to say, "Thanks a lot, Mr. Powell! Are you going to bring food to my house now for my family?"

Rick Morrow

Dear Editor:

Just who does Alex Powell think he is, anyway? I personally applaud the community-minded people at Vickers Field who had the courage to risk sidestepping the bureaucratic "procedure" (i.e., red tape) in order to bring additional jobs and money into Ashton.

> Councilman Don Essenpreis
> City Council District #2

Dear Sir:

Instead of going straight to the media, why didn't Mr. Powell approach the airport director or other airport officials to see if the problem could be quietly resolved without jeopardizing the Jet-Rep project? It's apparent by his actions that Mr. Powell was more interested in publicity and raising a scandal than in the welfare of our community.

> Jonathan Spire

To the Editor:

We the undersigned would like to publicly state our support for Alex Powell with regard to his recent dealings with Vickers Field. Many of us have worked with him for over ten years and know him as a man of absolute honesty and integrity. We will miss him.

> Custodial and Maintenance Crew Members,
> Vickers Field Airport—
> Joe Crain, Carlos Ramirez, Eric Seidler, Kevin Robinson,
> John Harney, Maggie Whitehead, Sue Setley, Kathy Fieler,
> David Smith, Maria Langer, Roger Franz, Scott Henderson,
> Richard Collins, Gary Sledge, Belinda Buckingham

Private letter from Pastor Maxwell:

Dear Alex and Cheryl,

I can only imagine the pain you both must be experiencing over this whole situation and the deep sense of loss Alex, especially, must feel. I can't begin to tell you how much I admire and appreciate your faithfulness in keeping your pledge to follow Jesus at all costs.

I deeply respect your continued refusal to answer the repeated attacks in the newspaper—especially since your accusers have so many wrong facts. If they only realized how you tried to "quietly resolve" the problem with the director or how much you lost by going public! I believe you're taking the higher road, as Jesus did:

"When they hurled their insults at him, he did not retaliate; when he suffered, he made no threats. Instead, he entrusted himself to him who judges justly" (1 Pet. 2:23).

As your pastor, I can only say "thank you" for your faithfulness, and promise that my thoughts and prayers will be with you as you walk through this dark time.

Pastor Michael Maxwell

II

THE WEEKS THAT FOLLOWED SAW SEVERAL INTERESTING
developments. One was the growing friendship between Rachel
Wingate and Jenny Paige.

Ever since the Sunday when Rachel talked to the older woman
about the V. C. Productions offer, the two had spoken regularly.
They met twice in the city for lunch, then Jenny invited Rachel
home for dinner. Rachel was overwhelmed by her first glimpse
inside the Paige mansion.

"I can't believe this!" she breathed, staring from the graceful
winding staircase to the small fountain near the entryway. The
floor was gleaming marble, scattered with costly Oriental rugs. A
heavy crystal chandelier was suspended from the raised ceiling in
the dining room to the left.

Jenny smiled at her reaction. "Not exactly cozy, is it? My
husband had this built during his high-roller days, and I hated to
sell it after he passed away. It has one advantage, though; if I get
upset with Roger, there's enough room here for him to stay out of
my way."

Rachel grinned. "Where is Roger, anyway? I haven't seen
much of him lately."

"He'll be here for dinner. I think he had other plans, but when he heard you were coming he suddenly decided he should spend more time with his dear old mother. Having a young, pretty girl here definitely adds to my charm."

Rachel laughed. "You're not a bit old. I can't even think of you as being my mother's age. You seem so much more—I don't know, alive or something."

Jenny was obviously pleased. "Well, I'm alive enough to be famished. Let's go see if we can hurry dinner along."

They were in the kitchen chatting with the cook when Roger walked in. He stopped short when he saw Rachel.

"Well, hello there!" he said, flashing her a grin. "I didn't know you were already here."

Clad in gym clothes with his brown hair tousled and sweaty, he used the towel around his neck to quickly wipe his face. Although his features were a little too blunt to be called handsome, he'd always been careful about his appearance. He was also acutely aware that, for most girls, his bank account greatly improved his looks.

Rachel hid an amused smile. "We were just scouting for food. Your mom and I have been working up an appetite wandering around this house. It's huge!"

Roger shrugged. "It's no big deal," he said with a smugness that belied his words. "Just a place to live." Reaching into the refrigerator, he drew out a wine cooler, twisted off the lid, and raised it in a mocking toast to his mother and Rachel before taking a long drink. "I guess I'll see you in a few minutes, ladies. I need to grab a quick shower."

Jenny and Rachel had already started eating when Roger came back in, his hair damp but combed. As he slid into a chair across the table, Rachel noticed for the first time how much he resembled Jenny in the strong lines of his face. His keen blue eyes were emphasized by the bright pattern of his shirt.

"So," he said pleasantly, "what brings you out to the Paige Mausoleum?" He served himself generously from a steaming platter of broccoli and ladled some gravy onto his potatoes. "We don't have many non-business visitors these days."

"Actually, your mom and I have been talking business. She was telling me about some of the property Paige, Inc., bought down in the south side a few months ago." Rachel looked at the older woman. "Have you already told him any of this?"

Jenny shook her head. "We were discussing the Jeffers Building, Roger. We came up with an idea that we both like."

The Jeffers Building was an old, run-down four-story structure situated at the heart of the roughest area of Ashton's south side. Long vacant, it had been repeatedly vandalized; most of its windows were broken out and replaced by steel bars. Since it was often used during the winter as a shelter by "street people," the air inside was pungent with the smells of urine and vomit. Drug deals and rape, even murder, were part of daily life in the area.

"The best idea for that eyesore is a bulldozer," Roger said firmly. "Even if we fixed it up, no business would want to locate there."

"That's the point," Rachel said. "There's only one thing it would be just perfect for—a gospel mission!"

Roger paused, fork in hand, to stare from Rachel to his mother. "A *mission?* You mean like a church?"

Jenny nodded. "But not like a regular church. It would be aimed at the street people in the area, and it would go beyond just preaching. There's already a kitchen downstairs that could be refurbished, and the upstairs could be equipped with cots and showers. It would be more like a shelter, a place where people could come in, hear a message of hope, then get a hot meal and a bed. Can you think of a more effective way to get through to them?"

Roger was cynical. "They'd just use the system to get what they want. Most of those people live the way they do because they *want* to, not because they have to. It would be a total waste of time and money."

"I don't think so," Rachel contradicted him. "But even if some of them 'used' the system, it would still serve its purpose for others. Anyway, we're going to talk to Pastor Maxwell about it and see what he thinks."

Roger looked at his mother quizzically, then briefly shifted his gaze to Rachel. What was it in their faces that suddenly seemed so—*vital?*

The atmosphere was tense in the tall Ashton Towers conference room as almost twenty store managers waited nervously for "Mr. B's" arrival. Rumors had run rampant ever since the meeting had been announced.

"I hear he plans to fire us all and replace us with people from his church," one man said. "He's on some Jesus thing where he only wants Christian managers."

"Well, if he tries that he's gonna be sorry," a woman said belligerently. "I'll sue him so fast he won't know what hit him. That's discrimination!" A growing rumble of assent was abruptly cut short when Cliff Bright entered the room and walked to the front. He greeted several managers by name, then called the meeting to order.

"I understand," he began, "that some of you are concerned that I called this meeting to fire everybody." He paused to smile. "Although there've been weeks when that might have sounded tempting, I assure you that's not why you're here."

Several people exchanged relieved glances. The woman who had spoken earlier settled back in her chair. In the front row Connie Garza listened quietly, her dark eyes on Bright's face.

He continued, "Actually, I want to announce some changes that I hope to introduce into the stores over the next few months, and also to get your advice and input about ways we can improve Mr. B's. You know your customers better than I do, and I thought you might have specific ideas about things you might like to see happen in each of your stores."

At his words, several managers nodded and whispered excitedly to each other. Bright waited for the murmur to die down before speaking again.

"You're all aware that, as of several weeks ago, Mr. B Food Stores no longer sell pornographic magazines. Although that decision has cost the company a considerable amount of money, I believe it was the right thing to do. We don't need money earned by selling trash."

Several of the female managers burst into spontaneous applause. Bright, startled but pleased, waited till it died down, then went on.

"The more I've thought about it, though, the more convinced I've become that there are other significant changes that need to be made as well. And frankly, they might end up being even more costly."

At his solemn tone, a worried silence once again descended over the room. What did he have in mind?

"Over these past two weeks I've made it a point to visit each one of your stores—not for the usual reasons—but to get a better feel for how we're serving the community. I must say that it left me with a lot of thinking to do. None of what I'm going to say next is a reflection on any of you. The products in your stores have always been my responsibility, not yours. But since that's the case, it's now my responsibility to correct some bad decisions I've made in the past.

"First, as your stores sell out of tobacco products, I don't want you to reorder. Too many people today are suffering and dying because of tobacco use, and even though I realize it's perfectly legal, I don't want to be guilty of contributing, even indirectly, to anyone's addiction." His eyes rested briefly on Connie's face.

"Second, I want you to follow the same no-reorder policy with all hard liquor. I don't claim to know a whole lot about alcohol, but it seems to me that the main purpose of buying hard liquor is to get drunk. For the time being, we will continue to carry beer and wine, but any store employee I catch selling to a minor will be instantly dismissed."

The news of those two changes alone was enough to leave the managers wide-eyed, but before it could all sink in, Bright opened the floor to discussion. Connie Garza hesitated, then slipped up her hand. When Bright nodded, she stood up.

"Lots of my customers work at the steel shop down the street," she said. "Several of them have asked me why we don't open a deli at Mr. B so they can buy fresh sandwiches during their lunch break."

Several managers nodded, and Bright jotted the idea down on

a notepad. "That's an interesting idea, Connie. I'll check into it. Anyone else?"

"If we're going to talk about opening a deli, why not a bakery too?" suggested one man. "Some of my customers buy the prepackaged donuts for breakfast every morning, but if we had fresh donuts—even a small selection—I'll bet we'd sell out. There isn't a donut shop for miles around."

The other managers, getting into the spirit, talked in low murmurs as Bright noted the man's comments. When he asked for the next suggestion, four people raised their hands.

"This isn't about a new product or anything," a woman said, "but my sister works in a Quik-Mart down in Tennessee, and after she got robbed one night, her boss installed a kind of cage of bulletproof glass around the counter. I don't know about anybody else, but something like that would make me feel a lot safer when I have to work alone late at night." Several others echoed their support of the idea, and Bright wrote it down.

The meeting continued for another hour, with manager after manager standing up to make suggestions. The atmosphere became jovial, with frequent laughter and a growing sense of camaraderie between Bright and his employees. When they were dismissed, many stayed behind to chat with Mr. B. Bright left that afternoon with a light heart. *I've never seen them so fired up about making their stores succeed,* he thought. *If anything will help us weather the rough months ahead, it will be that.*

12

THE FIRST CHURCH PLEDGE WAS NOW ENTERING ITS fourth month. The number attending the Sunday afterchurch meetings had steadily grown, and the regulars, now numbering more than 150, greeted each other with joyful familiarity. The common bond between them made it seem increasingly natural to share their experiences.

The growing success of the meetings, however, had led some of the deacons and other church administrators to complain of "cliquishness" in the church.

"Going to these 'pledge meetings' is getting to be like some kind of status symbol," Martha Robinson had muttered darkly at their last meeting. "If Pastor Maxwell doesn't put a stop to it soon, the Board is going to get some letters calling for his resignation."

"From what I've seen," one deacon said quietly, "a lot of people who've taken the pledge don't stay for the meetings, and some who attend the meetings haven't taken the pledge at all. Have you ever gone to one?"

"No, and I don't plan to, either. Doesn't the Bible say that we're all one body? I think this is just another way for people to be 'holier-than-thou.' "

This Sunday, however, Michael Maxwell noticed that several people were missing from the after-meeting—Jason Clark among them. He had excused himself right after church, citing a last-minute schedule conflict. Michael noticed he had carefully avoided Rachel's appraising look as he left.

Catching sight of the Powells across the room, Michael slowly worked his way in their direction. Alex had just started a new job in neighboring Guilford as an FAA inspector, so it looked like he and Cheryl wouldn't end up suffering too much financially. But the transition had been rough.

"How's everything going?" Michael asked, shaking Alex's hand warmly. "Do you have your new boss trained yet?"

Alex shook his head ruefully. "It's not easy calling a supervisor half my age 'sir'—especially when most of the time he doesn't know what he's talking about. He has a degree, but less than two years' airport experience!" He sighed. "It takes just about everything I've got just to get through each day."

Maxwell patted his shoulder. "Well, it might cheer you up to hear that last week, two men at the Vickers Bible study committed their lives to the Lord and asked to be baptized. The group gets bigger almost every week, and it wouldn't have happened without you, Alex."

Alex brightened. "That's good. That's great! Thanks a lot for letting me know."

After the opening prayer, several people shared testimonies and special prayer requests; then Cliff Bright stood up.

His usually florid face was slightly pale this morning, and he seemed to have lost some weight. Although Elizabeth had never relented in her opposition to his attendance of the First Church after-meetings, he hadn't missed a single one since he had taken the pledge. He had grown especially close to Ted Newton and Daniel Marshall.

Facing the crowd, Bright cleared his throat. "I'm afraid my news isn't as positive as some of the other testimonies this morning," he said slowly. "I put this off for as long as I could, hoping it would eventually take care of itself. But unless something dramatic happens soon, it looks like I'm going to have to close several of my stores."

His announcement left many people shocked. Even those who didn't know the store owner well had come to admire and respect him over the preceding months. His spiritual insight and thoughtful responses had caused many of them to look to him for leadership and advice.

Bright continued, "Most of you remember that soon after taking the pledge I decided to stop selling 'girlie' magazines and to pull all tobacco products and hard liquor from my stores' shelves. I made those decisions after a lot of prayer, believing that they were what Jesus would do in my place.

"I wasn't surprised when the company showed an immediate loss; the magazines were a big money-maker. But over the next few months, the additional losses from tobacco and liquor added up to a total income drop of over *31 percent!* No company can take a loss like that for long and stay in business.

"I called a meeting with all my managers to discuss ways we might be able to compensate for those losses, and they came up with great ideas which I think, in time, could be a great success. I've invested a significant sum of money in adding small delis to five of the stores and bakeries to another six. But the bottom line is, unless we get a major boost in sales over the next six to eight weeks, I'll be forced to make drastic cuts—most likely by closing stores."

He looked around the room. "What I'm most concerned about at this point are my employees. Several of them are in financial straits and couldn't afford to lose their jobs and health insurance. It isn't their fault that I'm no longer giving them the kind of products people obviously want to buy! I'd appreciate it if you'd all pray for me over the upcoming weeks that I'll make the right decisions."

Alex Powell was listening thoughtfully. "Cliff, have you decided yet whether or not you're going to pull beer and wine out of your stores, too? You'd talked about that before." Alex, with his near-shattering experience years before, was opposed to the sale of alcohol in any form.

"I'm not really sure at this point," Cliff said honestly. "I know a lot of Christians believe it's wrong to drink under any circumstances, and I can't argue the fact that alcohol has caused a lot of grief and misery. But from my understanding of the Bible, it's drunkenness that's condemned, not alcohol itself. I'd appreciate it if you'd pray with me about that as well."

After Cliff sat down, there was a moment of silence. Then Kim Newton impulsively stood up and faced the group.

"I don't know about the rest of you," she said, "but I have a lot of respect for what Mr. Bright is doing. Why don't we back him with our purchases as well as with our prayers? If every one of us here today made it a point to shop at Mr. B Food Stores from now on and encouraged our friends and neighbors to shop there, too, couldn't we make a difference? I bet lots of people would be willing to go out of their way if they realized what was happening."

Ted, surprised at his wife's spirited outburst, enthusiastically voiced his agreement. He was quickly joined by all the others.

Michael Maxwell stood up. "That's a great idea, Kim. The church can help, too, by buying the donuts and coffee for our fellowship breakfasts there from now on." Cliff listened in astonishment, overwhelmed by their promises of support.

Then Jenny Paige spoke up. "Cliff," she said briskly, "I can't help but think that, with the Christian community behind you, things will turn around quickly. But will you make sure to let us know how things are going, whether it's good news or bad?" Cliff nodded in agreement.

Jenny smiled. "Well," she said, "while I'm already talking I guess I might as well share some other news. For the past few weeks, Rachel Wingate and I have been working on an idea for an inner-city outreach down on the south side. If you're at all familiar with the area around Second Street and Chandler, you know it's overrun with drug dealers, prostitutes, street people, gangs— you name it. It's so rough the police have almost given up patrolling it.

"But right in the middle of all that is a big, vacant four-story building, the old Jeffers Building. Paige, Inc., bought it several months ago along with some other commercial properties downtown. Rachel and I would like to see it turned into a sort of street ministry where people could hear preaching, but also find food, clothing, temporary shelter and maybe even medical help. We're thinking of calling it 'Southside Mission.'"

In the audience, Dr. West quickly nodded, her face alight. Jenny smiled at her.

"I have to admit that at first, this whole idea sounded more like a nightmare than a dream to me. I'm a businesswoman, not a missionary, and in the past I've done my best to avoid involving myself with these kinds of people. But lately, I've become convinced that I need to start giving *myself* rather than just my money."

She stopped, groping for the right words. "Most of you know that I have been blessed financially. I've always prided myself on giving generously to the church, sure that I was doing my Christian duty. Ever since I took this pledge, though, I've started wondering. Is it really following Jesus to give away money you'll never miss? Or to support charities financially while refusing to get personally involved with the people they help? Where is the self-denial, the suffering, in that?"

She smiled gently. "So, here I am. I firmly believe the Lord has directed me to become involved with Southside Mission, and oddly enough, I'm starting to enjoy it! We hope to equip it with enough cots to sleep 125 and to have a dining area big enough to feed the same number. Pastor Maxwell has already talked to several other ministers in the area who might be willing to help. If all goes well, it should be ready to open within six weeks."

When Jenny sat down, a low murmur of excitement ran through the group. Dr. West leaned over to speak to Ted and Kim Newton; Lauren Woods and Terri Bannister also talked hurriedly. The idea of a street mission caught their imaginations. Suddenly, the very air suddenly seemed charged with divine possibilities.

Michael Maxwell stood up and motioned for silence. "Once

the mission opens," he said, "there'll undoubtedly be a great need for counselors and workers. Please pray about it, and let me know if you'd like to have a part in that ministry."

A few minutes later, Michael asked Cliff Bright to close the meeting. As Cliff rose and began to pray in his soft, earnest fashion, a hush once again fell upon the room. A distinct wave of spiritual power moved over those gathered there, causing many of them to feel a sudden deep yearning, a hunger to walk the way of sacrifice, to suffer something for Jesus.

Who could resist such a baptism of power? How had they lived all these years without it?

13

RACHEL DROVE BACK TO HER APARTMENT LOST IN thought. The First Church after-meeting had left her curiously restless, unable to settle down to her Sunday afternoon routine of housecleaning and laundry. Instead, she decided to write a long overdue letter to her parents.

Sitting at her small oak desk, she opened the drawer and pulled out a pad of rose-colored stationery decorated with music notes. After thinking a moment, she started writing in her precise long-hand:

Dear Mom and Dad,

Sorry it's taken me so long to write back to you, but a lot of exciting things have been going on here.

Last time we talked you were concerned about the church pledge I took, especially about whether I was getting into some kind of "cult" or "mind control" situation. I want you to know that nothing could be farther from the truth. In fact, if anything, this pledge has made me much more resistant to being pressured into things against my better judgment.

I'll give you one example, now that it's all over and I'm not still struggling with it.

Six weeks ago, a Chicago production company offered me a chance to audition for a part in a TV movie called *Secret Rage* to be filmed this summer. They had heard me sing in church and thought I'd be perfect for the part of a nightclub singer.

At first it sounded wonderful. The money was fantastic, and it would be a perfect opportunity to launch my singing career. The only problem was, both the movie and my part were, to say the least, morally questionable. On top of the unhealthy theme of the movie in general (a young man with multiple personalities kills both his parents), I'd have to swear and appear in at least one explicit "love" scene.

Still, I was going to do it anyway—until I remembered my pledge. To tell the truth, it made me mad at first to think that God would spoil something that exciting, and I came very close to breaking my promise so I could do what I wanted. I still don't know exactly what stopped me—unless it was the Holy Spirit.

I know, I know. That probably sounds very strange, especially coming from me! I've never been one to use "churchy" phrases like "Holy Ghost." In fact, if I ever thought about the Spirit at all, it was only in the vaguest terms, like some kind of religious theory.

But if there's any one thing I've learned over these last few months, Mom and Dad, it's that the Holy Spirit is real, the actual presence of God in my life. I mean—I feel now like I've spent years going through the motions of being a Christian without understanding where it all springs from, kind of like a flashlight trying to shine without batteries!

It's made a big difference in the way I pray. In the past, if I prayed at all, I never really expected to get an answer; it was more like positive thinking, "wishing" for things I wanted. But I can't tell you how many specific prayers I've seen answered just in these last few months alone, both for myself and for others. It's incredible!

Remember President Marshall out at my college? He took the pledge at First Church along with the rest of us, and several weeks ago he asked all of us to pray for a student who was having financial difficulties that might force him to drop out in his final semester. The poor guy was already working two jobs, but there was some kind of problem with his family. Anyway, we prayed that God would provide a way for him to stay in school and sure enough, he did! Lincoln College got a number of donations toward the student's tuition, and they added up to within twenty-five dollars of what he needed! Mr. Marshall made up the rest.

Then there's Ted Newton, the station manager at WFBB-TV. After he took the First Church pledge, he started running the station like he thought Jesus would— getting rid of some of the really offensive programs and trying to replace them with some wholesome family shows.

He came close to having to quit his job last month after he announced that he'd no longer accept heavily sex-oriented advertising. But despite our local newspaper's cynical comments about Ted's "Pollyanna ideas" and the other stations' victory parties, Channel 5's ratings immediately went up! Nobody in the business understands it, but that's a direct answer to our prayers.

And do you remember my mentioning Jenny Paige? She's a real estate developer whose family owns a lot of property in Ashton. She and I are working together now on a plan for a downtown outreach aimed at reaching Ashton's street people. Next time we talk I'll tell you all about it. We've got some really exciting ideas.

Anyway, I just wanted to let you know that everything is going well. I'll try harder from now on to stay in touch so you won't worry. Give all my love to Gram and Gramps, and tell Jimmy to stay out of trouble.

Much love,

Rachel

After a moment's hesitation, she added:

P.S. Jason also sends his love, and says he's looking forward to seeing you when we visit in November.

At that same moment, Jason Clark was also contemplating his and Rachel's plans to spend the Thanksgiving holiday with her family.

Sitting at the piano in his apartment, his long fingers skillfully stroked the keys to create a soft, sensual melody that closely echoed his thoughts. He paused briefly to make a note on the half-filled music sheet propped in front of him, smiling at the scrawled song title: "Rachel."

The lyrics he'd composed were as throbbingly suggestive as the music he played:

> *Sweet perfume fills the air*
> *Sunlight glints on auburn hair.*
> *A promise in your lovely eyes*
> *of us together—Paradise!*
> *I'm a moth drawn to your fire*
> *Beauty fills me with desire*
> *No voice but yours can blend with mine*
> *Our voices . . . bodies . . . all entwined.*

That morning, he had decided at the last minute not to tell Pastor Maxwell exactly why he was leaving so hurriedly after the service. With Rachel's birthday just weeks away, he needed time to finish the song he planned to present her as a gift. Although he considered it a perfectly valid reason for missing the after-meeting, Jason somehow doubted Pastor Maxwell would agree.

Maybe I should go ahead and give her the engagement ring we picked out, too, he thought. *She's been acting a little strange toward me lately; that might smooth things out.*

Her parents would probably expect them to delay any announcement of an engagement until after the Thanksgiving visit to officially ask their "blessing," but he suddenly didn't want to delay any longer. *They'll get over it,* he decided, and with that confident thought returned to his music.

14

IT WAS FRIDAY NIGHT, AND THE CROWD AT THE COLORful Mardi Gras Pub was boisterous. Roger Paige walked through the door to be greeted enthusiastically by the other regular patrons.

As he made his way through the noisy, smoke-filled room, Jo Lynn, the tall barmaid, called cheerfully, "Hi, honey. How ya doin'?"

"Great," Roger replied, shouting to be heard over the country music band. "How about you?"

" 'Bout the same. Life goes on."

Roger smiled an acknowledgment, then made his way over to a table where two of his racquetball buddies were already sipping drinks. Jo Lynn sat a drink in front of him, then flashed him a bright smile before disappearing back through the crowd.

After nodding companionably at Bruce and Dennis, Roger quickly scanned the packed room, spotting many familiar faces. The Mardi Gras drew a predictable crowd each weekend, mostly the younger, "work hard, play hard" set. The description fit Roger perfectly.

Tonight, though, he found himself once again battling restlessness. The conversations around him were all the same—forced, almost desperate gaiety that thinly concealed dark undertones of hopelessness. What was it with him lately? It was like nothing satisfied him any more. Even the music was depressing.

Maybe it's time for a vacation, he thought gloomily. *I haven't been diving for a while. I could take a week off and fly down to Cozumel—*

His thoughts stopped there abruptly. The last time he'd gone diving, it had been with Lisa. She'd made it plain at that time that marriage was on her mind. He'd made it equally plain that he wasn't interested in commitment. He'd heard since then that she'd become engaged to a stockbroker.

Better him than me, Roger thought bitingly. *I'm not ready to be tied down to just one woman yet.*

As if to contradict that thought, however, an image instantly sprang to his mind of wide, green eyes and auburn hair: Rachel.

Sipping his drink moodily, Roger recalled the way her eyes had sparkled as she talked about the church and the plans for Southside Mission. Rachel Wingate, he realized, had never acted particularly impressed with him, or like she even cared to be around him. He wasn't used to being so easily dismissed.

I'd like to get to know her better, he suddenly realized, somewhat to his surprise. *But I guess she and Jason Clark are pretty much committed. I don't know what it is about her, but she's really something.*

Over the next few weeks, First Church experienced an almost unprecedented flurry of activity. Volunteers made repeated excursions to the south side to work on the mission: painting it inside and out, tearing out and replacing worn kitchen fixtures, laying new carpet, and bringing in chairs, tables, and cots donated by sister churches.

Daniel Marshall astonished everyone with his untiring dedication to the project.

"It's not what you might think," he admitted to Michael Maxwell. "I'm not even sure this whole concept of a street mission can be made to work. But I've taught theology for years and written books about 'practical Christianity' and 'imitating Christ' without even considering that *I* could be more actively involved. I've always assumed that I was supposed to serve the Lord in Christian education, where I'm best qualified. But lately I've felt that I should be getting more involved in the secular community. This looks like a good way to do that."

Maxwell nodded. "I'm glad you're helping out," he said. "I've already heard two or three people comment that you've provided a cool head and logical approach to the work that needs to be done. And I guess you're responsible for all the Lincoln students who are showing up to help—a lot of them don't even come to First Church."

The college president nodded. "I've talked out at the college about what we're doing and invited some of them to help. I'm glad they're getting involved." The concerted efforts to prepare the mission to open were covered one night on Channel 5's evening news.

"An unusual sight is being observed in Ashton's south side these days," the young reporter announced. "A dilapidated building on the corner of Chandler and Second is being transformed, almost overnight, into a 'street ministry' called Southside Mission, due to open next week. The winos and street gangs who roam the area seem bewildered by the flood of middle-class churchgoers and Lincoln Christian College students who boldly park their cars next to burned-out buildings and greet them with smiles and comments like 'Jesus loves you.'

"I'm here with Jenny Paige, whose company, Paige, Inc., donated the facility."

The camera scanned the newly painted Jeffers Building, an oasis among the other dirty, graffiti-scrawled buildings on the street. The lens brutally captured the sight of the homeless, some severely emaciated, sprawled sleeping on "beds" of rags on the sidewalks. Then the camera turned to Jenny.

"The mission will serve dinner each evening to up to 125 people immediately after the church service," she said, "and issue clothing and shoes to those who need them. Up to one hundred people will be able to check in for the night, shower, wash and dry their clothes, and sleep on a clean cot. Dr. Patricia West has also agreed to donate one afternoon a week to provide *pro bono* medical services."

"How is the mission being funded?"

"We debated about taking money from some charity organizations, but decided against it because of all the strings attached. At this time, the mission is funded entirely by private donations. We've already received food, money, and clothing from over fifteen churches in the area as well as from various individuals and even one Girl Scout troop. No tax money is involved."

"Are there any rules about who gets to stay overnight?"

"Well, they have to be sober," Jenny replied wryly. "And to get a bed they'll have to attend the evening church service and be willing to abide by the 'house rules'—including leaving their weapons at the door."

"Do you think they'll do that?"

"I think they will. Besides, we'll return their things when they leave. Our goal goes beyond just feeding or clothing or disarming them; we want to see their lives changed. Once that happens, the rest will follow."

The news clip ended with some brief footage of Lincoln College students washing some newly replaced windows while black-clad gang members nearby made obscene gestures at the camera. It was a vivid image of stark contrasts, both promising and unsettling.

It was Wednesday evening, two days before the scheduled opening of Southside Mission, and the mid-week service at First Church of Ashton was unusually crowded. As Michael greeted people at the door, he marveled at how many new faces he saw. Many appeared to be young people, some recognizable as Lincoln students.

Connie Garza came up the steps, her face alight as she introduced Michael to her husband. Epimenio Garza, gaunt but smiling, shook the pastor's hand.

"Connie's been trying to get me to church for months now," he said. "Her boss comes here, and she's really been enjoying it. I figured it was about time I came along."

Michael grinned. "Glad to have you. I almost feel like I already know you—we've been praying for your recovery at the Sunday after-meetings."

Epimenio nodded, embarrassed. "Connie told me. I don't know that much about church, but she says you people have really helped her. All this has been pretty hard for us."

Michael shook the man's hand again. *We're starting to function as the body of Christ,* he thought excitedly. *This is what the church is supposed to be all about.*

That Friday night, Southside Mission officially opened its doors. Fliers had been posted throughout the area announcing the first service, and by late afternoon the mouth-watering aromas of freshly baked bread and simmering beef stew filled the city streets. As the six o'clock opening hour approached, a varied crowd began to gather on the sidewalk outside. The southsiders, ranging from obviously drunken elderly men to arrogant teenagers to wary, hard-faced women, jostled for position and eyed each other with varying degrees of hostility. It was a potentially explosive mix.

At exactly six, Jenny Paige and Michael Maxwell unlocked the front doors. There was an instant stampede, but it slowed a moment later when the first ones in reached the "check-in" station. Lauren Woods and two other First Church volunteers stood behind a counter, pleasantly explaining that mission rules required that all weapons, alcohol, and "controlled substances" be stowed in lockers before going inside.

The first man glared at Lauren. "You gonna take my bottle while I eat!" he said accusingly. When Lauren assured him that he could take the locker key with him he still hesitated, but finally the smell of lasagna and freshly baked bread from inside won him over. He grudgingly shoved his small bottle in a locker and went into the dining hall.

It was set up cafeteria style, with plastic trays and a serving line. Michael Maxwell watched unobtrusively from the far side of the room as the street people, the vast majority of them men, shoved their way through the line. The younger ones were treating it like a joke, laughing and sneering at the "church freaks" who were stupid enough to give away food.

"It prob'ly make them feel real good to help us po' hungry niggers," one remarked. "We be doin' 'em a big favor, eatin' this—." The expletive he used to describe the free meal drew sharp glances from the volunteers in the serving line.

"Yeah," another smirked. "And have you looked at these church women? I think they need a man." He leaned forward to leer suggestively at an older volunteer in the serving line. As he graphically described what he'd like to do, her eyes grew wide. The man burst out laughing and moved on.

Michael felt sudden doubt. Was it wise to expose the volunteers to such men and their crude language? The mission was such a small light in the midst of such great darkness; was it really worth the risk?

And yet, he knew the Holy Spirit had the power to melt even the hardest hearts, replace lust and hatred with perfect love. *This is where we belong,* he thought firmly, *with the same sick and sinful people Jesus reached out to.*

At seven o'clock, the evening service began in the chapel adjoining the dining hall. Those still eating looked up in surprise when they heard catchy music starting, and most went into the chapel, where about thirty-five people were already assembled. Jenny Paige was seated on the front row with Dr. West, Daniel Marshall, and a half-dozen other First Church members who'd come for the mission's first service. The room quickly filled as the latecomers noisily pressed inside.

When Rachel Wingate stepped up onto the small elevated stage, she was instantly met with a chorus of loud wolf whistles and drunken shouts. Ignoring them, she picked up a microphone as the pianist played the opening chords to "All to Thee."

The whistling and shouts abruptly died away as soon as Rachel started singing.

I have heard the voice of Jesus
calling clearly "Follow Me";
No one else could ever promise
*Life eternal and so free.**

The hardened crowd seemed riveted by the purity and sweetness of her voice. One wizened old man started sniffling, rubbing his bleary eyes with the back of his hand as he listened. Several young men wearing black bandannas knotted on their heads stared at the floor, scowling in an obvious effort to deny any emotional response.

Tho' unworthy of salvation,
Jesus sought me for His own;
On the cross He died to save me,
Now I long to make Him known.

Only Jesus is the answer
For the happiness we seek;
He alone can lift life's burden,
And give strength unto the weak.

Rachel was surprised when Jason Clark walked in and glanced around; she somehow hadn't expected him to show up. Her heart suddenly light, she asked the crowd to stand and join her in singing the chorus:

All to Thee, I give my all to Thee,
All to Thee, Thine only will I be;
All to Thee, O Christ of Calvary,
My prayer shall ever be, my all to Thee.

When the music faded, she handed the microphone to Pastor Maxwell. As she quietly stepped down from the stage to go sit beside Jason, she was startled by a deep voice that boomed: "Praise the Lord!" Heads turned toward the speaker, a tall, heavyset black man at the back of the room wearing a tattered shirt and cap. He smiled beatifically, revealing several gaps where his front

---

© 1966. Assigned to McKinney Music, Inc. (BMI). All rights reserved. Distributed by GENEVOX MUSIC GROUP.

---

teeth should have been. A ripple of laughter ran through the audience.

The moment Michael tried to speak, however, the ugly mood returned to the crowd. A harsh, almost angry murmur started across the room—whispers of "rev'rend from First Church . . . ," "big, fancy place in north Ashton . . . ," "rich white church"—and soon grew into drunken shouts.

"We don't need no fancy preacher in the south side!" someone shouted, while another called out, "Why don't you people stay in north Ashton where you belong?" A large man with a beard provoked gales of laughter by standing up to sing "Amazing Grace" in loud, nasal tones, gesturing for emphasis. "Hey, preacher," a woman shouted, "we got us a deal with God, see— we leave Him alone, and He leave us alone!"

Michael tried to regain control by raising his hands, then his voice, but it was hopeless. They were arguing and milling around, not even listening. In one corner two men started angrily shoving each other.

Finally, Michael stepped down from the stage and walked over to the small First Church group. Sitting on a folding chair, he covered his face with his hands and began to pray.

Rachel touched his shoulder. "Pastor Maxwell, should I sing again? Maybe that would calm them down."

Michael, near despair, looked up. "Thanks, Rachel. Maybe they'll listen to you."

She leaped up and quickly mounted the steps to the stage again, followed closely by the pianist. A moment later her clear voice was once again raised in song:

> *When peace, like a river, attendeth my way,*
> *When sorrows like sea billows roll;*
> *Whatever my lot, Thou hast taught me to say,*
> *It is well, it is well with my soul.*

She hadn't sung the first line before the southsiders were all turned toward her, sadly thoughtful, listening almost against their will. Before she finished the verse, the room was subdued and tamed. It lay like some wild beast at her feet as she sang it into harmlessness, her lovely face radiant.

Michael watched the transformation of the mob with awe, catching a sudden glimpse of what Jesus could do with a voice like Rachel's. It was a gift that could touch and heal those around her, that could bring peace in the midst of strife.

Dear Lord, he prayed, *lead her faithfully in the path You'd have her take. Let her life reflect Your great love.*

A few seats away, Jason Clark's eyes were also fixed on the singer. Unlike Michael, he was thinking that Rachel had never looked more beautiful, more appealing. His thoughts drifted into anticipation, and he smiled confidently as he recalled the words he'd written: *"our voices . . . bodies . . . entwined."*

No one noticed the unlikely presence of Roger Paige, who stood unobtrusively just inside the chapel door. On impulse, he'd left the Mardi Gras early to visit the mission opening that Rachel and his mother had talked so much about. Now, as he watched the young singer step down and Michael Maxwell turn to face the subdued crowd, he saw again the indefinable strength, the joyful radiance, in both their faces.

He hesitated for a moment, then turned to leave as quietly as he'd arrived. Neither Rachel nor his mother saw him as he slipped back outside and drove away.

Michael stood in front of the crowded room, feeling calmer this time. What would Jesus do before this kind of audience? Christianity had to be more than delivering slick, "professional" sermons to smug audiences who were already converted. Wasn't it about calling lost and weary sinners like these to repentance? How would He speak to these people?

Michael didn't realize it, but the deep compassion he felt showed plainly on his face, commanding the attention of his restless audience. Empowered by the Spirit, he spoke as never before of the love Jesus had for them and what a rich life He promised for those who became His followers.

When the meeting closed two hours later, the chapel quickly emptied, most of the southsiders heading back to the streets that spawned them. Only a handful stayed behind, among them Eddie Saenz, a painfully thin Puerto Rican teenager wearing a black bandanna on his head.

He approached Michael hesitantly. "I sleep here tonight?" he asked in broken English. "No cost me nothin'?" His voice, like his movements, was disjointed, and he jumped when two older teenagers also wearing bandannas moved close to him and spoke sharply in Spanish. It was evident that they were pressuring him to leave with them.

"You can stay for free," Michael confirmed. "You have to shower before getting a bed, and be up and out by seven o'clock tomorrow morning. If you stay, you'll get breakfast in the morning before you go. You can wash and dry your clothes here if you want, but if you leave tonight, you can't get back in. The doors are locked at nine o'clock."

Eddie listened carefully, then shot a nervous glance at his companions before bobbing his head twice, quickly. "Okay," he said. "Okay, I stay." After another sharp exchange in Spanish, his friends stormed out.

Eddie's hands visibly trembled as he turned back to Michael and searched for words. "I—I don' wan' be with them no more," he said with an effort. Dr. West had remained after the service, and she'd witnessed the entire exchange. Now she said quietly, "Look at his arm. That's why he's got the shakes so bad." Needle marks covered the teenager's forearms. She stepped closer to Eddie. "How old are you, son?"

The boy looked at her, then dropped his eyes. *"Quince,"* he murmured. Dr. West glanced at Michael, horrified. On the streets and an addict at only fifteen years old!

She turned to Michael decisively. "He'll need medical help and close monitoring, but I'm not scheduled for the clinic here until late next week. Do you think someone could bring him into my office first thing in the morning?"

"I'm sure we can arrange that, as long as he'll cooperate. Thanks a lot, Pat, for being here tonight."

"Wouldn't have missed it for the world," she said cheerfully. "See you later."

When Michael finally left at almost ten o'clock that night,

there were less than a dozen men signed into the men's dormitory—equipped for more than seventy—and no women at all. Not one person had responded to the altar call at the end of the service.

Driving away through the dark streets, Michael mused about the events of that night, his disappointment tempered by the memory of Eddie's amazement that the "lady doctor" would treat him for free, and a frail elderly man's gratitude at being given a clean blanket. Winter was approaching, and soon the street people would be huddling over trash fires to stay warm. Southside Mission could literally be a lifeline for those most vulnerable—the very old and very young.

He was turning a corner when he spotted a heavily made-up teenage girl he recognized from the service, laughing and talking to a balding man in a red Porsche. As he watched, she walked around and got into the car, smoothing her tight skirt with skill. The two quickly disappeared into the night.

With a sinking heart Michael realized that he'd just witnessed a prostitute being solicited. *Dear God,* he cried silently, *this place is like a festering sore. Show me how to reach these people with Your love!*

After the service ended that evening, Jason Clark had asked Rachel if he could take her home. Since she'd driven in early that afternoon with Jenny, her own car was at home. She gratefully accepted.

She was unusually quiet as they drove through the dark city streets. Jason reached over and gently pulled her toward him.

"Come over here," he said. "I haven't seen much of you lately because of all this mission stuff. Don't you miss me?"

Rachel unbuckled her seat belt and scooted over next to him, resting her head against his shoulder with a contented sigh. "Yes, I sure do. I was really happy you came tonight, Jason. I didn't expect you to show up."

He laughed. "Well, it wasn't exactly my idea of an exciting place to spend a Friday night, but since *you* were there . . ."

He let his words trail off as he leaned down to quickly brush her cheek with his lips. "When I walked in and saw you singing in front of all those filthy people, it was like stumbling across a diamond in—in a garbage heap! I wanted to sweep you out of that ugly place and—"

He impulsively rolled to a stop in the middle of the quiet street and drew her close to him, but even as his lips hungrily sought hers, he felt her stiffen in his arms. Irritated, he drew back and looked at her.

"What's the matter with you?" he demanded angrily. "I thought you said you missed me!"

She looked miserable. "I do, Jason," she said. "I guess I'm just not in the mood right now."

He put the car back in gear with a jerk and started forward again, speeding down the dark streets. Rachel studied his angry profile thoughtfully.

"Didn't you see those people in there tonight?" she finally asked. "Didn't you *feel* anything about them other than their 'filthiness'? A lot of them live in the streets, Jason, literally sleeping on the sidewalks. Some of them are borderline mentally ill and can't even care for themselves. They need help, and hope— and most of all, they need to know Jesus."

Jason gave her a sideways glance, and she suddenly felt embarrassed. To him, her impassioned words must have sounded incredibly naive.

"You're really into all this, aren't you?" he asked. "You've been acting different lately. I'm not sure I even know you anymore."

She looked back at him, unable to think of a response. *You seem different, too,* she thought. *Or maybe I'm just seeing you in a different light.*

They rode the rest of the way home in uncomfortable silence. When they finally pulled up at Rachel's apartment, Jason got out and walked her to the door.

"Listen," he said abruptly, placing his hands on her shoulders, "I'm sorry, okay? Lately everything I say to you seems to be wrong. I didn't mean to get you upset." His face was suddenly soft, his voice persuasive. "Can we just forget all this and go on? I'd planned a big surprise for your birthday tomorrow, and I don't want it to be spoiled by some silly misunderstanding. You know I'd never deliberately do anything to hurt or upset you."

He lifted her chin, forcing her to look him in the eyes. "Forgive me?" he asked ruefully.

His boyish grin and repentant manner made Rachel smile despite herself. "Okay, okay," she said, standing on tiptoe to give him a quick placatory kiss on the cheek. "And I *am* glad you came tonight. What time are you picking me up tomorrow?"

"I'll be here at five." He gathered her close for a gentle, lingering hug, then slowly released her, giving her a tender look that left her flushed.

"See you then," he said softly.

Rachel waved as he drove off, then went inside and bolted the door. But as she moved through the apartment absently straightening magazines and carrying a dirty cup into the kitchen, the vague uneasiness she'd felt in the car slowly returned. What was it about Jason that left her so unsettled? She loved him, wanted to spend the rest of her life with him—didn't she?

Pulling a clean mug from the cabinet, she went to the kitchen sink and turned the water on, letting it run over her fingers as she waited for it to warm up. She hoped relaxing with some hot tea would help her see things more clearly.

Lost in thought, she didn't notice how quickly the water was heating up. By the time she shouted, "Ouch!" and belatedly jerked her hand back, her slender fingers were scalded. Tears abruptly welled in her eyes—but not just because of her fingers. Wrapping a dish towel around her hand, she walked into her room and sat on the edge of the bed.

Oh, Jason, she silently cried, *I love you so much. Why do you leave me so confused?*

15

THE SUNDAY AFTER-MEETING WAS MORE CROWDED THAN ever, despite the overcast weather. Fall was setting in, and the bright greens of summer were slowly changing to autumn hues. The air was slightly damp.

Inside the First Church sanctuary, people were still milling around exchanging greetings. Alex and Cheryl Powell were chatting with an older couple attending for the first time; Lauren Woods and Terri Bannister huddled near the front talking animatedly. Terri's husband, Ray, had come to church with her and the kids that morning for the first time, so she'd be leaving early. Jason stood with a possessive arm around Rachel as she and Kim Newton discussed some of Ted's latest ideas for Channel 5. Cliff Bright and Jenny Paige, their faces grim, appeared to be engaged in a serious conversation.

When Michael called the meeting to order, they all quickly found seats. Daniel Marshall opened with prayer, then Michael began to tell about the first service at Southside Mission.

"I think that most of us who went there Friday night saw and heard things that made us uncomfortable," he said, "but I think we also became a lot more aware of the kind of problems that exist in the south side. Many of the young people in the area are dropouts who've either run away or been thrown out of abusive homes, and they've gone to the only people who take an interest in them—the pimps and pushers. Others have ended up in street gangs.

"I talked at length with a fifteen-year-old boy named Eddie who joined a gang called the 'Second Streets' over a year ago. Several of them came to the mission Friday night to eat and cause trouble, but Eddie ended up staying for the night. He went to see Dr. West yesterday to begin drug treatment."

Michael smiled at Patricia West. "Eddie doesn't speak much English, but Dr. West tells me he's been asking a lot of questions about *'el Cristo.'* We need to find someone who speaks Spanish to talk with him in more detail."

Several rows back, Connie and Epimenio Garza exchanged a quick glance. Connie raised her hand.

"Pastor Maxwell? 'Menio and I could talk to him—," then she added, casting an impish smile in Cliff Bright's direction, "if I can convince my boss to let me off early some afternoon."

Cliff's troubled face momentarily cleared. "I think that can be arranged," he said, grinning back at her.

"Great!" said Michael. "Jenny, can you help them get together with Eddie?" Jenny Paige nodded.

Terri Bannister raised her hand. "How many of the southsiders responded to the altar call on Friday?"

"No one came forward either Friday or Saturday," Michael admitted, "but I don't think we should be discouraged by that. The south side has been a stronghold of evil for a long time, and it'll probably take awhile to break through that. But I talked to Pastor Snyder from Ashton Park Baptist early this morning—he preached at the mission yesterday—and he said that two of the men who stayed last night prayed later to receive Jesus."

There was an excited spatter of applause. Michael waited for it to die down.

"We need to remember the mission in prayer," he said. "I've committed to preaching the Friday night services for the next three months, but Jenny tells me they need volunteers during the week to help with some of the kitchen and maintenance duties as well as with counseling. Right now they've only got three permanent staff members."

He paused then and glanced around until he located Rachel and Jason. "Now," he said, "I think there are two people here who'd like to share some exciting news. Jason? Rachel?"

With self-conscious smiles, the young couple rose and turned to face the crowd. Jason smiled down at Rachel, then gently took her left hand in his.

"Last night, I took Rachel out to a nice restaurant to celebrate her birthday," he said, "and after the meal I had roses brought to our table. While she still had her arms full of flowers, I got down on my knees in front of everyone and asked her to marry me."

A murmur of satisfied approval ran through the crowd, and several people laughed. Jason proudly lifted Rachel's hand high to display the sparkling diamond ring on her finger.

"She probably just said yes to keep from embarrassing me," he said modestly, "but now she's stuck with me. Since we've talked about getting married for almost a year now, we've decided not to put it off too long. We're tentatively planning a December wedding, and we'd like all of you to come."

This time the applause turned into cheers and congratulatory shouts. Only Jenny Paige, studying Rachel closely, caught the fleeting expression—was it doubt?—that shadowed her lovely face. The next instant, however, as Rachel smiled up at Jason, she looked as radiantly happy as any newly-engaged young woman.

After they sat down, Ted Newton stood up to share his news about a new local series WFBB-TV would soon launch called "The Hero Next Door."

"It'll be similar to some of the other 'reality shows' that are so popular right now, but with a different twist," he said. "Instead of featuring trained rescuers doing their jobs, it'll focus on ordinary people who, in a moment of crisis, willingly risk their lives for strangers—like the Chicago man last year who helped a woman being attacked by armed muggers, or the two high school students who jumped into a fast-moving river to rescue a toddler trapped inside a sinking car. Ordinary people doing extraordinary things—or, in Christian terms, 'doing unto others as you'd have them do unto you.' It won't be overtly religious, but many of these 'heroes' appear to have a strong element of Christian faith in their lives. At the very least, it'll be an encouraging, uplifting show, some good news in a bad news world."

After Ted sat down, Michael commented, "Well, it sounds like God is really moving in people's lives! Anybody else have anything to share today before we close? A prayer request or another testimony?"

Jenny looked pointedly at Cliff Bright. The store owner sighed and slowly stood up.

"I hate even to share this after all the exciting news," he said, "but I guess I need to. Remember last month when I mentioned that, due to the financial losses my company had suffered because of changes I'd made, I might have to close several stores? I know many of you have made it a point to shop at Mr. B Stores since then, and I really appreciate your efforts, but unfortunately it's still not been enough. Next week my Ray Street and Sunset stores will close."

The announcement was met with a moment of stunned silence. Several people turned to look at Connie Garza, knowing she worked at Mr. B. She shook her head; neither of the stores being closed was hers.

Cliff went on, "I'm hoping that, by downsizing now, I can prevent any more store closings from becoming necessary. But I have to tell you—" His voice broke, and he had to clear his throat and wait a moment before continuing. "I have to tell you that this has been very difficult. Elizabeth doesn't understand why I'm doing this, and she—she—"

This time it took him longer to regain control of his speech. As he stood, his balding head half bowed, Michael walked over to put a hand on his shoulder; Alex Powell and Daniel Marshall quickly followed suit. When the store owner looked up again, he was surrounded with supporters.

"Cliff," Michael said, "I don't know what to say. I wish I had some kind of answers for you to make it all easier, but I don't. Can we just pray for you, and for Elizabeth?"

Cliff nodded wordlessly. Michael, his hand still firmly on Cliff's shoulder, closed his eyes and bowed his head.

"Lord, we know that You're present in our midst, and that You're intimately aware of all the setbacks Cliff has encountered as he's tried to honor his pledge to follow You. We don't understand why his faithfulness in business seems to have been rewarded with failure, or why his devotion to You has brought such pain and strife to his home. But regardless of how it looks, we know that You're a good and loving Father who works all things together for good. Lord Jesus, please let this whole situation somehow work for Cliff's and Elizabeth's good."

There was a moment of silence, then Alex Powell's deep voice quietly continued the prayer, "Dear Lord, we want to stand with our brother in this difficult time. Please grant him Your strength and peace in the days and weeks to come, and show the rest of us what we can do to help bear his burden."

One by one, various others spoke out to ask God's peace and blessing on Cliff, and to intercede on his behalf. There was an almost tangible sense of the Spirit's presence in the room, and by the time the prayer ended there were few dry eyes. When people slowly looked up, still half distracted, the unseen bond between them brought to mind the words of Psalm 133:1: "Behold, how good and how pleasant it is for brethren to dwell together in unity" (KJV).

September turned to October, leaves fell, and the weather turned cold. In the south side, the poor and homeless braced for another long winter of hardship.

But this year, the word was slowly circulating in the streets: Southside Mission was "for real," a safe place to find food, clothing, and medical help. In the three weeks since it had opened, the mission had gone from housing less than a dozen men to more than fifty each night, and seventeen men and two women had made the decision to follow Christ. The women's section still remained largely vacant, though, and fully a third of the new converts had soon disappeared back into the streets. To everyone's sorrow, young Eddie Saenz was one of them.

On this Friday night, the dining hall was crowded to capacity with people driven inside by the season's first snowfall. Michael Maxwell noticed many new faces, but he had learned enough by now not to approach them directly. Southsiders were, of necessity, wary.

The minister had also learned not to show up in a suit and tie. Tonight he wore jeans, tennis shoes, and a pullover sweater. At first it had felt odd and uncomfortable to preach in such casual garb, but he had finally adopted the apostle Paul's attitude: "I have become all things to all men, so that by all possible means I might save some."

Now, moving through the crowd, he warmly greeted some of the "regulars." "Hi, Nick," he called to a tiny, birdlike elderly man huddled in a corner with a plate of lasagna.

Nick looked up, his gray face lighting up in a smile. "Hi, Father," he answered. "Nice dinner tonight." Michael grinned and shook his head; the man, who was mildly retarded, had been raised Catholic, and no amount of explanation could shake his habit of referring to him as "Father Maxwell."

More women were present than usual, both the older "bag lady" variety and some of the district's many prostitutes. *It must be the cold that's driving them inside,* Michael thought. *Maybe we should pray for a long winter!*

At 7:30 the evening service began. This time when Rachel nimbly stepped up on the stage and motioned to the pianist, there were only a few ribald shouts and wolf whistles. Those seated around the troublemakers quickly quieted them as Rachel picked up the microphone. Over the past few weeks that she'd been coming to sing, the southsiders had grown increasingly respectful toward Rachel, impressed by the unselfish giving of her time and talent.

She started the service tonight with a fast-moving song called "Suddenly Eternity."

> *We all go through this life*
> *as if we're here to stay,*

Making plans, working hard,
taking it day by day.

We all think that someday soon
we'll take time to make things right,
But when that call comes through for you
it's like a thief in the night!

Suddenly eternity! Your plans have gone astray.
Suddenly eternity! Today is the day.
Suddenly eternity! What you are is all you will be.
There is no more time . . . There is suddenly eternity.

The southsiders listened with varying degrees of visible response. A thirtyish woman wearing a tight, black jacket looked stricken, as if she'd just caught a horrifying glimpse into her future; a man a few years older stared, unseeing, at his own hands. Rachel started into the second verse:

But if we try to live our lives
as if each day is the last,
If we put our trust in Him,
hold our commitments fast.

Someday when that moment comes
that our lives will be required . . .
We won't have to be ashamed
in that sudden hour!

By the time she'd finished the second chorus, she had the undivided attention of every person in the room. When Michael stood up to speak, he sensed immediately that something was different tonight; the normally rowdy audience was as quiet as his affluent and sophisticated First Church congregation ever was.

That Friday night there occurred some of the most remarkable scenes he and his small group from First Church had ever witnessed. Although there was nothing especially new in his simple message of God's love and forgiveness, as the Holy Spirit swept across the room, the hardened audience was unaccountably touched. Before he was finished speaking, there were the sounds of open weeping in the crowd. When Rachel finally rose and began to sing, the southsiders moved almost as one toward the platform.

> *Softly and tenderly, Jesus is calling,*
> *Calling for you and for me . . .*
> *See, on the portals He's waiting and watching,*
> *Watching for you and for me*
>
> *Come home, come home!*
> *Ye who are weary, come home*
> *Earnestly, tenderly, Jesus is calling,*
> *Calling, O sinner, come home!*

Michael hardly said a word. Stretching out his hand with a gesture of invitation, he waited for all those who stumbled forward, weeping, to kneel at the front. As he went among them to pray, he saw Jenny Paige kneeling with an older woman and Rachel Wingate holding a weeping young prostitute.

As the southsiders continued to crowd in a double row around the platform, a well-dressed young man suddenly pushed his way through to kneel among them. Michael, catching sight of him, stared in astonishment. It was Roger Paige.

It was nearly midnight before the service ended. Michael stayed up long into Saturday morning, praying and talking with many of the new converts who, bewildered by the emotional upheaval they'd just experienced, clung to him as though their lives depended upon his physical presence. Roger Paige was among those who stayed.

Rachel had spoken to Roger briefly before she and Jason left. Her face was soft as she approached and extended both her hands to him.

"I'm so happy for you," she said quietly, her eyes shining with tears. "Your mom and I have prayed for you so often."

Roger awkwardly took her hands in his own. "Thanks," he murmured. "I don't know why I ran from God for so long. Guess I was just being stubborn."

He glanced over to where his mother sat counseling a young woman. Feeling his gaze she glanced up, her weary face reflecting her joy at his presence. He smiled at her before turning back to Rachel.

"You and Mom—you were really the ones who got to me," he said. "That night at my house, when you were talking about the mission, all of a sudden it seemed so—*real*. You were both so happy! I couldn't figure it out." He laughed suddenly, his face alight with new joy. "Now I think I know what the excitement was all about."

Rachel grinned, then impulsively stepped forward to give him a hug. She was startled when Jason stepped forward to intercept her.

"Hey, what's this?" he said only half-jokingly, putting his arm possessively around her shoulders. "Go find your own girl, Paige. This one's mine."

His words embarrassed Rachel. "Jason, stop it. I was just congratulating him. He came to know the Lord tonight! Isn't that great?"

"Yeah, sure, that's great." After only a moment's hesitation he put out his hand, and Roger shook it warmly.

Jason abruptly turned back to Rachel. "We really need to go now. Are you ready?"

"I guess so. See you at church on Sunday, Roger?"

Roger nodded. "Yeah, see you then."

It wasn't until they were in the car that Jason asked tersely, "Why'd you do that?"

Rachel looked at him, puzzled. "Why'd I do what?"

"Grab Roger like that. You're supposed to be engaged to me. I wish you'd start acting like it!"

Rachel stared at him in utter astonishment. "What are you talking about? Didn't you even see what happened there tonight? Didn't you feel the presence of the Holy Spirit? It was the most powerful, most awesome—"

Words momentarily escaped her. How could he have sat in the same room, watched all those men's and women's lives be transformed and yet remain untouched?

Her thoughts turned to the sights they had witnessed earlier that night: the tear-stained face of the "fallen woman" Jenny had enfolded in her arms as she gently led her to the Savior and the shining face of the elderly man who had knelt beside Michael to exchange his life of drunken debauchery for a new life as a child of the King. And Roger Paige's humbled expression as he knelt among the people Jason had once referred to as "garbage." Those faces—men and women touched, for the first time, with the Spirit's glory!

Studying Jason's stony profile, Rachel realized with sudden, painful clarity that he had no respect at all for the supernatural events they had witnessed. She felt a sudden sense of revulsion. All the time she had been singing with the complete passion of her soul, he had been unmoved—except, perhaps, for his longing to physically possess her. She unconsciously twisted the diamond ring on her slender finger, suddenly feeling smothered. "Take me home," she said. *"Now."*

16

ONCE INSIDE HER APARTMENT, RACHEL HARDLY REMEM-
bered telling Jason goodnight. She paced restlessly, trying in vain
to sort through her conflicting emotions.

Did she truly love him? Had she ever? *Yes. No.* "I don't know!"
she finally whispered aloud, then stopped, appalled at her own
words.

Sinking onto the couch, she hugged her knees, tears streaming
down her cheeks. What was the matter with her? Jason was
handsome, charming, the perfect companion. When she was with
him, he made everything seem so right.

But that's part of the problem, she thought, remembering how
he'd urged her to take the movie part even though it meant
"temporarily" compromising her morals. It had seemed right
when he'd explained it, and yet—it was just plain wrong!

With that thought, she walked over to the stereo and slid a
hand-labeled cassette into the tape player. When the music
started, she settled back on the couch and closed her eyes to
listen.

Sweet perfume fills the air
Sunlight glints on auburn hair . . .

———

351

As Jason's smooth tenor voice sang the words that had so thrilled her when he sang them to her, she discovered she felt curiously detached. Why wasn't it moving her?

I'm a moth drawn to your fire
Beauty fills me with desire . . .

Suddenly nauseated, Rachel leaped up and jabbed the "stop" button—then stood frozen, lost in thought.

What was Jason really to her, or she to him? Undeniably, they both felt a strong physical attraction. But, beneath his easy charm and wit, was there the inner strength and determination of a man truly committed to the Lord? Most important of all, did she respect him enough to give him her trust, her life?

"No. No!" she said aloud, and with those words she knew her choice had been made.

The realization brought an instant cloud of distressing thoughts. She and Jason had made so many plans together—picked out their living room furniture, imagined the kind of house they'd buy, even chosen names for their "first few" kids. She couldn't even imagine a future that didn't include Jason. Without him, all her most cherished dreams were dead.

And what about all the people at church? They'd been so excited about their engagement! And her parents—they'd already sent the plane tickets for her and Jason's visit at Thanksgiving, less than a week away. How could she just cancel out like this at the last minute?

Despite all the dark and confusing thoughts, however, she suddenly felt a strange sense of relief. Deep in her heart she knew she'd made the right decision, regardless of the pain it brought. She'd just have to face the consequences as they came. She slipped the diamond ring from her finger and carefully placed it on the corner of her desk. She'd get a few hours of sleep, then go talk to Jason.

There was a heightened sense of excitement among First Church members that Sunday morning. News of the revival that struck Southside had swiftly spread, and the attendance, which had been tapering off for months, was slightly up.

Michael faced the congregation with a deep sense of humility and gratitude, aware that a new, unspoken camaraderie was developing between them. The more literal imitation of Jesus that had begun with a small group of volunteers was working like leaven through the entire church, and as he looked from face to face he felt a strange but vivid change of setting, back to the first century when the disciples had all things in common. They were slowly developing the kind of trust in their Lord that the early disciples had as they faced loss and death with courage and even joy. At the close of his message, he asked the church to remember the new life that had begun at Southside Mission.

"We've already lost many of the earlier converts back to the streets," he said. "The pull of drugs and friends has been too much for them to resist. We need to pray that the Holy Spirit will thwart the drug dealers and pimps and gang leaders who deliberately lure people away."

The after-meeting was the largest it had ever been. Jason Clark was one of the few missing, a fact Michael noted without surprise. He and Sharon had spent hours the previous afternoon counseling with Rachel after she had returned, distraught, from breaking off the engagement. Jason had also apparently taken it hard, not even attending the regular church service that morning.

There were many excited questions about the moving of the Spirit at the mission, and several more people offered to help with the ministry. Michael directed them to talk to Jenny Paige, then with a smile asked Roger Paige to stand up.

"Roger was at the mission Friday night, and he asked if he could say something this morning," he explained. "For those of you who don't know him, he's Jenny's son. Roger?"

Roger looked slightly red as he stood up and glanced around at all the expectant, upturned faces.

"This is more embarrassing than I thought it would be," he admitted. The crowd laughed quietly. "I've been going to this church since I was a kid, but it's only been these last few months that I've started really wondering what it was all about. More than anything else, it was because of this pledge thing.

"I'd always thought of God as somehow distant, not connected to real life. But after my mom took the pledge to live her life by asking, 'What would Jesus do?' I started seeing a lot of changes in her. All of a sudden she was doing things I never could've imagined her doing, but she was also happier than she'd ever been before! After awhile it got to me."

He paused to smile ruefully. "I went to the mission the very first night it opened, but I was too proud to go inside. When I went again on Friday, though, I just couldn't help it. There was—there was something—"

His voice faltered, and he hastily blinked back tears. Jenny reached up to take his hand as he went on in a low voice. "There was something there in that room, a kind of love, I guess, that made me feel like a kid. Before I knew it I was at the front bawling like a baby." He took a deep breath. "I guess what I'm trying to say is, thank you. If you people hadn't taken this pledge, I don't think I'd have ever thought twice about how I was living my life."

He started to say something else, then shook his head and sat down. Jenny hugged him as the others clapped and murmured their congratulations.

It was a short meeting, but before the group broke up there were several other confidences. Alex Powell shared that he'd had the joy of leading a co-worker to Christ early that week, and a young newspaper reporter who'd been coming barely a month told how he'd been fired for refusing an assignment that would have required him to spend an evening in a topless bar.

Another young newcomer stood up, trembling, to make a public confession: he had gone that Friday to the owner of the camera shop where he'd worked for more than two years to confess that he'd stolen several valuable cameras in the past, and to arrange to repay the owner for his loss. He'd fully expected to be fired, but to his utter amazement, his boss had kept him on. Even more exciting, though—it had opened the door for him to share *why* he'd confessed his thievery. He and his boss had talked about the Lord for almost two hours.

The First Church group counseled together and prayed for each other, and when they finally went home all of them were filled with the Spirit's power.

Rachel Wingate walked out with Jenny and Roger. Jenny let Roger move a few steps ahead, then put her arm around the younger woman.

"Are you okay?" she asked quietly. "You look a little down today."

"I'm all right. I guess you already know that Jason and I aren't—" She held up her left hand, letting the empty ring finger complete the sentence.

"I heard," Jenny admitted. "Is that why he didn't show up for church today?"

Rachel nodded. "When I left yesterday, he was furious. He accused me of 'betraying his trust' and just about everything else you can think of. Said that if that was the way so-called Christians acted, he wanted no part of it! Can you believe that?"

"I'm afraid I can. I'm actually a little relieved, if you want to know the truth."

"Why?" asked Rachel, a little startled.

"Because I never thought he was right for you. There was always something—I don't know—*false*, about him, like he was playing a part. I was surprised that he took the pledge. I assumed it was probably just for your sake."

Rachel was silent for a moment. "I really thought I loved him," she said painfully. "He was so much fun, and he knew how to make me happy. It was only when I was away from him that I started questioning what we were doing."

Rachel paused, suddenly aware of the amazing changes that had taken place in her thinking. Where would the Lord lead her next?

Even as the Sunday after-meeting was breaking up that day, another meeting in the church was still going strong. It was a small, informal gathering consisting of four deacons, two members of the building committee, the chairman of the foreign missions board, the financial director, and the church treasurer. They had decided to meet in one of the Sunday School rooms where Michael Maxwell wasn't likely to walk in on them.

"I think we're all agreed," Martha Robinson was saying, her pudgy chin quivering with indignation. "Even though this morning's attendance and offering were up compared to the last few weeks, the offering was still down almost 20 percent from what it was seven months ago before Pastor Maxwell started this pledge thing. I think we've been patient enough. If we don't do something now, there might not be a church to worry about in another seven months."

There was a murmur of agreement. "It was Pastor Maxwell himself who said that any church that isn't growing is dying," said Frank Boykin, the financial director. "But when I tried to talk to him about going back to some of our more successful advertising, he just said, 'I've pledged to follow the Lord regardless of the outcome, and I don't believe that's what He would have us do.' He won't listen to reason."

"It's more than that," interrupted John Roberts, one of the deacons. "The biggest thing is, he's concentrating all his time and attention on one small group of people—the ones who've taken his pledge. He's totally ignoring the needs of the rest of the flock."

Martha nodded vigorously. "That's exactly what I thought. Then it's all settled. Frank, are you going to draft the letter to the board?"

"It'll be ready to mail tomorrow. It will probably take them a few weeks to respond, but in the meantime I think we should get the support of a few more of our most prominent families. Maybe we can even start making some quiet inquiries about other pastors that might be interested in taking over."

As they disbanded, the furtive glances and mean-spirited whispers formed a sharp contrast to the spirit of peace that had reigned over the other group just minutes earlier.

*　*　*

It was Thanksgiving weekend, and Rachel Wingate was in Virginia visiting her family. For the first time in almost two months she wouldn't be singing at Southside Mission that Friday night. A choir member from Villa Drive Lutheran Church had volunteered to stand in for her.

There was now a regular contingent of First Church members who faithfully attended the mission each week when Michael preached, including Daniel Marshall, Alex and Cheryl Powell, Connie and 'Menio Garza, Lauren Woods, and, of course, Jenny Paige. Several others, Dr. West among them, came as often as their schedules permitted.

Roger Paige had also faithfully attended since he'd first come forward at the mission. But even though he enjoyed the time of worship and Michael's straightforward messages, he felt increasingly restless. He didn't really fit in with the other First Church members who stayed afterward to pray with and counsel those who had responded to the message.

Even though he was devouring the new "plain English" Bible Pastor Maxwell had presented him the day he was baptized, he didn't yet feel equipped to address the problems many of the southsiders faced. What he really wanted was to find a way to reach other people like himself—the outwardly content men and women who drifted from one club to the next in an endless search for something to fill the emptiness in their lives.

On the way home from the mission that night, he talked to his mother about it.

"It isn't that I don't like the mission," he assured her. "You're doing a great job of reaching people who've slipped through the cracks with traditional churches. But what about people like my friends, Bruce and Dennis, who think church is a joke because of all the hypocrites they read about and see on television? Who's doing something to reach them?"

Jenny looked at her son, a small smile playing at her lips. "It sounds to me like the Holy Spirit might be nudging *you* to do something. Did you have anything specific in mind?"

Roger grinned. "Not really. Right now I'm just complaining! But I know there's got to be a way to get through to them the way you and Rachel got through to me. The problem is, Christians don't usually hang around in nightclubs or bars, so the 'party' crowd rarely sees them. And I don't think many of my friends would even think of coming to church with me. They'd consider it a huge waste of time."

Jenny nodded. "Well, why don't we start praying that the Lord will make it clear to you what you should do? That's the best way I know to come up with some answers."

On that same holiday weekend, several tragedies simultaneously struck the First Church of Ashton.

First, Michael and Sharon Maxwell were awakened early Saturday morning by the insistent ringing of the telephone. Sharon answered it groggily, then, suddenly alert, handed the receiver to Michael. It was Terri Bannister.

She was crying so hard that he could barely make out her words. "Pastor Maxwell, it's Ray," she sobbed. "The kids—we heard a shot in the den and little Bobby ran in to see—Ray's just lying there on the carpet, he's—he's—I don't know what to do! Oh, dear God, I don't know what to do!"

Michael was already out of bed and reaching for his pants. "Terri, I'm on my way. Have you called an ambulance?"

"Jennifer called 9–1–1." She made an obvious effort to control her voice. "Pastor, why—why would he do this? He was going to be baptized tomorrow!"

"I don't know, Terri. Listen, I'll be there in just a minute. Just hang on, okay? Get the kids and go sit in the bedroom until the ambulance arrives."

He wasn't sure if she understood, but when the phone clicked he hung up and turned to Sharon. "I don't know for sure, but it sounds like Ray must've shot himself. Terri and the kids are there alone. Call Jenny and Cheryl and get them to pray, okay? I'll call you as soon as I know what's going on."

At the Bannisters' house, Michael walked into a situation out of a nightmare. Paramedics were gathered around Ray's blood-soaked body, carefully lifting him onto a stretcher as two policemen tried to calm a hysterical Terri. One look at Ray's head told

Michael that there was no hope for his recovery. The gun he had used was still on the floor.

He had written a short, pathetic note addressed to his wife in his final moments. In barely coherent words, he explained that he'd been involved in an embezzlement scheme at the bank where he worked, and that he'd been alerted by a call early that morning that some of the missing funds had been traced to him. "I've been trying to figure out a way to pay it all back without anyone knowing," he wrote, "but now it's too late. May God forgive me."

Terri clutched the note until a policeman gently took it from her, explaining apologetically that it was evidence. Michael called Sharon, who soon arrived with Cheryl and Jenny. They all stayed with her and the kids until Terri's brother and sister-in-law showed up late that afternoon.

The second near-tragedy occurred that same night, when Martha Robinson's car was violently rear-ended as she sat at a red light. The impact totaled her car and left her with a painful neck injury and two broken toes. Michael received the phone call only moments after he returned from Terri Bannister's house. He went straight to the hospital.

Martha was already recovered enough to be thoroughly enraged at the other driver. "Imagine!" she told Michael, "I was just sitting there minding my own business when this—this *fool* of a woman ran right into me! And she doesn't even have insurance on her car!"

She brusquely waved aside Michael's offers of help. "The doctor says I can go home tonight, as soon as he finishes wrapping my toes. My nephew is coming to pick me up."

"Well, I'm just glad you're okay," Michael said wearily. "Let me know if there's anything we can do for you." He decided not to mention Ray Bannister, although the news would be out soon enough; Martha had a reputation for embellishing stories in the re-telling. Terri would have enough to deal with in the days and weeks to come without any "well-meaning" gossip.

The following morning the *Ashton Herald*'s Sunday edition ran a front-page account of Ray Bannister's suicide, mentioning his implication in an embezzlement scheme. Terri didn't come to church. Michael had learned that Ray's funeral date couldn't be set until the investigation and autopsy were complete.

The message he preached that morning was about forgiveness. He chose his text from the Book of Ephesians:

Be kind and compassionate to one another,
forgiving each other, just as in Christ God forgave you.
      Ephesians 4:32

"As Christians we tend to talk a lot about forgiveness," he began. "We're very self-righteous about overlooking 'little' sins— 'white' lies, angry outbursts, momentary lapses. But the true test is in how we react to the brand new believer who's struggling to overcome a sordid past, or to the older brother or sister in the Lord who stumbles into what we consider *serious* sin—things like adultery, thievery, drunkenness. Do we freely forgive them when they repent, or do we turn our backs on them, leaving them to deal with it alone?

"What would Jesus do?"

He paused, then continued after a moment. "If we're to be imitators of Christ, we need to grasp firmly one central fact: *Forgiving others is a requirement, not an option.* We can't use religious excuses to withhold from others the very forgiveness God extends toward us. We can't call it 'discernment' when we're passing judgment on people, or cloak damaging slander in the righteous robes of making a 'prayer request.'

"Listen to the instructions Paul gave to the Corinthians about dealing with a brother who had gotten caught up in sin.

Now instead, you ought to forgive and comfort him,
so that he will not be overwhelmed by excessive sorrow.
I urge you, therefore, to reaffirm your love for him."
      2 Corinthians 2:7–8

He rubbed his forehead wearily, then said with obvious difficulty, "We had a new brother who I had planned to baptize today. He came to the Lord with the burden of a past he felt compelled to conceal, apparently hoping to deal with it on his own. When he learned it was going to become a public matter, he didn't have enough confidence in God's—and our—willingness to forgive and stand by him. I pray that we will become the kind of church and the kind of people who are known for our ability to forgive."

After the closing prayer, Michael announced that the regular Sunday after-meeting would be replaced that day by a prayer meeting.

"The Bannister family needs our support, and as some of you know, another of our members, Martha Robinson, was involved in a car wreck late yesterday afternoon. She's not seriously injured, but she's going to have trouble getting around for a while. We need to remember her in prayer as well."

He hesitated, seeming to study their faces. "It's been almost eight months since many of you took the pledge to live one year by asking yourself, 'What would Jesus do?' Looking out over this congregation, I see a number of people whose lives have been radically changed as a result—and their actions, in turn, have affected many others.

"Sometimes when you're following the Lord, you run into some pretty serious opposition. Peter wrote:

Be self-controlled and alert.
Your enemy the devil prowls around like a roaring lion
looking for someone to devour.

    1 Peter 5:8

"Now, more than ever, it's time to watch and pray. I hope many of you will stay today."

Most of the people who usually attended the after-meeting remained, joined by a number of others who'd never found time before. The shocking events of the previous day seemed to draw them together, to make them more willing to overlook petty disagreements in an all-consuming desire to seek God's face.

They had hardly begun to pray when the Holy Spirit swept over them, leaving many in tears. Earnest prayers were offered on behalf of Terri Bannister and her children, for Martha Robinson, for Southside Mission, and for the church as a whole. When the final "amen" was spoken, most were astonished to discover that over an hour had passed.

Lauren Woods lingered for a moment after the meeting was dismissed. "Pastor Maxwell," she said, "while we were praying God really laid it on my heart to do something to help Martha. Do you know if she needs help around the house or maybe someone to run errands for her?"

He thought for a moment. "She lives alone, and I think the only relative nearby is a nephew. She'd probably appreciate the offer." He gave her Martha's phone number.

On the way home Michael was unusually quiet. Sharon finally asked him what he was thinking about.

He smiled. "Lauren, actually. Have you noticed the change in her, Sharon? She's not even like the same person anymore. I used to cringe every time she called or walked up to me because she was always so clingy, obviously trying to attract attention to herself. But now it's like she's found her niche. She's turning out to be one of the strongest, most spiritually insightful women in our congregation."

On Wednesday Ray Bannister's body was finally released for burial, and the funeral was held the next day. It seemed to Michael that the entire congregation of First Church turned out for the service, surrounding Terri and her children with a public display of loving support. He could hardly believe it was the same group of people who, just seven months before, had been so scandalized when a feverish young mother had committed the "crime" of disturbing their church service. Now, the disgrace Terri and the kids were having to bear as the result of Ray's actions was being willingly shared by the many, diffusing its devastating effect.

"Did you see what happened there?" Michael later asked Sharon. "The church is finally pulling together, putting aside differences to function as the body of Christ. Did you see John Roberts? He has opposed almost everything I've done for months, but he showed up today and actually asked me if there was anything the family needed." He added thoughtfully, "He stayed for the prayer meeting on Sunday. Maybe that's what finally got through to him."

He was still musing about the changes in the church when the phone rang. It was Dr. Carl Bruce, pastor of the Nazareth Avenue Church in Chicago.

Michael's face lit up when he recognized his long-time friend's deep, slightly raspy voice, but his smile quickly faded when he learned why he was calling.

"Michael," Carl said carefully, "have you had some trouble lately at First Church with the deacons or the financial committee?"

"Nothing outstanding. Just the usual griping I get whenever offerings drop or whenever I've announced that we're changing the way we do things. Why?"

Carl sighed. "I thought it was probably like that. Look, you've got problems—*big* problems—with some of your people. I got a call this morning from a friend on the board; apparently a number of your deacons and some others on the financial committee wrote to them several weeks ago asking for your removal. They accused you of everything but fraud: mismanagement, fanaticism, you name it. My friend on the board who knows we're close asked me to call you and find out what's going on."

The news hit Michael like a physical blow. He sat down slowly, his fingers white as he tightly gripped the phone receiver.

"Michael? Are you there?"

"I'm here. I don't know what to say, Carl. I just came back from preaching the funeral of a new convert who committed suicide last weekend. He left a wife and three children. I was so proud of the church for making such a big effort to turn out to support the family—" His voice trailed off.

Carl waited a moment. "Why don't you just tell me what's been happening at the church the past few months? All the complaints in the letter seem to center on that."

Michael didn't know where to begin. "It all started back in the spring," he said slowly, "when a young woman named Brenda Collier came to our church with her little girl, hoping to find help . . ."

He went on to detail the events that had eventually led to his challenging the congregation to take a year-long pledge to live their lives by asking, "What would Jesus do?" and then told of the many events that had followed, both in his own life and in the lives of other church members.

"I can't tell you what a difference it's made," Michael said, a flicker of his earlier excitement returning to his voice. "It's not only making a difference in our church, but it's spreading out into the community. People who'd never darken the door of a church are being touched because of how His people are acting in business and their family life. One of the most effective preachers in all of Ashton right now is Cliff Bright, who owns Mr. B Food Stores. His commitment to the Lord has cost him a lot, but his life has been a testimony to more people than I can count."

Carl Bruce had listened, fascinated, to the whole story. When Michael finished, the Chicago pastor was openly excited.

"Listen," he said impulsively, "I have an idea. Why don't I drive down to Ashton next weekend and see everything for myself? I can go to Southside Mission with you on Friday night and attend First Church on Sunday. It'll give us a chance to catch up."

"We'll be glad to have you. But while you're here, why don't you plan to preach at the mission Saturday night? The pastor who was scheduled that night called yesterday to say he has to go out of town, so I was looking for a replacement for him."

Dr. Bruce replied quickly, "I'd love to. But I'm not at all sure I'll know how to speak to that kind of audience."

Michael laughed. "It's quite a change from Sunday mornings; I'll tell you that. But it'll be good for you, Carl."

The moment he hung up, Sharon asked anxiously, "What's going on?" From his end of the conversation she'd been able to tell that something serious was happening.

Michael shook his head. "Looks like a lynch mob is forming at church. I've apparently upset some people, and now they've written to the board asking for my removal. A friend of Carl's on the board called and told him about it."

Sharon's lips tightened. "If somebody wants you to leave, why don't they talk to you face to face instead of sneaking around like this behind your back?"

Michael smiled without humor. "It rarely works like that, honey. I've seen it before, even if it's never been directed at me. It starts with a few whispers and complaints and slowly escalates into an ugly feud."

"Just what we need right now," Sharon said glumly. "What are we going to do?"

"I don't know. I think I'd like to talk to Alex and Daniel before I do anything else. The bad thing is, once these things start they almost never resolve peaceably; it only takes a few trouble-makers to turn a church upside down. I'd hate to see everything that's been started at First Church destroyed over something like this."

Sharon searched his face. "What if we can't work it out?" she asked, seeing his doubt. "You're not going to let them bully you into resigning, are you?"

Michael sighed. "This is one case where it's hard to know what Jesus would do, isn't it? I just don't know. That's why I want to ask Alex and Daniel, and maybe Cliff Bright, to pray with me. I don't think I can trust my own judgment on something like this."

17

THAT FRIDAY, THE SEASON'S FIRST SNOWSTORM BLAN-
keted the city of Ashton. Southside Mission opened its doors four
hours early to serve a hot soup lunch to the shivering crowd,
many of whom had never been inside. Michael Maxwell and Dr.
Carl Bruce carefully made their way downtown at around four
o'clock.

Rachel Wingate was already there. Michael introduced her to
Dr. Bruce, then asked, "What brings you here so early, Rachel? I
didn't expect you until closer to the service time."

"They let us out of class early today because of the storm," she
replied. "I knew the mission would be short-handed, so I came
straight here. It's a good thing, too; three kitchen workers have
already called to say they can't make it." She smiled and held up a
wooden spoon. "I'm not much of a cook, but I guess I'm better
than nothing. They have me stirring the cheese sauce."

Michael and Carl both laughed. "Michael has been telling me
good things about you, Ms. Wingate," said Dr. Bruce. "He says
your singing ministry has touched a lot of people who've become
immune to preaching. I'm looking forward to hearing you."

Rachel flushed. "I just hope it goes well. Lots of new people are here tonight because of the storm."

Roger showed up a few minutes later with Jenny. He looked startled to find Rachel in the kitchen.

Feeling his glance, she looked up and smiled. "Well, hello!" she said warmly, brushing a long strand of auburn hair from her face. "What are *you* doing here?"

Roger seemed uncomfortable. "Mom thought they might need an extra hand tonight, so I offered to come in and help." When he hastily retreated from the kitchen, Rachel stared after him with a puzzled expression. What was wrong with *him?*

The service that night was standing room only. Dr. Bruce sat on the front row between Jenny and Roger, listening with interest as his old friend from seminary delivered a down-to-earth sermon that could hardly be called simply a "message"—it was more of a ringing challenge to the wayward to discard their sin-filled lives in exchange for a new life in Christ.

I would never have expected to find Michael Maxwell in a place like this, Dr. Bruce thought. *When I heard him preach two years ago, he'd never have dreamed of using the word 'sin' in a sermon. He was a great speaker, but it never meant much. Now he's different— less eloquent, but also much more powerful.*

At the conclusion of the service, Rachel stood to sing "Amazing Grace." As her sweet voice rang out with the familiar words, she was joined by many in the audience:

> *Amazing grace! How sweet the sound*
> *that saved a wretch like me,*
> *I once was lost, but now I'm found*
> *'twas blind, but now I see.*

Before she reached the second verse, the area around the platform was crowded with weeping men and women. Dr. Bruce quickly joined the other First Church members who moved among the crowd to pray. Within minutes, kneeling with his arm around a black teenager, he found tears streaming down his face as well.

'Twas grace that taught my heart to fear,
and grace my fears relieved!
How precious did that grace appear,
the hour I first believed.

Dr. Carl Bruce preached the next night at the mission. He was amazed to discover that he not only enjoyed it, but that he was effective, as well. He prayed with four people that night.

It was late Sunday night when he finally arrived home in Chicago. Unable to sleep, he sat up in his Nazareth Avenue Church study with pen in hand, searching for the words to effectively describe what he'd experienced that weekend in Ashton. He had returned both thoughtful and agitated.

He decided to write it all down in letter form to his friend on the board, the Reverend Patrick Corridan.

Dear Pat,

It is late Sunday night, but I'm so awake and excited after my weekend visit to Ashton that I feel driven to write to you now, while it's all still fresh in my mind.

As you know, I drove down Friday to spend a few days with Michael Maxwell and to see for myself what effect his actions this past year have had on First Church. Michael and I have been friends since seminary, although our methods have always been rather different. He was always more of a popular "sermonizer," while I tended to be more of a teacher. When he was called to First Church of Ashton within months of graduation, I thought to myself, "They made a good choice. Michael's preaching will fill their pews in record time."

He's now been there almost eleven years, and until about eight months ago he apparently did just that. He took First Church from its small beginnings and aggressively built it into one of the largest and most affluent congregations in the city. The music ministry, which included a full band as well as some very talented vocalists, regularly gave concerts in the community. Michael commanded a rather impressive salary that enabled him and his wife, Sharon, to take exotic vacations every year. It was the kind of position that most pastors—myself included—would consider ideal.

But then, in the spring this year, Michael made a totally uncharacteristic proposition at the end of the service one Sunday morning. He challenged members of the church to volunteer, with him, not to do anything for one year without first asking the question, "What would Jesus do?" As you can imagine, it sent shock waves through that comfortable, well-heeled congregation!

What has happened since then strikes me as so remarkable that I'm not quite sure how to even describe it. Probably the best and easiest way will be for me to tell you about some of the people I met in the church who, along with Michael Maxwell, took what they now refer to as "the pledge."

First of all, Michael tells me he was astonished that several of the most prominent members of the church responded to his rather controversial challenge. One was Ted Newton, the president and general manager of WFBB-TV in Ashton.

Ted has, in less than a year, succeeded in making significant changes in the station's programming to make it a more positive influence in the community. I don't have time to list all the changes, but among other things, he has replaced the most violent and indecent shows with family programming and refused to accept sex-oriented advertising. I understand that Ted is going to be honored in January by a national watchdog group supporting excellence in television.

Another member named Jenny Paige, owner of Paige, Inc., a real-estate development corporation, has devoted a large portion of both her time and money to establish an inner-city church outreach called Southside Mission, which I'll discuss with you sometime soon in more detail.

Cliff Bright, owner of the Mr. B Food Stores chain, has dropped pornographic magazines, tobacco, and hard liquor from all his stores.

Rachel Wingate, the lead female vocalist in the First Church worship team, turned down a lucrative TV movie opportunity several months ago, solely because of her conviction that the part was immoral—not "what Jesus would do."

Although Michael has no idea I know about this, I found out he and Sharon gave up a planned three-week vacation in Italy this year in order to help a family of six they met at the mission. The family had fallen on hard times after the father lost his job, which left them stuck with enormous medical bills for one of their children. The money got them into a clean apartment and bought them a second-hand car so the father could get to and from work. I've never seen a face so transformed with joy as that man's, when he told me what a difference Michael had made in their lives.

The impact of the First Church pledge has also apparently spread beyond their own congregation. At Southside Mission Friday night I met a young man, Keith Walton, who works with Ted Newton at WFBB-TV. His church has become involved with the mission, and he said that his pastor gave essentially the same challenge to their congregation several months ago. He also said he knows of at least two other churches which have done the same thing.

But I'm starting to ramble. What I really want to share with you, Pat, is what I observed as it relates to the accusations you received that Michael Maxwell's "fanatical" actions are causing the church to deteriorate.

In my mind, nothing could be farther from the truth! The fact is, the pledge seems to have resulted in bringing about a new spirit of fellowship in the church that Michael tells me never before existed. He compares it to what the early Christian churches must have experienced, and I can't much argue with him.

There seems to be a genuine sense of caring and interdependency that brings to life the Scripture about the early disciples "having all things in common." It's a refreshing change from the self-centered congregations in so many churches today—including mine!

As for the "deteriorating" condition of First Church, I guess there are several ways of looking at it. From a sheer numbers viewpoint, a case could probably be made that Michael has "scared off" some members. He says they lost about 10 percent of their congregation immediately after he announced the pledge eight months ago, and over the next few months they lost another 5 percent. There is no doubt that this pledge was viewed by many as highly controversial.

Despite the initial loss in numbers, however, the "core" of committed members has remained, and it now appears that the church is once again starting to grow, albeit slowly. At the service this morning, their attendance was the highest it's been since the Sunday when the pledge was first announced.

The main source of discontent seems to rest with a rather small faction in the church who continue to regard those who have taken the pledge as radicals; I suspect it's among those people that you'll find the authors of the letter sent to your board.

Overall, though, their divisive attitude seems to have been held in check by the continued presence of the Holy Spirit in the church, and also by the fact that many of the most prominent members have allied themselves with the pledge movement.

I'm not sure I agree with Michael in everything, but I have to say that what I saw at First Church moves me to strongly re-evaluate my own life and ministry. Although it has been years since I've been moved to tears in church, I found myself weeping both at the Friday night service at the mission and again during the worship service this morning. It wasn't what was said nearly so much as it was that indescribable sense of closeness to my Father. I found myself asking, "How is it that so many of us have let that closeness, that first love, slip away without noticing—without even grieving its passing?"

At any rate, I spent much of my time asking people questions about this "literal imitation of Jesus" the church has embarked upon. Michael tells me that, so far, no one has interpreted the following of Jesus in a way that would compel them to abandon their earthly possessions, give away all their wealth, etc., although several members have, in following their convictions, suffered financial loss. But they're all quick to add that, if anyone were to feel that in his or her particular case Jesus would do that, there could be no compromise. The pledge is to follow Jesus without thought for the results.

I should point out that those who have suffered the loss of either money or job positions have immediately been helped by others in the church. I witnessed part of this myself this morning when I attended the church after-meeting with Michael. A young reporter who'd recently lost his job stood up to share that he had not only been flooded with gifts of money and cards of encouragement over the past few weeks, but that Ted Newton had just found him a job at the TV station!

It was clear, as I looked across the room, that none of those people felt themselves to be alone in their Christian walk. I never dreamed that such close Christian fellowship could still exist today! It left me almost speechless—and, I must admit, more than a little jealous.

Which is why I now come to the real heart of this letter. After we left the church this afternoon, Michael and I talked for several hours about how great an impact this one small group has already had on Ashton and the surrounding communities. And the longer we talked, the more excited we both got.

"What do you think would happen," Michael asked me, "if Christians all across the country made the pledge and lived up to it? What if, in every city and county, just a handful of Christians firmly set their hearts and minds on following Jesus, regardless of consequence? What a revolution it would cause! People would be able to say of us now what they said about the early disciples—that we were 'turning the whole world upside down!' "

From that point on we talked rather wildly, I'm afraid. We imagined encouraging other pastors to form "pledge meetings" like the one at First Church. If their group caused so many changes in just months, how much more could be accomplished with churches all across the country joining the effort, volunteering to simply do as Jesus would?

It would cut the ground out from under those who repeatedly claim that all Christians are hypocrites; instead of having only a few "token Christians" to point to, they'd be exposed to them everywhere—in the workplace, in the schools, in the media, in homes—showing Christ's love by their actions. Can you imagine a more effective message than that?

But this is where I find myself suddenly hesitating. I can't help but ask myself, what would happen if I put this idea to my own congregation at Nazareth Avenue Church? I can think of very few men and women who, to my sure knowledge, would be willing to risk everything they hold dear for such an experiment. Would anyone even respond to the call, "Come and suffer"?

What I saw in Ashton this weekend left me shaken but also deeply hungry for more of the Spirit's power to be manifested at Nazareth Avenue. But I also have to ask, "Am I myself ready to take this pledge?" I dread the question, dread the honest answer. I know that, if I promised to closely follow in His steps, painful changes would be necessary in my life.

At any rate, Pat, I've tried to share my sincere, if somewhat jumbled, thoughts with you about Michael Maxwell and his congregation, and maybe even to leave you with the same dilemma I now face. Should I stand up in front of my people next Sunday and say, "Let's all pledge, from this day forward, not to do anything without first asking, 'What

would Jesus do?' " That would undoubtedly startle and upset many people. But why should it?

I'm just not sure I have the courage. Do you?

In Christ's love,

Carl Bruce

18

IT WAS MID-AFTERNOON ON CHRISTMAS EVE, AND Southside Mission was gaily decorated with red and green streamers. In one corner of the dining hall stood a tall, fragrant pine tree, decorated with tinsel and shiny red bulbs.

The smell of turkey and dressing wafted through the rooms, making everyone anxious for the dinner hour to arrive. Outside, the swelling crowd of hungry people overflowed the sidewalks as they jockeyed for position in the food line.

"How does that look?" asked Lauren Woods, centering a pot of poinsettias on the long serving table. Rachel Wingate, holding a silver garland bunched in one hand, stepped back to admire the effect. "Perfect," she replied.

The two young women had been working for several hours to "dress up" the mission for the holiday meal. As they hung decorations and spread paper tablecloths, Lauren had told Rachel for the first time about her idea for a program aimed at helping girls in the south side who'd become mothers at a very young age.

"I'd like to call it 'Parents Too Soon,'" she said. "Some of the girls I've talked to here are only thirteen or fourteen, but they already have one or two babies. They don't have a clue about how to take care of their children; they're only children themselves. I started working with a couple of them—teaching them things like personal hygiene and makeup application—and they just blossomed! So I started thinking; if I could get together with them once a week, teach them some basic 'life skills' like child care and job hunting, and maybe even take them on occasional outings to expose them to a different life, it might break the cycle that keeps them locked into the south side."

Rachel was impressed. "Lauren, that's a wonderful idea! Have you talked to Jenny about it? I'll bet she'd help fund it to start with."

Lauren's face brightened. "Do you really think so? That was my only real concern—I have the time, but I don't have much extra money." She hesitated for a moment before asking, "Would you go with me to talk to her about it? Jenny kind of scares me."

Rachel laughed. "She puts up a tough front, but I don't think I've ever met a softer touch. But I'll still go with you, if that's what you want." She paused to arrange some Christmas napkins in an attractive fan, then asked, "By the way, how's Martha? I heard you'd been lending her a hand ever since her car accident."

This time it was Lauren's turn to laugh. "I don't know whether I've been helping her or driving her crazy, but I've been trying to stop by every other afternoon or so to straighten up her house and make sure she's got plenty of easy-to-cook food in the fridge.

"As far as I can tell, her nephew hasn't done a thing for her, and she's still pretty miserable. She keeps complaining that her neck is getting worse, not better. I don't think she's used to having anyone help her."

"Well, I'm glad you're doing it, anyway. Even if she never thanks you, you're still earning—"

"I know, I know," Lauren interrupted with a smile, "I'm earning 'treasure in heaven.' That's what I keep telling myself. Every time Martha gripes that I don't clean the kitchen the way she does, or that when *she* scrubs the floor it's like a mirror, I'm tempted to walk out and let her try to do it all herself. But—" she shrugged her shoulders, "that's not exactly what Jesus would do, is it?"

Rachel grinned. "No, but it's probably what *I* would do. You must be getting positively *rich* in heaven if you're putting up with that!"

A few minutes later, Jenny and Roger Paige came in. Roger, as usual, disappeared into the other room the instant he saw Rachel. Rachel looked after him with troubled eyes.

Jenny noticed her glance. "Have you and Roger quarreled over something, Rachel?" she asked, puzzled. "I've noticed that he's been rather abrupt with you for weeks now."

"We haven't talked enough to get a chance to fight. The last time I exchanged more than just a couple of words with him was the night he came forward. But then Jason interrupted and dragged me away."

The mention of Jason cast a pall over her lovely face. She had heard several days before that he had accepted a job at a local "men's club"—a high-class topless bar—as a lounge singer. His rejection of God and his faith had been complete.

She took a quick breath and forced herself to smile. "I wouldn't worry about the way Roger's been acting," she added lightly. "It's probably just a leftover from his early childhood. I hear his mother's a real storm-trooper."

Jenny and Lauren both laughed, and the tension in the air disappeared. Soon they were all chatting happily about Lauren's plan for "Parents Too Soon."

But that night, after Jenny got home, she called Roger into her room. Her son plopped down on the small rose-colored love seat in the corner and looked at her inquiringly. She returned his gaze with an equally inquiring look.

"Rachel Wingate," she said carefully, "is an exceptional young lady. I've never met anybody else her age willing to accept responsibility or work as hard for others."

Roger cleared his throat. "Yes, she's a hard worker, all right," he said noncommittally.

Jenny studied him, puzzled. "I don't know many other girls as talented as she is who'd have turned down a movie part because of her convictions, either. Do you?"

"No," Roger answered briefly.

Jenny decided to drop all pretense. "Then why are you being so rude to her?" she cried. "When she walks in a room, you walk out. If she speaks to you, you barely answer. I saw the look in her eyes tonight; you hurt her feelings! Why on earth are you treating her like this?"

Roger jumped to his feet in agitation and began to pace, keeping his back toward his mother. Finally, he whirled to face her. "Don't you know how I *really* feel?" he demanded.

She stared at him, then slowly a look of understanding crept over her face. "You—?"

"I think I fell in love with Rachel that very first night you brought her here," Roger said almost angrily. "I didn't know it at the time, but it was never the same after that. She was different than any girl I'd ever met." His voice suddenly grew soft. "I think what struck me most about her was the—I don't know—the love, I saw in her face. I didn't recognize it then, but it was her love for Jesus."

He paused, then continued after a moment, "If it had been anybody else, any other girl, I would've gone after her, Jason Clark or not. But with her—" His voice trailed off, and he shrugged. "Somehow I just couldn't bring myself to play those kinds of games with her."

"But why haven't you said something since you've come to the Lord? You could at least ask her out instead of treating her like dirt!"

He was already shaking his head. "Don't you understand, Mom? Rachel is—Rachel is *pure,* for lack of a better word. She'd never be interested in someone like me. I mean, I know that in Christ I'm a 'new creature' and all that, but when she looks at me she'll always see a spoiled playboy. She could never take me seriously enough to love me, not in that way."

Jenny didn't say anything. She didn't agree with her son's conclusion, but she knew better than to try to reason with him when he was being hard-headed.

He doesn't realize it yet, she thought, *but he's already being transformed from a moral weakling into a man of strength and courage.* Someday, he might be the very kind of man to whom Rachel would gladly give her heart.

For much of Ashton's young adult crowd, the new year began as many previous years had begun—with drunken partying from club to club. Roger Paige, however, found greeting the new year without his friends at the club a thoroughly disorienting experience. Several people at church had invited him over to play board games or watch videos, but he couldn't work up enthusiasm for the idea. For the hundredth time since his conversion, he found himself thinking, *Aren't Christians allowed to have any fun besides playing Monopoly?*

Sitting up alone late that night, an idea slowly began to form in his mind. After a few minutes, he jumped up and jogged downstairs in search of a notepad and pencil, then fixed himself a sandwich and sat down at the kitchen table.

He thought for a moment, then quickly scrawled:

Celebration Station—A Christian Nightclub
Non-Smoking Soda Bar,
Contemporary Christian Bands, Great Food,
Live Entertainment.

He stared at the words until they became a blur. Was it possible? Could it work?

It was a chilly mid-January morning, Martha Robinson's first Sunday back in church since her accident. She was edging her way down the aisle, trying to keep her still-sore toes from being trampled by other worshippers, when Larry, a suit-clad deacon, approached with a smile.

"Martha!" he said loudly. "Glad to see you back. It's been weeks!"

She gave him an irritable look. "*Six* weeks," she replied with a distinct edge to her voice.

Larry didn't notice. Instead, he pulled her aside. "Listen, have you heard back from the board yet?" he asked, glancing around to make sure no one could overhear. "It seems like they'd have decided *something* by now."

"No, I haven't heard anything," she said uncomfortably. "And really, you know, I've been thinking—" She broke off, obviously reluctant to continue.

"What? What have you been thinking?"

She glanced at him sharply. "Let me ask you this, Larry. During all these weeks I've been out of church, how many times did you visit or even call to see how I was doing?"

"Uh, I—well, Martha," he said uneasily, "you know I work long hours. Besides, wasn't your nephew helping you out?"

"My nephew," she replied coldly, "is useless. In fact, as far as I can tell, most of you who I thought were my friends are useless. The only one in our group who did anything to help me was John. He came over twice and brought groceries."

She adjusted her glasses. "You know who kept showing up all those weeks? Lauren Woods and several others from the pledge group. Pastor Maxwell even found time to come over several times a week. Lauren and the pastor prayed for me each time they were there. I don't know what I would've done without all of them."

Larry looked embarrassed. "I'm sorry, I really am. But that doesn't change the fact that this pledge thing is slowly killing the church. We still need to do something about that."

"Well, I've had plenty of time to think about that. And you know what? I was wrong. The church is growing again—slowly, but it *is* growing. I think we should just let it go."

He stared at her, bewildered, but before he could say anything she quickly added, "I already wrote a letter to the board to tell them how I feel. Now you'll have to excuse me, Larry. The service is about to start."

He watched, open-mouthed, as she slid into a pew next to the Powells. Wait until the others heard about this!

Rachel Wingate was walking into the Ashton Christian Bookstore when a young man burst through the door, almost knocking her down. At her startled shriek, he quickly grasped her elbow to keep her from falling. She looked up to discover that the strong arms supporting her belonged to Roger Paige.

"Rachel!" he said, his clear blue eyes alight. "Are you all right?" But almost instantly that guarded look returned to his face. He reluctantly released his grip on her. "I'm fine," she said. "I was just coming in to buy some sheet music for our concert next month. Where are you going in such a hurry?"

"I have some phone calls to make." He paused, then asked, "Have you talked to my mom lately?"

Rachel shook her head. "We've both been so busy we haven't had much time. Why, what's going on?"

He hesitated again, but the subject seemed safe enough—and he was dying to talk to somebody about it. He decided impulsively to confide in her.

"Well," he said, "a few weeks ago, I got this idea for opening a kind of Christian nightclub, a place where Christians can go on weekends to listen to good music and maybe even bring along some of their unsaved friends."

He held the door open and allowed Rachel to precede him back into the bookstore. As they walked through the aisles together, he excitedly described some of his ideas.

"I found the phone numbers of some local Christian bands that we could book on Friday and Saturday nights," he said, "and I've already talked to a DJ from a Christian radio station who said he'd like to act as emcee. The way I see it, we should have a sandwich menu and soda bar and maybe a bunch of small tables where people could sit around and talk. We could even have a couple of pool tables—but without the haze of cigarette smoke."

His face was transformed by his enthusiasm for the idea. Rachel noticed with approval the new strength and purpose in his manner.

He continued, "If we did it right, I think we could not only reach the 'party' crowd for Christ, but actually make it succeed as a business. Mom and I have been looking at a property in North Ashton that seems just perfect—it already has a small kitchen, hardwood floors for a dance floor, everything. If we can get it for a reasonable price, we're going to buy it."

Rachel exclaimed, "What a great idea, Roger! What made you think of doing something like that?"

He laughed. "Desperation, mostly. It was on New Year's Eve when I was bored stiff. I'm not like a lot of 'regular' Christians, I guess; I just don't fit in with most of the people who teach Sunday School or help out at the mission." He smiled to take the offense from his words. "But the biggest thing is, I keep thinking that nobody is even *trying* to reach the kind of people I used to hang around with! I've been praying about how the Lord could use me to get through to them. I think this might be the answer."

After Rachel paid for her music, she and Roger walked out together. They paused just outside the store, both suddenly stricken with an inexplicable shyness.

"You know," Rachel finally said, "you seem like a totally different person than you were few months ago. You used to be so smug and cynical, but now you're so much more—I don't know, *real,* I guess, about God and about your life."

He looked embarrassed. "I guess God is working on me little by little, but I still have a lot of catching up to do."

"Maybe not as much as you think. I really respect you for the stand you've taken, Roger, and for your dedication to the Lord."

There was a moment of awkward silence, then he said uncertainly, "Thanks—thanks a lot, Rachel. That means a lot to me." He looked down at her, and their eyes met. In that instant, Rachel read his true feelings for her in his face.

She drove home a few minutes later, aware of a glad, new joy stealing over her. *Roger is everything I kept trying to make myself believe Jason was,* she thought, recalling his animation as he spoke of reaching his old friends for Christ. *I think I might be starting to understand what it means to be loved by a real man.*

And Roger, as he drove home, felt a new surge of hope as he remembered the warm look in Rachel's gray-green eyes.

19

Winter had passed and the year was nearly ended—the year Michael Maxwell had set as the time period for the First Church pledge. As the anniversary Sunday approached, several people suggested that it be marked by a special service with a "dinner on the grounds" to follow at a nearby park. Michael agreed that it was a good idea, and preparations were begun.

The past three months had been marked by several notable events, among them Martha Robinson's change of heart toward the whole pledge movement and the budding romance between Rachel Wingate and Roger Paige. On Valentine's Day Sunday, Rachel had come to church with a lovely rose corsage and a radiant smile, holding Roger's arm. Jenny Paige was said to be overjoyed.

The other big news involved the new Christian nightclub Roger Paige had opened in North Ashton. Dubbed "Celebration Station," it had created an instant stir in both the Christian and secular communities.

"This is great!" exclaimed several surprised visitors dragged in by Roger. His friend Dennis even admitted, "I always thought

Christian music was old hymns and stuff. But the bands here sound better than the ones at the Mardi Gras!"

Although Zack, the Celebration Station emcee, avoided long "preachy" speeches, he managed to work in quick comments between each song set to point people toward Christ. By the fourth week, the club was regularly packed and starting to show a profit. Several traditional nightclubs, the Mardi Gras included, were even complaining loudly that their business was dropping off. Celebration Station's atmosphere of Christ-like love and joy was proving a formidable rival for the smoke-filled rooms where peace and joy came from a bottle.

Nonetheless, there were still many Christians—Michael Maxwell among them—who found the whole nightclub concept troubling. "Isn't it just 'whitewashing' worldliness to practice it under a Christian heading?" he asked Sharon after attending Celebration Station's grand opening. "It seems a little cheap for Christians to stoop to imitating the world like that—dancing to loud music and drinking 'fake' alcohol."

"I don't think it was exactly worldly, Michael," Sharon protested. "I mean, nobody was talking or dancing in a vulgar way or anything, were they? The song lyrics kind of discouraged that. Were you listening to those girls at the next table? Two of them were telling the other girl about how they'd come to know the Lord since coming to the club. Maybe Roger was right in thinking it would be an effective way to reach the party crowd. You said it yourself when you were talking about preaching at the mission—to reach some people, you have to become enough like them so they can relate.

"Besides," she added mischievously, "if you're going to complain about dancing, you'd better go back and read about King David again!"

"That's not the same thing and you know it," Michael retorted. Her comment made him grin, however, and he finally conceded, "We all agreed not to judge other people's decisions as they tried to follow Jesus as best they knew how. I just hope this doesn't lead any young Christians astray."

* * *

With the anniversary Sunday two weeks away, Rachel Wingate came up with an idea.

"I've stayed in touch with the Andersons, little Hallie Collier's grandparents," she told Michael Maxwell. "I was just wondering—do you think we could invite them here for the anniversary service, kind of as a memorial to their daughter?"

Michael nodded thoughtfully. "Good idea. It might be a comfort to them to see what Brenda started here, and what's come of it."

"I'll call them. I just hope they can come; I'd love to see Hallie again. I've talked with her on the phone a few times, and she sounds so cute. She calls me 'Way-tull.' I'll bet she's grown so much in the last year!"

Back at home, Rachel quickly looked up the phone number, and a few minutes later she was talking to Mrs. Anderson.

"Rachel! How are you doing, honey?" Mrs. Anderson was always glad to hear from the young woman.

Rachel explained why she was calling, and after a brief conversation, the Andersons said that they'd love to come to Ashton for the anniversary service. Jenny Paige suggested that the older couple stay with her at the mansion.

Over the next two weeks, the church was filled with a meditative spirit, a sense of quiet reflection about the year now almost gone. Some wondered aloud, "What will happen now that the pledge is ended?" while others looked to the years ahead with renewed excitement. One thing was certain; none of those who had taken the pledge and kept it faithfully had remained the same.

Michael Maxwell prepared his message for the anniversary Sunday based on the text, "What is it to thee? Follow thou me" (John 21:22, KJV). As he thought back to that day almost a year before when his sermon preparation was interrupted by a stranger at the door, he was struck anew by the changes that had been wrought in his own life. Now, instead of counting on clever phrases or a gripping delivery to bring his messages home, he prayed long and hard for each service to be visited by the divine

Presence who could bring life to faltering words, living water to thirsty hearts.

Then, almost before the members of First Church knew it, the anniversary Sunday was upon them. Unlike the morning the year before, it was rainy and overcast; tables for the picnic lunch afterward were hastily moved to an indoor facility. Despite the rain, the sanctuary was filled to capacity. Dr. Carl Bruce had driven down from Chicago at Michael's invitation to attend the service.

As Rachel sang the opening choruses with the worship team, she smiled down happily at Hallie, wedged between her grandparents on the front row with Jenny and Roger Paige. When she finally joined them, she sat next to Roger and held her arms out invitingly to Hallie. The little girl smiled and crawled over Mrs. Anderson to sit on her lap. Roger grinned at her and reached over to tweak one of her small, dark brown braids.

The service that morning was characterized by a spirit of solemn joy that touched—and in some cases puzzled—many first-time visitors. The audience listened attentively as Michael read the story of the rich young ruler, then spoke of "losing your life to find it." He related Christ's call to "come, follow me" to the experiment the church had embarked upon exactly one year before.

"Many of you gathered here today can think back and marvel at the changes that have occurred in your lives and homes as the result of that experiment," he said.

"Many others probably wouldn't even be sitting here today if it hadn't been for someone who demonstrated the love of God toward them."

Epimenio Garza smiled at his wife, then they both glanced over at Cliff Bright. His round face, drawn from the long months of difficulty both at home and at work, brightened momentarily at their grateful nods. On the front row, Roger Paige gently tightened his arm around Rachel's shoulders. Across the church, numerous small smiles and gestures acknowledged lives tightly interwoven by Christ-like love.

"None of us imagined at the time," Michael continued, "all

the miracles that would happen, the doors that would be opened, when just a few people started living their lives by one simple rule: asking, 'What would Jesus do?' and then doing it. For many of us, it has been an experience that we are now unwilling to leave behind."

He paused, his eyes resting briefly on Mr. and Mrs. Anderson. "I will always regret that it took a tragedy to wake us up," he said softly. "But now that we're awake, it is my fervent prayer that we'll all continue to live our lives, day by day, week by week, by that same simple rule."

The message was somewhat shorter than usual, but instead of closing with the usual prayer, Michael asked that the congregation spend a few moments in silent reflection, asking the Holy Spirit to move in their own individual lives. In the quiet of that time, a holy reverence settled over the sanctuary; many, sensing the Presence in their midst that went beyond their human understanding, bowed trembling hearts in solemn acknowledgment.

Finally Michael prayed aloud, asking God's continued blessing in their lives as they sought to follow in His steps. Afterward, the audience only slowly stirred, still caught in the glory and wonder of what they'd experienced.

Dr. Bruce lingered behind with Michael long after most of the congregation had left for the picnic area. His face was pale, but determined, as he warmly clasped his friend's hand.

"I made a decision today, Michael," he said without preamble. "I've been wrestling with myself ever since I came here and saw what you and First Church were doing." He paused, shaking his head. "I'm ashamed to say that I've been too cowardly, or maybe too selfish, to take the kind of step you've taken here. I can't imagine my Nazareth Avenue congregation rising to a challenge to make even the simplest sacrifice in their lives, but maybe I'm misjudging them. At any rate, I've decided to go back to Chicago and put it before them."

He met Michael's eyes and found there a strong bond of sympathy. Dr. Bruce smiled grimly before going on, "Now I'd like to ask you a favor. Could I convince you, and maybe some of your people, to come to Chicago and speak to my congregation about what's happened here in Ashton?"

Michael thought about it for a moment, then nodded. "I'll be glad to come, and I can probably get Alex, Cliff, Ted, Jenny, and a few others to come with me. Would three weeks be soon enough?"

"That'll be great. Thanks a lot, Michael, and tell the others thanks, too. I'd like to stay today for the picnic, but I've got to get back to Chicago. Can I call you sometime next week?"

"That's fine. And Carl—," Michael put his hand on the other man's shoulder. "You might be surprised at how your people react. I know *I* was at First Church."

At the picnic that afternoon, Michael was able to talk to everyone but Cliff Bright. Elizabeth didn't care for picnics; at her insistence they'd gone straight home after church. But Jenny, Roger, and Rachel all enthusiastically agreed to go along to Chicago, as did Alex Powell and Ted Newton and their wives. Daniel Marshall and Dr. Patricia West were also interested, but they wouldn't know until closer to that time if they'd be free. They promised to let Michael know.

A few days later, Michael called Cliff Bright at his office. After explaining the purpose of the Chicago trip, he asked the store owner if he could find time to go. Cliff answered quickly that he'd be glad to but added unnecessarily that he doubted Elizabeth would want to come along. The same day Rachel called to let Michael know that the Andersons, at Jenny Paige's urging, had decided to extend their stay in Ashton for the next few weeks, and that she thought they'd like to go with the Chicago group as well.

"The more the merrier," Michael said cheerfully. "I talked to Carl this morning, and now that he's committed himself, he sounds really excited. He's been meeting with a small group of deacons especially to pray for the service, that God will touch people's hearts."

Over the next week, as word spread through First Church about the Chicago church's upcoming "special service," many members made it a point to earnestly pray for the other congregation, and the next Sunday after-meeting at First Church was devoted almost entirely to prayer for a sweeping move of the Holy Spirit at their sister church. As the day grew closer, believers in both Ashton and Chicago prayed as never before, spurred by a deep sense of urgency they only half understood. An unseen cloud of intercession rose to the heavens like sweet incense.

The following Saturday afternoon, Michael and Sharon Maxwell drove to Chicago. Carl Bruce and his wife, Kathy, had invited them to stay overnight so he'd be rested and ready for the service the next morning. Jenny, Roger, and Rachel also drove over that afternoon and checked into a hotel near the church. Most of the others planned to drive up early Sunday morning.

That evening the Maxwells and Bruces enjoyed a quiet dinner, then talked at length about the state of modern Christianity. How had the church in America come to be so far removed from Christ that many lost and dying people could no longer find Him there? How had Christians been lulled into believing that the "way of the cross" could be traded without consequence for lives of greed and self-indulgence?

"Whatever happens in the morning," Carl finally said, "I firmly believe that it's by the Lord's clear leading that I am to challenge this congregation to follow more literally in His steps."

Late that night, long after the others were all asleep, Michael remained wakeful. As he stared up into the darkness, he couldn't stop thinking of all the things he and Carl had talked about. Was it true that the church in America had, for the most part, lost its power to touch and restore the very kind of lost and hurting people which, in the early ages of Christianity, it had reached in the greatest numbers? Was it true that today's Christians would, as a rule, refuse to walk in Jesus' steps if it meant suffering at all for His sake? *Oh, Father!* Michael cried silently into the darkness. *Bring a spiritual awakening to Your people!*

Suddenly, he could no longer stay in bed. He got up and went quietly into Carl's study, where he knelt beside the couch and began to pray. As he continued to intercede for the church, he was filled with an inner agony that left him almost moaning. He had never felt such a deep wrestling in his soul, not even during his strongest experience in Ashton. He prayed, wept, and prayed again, pleading repeatedly for the Spirit to move in the church across the nation.

He spent nearly all that night in prayer, finally rising just before dawn to return to bed for a few hours' sleep.

20

ON SUNDAY MORNING THE LARGE NAZARETH AVENUE Church was crowded to capacity. Michael Maxwell, stepping into the pulpit after his all-night vigil, instantly felt the deep sense of curiosity among the people in the congregation. Most had heard of the Ashton movement, and many of them had come specifically to hear about the First Church pledge and how it had all started. Perhaps a few, at least, had come prepared to mock the whole idea.

But Michael also sensed something deeper, something more serious than mere curiosity, in their faces. He glanced over at Dr. Carl Bruce, sitting on the front row. *There's so much I want to say to these people,* he thought. *Dear Lord, please give me the right words to deliver Your message to them today.*

He started very simply by telling how, just one year before, a stranger had come to his door in Ashton looking for help—only to be turned away. As he painfully related what had later happened to young Brenda Collier, his voice faltered and his hands visibly trembled. Although there was none of the polished eloquence of his former distinctive preaching style, the congregation felt the complete sincerity and humility of a man who has been confronted with a great truth.

"Like many other Christians," he said, "I had allowed myself to become self-satisfied, immune to the hurts and needs of other people around me. I forgot what the Bible has to say about people who practice an empty faith:

"What good is it, my brothers,
if a man claims to have faith but has no deeds?
Can such faith save him?
Suppose a brother or sister is without clothes and daily food.
If one of you says to him,
'Go, I wish you well; keep warm and well fed,'
but does nothing about his physical needs,
what good is it? In the same way, faith by itself,
if it is not accompanied by action, is dead."

> James 2:14–17

On the front row, Mr. Anderson reached over to take his wife's hand. They both gazed up steadily at Michael's face.

"I will regret for the rest of my life," he said quietly, "that when Brenda Collier came to my house that day, I wished her well and sent her away empty-handed. But I can truly say today that, because of her tragedy, Ashton has seen a spiritual reawakening which has already changed the lives of countless people."

He went on to tell how he had come to challenge his own church to join him in pledging for one year to do as Jesus would do, then shared some of the results at First Church.

"I'm sure many of you here in Chicago are already aware of the dramatic programming changes made this last year at WFBB-TV," he said, "but you might not be aware that those changes came about solely because of the station manager's pledge to live his life by asking, 'What would Jesus do?' and then doing it." He nodded slightly at Ted Newton in the audience. "That decision has already provided a living testimony of God's love to countless other people, including eighteen children who've found permanent adoptive homes through Channel 5's new 'Wednesday's Child' program.

"Another result many of you will probably recognize is the removal of all pornographic magazines, tobacco products, and hard liquor from the Mr. B Food Stores chain. Those changes have cost the owner a great deal of money, and recently the loss of two entire stores, but it has also provided a testimony in the community that has already resulted in lives being transformed." In the audience, Cliff Bright looked down self-consciously.

"I could give example after example. Southside Mission that has, in barely eight months, seen more than seventy-six men and women make decisions for Christ, was started by two women who believed Jesus would use their money and talents to shine a light in the darkness of downtown Ashton. The weekly prayer group at Vickers Regional Airport that now numbers more than one hundred was started by a manager who believed Christ would treat His employees with both fairness and love.

"But for every one of these 'big' success stories, there are many, many more 'small' stories, where just one person, by simply acting as Jesus would in an everyday situation, has touched someone else's life in a significant way."

He paused to look down at little Hallie, who was bouncing happily on Roger's leg. As he lifted his eyes to briefly gaze across the audience, there was an almost studied stillness in their faces.

"Several weeks ago, I baptized a young man who had a strange story to tell about how he came to know the Lord. It seems that he was driving his rather beat-up car one day not long ago when he ran out of gas and had to pull off the road. Since he didn't have a gas can, he got out and started pushing the car along toward the nearest gas station, which was almost a mile away.

"But he'd gone only a short distance when another car carrying a well-dressed young couple pulled up beside him. To his astonishment, the other man immediately called out, 'Here, let me help you!' and jumped out to push from behind. Together, they pushed the car all the way to the gas station, the young woman driving along behind them with her hazard lights flashing.

"But that wasn't all. When they finally got the car up to the gas pump, the well-dressed young man, whose clothes by now were sweaty and dirty, asked the other man, 'Can I fill it up for you?' apparently concerned that he might not have any money with him.

"The first young man was so bewildered by all that had happened that he blurted out, 'Why are you doing all this for me?' "

Michael smiled, not seeming to notice a flushed young couple—Roger and Rachel—sitting on the front row. "You can guess at the reply. The young couple who had stopped to help the stranger had both taken the pledge to live every day by asking themselves, 'What would Jesus do?' and then doing it."

He fell silent for a moment, sensing the Spirit's presence in the quiet sanctuary. When he continued, it was in a thoughtful voice.

"The point is, it's rarely the great sermons or extravagant programs that reach people for Christ. More often than not, it's the Christian homemaker who takes a meal to a neighbor who's ill; the Christian teenager who mows an elderly widow's yard; the Christian father who makes time to spend with the child of an overworked single mother. It's those individual acts of sacrificial love that not only change other people's lives but also bring great joy to the giver.

"In Matthew, Jesus used two parables to illustrate the Christian lifestyle:

" 'The kingdom of heaven is like treasure hidden in a field.
When a man found it, he hid it again, and then in his joy
went and sold all he had and bought that field.
Again, the kingdom of heaven
is like a merchant looking for fine
pearls. When he found one of great
value, he went away and sold everything
he had and bought it.'
Matthew 13:44–45

"Jesus never preached that following Him would result in a carefree, comfortable existence; to the contrary, He talked about people who willingly gave up *everything they had* for His sake! But the point is, the sacrifices were all for a purpose, not just for the sake of suffering—and the end result was always great joy."

He carefully closed his Bible. "Over this last year, many of us in Ashton who took the pledge to live our lives by asking, 'What would Jesus do?' have been accused of being radicals and religious fanatics, of having gone too far in our attempts to literally follow in Jesus' steps. It appears that today's church, the church that is called after Christ's own name, can come up with a million excuses for not following Him if it might mean inconvenience or personal suffering. We think we're somehow entitled to our ease and comfort, that we're doing something special if we donate to a worthy cause or sit on a committee. But I think one of our First Church members put it very clearly," his eyes went briefly to Jenny Paige, "when she posed the question: 'Is it really following Jesus to give away something you'll never miss?' We forget that the only sacrifice God finds pleasing, the only sacrifice that touches people around us, is when we give *ourselves.*"

Michael took a deep breath and looked out at the audience. "I want you to think with me for a moment," he said, "about what would happen if today, in this very church, Jesus were to stand here and call some members to do just what He asked of the rich young ruler—to give up their wealth and literally follow Him? Could they do it? What would happen if he called others to run their businesses in ways that, while less profitable, would bring Him more glory? Would they be willing? *What, today, is the test of Christian commitment?* Isn't it exactly the same as in Christ's own lifetime, when He said, 'Any of you who does not give up everything he has cannot be My disciple'?"

The congregation sat motionless, their eyes riveted on Michael's strong, passionate face.

When he continued, it was in a low voice, almost a whisper.

"Can you even imagine," he said, "what would happen if every Christian here in Chicago woke up tomorrow morning and suddenly began to do as Jesus would do? It staggers the mind! What would Jesus do about the many homeless families, mothers abandoned with small children, who live miserably in group shelters downtown? Would He turn His back on them? Claim it was none of His business?

"What about the low-income housing projects, where men and women live in desperate hopelessness, believing drugs and alcohol are their only respite? Would Jesus stand idly by, allowing a tidal wave of evil to sweep them away?

"What would Jesus do in the middle of a society that races so hard after money that they don't have time or energy left for their spouses and children? What would He say about the soft, selfish lives many of His people lead while turning a deaf ear to the cries of penniless missionaries? Would He do nothing, say nothing, feel nothing?

"I believe that it's time for a new commitment to Christian discipleship, following Jesus like the early church did without regard for cost or sacrifice. If our definition of being a Christian is simply to enjoy a good, comfortable life surrounded by friends and luxuries while steadfastly avoiding the pain and trouble of the world around us—if that's our definition of Christianity—then I'm afraid we're a long way from following in the steps of the One who was called a 'Man of sorrow'; who sweat, as it were, great drops of blood; who cried out as He hung in anguish upon a rough cross, 'My God! My God! Why hast thou forsaken me'!"

When Michael Maxwell finished his sermon and bowed his head, a great silence fell over the congregation. Into the silence, there slowly came the sound of muffled sobs—and a consciousness of the divine Presence that left the people trembling. Although many had expected Michael to ask for volunteers to pledge to do as Jesus would do, he didn't utter a word. He just remained standing at the pulpit, eyes closed, head bowed in silent prayer.

Then, unbelievably, there followed a scene that neither Michael Maxwell nor Dr. Carl Bruce would ever have imagined occurring at the fashionable Nazareth Avenue Church. One by one, men and women quietly rose and slipped out into the aisle to make their way to the front. When Michael finally looked up, he was surrounded by a crowd of people offering their earnest

promises to do as Jesus would do. It was a spontaneous movement prompted by the Holy Spirit, not by a clever or persuasive
sermon. Michael saw, in that joyous moment, all his prayers of
the night before being answered far beyond his wildest hopes.

Then he noticed Mr. and Mrs. Anderson frantically beckoning
to him. They were standing at the front, their arms around a
sobbing, painfully thin, young black man. Michael made his way
over to them.

"Pastor Maxwell," Mrs. Anderson said tearfully. "Do you
know who this is? It's Jim, Hallie's father."

Michael stared incredulously, taking in the young man's
gaunt, stricken face. *How—?*

With obvious difficulty, Jim Collier turned to face Michael. "I
think I talked with you on the phone once a long time ago," he
said in a low voice, "but I was so high I don't remember much
about it. There were whole weeks back then that went by in a
fog." He drew a ragged breath. "Then yesterday I ran into Tim
Mott, a guy I used to buy dope from down in Ashton. He started
telling me about how he's into this Jesus thing now, working as a
counselor at Southside Mission. He bought me lunch."

He looked down, embarrassed. "I hadn't eaten in a long time;
I got caught with some pills last month and lost my job. Anyway,
Tim told me my—the Andersons would be here today with Hallie. I just thought—I don't know. It had been a long time, and I
just decided—" He stopped, unsure of what to say.

Mr. Anderson said quietly, "He came to see Hallie, Pastor
Maxwell, but the Lord touched him during the service. He says
he wants to turn his life over to Christ."

Michael searched the older man's face, seeing the deep pain
reflected in his dark brown eyes. This was the young man who
had callously abandoned their beloved daughter, ignoring all his
responsibilities in his lust for drugs. Only the power of the Holy
Spirit could put it in their hearts to tolerate, much less forgive,
such a man.

Just then, Jenny Paige quietly joined them. "Pastor Maxwell,
Dr. Bruce asked us to stay after the service to help counsel with
the people who came forward today. He's moving everybody into

the church conference room." She gave the Andersons a reassuring smile; over the two weeks that they'd been her guests at the mansion, they had spent many hours talking about the Lord. Now, they walked as a group to the conference room, where more than seventy people were already waiting.

That was a remarkable day in the history of the Nazareth Avenue Church. Michael Maxwell and his small band from First Church stayed long into the afternoon, talking and praying with those who'd come forward. In many ways, the after-meeting that day resembled many of those they'd experienced in Ashton. Many church members solemnly took the pledge to do as Jesus would do, and toward the close of the meeting the Holy Spirit moved upon those gathered there, leaving them filled with almost indescribable joy.

Afterward, the First Church group ate lunch with Dr. Bruce and his wife. Cliff Bright, Ted and Kim Newton, Roger and Jenny Paige, Rachel Wingate, and Alex and Cheryl Powell were all there along with Michael and Sharon Maxwell. They spent the meal in a joyous recollection of the morning's events. Jenny shared that the Andersons had decided to stay overnight in Chicago while they talked further with their former son-in-law. Jim Collier had prayed that day to accept Christ as his Lord and Savior; rising from prayer, his tear-stained face had been literally transformed with joy. He was anxious to learn more about his new Lord, and had asked Dr. Bruce to baptize him that very night.

It was late that evening when Michael and Sharon finally arrived back home in Ashton. Long after Sharon went to bed, however, Michael sat up in his study, thinking over, once again, all the experiences of the last year. As he reflected on all the changes that had come to his life as he had tried to follow Jesus more literally, he was conscious of a deep stirring in his spirit, a call to prayer. He finally slipped out of his chair and knelt beside it, resting his head wearily on his hands.

Almost immediately, he experienced a vivid waking dream in which he saw distinctly a series of future events—a vision planted in his heart and mind and soul by his Creator.

He saw himself going on to live his daily life in a simpler, more unselfish fashion, increasingly willing to reach out to those around him in need. He also saw, more dimly, that the day would come when the divisive element in his church would grow stronger, causing him to suffer more as he increasingly sought to imitate Jesus and His conduct.

My grace is sufficient for thee, he heard through it all.

He saw Rachel Wingate and Roger Paige married, melding their lives and youthful talents in joyful service to their Lord. Roger he saw continuing to minister to the affluent "party" crowd, while Rachel's pure voice sang on into the darkness of sin and despair at Southside Mission, eventually, he saw dimly, to reach far beyond Ashton to draw lost souls all across the nation to Christ.

He saw Alex Powell continuing to work faithfully in a job not to his liking, but shining ever brighter as a witness for Christ because of his attitude of genuine humility and loving concern for all those around him.

He saw Cliff Bright suffering even more harshly in his marriage and meeting with additional business reversals, but growing through his suffering into a deeper knowledge of his Master and emerging from his reverses with Christian honor and integrity that would become an example in the community.

He saw Ted Newton defining a new, more responsible approach to television programming that would, in time, come to be recognized as a leading force in the nation, eventually spawning similar programming changes in television stations across the country.

He saw Ashton Christian College president Daniel Marshall becoming embroiled in national controversy because of his outspoken conviction that Christian students should minister to the world physically as well as spiritually, considering a Christian influence in such "secular" fields as the arts, journalism, literature, and film and television to be as important for the kingdom of God as pastoral ministry or foreign missions.

He saw Jason Clark, who had coldly turned his back on his faith, rising to national fame as a composer, writing cynical songs that, while popular, dripped with scorn for everything he'd once claimed to hold sacred.

He saw Lauren Woods continuing to work with young unmarried girls in Ashton's south side, growing in both wisdom and grace as she found, in following Christ, the fulfillment she had once believed could only be found in a man.

He saw Dr. Bruce ministering to his Nazareth Avenue congregation for a time, then resigning to begin a new ministry among Chicago's roughest housing projects, where he would fearlessly venture into the dull, dark, terrible places with the good news of Christ's redemption.

He saw Jim Collier and Tim Mott and a great crowd like them redeemed and giving in turn to others, living testimonies to the reality of the new life Christ offers, even to the most hopeless and ruined of people.

And then he saw a familiar figure, One whose face shone brighter than the sun as He beckoned with nail-scarred hands. Somewhere an angel choir was singing, and there were many voices and triumphant shouts of joy. The figure of Jesus grew more and more splendid, until Michael felt he had to avert his eyes.

"Lord Jesus!" he cried, still not sure if he was speaking aloud or in a dream, "open our eyes to the needs of the world around us! Let Your church begin to follow You more faithfully! Refocus our lives so Your Spirit can do His work in the world through us."

When he rose at last, weary but joyful, Michael felt, as never before, the weight of human sin and misery in the world, and the great responsibility of the church to penetrate the darkness by allowing God's love to shine through His people's lives.

And with a deep sense of both awe and gratitude, Michael Maxwell went to bed to dream of a church renewed, a church "without spot or wrinkle," obeying Jesus joyfully, following closely in His steps.